Skating the Line

ISABELLE MARTENS

Paperback ISBN: 979-8-9938406-1-1

eBook ISBN: 979-8-9938406-0-4

This is a work of fiction. Names, characters, places, and incidents either are the product of the author's imagination or are used fictitiously. Any resemblance of actual persons, living or dead, events, locales, and to existing social media usernames, handles, or accounts is entirely coincidental.

Front cover art by Alex.

Interior formatting by Isabelle Martens.

To you, my reader.
Without your support, this book, this dream, would be nothing.
Literally.
So... thank you.

To my reader,

While this is a YA romance, some themes in this story may be triggering. I take everyone's boundaries very seriously, so please read the next paragraph if you feel you need a warning. If you believe trigger warnings are spoilers, then feel free to skip the following paragraph and get straight into the story.

This book contains detailed portrayal of an eating disorder, including restrictive eating behaviors, purging, and negative body image thoughts. There are a few mentions of medical emergencies, including descriptions of blood. We are also dealing with teenagers, so there are a few moments of strong cursing and complicated relationship choices.

Please be advised, and if you choose to do so, continue reading with care.

Chapter 1

Clarity

Having figure skating practice scheduled on the same night as All-You-Can-Eat-Endless-Pasta-Bowls, AKA the last Wednesday of every month, is never a good idea. Granted, I wasn't supposed to work tonight.

Not until Stella texted me six hours ago, begging me to take her shift because she hasn't left the bathroom all day, thanks to the seasonal stomach flu that's starting to go around. Practice starts at 6:30 p.m., so I bartered with her. I'll stay until six, then Nicole needs to come take over.

The only good thing that comes out of this situation is the tips, which help cover some of the costs of my skating. But what good will that do me when Coach Ortiz kicks me off of the team for being late to practice?

"Behind! Coming through!" I shout over the symphony of noise that's coming from the kitchen, holding a tray over my head piled high with plates of food as I navigate my way down the line.

Pots and pans clang together, creating an awful soprano. My twin brother, Cole, pulls a pan of blackened garlic bread out of the raging oven as he argues with dad, our boss.

The cook, Antonio, stirs his sauce and sings along to the radio in a tenor that makes me wince as I breeze by.

Line cooks chop knives on cutting boards. Vegetables sizzle as they hit hot oil. The fires in the pizza ovens roar. The dishwasher in the back slams shut.

My shoulder aches as I reach the double doors. Spinning on my heel, I glance up at the clock hanging on the wall. The hour hand sits directly on the number six.

Where is Nicole?

Gritting my teeth, I use my backside to push the doors open while navigating the tray through. All of my years of practice pay off, though: whether it's the balancing skills from figure skating, or helping out around the restaurant since I could walk, it's hard to say.

The doors swing shut behind me, cutting off the noise from the kitchen, and the silence in comparison makes my ears ring. Soft jazz music guides me down the hallway, progressively getting louder until I turn the corner. Silverware clinks on dishes and guests chatter over glasses of wine. I can finally hear myself think.

I smile politely as I weave through the dining room before coming to a stop at a booth on the other side of the restaurant. The guests are practically drooling by the time I finish passing out their plates. I make quick work of putting the tray stand back, grabbing the water pitcher that they've already drained dry, and hurrying off so they can enjoy their dinner.

I clench my jaw as I burst through the kitchen doors again, the hinges swinging so fast that the doors clang against the walls. The sound makes me grimace. Dad will definitely be grumbling about that tomorrow.

"Sorry, Dad," I mutter to myself and check the clock on the wall again. 6:05. I start to jog, dodging and weaving my way around the line cooks despite Mom's age-old advice that's ingrained in my brain: *absolutely no running through the kitchen!*

I snatch a microfiber towel out of a clean laundry bin as I pass on my way to the ovens.

"Cole!" I shout over the noise.

Cole's eyes lift as he closes the oven door, a rivulet of sweat racing down his nose. His nostrils flare against the heat, and a small wisp of black hair escapes his hairnet. He relaxes when he notices that I'm not missing a limb, and scrubs his arm over his forehead.

"Good grief, you're lucky I didn't burn my hand off."

"Listen." Untying my apron with one hand, I thrust the empty water pitcher into his arms with the other. "You need to wait on table twelve. And sixteen. And eight. Like, right now. Until Nicole gets here."

He blinks. "Wait, what? But I'm on bread duty."

"And if I don't make it to practice, I'll be waiting tables for the rest of my life. I'll tell Antonio to send someone over on my way out."

"Excuse me, but Antonio will not be sending anyone over here. Cole has a station to maintain, as do you, young lady!"

I freeze, caught in the middle of dropping my apron in his arms. My eyes flash to his, and he quirks an eyebrow.

You could've told me that Maureen was behind me. I let my facial expression speak for me as I glare at him.

Cole smirks, his eyes communicating in response. *It looks like you might be stuck waiting tables for the rest of your life after all.*

Stupid twin telepathy. Or lack thereof, in this case. I scratch my temple with my middle finger. Then, shifting my weight over my toe, I spin around and fix my gaze on the bane of my existence. Maureen.

She should look the same age as Mom, but a lifetime spent spitting on teenagers' dreams and in unsuspecting customers' soup has aged her immensely. She's short, stout, and currently steaming like a teapot.

"Look," I begin to say, "usually I would agree with you, but if I don't leave right now, I am going to be extremely late to practice."

Maureen crosses her arms. "For your silly figure skating? You're still doing that? This dream of yours is causing you to wither away to skin and—"

Whatever she was about to say is cut off by the worst sound any kitchen staff can hear: a pan of sauce tumbling to the floor.

My eyes widen and my neck snaps to look over at the culprit. Antonio.

His shoes are covered in red sauce, as is the floor surrounding him. His sous chef is already in action, grabbing a forgotten pan off the counter to recreate the recipe.

Maureen turns her attention away from me, simultaneously shouting orders at the line of cooks and vulgarities at Antonio. He looks past her to meet my eyes, and he winks, chancing a small smile. My heart swells.

Cole reaches around and shakes my shoulders. "If you're going to leave, you better do it now while she's distracted."

"You are amazing! And tell the same thing to Antonio later," I say as I use the towel in my other hand to wipe the sweat off Cole's face. He winces at the pressure, then yelps as I rip the hairnet from his head.

"Ow!"

"Oh, whatever." I lick my fingers and ruffle up his hair. Taking a step back, I grin at him. "There. You should actually be thanking me. Table eight is a group of businesswomen in town for a conference, so put on your best smile and dazzle them. I'm leaving. Tell Mom and Dad I said bye."

"When you see Victor, tell him that he still owes me five bucks," Cole says over his shoulder as he starts to walk away, pulling the black apron around his hips and tying it behind his back.

"Not my problem!" I call back before hustling out of the kitchen. My shoes squeak on the tile as I dodge our two dishwashers coming around the corner with a mop bucket.

I run down the hall, then slide around the corner into the back room, where the walls are lined with metal cubbies for employees' personal belongings. After snatching my duffle bag out of the lowest cubby, I continue my mad dash out the back door and into the rear parking lot. I duck my head against the cold September rain that's pouring down.

An old, rusted SUV is waiting right outside the door, lit by the nearby light poles. Tonight it looks like Cinderella's royal carriage. Annabelle, my best friend and soul sister, honks the horn as I take the final few running strides to the passenger door and fling it open, throwing myself onto the seat.

"Drive!" I yell as I roll over to push my bag to the floor.

Annabelle is already taking off across the parking lot before I can get the car door closed. She hoots and points at the time. "Only two minutes late! And you can't be mad at me this time, because it isn't me that's holding you up."

I grin and glance over at her as I pull open the zipper at the top of my bag. Her brown eyes are glimmering, her curly hair is a frizzy mess, and her hands are at ten-and-two as she focuses on the road. My knight in shining armor.

"What?" I laugh and pull out a pink windbreaker. "Me, mad at you? Never."

"Next week, when I'm running behind, remember this moment."

Snorting, I set the windbreaker on the center console. "Seriously, thank you for taking me to practice. I am *so* over sharing a car with Cole. He is such a hog."

As I speak, her car begins to make a warning sound to let me know that I am still not wearing my seatbelt. That is a fact that I'm very well aware of as I kick off my serving shoes, hover my hips over the seat, and wiggle out of my work pants. When I know I'm going to be in a time crunch like this, I've learned to wear leggings underneath.

"Where in the world does he have to be tonight?" Annabelle takes a moment to look over her shoulder before switching lanes. The windshield wipers squeak on the glass.

I take out my sandals and slip them on. "The gym, I guess. He and the boys are gearing up for hockey season."

"Really?" She takes a moment to look at me with wide eyes. "Practice doesn't start for another two weeks."

"Your dad should be happy that they're putting in the extra effort before practice starts." I make sure there's no traffic in the lane next to us before stripping off my work shirt. I toss on the windbreaker equally as fast.

Annabelle chuckles, but her smile tightens as her eyes catch on my ribs. I pull the shirt the rest of the way down and bite my tongue.

"He'll be happy all right. Honestly, he will probably fall out of his chair when I tell him tonight. Speaking of, Tiffany was starting rumors earlier at lunch."

I grimace as I flip the sun visor down, opening the tiny mirror. Thinking about Tiffany makes me want to stick my head out of the window and hurl.

She continues, unfazed. "According to her, Jason's dad is getting involved with our varsity hockey teams this year. He's partnering with some AI company to make hockey sticks that track swings, power output, stuff like that. We're the test monkeys, I guess."

I stop in the middle of pulling bobby pins out of my bun when she says Jason's name. "What did he have to say about that?"

"You know Jason," Annabelle replies with a shrug. "He was smug, puffing out his chest, acting like he's all that and a bag of chips."

Rolling my eyes, I reiterate, "What did he *really* say?"

"That he doesn't want word of that to get around until he has all the facts. Which was too late, because Willie was already texting the JV teams to let them know what they're missing out on."

"Typical," I murmur as I unwind my black hair, letting it fall over my shoulders. My scalp aches with relief. "Well, good for Jason. I'm sure Jesse will let him help with that project. It would look good on college applications." It's hard to sound enthusiastic at the thought of him hanging around the rink again when I'm finally making peace with his absence.

"For sure. We all know how much he loves working with his dad." Annabelle rolls her eyes and dials down the heat.

"Don't get too excited. You'll have to work with Jesse too, if that happens," I remind her.

Annabelle used to play hockey until she fractured her collarbone in middle school, putting a pin in her athletic career. Her dad is the head coach of the boys' high school varsity hockey team, and he immediately took his daughter under his wing after her injury, turning her into the team's assistant coach/wrangler of teenage boys.

I pull my phone out of the bag as Annabelle groans. "I could go the rest of my life never seeing Jesse again and I'd die peacefully. Jason is so sweet. How did he end up being associated with monsters like him and Tiffany?"

Tiffany was never a monster to everyone. Just to me.

I shake my head. I don't want to get into it because Annabelle will say what she always does, and I don't have the energy to hear it.

She lets it go and starts to talk about her plans for this hockey season, but mentally I'm still tied up. Despite Tiffany's past friendship with me and Annabelle, there's been a bigger conflict of interest since she and Jason started dating at a party last autumn.

Jason Forbes is an All-American boy, wrapped up in a pretty blond hair and green-eyed package. He is Cole's best friend, and those two have been practically inseparable since elementary school. They played on the same hockey team their entire life up until a few months ago.

He and I are close—no, *were* close. Not so much anymore.

I finish pulling myself together for practice by the time Annabelle pulls into the parking lot of the rink. I jump out of the car with my bag, leaving her to follow. The phone vibrates in my hand, and raindrops splatter against the screen as I glance at the notifications. During my short work shift, over one-hundred people have already liked my newest blog post breaking down Victor and I's twizzle sequence, and there's thirty new comments. I clear it all away. I'll deal with that later.

At the same time, the screen lights up with a phone call. Speak of the devil.

As I start to answer it, the front doors of the rink open. Victor steps outside under the awning, his narrow eyes slanted with concern until he looks up. His shoulders crumple with relief, and he takes the phone down from his ear to hang up.

"You're cutting it a little too close for comfort, ladies." Victor steps back and holds the door open for us. He regards Annabelle as he asks, "What was it this time? A gaggle of geese crossing the road? A shirtless man running down the sidewalk?"

"I wasn't going to run those poor geese over!" Annabelle counters.

I breeze through the second set of doors, and a cold rush of air greets me. "That's because I was the one who jumped out of the car and chased them to the other side of the road."

Annabelle shakes her finger at me, then turns to Victor as we enter the lobby. "Besides, you would've slowed down for that runner, too. His back literally had hills and valleys. Mr. Wagner could've used his little plastic army men to reenact World War I on that expanse of space, if you know what I mean."

Victor smirks and grabs my elbow, dragging me toward the North Rink. "I know *exactly* what you mean. See you later."

"Enjoy practice." Annabelle waves at us before disappearing down the hallway that leads to her dad's office.

"She's really got to start driving faster," Victor mutters and glances at his phone, using his lanky legs to match my pace as we turn the corner. "Or you need to tell Cole to pass over the car keys every once in a while."

I let out one singular bark of laughter. "We both know how that would end. At least I'm dressed for practice this time."

Victor runs a hand over his straight black hair. "I think Coach Ortiz would rather see you skating in work pants than be a single minute late."

"She wouldn't even let that slide. May as well cancel practice at that point." I stop talking for a moment to catch my breath as we begin to descend the stairs. "Not that I'd let that happen."

"No, you wouldn't." Victor takes my bag from me, tossing it over his shoulder. "Remember last year? When you didn't let me stay home that one night I had a hundred-degree fever and diarrhea? That was a short, crappy practice. No pun intended."

I nudge him with my elbow. "Let's be honest, you're as dedicated as I am. That's why I love you so much."

"No chance of that here, girl." Victor chuckles and proves his point as we both turn our heads to check out a cute brunette boy that runs up the stairs in the opposite direction, his skates thudding against his back.

We reach the benches on the side of the rink and sit by his gear. He puts my bag between us and I dig out my skates just as Juliette and

Montgomery, our old competitors that recently turned into teammates, come stumbling off the ice.

I've already learned my lesson about inserting myself into other people's lives, so I try to forget the fact that a few months ago I would've happily ignored her and instead act like what we are: team mates.

Juliette returns my smile as she steps past, not one blonde hair out of place. She has always reminded me of the porcelain dolls that my grandma keeps up high in a cabinet and she swears we could sell for thousands of dollars once she's dead.

Montgomery's mouth hardens into a flat line, like someone brought a Greek sculpture to life and stuck a stick where the sun doesn't shine.

"Are you guys done early, or are we behind?" Victor asks as he finishes lacing up.

"I hate to say this, but I think you're late." Montgomery lifts his wrist to glance at his watch. "By three minutes."

Great. My fingers shake as I tie off the last knot. Victor gets to his feet and goes over to the rink door, taking a moment to pull off his blade guards.

"We left Ortiz in a good mood for you guys. You'll be okay," Juliette says as she grabs her water bottle.

"I appreciate the positivity, but let's be real. She's not going to be happy." I launch up and pull my hair into a ponytail as I hurry after Victor. "Let's do this."

"Take a breath, guys. Good luck. I've got the door." Montgomery gets up to latch it behind us as we step onto the ice. I push off first, my fingertips numb with adrenaline.

"Jansky! Kerr!" Coach Ortiz's voice echoes in the rink, causing other skaters to look over their shoulders to see who's in trouble. "You're late."

Victor's eyes bore into my back, though he knows better than to offer empty excuses. The second we're on the ice, we're not two separate people anymore. We are one unit. One person's mistake is both of our mistakes.

I swallow, and my pounding heart drowns out my words. "Yes, ma'am. We know we're late, and we're sorry."

"Our apologies," Victor echoes as he comes to a stop beside me, right in front of Ortiz, her silver hair tied back in a tight bun.

"There are twelve hours until we fly out to Colorado for the Fall Classic. That means one more practice." She lifts her watch to read the time. "And we've already wasted five minutes. Do you understand me?"

Of course we do. In the eleven years Victor and I have been a pair, we've been late only a handful of times, including tonight. I bite my tongue and keep that thought to myself.

Victor stiffens. He's probably thinking the same thing, but he replies, "We understand."

She sniffs, unconvinced, then flourishes her hand. "Take ten laps together to warm up, matching pace and tempo. Kerr, watch your pesky left leg. Don't let it drop heavily."

We say another yes ma'am in unison before taking off to the rail. The ice chips away under our blades, and other skaters move out of our way as we begin moving counterclockwise.

"Sometimes I imagine taking my skate and throwing it at her face just to wipe off that stupid scowl," Victor mutters under his breath.

Out of the corner of my eye, I watch his footfalls. Left, right, left. I adjust my stride and move my feet a little quicker. Within seconds, we sound like one body, the blades of our skates striking at the same time.

I risk my life by whispering in response, "It's not worth the fight, Vick. We need her." Even if lately my nervous system has been mistaking skating practice as being hunted for sport.

"Yeah, the same way I need a hole in my skull." Victor shakes his head as I cast him an unamused look. We become silent, focusing on our warm-up. The next corner comes up fast, and even though there's nobody beyond the plexiglass windows, I glance at the West Rink out of habit.

The Greater Midwest Ice Complex is a huge facility that hosts three full-size skating rinks, a lobby with a concession stand, offices for the coaches, locker rooms, and even a second-level viewing deck overlooking multiple rinks. Ortiz leases out the North Rink for her skating team year-round, while the local high school uses the West and South Rinks for their ice sports, mainly hockey this time of year.

Coach Lloyd always claims the West Rink for his boys, so for most of my high school career, I could check in on my brother and his friends from afar. Growing up has already begun to pull us all in different directions, not leaving any time to see each other outside of school. I've found solace in glancing past the scuffed glass windows, watching as they become amazing athletes. It won't be so quiet in two weeks when they all go back to practice.

Well, not everyone.

My stomach aches with the reminder that I'll never catch a glimpse of Jason on the ice again. Their last practice was back in March, right before the semi-final game that stripped him of his role on the hockey team. All of those years, that hard work, erased.

The empty rink mocks me because, even when the boys start practicing again, the team will never be complete.

My right foot betrays me by sticking the toe pick into the ice, causing me to stumble. I catch myself and right my center of gravity so I don't end up crashing into the windows like the hockey players do.

Victor raises his eyebrows and waits for me to catch up. "Are you good? What's wrong with you?"

"I'm fine. Nothing." I continue along, my cheeks flaming as Ortiz reprimands me from across the ice.

Once we finish our warm-up, Ortiz coaches us through the individual sections of our choreography where we've been slacking. I sense each passing minute as if a clock were ticking inside of my chest, counting down the time until we step onto the performance ice in Colorado.

"Okay, let's put all of that together." Ortiz skates over to us as Victor sets me down from a combination curve lift that we've been practicing for the past ten minutes. I'm panting, sweat is dripping down the side of my face, and my body has forgotten the 823-calorie lunch that I fed it nearly seven hours ago.

"The entire routine?" Victor clarifies as he reads my mind and puts his hands on his hips. He's unaffected by our hard work. I'm too busy catching my breath to talk, fighting nausea.

"No, only until the combination lift." She slides backward, then points at the center of the rink. "Get in position and I'll count you down."

Victor starts off in that direction. My heart is pumping, pumping, pumping as I catch up with him. My lungs ache, fighting the cold exterior air and my hot interior oxygen.

He spins on the balls of his feet we reach the middle mark, his mouth pulling down into a frown. "Seriously, Clarity. You seem off."

"It's nothing." I put my back to him and raise my arms delicately. Digging my heels into the ice, I breathe. In, out. "Pre-competition jitters."

Victor huffs, and out of the corner of my eye, I catch him adjusting the position of his arm to mirror mine. "You don't get nervous."

I don't know how to respond, but it doesn't matter. Ortiz calls out, "One, two..."

Breathe.

"Three!"

Exhaling, I break away from Victor in a flash of movement as the song begins, keeping an eye on him as he backpedals away from me.

I push off each foot rapidly, then launch into a simple 360-degree spin. Behind me, I know that Victor is doing a 180-degree spin, pausing, and taking off after me. Slowing my speed, I press into my heels and sense him burst around my side as he flies backwards in an arc to face me.

We have been working together for so long that I feel like he is an extension of me. I know where he is going to be as I put myself in position for moves, and I know where he is even when my eyes aren't on him. And, more importantly, I trust him to be there when I can't see him.

My path and momentum take me right into his arms. He grabs my waist and picks me up for a moment, then pulls me toward his body, his abdomen against my back. I grab his forearms as he lets me back down, but keeps his hold on me to guide us in a spinning circle.

I raise my left leg parallel to the ice at the same time he does with his, and our circle gains speed.

Nausea hits me—

No. Not again. Not now. I ignore it.

"Hold that position right there! Count your rotations!" Coach Ortiz yells over the sound of scraping ice.

Right on four, Victor and I melt into our next move. We straighten and he grabs my left leg as I raise it vertically into the air. Grabbing my left foot with my right hand, Victor puts his arm around my back and guides me into another series of rotational spins.

"Beautiful, Jansky. Kerr, more passion! More passion!"

I'd rather hear her say that than, *"Stop! Try again!"* The quicker we finish, the sooner I can take a minute for myself.

Victor keeps his hands on me, a gentle barrier as I put my leg down and spin around. We latch hands to use each other as an anchor for a moment before coming back together.

I transition into a catchfoot spin as Victor lowers into a sit spin, keeping his hands on me for guidance. As fast as we came into the move, we move out of it again and split off into another game of chase.

As we progress through the routine, so does the complexity of our moves. My heart is in my throat as he begins to position himself for one of our hardest lifts, a reverse rotational with an upside-down hold.

I send up a quick prayer, allowing Victor to swoop in and throw me upside down over his shoulder as he spins. Straightening my legs, I hold the splits.

There's no one else I would trust for this. We've practiced this lift so many times, but tonight, my vision blurs. The edges of the rink are like smeared watercolor as he builds momentum.

Vertigo brushes against my waist as Victor begins to unfold out of the lift. He inhales sharply, yanking me back into his arms as I start to fall.

Black dots swim at the edge of my vision as he sets me upright on the solid ground. His hands grip my forearms, and his lips move silently, asking the same question that's lit in his eyes.

All of my senses fire up again at once. I wince against the bright lights reflecting off the ice, the earthy scent of his cologne mixed with sweat, the pressure of his fingernails digging into my skin, and the sound of Ortiz yelling.

"Excuse me, what was that?" she barks, the blades on her feet flashing as she approaches. "Did you not hear me when I said we're leaving tomorrow? Where are my athletes that were ready to sweep the competition?"

"I'm sorry," I apologize around my heaving breath. So many empty apologies tonight. "I lost my balance."

"New skaters lose their balance, Jansky. Baby giraffes lose their balance. You? No." She eyes me, sharp and cutting. "You lost focus. Rewind" —she circles her finger in the air— "and do that lift again. You have more eyes on you than ever this season, so start acting like it. Kovalenko only takes the strongest athletes, and right now, you are not it."

Anya Kovalenko. The legendary Team USA trainer who is scouting my senior year. Ortiz told me so one month ago.

The back of my throat stings, desperate for water. My stomach growls, needing sustenance. Right now, none of that matters. I need to impress Kovalenko, my blog, the world.

"Do you need a break first?" Victor asks.

"Nope. I'm ready." I turn away from him, leaving no room for argument.

He huffs in annoyance. "You better not be lying to me."

"When have I ever lied?" I reach for his hand as he enters my space. The look he gives me almost makes me laugh. Almost.

"Less talking, more practicing," Ortiz snaps.

Victor's jaw ticks as we push off, taking half a lap to regain speed. He begins to set himself up again as we fly down the center of the rink, his hand tightening around mine.

Hot air up, cold air down. Inhale, exhale, *lift*. Swing up, head down. Down below, ice rushes past. Legs split. Vertigo doesn't brush against me this time. It yanks.

My center of gravity is thrown, and I yelp, bucking my legs. Victor lets out a string of curses, his stability compromised, balance lost.

The ice rushes to greet me. I resist, instinctively grabbing the first thing I see—Victor's arm—and twisting as I fall. A loud crack echoes across the rink, and this time it's not from the hockey players practicing. His cursing turns into screaming as my blade misses the hard ice, slicing down his leg.

We fall hard.

Sparks of pain shoot up my knees. Victor's head bounces off the ice, and he's gasping. Short, quick, shocked breaths. Something warm and wet is soaking my leggings. Blood, rushing out of his thigh. I push onto my knees and stare at the red pooling onto the white ice.

"Stay still! Don't move." Ortiz flies over, her annoyance erased from a moment ago. For the first time in a long time, fear is drawn on her face as she squats down, carefully positioning Victor's arm against his body. Her gaze slides past me, focusing on a skater somewhere behind us. "Darika! Get the first aid kit, now!"

"I'm sorry," I whisper.

Victor blends in with the ice, he's gotten so pale. His gaze bounces to mine, reflecting the same sorrow and pain.

Ortiz doesn't hear me. Her hand falls on his cheek, and she taps him. "Victor? Kerr, are you with me?"

"Yes," he croaks.

"Hold your arm there. Yes, like that. Clarity, listen to me. I need your help. We need to get him to my car and to the hospital immediately. Let's get him up."

I don't know what to do other than obey. My limbs are filled with TV static as Ortiz walks me through the steps. Put our hands under his shoulders and back. Haul him up. Be grateful he's skinny. Ignore his cries of pain. Get him off the ice.

Darika is waiting outside of the boards with a red case in her hands. The poor young girl's brown skin is ashen as she stares at the gash in Victor's thigh.

Ortiz pauses our pitiful parade to prop him on the bench, using a scissor to cut a hole in the leg of his pants. She presses the gauze against the bleeding wound, her mouth set in a straight line as she adds a second layer before wrapping the tape around it. When she's satisfied that he won't bleed out, we change into shoes and continue to the elevator down the hallway.

My fingers and toes are still numb with shock as we limp toward the lobby doors. Darika is already waiting with our bags, her hands trembling as she opens the doors for us and follows us outside. The rain has lightened to a drizzle, and it almost feels warm compared to the cold rink.

Ortiz's Mercedes SUV chirps as we approach, and she nods her head at the back door. Darika jumps forward, pulling it open. The interior is show-room-perfect, the leather seats polished to a glimmering shine. Pain flashes across her eyes as Victor slides inside, leaving behind a small trail of blood that has begun to seep out of the dressing.

Darika sets our bags inside, tears shining in her eyes. "I'm so sorry, guys."

We make eye contact, and her lip wobbles. I wish I could hug her, but Ortiz practically pushes me into the backseat with Victor, handing me another package of gauze. "Hold that on his leg."

"Yes, ma'am," I whisper, my voice cracking as the package crinkles in my hand. She slams the door, says something to Darika, then runs around to the driver's seat. My fingers finally began to tremble, and it takes me four tries to open the plastic.

Victor groans as the engine roars to life, cradling his arm against his chest. He knocks his head back against the headrest. "I don't feel good."

"I wouldn't think so." Ortiz starts to peel out of the parking lot. "Just don't throw up in my car. We'll be at the hospital in a few minutes. Clarity, you better call someone to sit with you. I'll stay with Victor when we get there, but you'll need to get your head checked."

Sit with me? Annabelle is busy with her dad. Cole is probably at the gym by now. My parents are at work. I could call the restaurant, but it's the busiest night of the week, and I don't want to disrupt any of them. Besides, they'd all freak out. I can't handle any more panic beyond my own.

I press the gauze against the rivers of blood that are running down Victor's leg with one hand. With my other, I weasel the phone out of the pocket in my bag at my feet.

There's only one other person I can think of that's sitting around tonight.

I haven't spoken to him since last Thursday during lunch, and even that conversation lasted ten seconds.

Shock pricks my skin when he picks up on the first ring. His voice is laced with concern, muffled through the speakers. "C.J? What's wrong?"

Something about hearing his voice makes me crack.

"Jason," I sob. "I need you."

Chapter 2

Jason

Dad has reminded me every week for the last six months that I'm lucky to have a backup plan to fall back on since I had to go and blow up my hockey career. His words, not mine.

Hockey was supposed to be my escape. It was going to be my one-way ticket to leave Minneapolis and go somewhere else. Maybe I could've signed with the Boston Bruins and moved to Massachusetts, or gone to Canada with the Montreal Canadiens. I would've gone anywhere to move away from this city that has turned into a time capsule of memories.

Not even twenty-four hours after Coach Lloyd looked me in the face and told me to pack my gear and not come back, I started chasing a new dream. Dad hooked me up with an internship at SporTech, the multi-million-dollar sports technology business that he breathed life into during college. He said it was to keep my mind off of things, but being his only child, I know he expects me to take over one day.

I worked there all summer and I clock in every afternoon after school, yet I'm still waiting to feel that sense of belonging and camaraderie that every other person on the payroll seems to have.

I'm surrounded by research and development teams, all types of engineers, a hierarchy of finance analysts, and that's barely scratching the surface. These people are solid in their careers. Personal belongings litter their desks, and during work hours, conversations that sound terribly important fill the stations. Everyone has a place. Everyone is a part of this great machine. If one part fails, the entire operation would fall apart.

Me? I'm a loose bolt that's rattling around inside. Not necessarily doing any damage, but annoying all the same.

The test results of the latest development project are typed, printed, and punched with three holes, clipped inside of the binder that's under my arm. Two software engineers that I don't remember the names of are the only ones left in the bullpen, absorbed in their work. Everyone else has gone home for the day, save for me and dad.

I walk down the hallway and pull at the collar of my button-up shirt before slipping into Paul's office, the product and development manager. Light from the hallway spills over his messy desk. This is the last thing I have to do today, so I add the binder to the chaos and turn around to go home.

The phone in my pocket vibrates as I close the door. I scowl and pull it out, expecting to see Tiffany's name. No, it's better.

Wait. Worse.

Clarity? We haven't spoken in ages. This can't be good, not without a pre-warning text.

I grab the doorframe with one hand, immediately answering with the other. "C.J? What's wrong?"

This must be a joke. Maybe she dialed the wrong number or Cole needs something but his phone died. That's why my stomach drops further when she begins to sob and chokes out the words, "Jason, I need you."

I start sprinting toward the back exit. One engineer looks up as I pass, then goes right back to work.

"I'm coming, don't worry," I try to soothe her, even as my voice shakes with panic. The only reason I pause is to grab the jacket at my desk, then I'm moving again, right out into the main hallway. "What's going on? Where are you?"

"I—In—I'm in the car," Clarity stutters, then hiccups. I hit the button to summon the elevator, then run a hand over my blond hair. "I was at skating practice with Victor, but I fell. He might've broken his arm trying to catch me, and I sliced..." She fades off, her voice cracking as she starts to cry again.

In the background, I hear Victor say, "Relax, would you? We're not heading to get me cremated."

My heart pounds in my ears as I step into the elevator and hit the button for the first floor. "Take a breath. It's going to be okay. Who's taking you?"

She takes another shuddering inhale. "Coach Ortiz."

I squeeze my eyes shut with gratitude. At least she isn't driving him alone. "Okay. What hospital are you guys going to?"

"North Memorial, I think." She pauses and a female voice mumbles in the background. "Yeah."

"Alright, I'm leaving the office. I should be at my car in a minute, and I'll be there in thirty. Can I bring you anything?" I ask as I watch the elevator numbers tick by. Finally, the doors slide open, and I hurry out.

"No, no. I've already got our bags and everything. Ortiz said I should have someone pick me up while she sits with Victor. Everyone else is busy, or at work."

That makes more sense. My stomach pinches knowing that I was her last resort, however I'm grateful that she called. Those are two awful thoughts to have while she's holding pieces of her friend together. I immediately shake those thoughts away, refusing to entertain them. She is my priority. Nothing else.

"Let me know if anything changes." I continue my jog outside. The brittle cold steals the air from my lungs, and the rain doesn't help. Thankfully, the parking lot is covered, so I'm not completely soaked by the time I reach the Range Rover. "I'll be there soon."

"Okay." She's stopped crying, but the silence is almost worse. "Thank you. Drive safe. See you soon."

She disconnects the call first. I jump behind the wheel, and I won't admit to her I drive anything but safe.

The thirty-minute drive almost gets shaved down to twenty, yet they still beat me here. I wasn't expecting to see anyone in the waiting room, but there's Clarity, pacing along the back wall, chewing her thumbnail as she texts with her other hand.

I haven't seen her since last Thursday: she's been taking advantage of extra study halls instead of lunches so far this week. She's a wreck with her messy ponytail, smeared mascara, and pink windbreaker smeared with either dark paint or blood. I'm betting blood. I don't care. She's a sight for my sore eyes.

The receptionist behind the desk lifts her head, a tired smile crossing her face. "Evening, sir. Can I help you with something?"

"No, thank you," I say, and Clarity spins around at the sound of my voice. "I'm here for her."

She meets me halfway and I pull her into a hug, burying my face in her hair as she hides hers against my neck. Her shoulders shake. I rub her back, allowing the faded scent of her perfume to ground me, remind me she's safe in my arms.

Clarity sniffles as she steps away and wipes the tears off her cheeks. Her eyes widen as she stares at the shoulder of my shirt. "Oh, no. I don't know if that's mascara or blood on your shirt. Maybe it's both. I'm so sorry."

"Don't worry about it. It's just a shirt." I let her go. She drops into a nearby chair like the air got knocked out of her.

I don't know what it is about this waiting room; maybe it's the lack of people, the bright fluorescent lights, or the large windows that make everything else feel small, but she appears impossibly slight and fragile, like the chair is about to swallow her whole.

The chair next to her squeaks as I sit down and lean on the armrest between us. "Not ready to go home?"

Another strand of hair falls out of her ponytail as she shakes her head. "No. They brought Victor back to get cleaned up and take x-rays. A nurse already checked my head, and I'm fine. I'd just like to see him before we leave. Make sure he's okay." Her breath hitches, and her eyes flash up from the floor, hooking into mine. "It's my fault that he's hurt."

"That's not true."

"It is." Clarity wraps her arms around her stomach at the same time it lets out a low whine. She hesitates. "I panicked and lost my balance. That's never happened before."

I hold a steady expression on my face, refusing to show my shock. She's right. I've seen her practice on the other side of that rink window for years. I've watched every video that she has posted on her blog. Not once have I witnessed her lose control. Crash and burn? Sure, we all do from time to time. Would I describe those times as a result of *panicking?* Absolutely not.

Clarity lets out a slow exhale. "We were supposed to fly out tomorrow with the team for a competition in Colorado, but that's not happening."

"Do you have pre-comp anxiety?" I ask gently. "Is that what threw you off?"

She snorts. "No way. I don't get nervous." Her hand sub-consciously slides over her stomach as it growls loudly again. I cast my eyes to the clock on the wall. 7:32. Way past dinner time.

"I'm going to get something from the vending machine," I say as I stand. "Need anything?"

Clarity pulls her ponytail over her shoulder and grimaces. "I don't have cash on me."

"That's not what I asked."

She blinks and bites her lip. "Surprise me."

That's what I thought. I stuff down my smile as I turn away, walking over to the vending machines on the far wall.

I get a Gatorade for myself—light blue, the best one—and a zero-sugar lemonade Vitamin Water for her. Her favorite. The snack machine is a little more intimidating. I decide on a bag of honey mustard pretzels that's the same brand she used to eat in sixth grade.

Clarity sits up as I return. Her dark eyes light up as she takes the pretzels. "Wow, I haven't had these in years. They're my favorite. How did you know?"

I shrug and crack open my drink as I sit back down. "Lucky guess."

"Thank you." She pulls her phone out. Instead of attacking the food like I expected, she opens up her calculator and starts adding the calorie count.

Pausing mid swig, I raise an eyebrow and slowly take the bottle away from my mouth. I don't get the chance to say anything because the elevator dings, opening the doors to reveal Alanna Ortiz stepping out.

Despite how often we practiced next to the figure skaters when I played hockey, I've never spoken to her. Except there's no forgetting her cold eyes, her foxish face. Coach Lloyd is a hardass, but there was always a running joke on the hockey team that we should be grateful we're not skating for Alanna.

Clarity's already on her feet, gathering her things as she says, "That didn't take long."

"They're finishing in the exam room, but he should be in the inpatient room by the time we get upstairs." Her attention lands on me. "Jason. I remember you. You're one of Ralph Lloyd's boys."

"Yep, you got it." I get to my feet while offering Alanna my hand. I should correct her and say I haven't been one of Lloyd's boys for months, except she doesn't seem like the type to appreciate that. Instead, I leave it at, "It's nice to officially meet you."

"Likewise." Her handshake is steely, as is the expression on her face when she notices the bag of pretzels in Clarity's hand. Suddenly, I wish I would've greeted her with an uppercut.

Clarity recoils, tucking the pretzels under her arm, out of sight as we follow Alanna to the elevator. "How's Victor doing?"

"Better. They cleaned up his leg and we'll have a solid answer on his arm soon. Miraculously, he doesn't have a concussion." She presses the elevator button, and we file inside. "But the doctor used his judgement, and he thinks Victor's wrist is broken. If I had to guess, it'll likely take twelve weeks to heal. The gash in his thigh will take a minimum of four."

"You're kidding," I mutter. Given the glint in Clarity's eyes, she'd probably like to use a stronger word.

"What are we going to do?" Clarity's tone edges toward dismay. "Competitions have already started! It's too late to sign me up for any solo performances this season. If I can't see our competition schedule through, I'll be a sitting duck until next year. This season is my chance to get rooted at the senior level, and the USFSA—"

"Clarity," Alanna cuts her off sharply. "Enough. I am well aware of the situation, however we need to focus on one problem at a time."

The elevator opens and Alanna strides down the hallway. Clarity rolls her shoulders back, jaw tight, eyes glassy as she follows in her coach's wake. Despite my long legs, I have to hustle to keep up with them, my gut churning. The energy in the air makes me feel like I've been here before, running after Lloyd, yelling, "*I didn't do anything wrong!*"

He had spun around, suddenly appearing ten years older. There was no anger in his voice, just disappointment when he said, "*Yes, you did, Jason. You violated the code of conduct. I'm sorry, son, but you're done.*"

Done. The period at the end of a sentence, the pin on the cork board holding up the leftover fragments of a dream. The end never seems possible until the door is shut in your face.

We walk past the closed doors of rooms 301, 303, and 306. 309 is open and Alanna steps inside. "Good, you're back."

Clarity and I are right behind her. She immediately flies to Victor's bedside, throwing her arms around his neck to avoid the brace that's holding his right arm to his chest.

I hover in the doorway to take in the scene. I haven't seen Victor for quite some time, yet nothing has changed. He's got the same thick black hair, flat nose, and wiry build. His eyes well up with tears as he returns the awkward hug.

Clarity pulls away and lets out a choked laugh. "Hey, don't make me cry again." She sets down her snacks and grabs a tissue out of the box on the side table to hand to him. "It's okay."

"No, it's not." Victor takes it and dabs his tears. "I should've put my foot down when I noticed something was wrong. We could have avoided this."

Clarity lowers her chin as she settles in the chair next to him, picking at a thread on her sleeve.

Victor rolls his head toward me, his eyes widening in surprise. "What are you doing here?"

"I called him," she says, and glances up.

He quirks an eyebrow. "You did? *Him?* When?"

My gut pangs with the tone he uses. What's that supposed to mean?

"You were sitting right next to me when I did."

"I was also bleeding out and holding my arm together. I apologize that I wasn't an active participant in your conversation."

"Actually, you were."

I open my mouth to agree, but Alanna raises her hand, regaining our attention. "What's done is done. We have to move forward."

Victor starts, "I could have paid more attention—"

"Don't." I step forward. "It was a stroke of bad luck. Don't play that game with yourself." I meet Clarity's eyes, and the despair I see makes my stomach pang. "Either of you."

She looks away. Victor eyes me. "Bad luck or not, we're screwed for the season. Best case scenario, I'm ready for light practice again in three months. Worst case scenario, I'm out until next summer. Either way, I sure as hell won't be ready for the Ice Dance Invitational in November."

"Right now, we're glad that you're going to be okay." Clarity lifts her chin. "Personally, I'm more worried about my best friend."

That answer doesn't match her concerns in the elevator, although that's none of my business. Victor stares at her and waits. She sighs and drops her eyes, confirming my thoughts by saying, "And I'm really worried about what this skating season is going to look like. Anya Kovalenko has been sniffing around, and now I have Shawn Duarte in my comments asking where we're going to be competing this fall. What am I supposed to tell him?"

Those names sound familiar, but I can't place them. Given the look that flashes across Victor's face, I know they're important.

"We can deal with that tomorrow." Alanna walks to the other side of the hospital bed to pour herself a glass of water.

Victor winces as he attempts to sit up straighter. The pain in his eyes spurs me to move forward and help, except Clarity beats me to it, jumping to her feet to help him readjust.

"Thanks," he says, then visibly bites his cheek.

Clarity shuffles backward. "What is it?"

Victor chuckles, the sound devoid of humor. "I'm going to sound crazy."

"Nothing can be crazier than this." She flourishes her hand around the hospital room.

Victor closes his eyes for a moment, his eyebrows bunching together. "Ortiz, correct me if I'm wrong. As a pair, Clarity and I have enough points for the season where we could skip the Fall Classic and go straight to the Invitational."

"Correct. But you won't be able to skate by then," Alanna says, echoing his earlier statement.

Victor opens his eyes and holds up his good hand. "Okay, so we have four days to make adjustments to the team. File a partner substitution. Team edits close October first."

"Kerr, you know that all of our backup options already have a partner."

"I don't trust any of them, anyway," Clarity grumbles.

Victor straightens up more, the sheets wrinkling loudly in protest. "There is one person I have in mind."

"Okay, smart guy. Enlighten us." Clarity quirks her head dramatically.

Victor points. At me.

My breath hitches.

Alanna chokes on her drink.

Clarity's jaw drops, and she also points at me. "*Jason?*"

My stomach drops to my shoes. The last time I approached her to ask if she wanted to work together, she all but told me that there was never, *ever* going to be a chance at that. She had her path, and I had mine. I made peace with that.

Now, our paths are joining, paving a two-lane highway.

Our eyes clash, her fear mirroring mine.

"He—You're the only option," Victor says to me as Alanna starts coughing. "Jason, think about it! You already know how to skate. Very well, may I add. It won't take much to put figure skates on your feet and show you the ropes."

I stare at him in disbelief. Me, the ex-hockey player, trading shoulder pads for tights? Explaining to my dad that I'm walking away from my internship to return to the ice? Heaven forbid, explain to my *girlfriend* that I'll be spending every night of the week with someone else? She's going to get mad, then I'll apologize for something I didn't do, and we'll pretend everything is fine until the next fight. We've done this dance since we first started dating, and I'm starting to wonder how many more rounds I've got left in me.

Except the more he talks, the more the cogs in my brain spin. I remember Clarity's fingers running over my face, pulling at my hair. The way my rough calluses scratched over the smooth skin on her hips.

"You're not committed to hockey anymore. You have time to practice. If you put the pedal to the metal, you can learn enough to get through the Invitational. After that, you guys would have two months to prepare for Nationals in January." Victor turns to Alanna. "I can help coach. We can make this work."

"Okay, that's a lot to ask," Clarity says, her words strained.

Is it really when the answer suddenly seems so obvious? I have the skills and talent to pull myself into something respectable for her. I dedicated myself to hockey for years, so what's another few months of practice?

Besides, I'm freaking out over nothing. The kiss we shared last summer didn't mean anything. Clarity made that very clear to me when we
promised to never talk about it again. We're just friends, even if tonight
is the most we've spoken since junior prom.

Alanna sets her cup down with a loud thud. "Well, he'd certainly need
all of the help he can get. I'm just not sold—"

"I'll do it."

The words tumble out before I can stop them.

Everyone turns to me wearing varying levels of surprise. Clarity stands
with her hands on her hips, lips parted like she's about to question my
judgement.

I repeat myself, leaving no room for questions other than my own as
I turn to Alanna. "Let's do it. When do we start?"

November 2008 - Age 9
Clarity

My hands haven't stopped shaking for the past hour. My tongue is going to be ruined forever, permanently indented with teeth marks. The taste of blood refuses to leave my mouth as I continue to swallow down bile to keep from making any noise.

I'm finally alone in the bathroom stall, and I let the tears run down my cheeks silently as the hockey girls start to come into the locker room. Gritting my teeth together, I hear seams splitting as I tug this awful dress off. Last week I couldn't wait to wear it. Tonight, I can't wait to throw it in the garbage. Even my leggings feel tight as I pull them on, and my skin squishes together at my waist. *Fatty.*

"Clarity? Are you still back here?" Annabelle calls out.

I smear my hands over my face, wiping away the tears as I grab my bag from the floor and unlock the stall door. "Yeah, coming."

I step out and nearly run into her. Her curly hair is a frizzy mess, and her arms are crossed.

"That took a while." Tiffany walks around Annabelle's backside, still wearing her hockey pads from practice. She raises her eyebrow at me. "Why are you crying?"

"I'm not." I clench my jaw.

Annabelle frowns. "But your eyes are red. Didn't you and Victor get to practice in your new outfits today?"

"Coach Ortiz said I was fat," I whisper before I can stop myself. The tears start to spill again.

Tiffany eyes me and shrugs. "My dad always says to listen to our coach."

I blink, stunned. Annabelle whirls around. "*Tiffany*. Why would you say that?"

"What?" She raises her hands. "I'm not the one who called her names."

Annabelle spins back around and walks over to me, brushing the tears off my face as she whispers just for me to hear, "Don't listen to her."

I don't reply. It's too late for that. They're confirming my worst fear, and I can feel the truth taking root. I know one thing is true: nobody will ever look at me and be able to call me fat again.

Chapter 3
Clarity

I grip the duffel bag in my lap with trembling hands and listen to the quiet lull of Jason's music with the man himself driving beside me. It's like I've stepped into the Twilight Zone. How is it that a few hours ago I was skating with a whole and healthy Victor?

At any moment, I'll wake up from this nightmare. I already told Jason that I wanted nothing to do with him after he showed up at our house last July, begging me to love him back. Even though I felt the same way, I just couldn't admit it. I couldn't let him be a distraction, or change the dynamic between me and Cole. I promised myself he would always be at arm's distance.

But if that's the case, why did I reach out to him tonight?

Here's the better question: *why did he agree to help me?*

After everything I put him through, he shouldn't have even answered my call.

I stop watching raindrops race down the window and turn to face Jason. Backlit by the passing streetlights, the strong angles of his face are hidden in shadows. He appears lost in thought, one hand steady on the wheel, his other elbow leaning on the windowsill, staring thousands of miles into the distance.

I clear my throat. He flinches, coming back to life as I ask, "Do you know what you're getting yourself into by doing this?"

"Doing what? Driving you home?" Jason teases. His smile falls as I shoot him a pointed stare and he tries again. "Yeah, I understand."

"Holy cow," I murmur as reality hits. He's my partner now. I'll have to tell thousands of my followers that Victor is out and Jason is in.

A sudden wave of dizziness forces me to lean forward and hold my head in my hands. Inhaling slowly, I'm hit with a scent that's entirely Jason: citrus, musk, vanilla. This car reeks of him, understandably so, but it's driving me crazy. The last time I was surrounded by these scents, my tongue was in his mouth. Kissing...

I can't be thinking like this. He has a girlfriend.

I pop my head back up. "What are you going to tell Tiffany?"

She never liked to share when we were younger, and I'd bet my life savings that hasn't improved with time. Besides, she already hates me, and I can't even begin to imagine how those emotions will deepen when she finds out I'm stepping back into the picture.

I mean, she could've prevented this by never approaching the boy who was mine first to begin with, but that's none of my business. I promised myself I wouldn't get involved when they started to see each other—not that there's any reason for me *to* get involved. There's no law that says two of my childhood friends can't date each other. All of it is water under the bridge.

"Leave Tiffany to me," Jason says firmly and returns both hands to the wheel. "She's not your problem. She'll be fine. Besides, in a few weeks, she will be busy with hockey. Our practice times align, so it's not like she has anything to worry about. Our lives will continue to be the same."

"Jason, you are my friend, and you deserve to know that nothing about your life will be the same for the next six months." I hold up my hand and start rattling things off on my fingers. "Practice for an hour and a half every night, six days a week. Yoga and strength training. Memorizing routines."

"It's not that different from hockey."

"Oh, it is *completely* different—"

"C.J, are you trying to talk me out of this?" He tosses another mischievous grin in my direction, but it doesn't quite reach his eyes. *Ah ha.* So there *is* something else going on in his head. He's probably going to use skating as a rebound after getting banished off the ice.

"I wouldn't say that. Let's call it making you absolutely one hundred percent aware of what you're signing up for before it's too late. Oh, no." I groan and knock my head back. "What about your dad?"

"He will live. Everybody will live, trust me." Jason takes his eyes off the road to meet mine for a moment, sparking my nerves further. "Victor had a point, and you know it. I have the time and the talent. The only thing you should be concerned about right now is making sure that *you're* okay before we start practice next week."

That's a silly thing to be worried about, considering I'm totally fine. Maybe a little concerned that I'm about to be spending over ten hours a week in close proximity with him.

It's fine.

I angle myself toward the window again, grateful that we're merging onto the highway and into the darkness so he can't see my emotions going to war. The windshield wipers move soundlessly over the glass. The phone buzzes in my lap, and I spare a glance at it. More people have found my latest blog post, and the newest comment makes my stomach sink like a rock.

> **@ster_it_up** Why waste your time skating? You might as well jump straight to sports commentary. I could listen to you talk all day... guess some things don't change ;)

Sterling. My ex-boyfriend. I swallow bile and shut my phone off as a message notification from Jason's phone pops up on the car's center screen. Reading Tiffany's name almost pushes me over the edge.

Jason scowls and clears the message away, and the second one she sends. "Look, I know that in the past I—"

The phone in my lap begins to ring, making me flinch. If it's Sterling calling, I'm opening this car door and jumping out.

Jason cuts himself off and chews his lip as he glances over, watching me fumble in my haste to pick it up. I deflate. Annabelle is calling me back. She must've seen the texts I sent her in the hospital.

"I'm so sorry." I show him my screen. "I should take this."

"No, yes. You're good. Go ahead." Jason waves his hand, his shoulders falling.

I mouth the words *thank you* before accepting the call, preparing myself further by holding the phone a few inches away from my ear. "Hey."

"Clarity Donna Jansky!" Annabelle yells, and I wince. "Excuse me, but what the hell is going on? Where are you? How are you? Is Victor still on this side of the dirt?"

"I'm fine. Victor... will be fine, in, like, three months." I cast a sideways glance at Jason. "I'm with Jason now. He's bringing me home."

There's a moment of silence, and I take the phone away from my ear to see if the call dropped. I'm glad I did, because that's when she lets out a hair-splitting screech. "*Jason?* Jason Forbes?"

Jason looks over, hurt flashing across his face as he whispers, "Why do you guys keep saying it like that?"

I shake my head and turn down the volume on my phone. "Yes, that's the one. My parents are working—well, they're probably leaving soon, but that's beside the point—and you were busy, too."

"You could've sent someone to get me! You're practically my sister. I would've told my dad to kick rocks if it meant driving you to the *freaking hospital.*"

It takes the rest of the drive home for me to convince Annabelle that the world is still spinning on its axis, and to fill her in on Victor's condition. Jason pulls into the driveway of the townhouse and parks before turning to me, his eyes darting between mine, brimming with unspoken words.

I don't feel bad because in a few days we'll have plenty of time to talk. I unbuckle the seatbelt and grab my bag while letting Annabelle drone on and on about her cousin that never completely recovered from his wrist surgery. I take this moment to mute her and say to him, "Thank you for everything. You don't know how much this means to me."

"There's no need to thank me."

"Yes, there is. I'm going to spend the rest of my life paying you back." I open the car door, bracing myself against the cold. "I'll stay in touch."

"Sounds like a plan." Jason leans on the center console as I get out. He hovers there, tense, like he's one second away from vaulting over the seats and following me inside. His lips press together as a blond piece of hair falls into his green eyes.

Turning away, I slam the door shut and leave him where he belongs: far behind me. Maybe I should hang up on Annabelle and give Ortiz a call to plead my case.

Sorry Ortiz, I know that I want to compete in the Olympics, but I think that dream needs to go on the back burner. Why? Because I still can't seem to control myself around my brother's best friend, I guess.

Annabelle doesn't notice when I take her off mute. She finishes her story by the time I unlock the front door, shoving it open with my shoulder when it sticks. Jason's headlights flash across the porch, and my heartstrings pull. He waited to leave until I got inside—

No.

I'm not starting that. He did what any kind person would do. That's it.

Annabelle suddenly gasps as I kick off my shoes. "Hang on a second. What are you going to do about your skating? Are you going solo?"

I put her on speaker as I drop my bag on the foyer floor, leaving it as a problem for later. I wander into the kitchen and pull a water bottle out of the fridge. "Well, not exactly."

"Please don't tell me you're skating with Tyler."

"Absolutely not." I crack open the bottle as I shut the fridge with my hip. "He got paired with a different girl on the team last month. I'll do you one better. I'm going to be training with Jason."

I put my phone on the kitchen counter and push it away, expecting to hear another glass-shattering scream. Instead, it's pin-drop quiet. I scowl. "Annabelle?"

She sighs. Loudly. "Clarity. Are you pulling my leg? You're pulling my leg."

"No, I'm not." I almost wish I were.

"Oh, my god. Only you."

"Only me, what?"

"Only you would be stupid enough to work with your crush!"

I pick up my phone to respond and point at the microwave as if she's in the room with me. "He is *not* my crush. The only reason why I tolerate having him around is because of Cole."

Annabelle laughs. "Okay, I'll play along." I take a frustrated sip as she continues, "You don't care for him. We get it. But—Oh, look! I just got breaking news on my phone. Let me see what it says." She pauses for dramatic effect. "*Jason Forbes, disgustingly in love with his long-time best friend's sister...*"

"Annabelle, stop that. That's gross. He has a girlfriend."

"Because you broke his heart and turned him away!"

"Because I don't like him!" I counter and whirl around, pacing past our dining room table. "Not like that. He's going to talk to Tiffany, he's going to help me win a National title, and then he'll go back to working with his dad and I'll join an international team far, far away. One year from now, we're going to look back and laugh."

Car doors slam in the garage, and my parent's laughter echoes.

Annabelle scoffs. "One year from now, I'm going to be laughing at *you* when you come to me and say that you're getting married—"

The door to the garage flies open and Cole walks inside. His face twists in confusion. "Who's getting married?"

"Nobody!" I yell over my shoulder. "Sorry Annabelle, I should let you go. My family is home and I need to talk to them."

"We're not done talking about this. Text me later, okay? Love you."

"Love you. Bye." I disconnect the call and turn around to face Cole, Dad, and Mom, who are pulling off their layers and wearing three different expressions of confusion.

"Hi, Claire-Bear." Dad hangs his jacket on the coat rack as he takes in my bloody clothes, my haggard expression, and my spot in the kitchen, all of which are extremely uncharacteristic for me. "I'm afraid to ask."

Mom rushes over, throwing her purse down on the counter before grabbing my shoulders. "Clarity! Oh my word, honey. What happened?"

"Did you kill someone?" Cole wanders over and snags a few cookies out of a jar.

I frown. "What? No. What are you doing here? I thought you were going to the gym."

"Nick got sick and Willie cancelled to help his latest... situation... rearrange his room."

"Is that what you kids call it these days? Rearranging?" Dad goes over to the sink, rinsing out his coffee mug from the car.

Cole ignores him as he continues around a mouthful of cookie, saying, "I kept thinking about my bed and the new *Mafia 3* that's coming out, so I'm replaying the other ones. Long story short, gym sesh got cancelled. Why do you look like a freak?"

I roll my eyes and share the same story with them that I told Annabelle: the dizziness, crashing and burning, running to the hospital, waiting in agony, and the final diagnosis.

"Well, thank God you're both going to be okay," Dad remarks as he rubs the peppered scruff on his chin. That's kind of him to say, considering he's poured nothing but time and money into this dream that's on the brink of crumbling. If it weren't for my passion, maybe he could've moved us to a real house with some land and chickens, like he's always dreamed.

"But your competition in Colorado..." Mom starts and fades, eyes wet with sadness.

I laugh, but it falls flat. "Yeah, we can cancel those plane tickets."

"Damn." Cole passes a cookie to Dad when he holds his hand out. "What are you going to do now? Are you just S.O.L. until Victor heals?"

I open my mouth. Close it. Swallow. "So, I forgot to mention that I called Jason on the way to the hospital. He met us there so he could take me home, but he went with me to see Victor. We came up with a plan."

Cole walks around the counter and points at me. "No way. Uh-uh. You are *not* skating with Jason."

I turn on him. "How did you guess?"

"Because I'm not stupid, unlike you. What are you thinking? Do you really expect him to become this talented ice dancer overnight? He's a hockey player!"

"Not anymore. We have a month and a half to practice until the Invitational. He'll get it."

"Jason?" Mom clarifies. "Wow, I haven't seen that boy in forever."

"How's he doing these days? I miss seeing him around," Dad adds.

"Guys! Now is not the time." I rub my palms against my face. "It's going to work. It has to work."

"Oh, that boy adores you, honey. I have no doubts that he'll work twice as hard to get caught up." Mom taps her nails on the counter.

Cole throws his hands in the air. "That's just the problem, isn't it? Of course that idiot agreed. All he wants is—"

"Keep it PG," Dad warns.

"No." I hate the way my chest aches. "No, he's just helping. End of story. I'm going to change my clothes."

Dad nods and pushes himself onto his feet. "Good idea."

"Invite him over for dinner sometime," Mom calls after me as I walk out of the kitchen, toward the staircase. I don't answer. The blood is rushing in my ears again.

Cole follows me upstairs, refusing to give up. "Is there seriously no one else to skate with on your team? Do I have to remind you that this is the same guy who has been pining after you since the fourth grade?"

"That means nothing. He has a girlfriend." I hurry down the hallway to the bathroom. My stomach lets out a warning growl as it clenches.

Jason. What *was* I thinking? That he would table a lifetime of memories, shove it all to the side to perform alongside me?

"Don't get me started on Tiffany. I can't stand that witch. He already has a lot going on. I just don't think he's going to be committed."

And why should he, after I told him there's no chance of *us?*

I can't do this right now. I can't do anything right.

But I need to make this right.

My vision blurs as I close the door in Cole's face and stumble to the toilet, falling on my knees, using two fingers to press the back of my throat.

Vomit rushes up immediately, and I squeeze my eyes shut so I don't see what I've eaten today. I blindly press my throat again for good measure. And again. And again. Until I'm choking on air, stuck with nothing but an empty stomach and the crushing weight of my guilt.

Keeping my eyes closed, I feel for the handle and flush the contents of my stomach down the pipes. When it's safe, I open my eyes and use toilet paper to wipe my mouth, tossing that in the bowl before leaning sideways against the tub, my entire body hot and shaking.

Light from the hallway stretches over my legs, and I glance at the doorway, a headache forming behind my temples.

Cole shuffles inside, panic etched on every line in his face as he crouches beside me. "Clarity..."

I break apart.

Chapter 4

Jason

I pull into our gated driveway with no recollection of driving home. I have no idea how fast I was going or if any of the stoplights were actually green. A cop could've been tailgating me with their lights flashing the entire way home for all of the attention I was paying, and that's because of Clarity.

I've spent the last twelve months trying to convince myself that I don't need her anymore. Twelve months of figuring out how to live without her, to look the other way when she entered a room, and strategically convincing Cole to hang out when she would be at practice. All of that work, and it unraveled in an hour. There won't be any more opportunities to run away when we're going to be working side-by-side for the next four months.

In a few days, Clarity's touch won't be a phantom sliding over my skin. It will be very, wickedly, real.

So will the intensity of her gaze, and the sound of her voice, forming words that I can actually hold on to. Not like the ones that burn away in my dreams, like the heat of the sun evaporating a morning mist. That's the agonizing truth—for the last several months, years, even, I've been stuck with only seeing her in my dreams. But not anymore.

That thought gives me joy, and an eye-watering amount of anxiety.

Nerves sit on my chest, as heavy as an elephant, squeezing the air out of my lungs as the car rolls over the hill. The garage door is wide open, and red taillights from Dad's sports car reflect on the wet pavement outside. I was hoping to wait until tomorrow to have this conversation, however it seems like the choice is being made for me.

Dad steps out of his car as I park, sharp as ever despite working twelve hours. Not a hair is out of place as he walks around the front bumper and pauses a moment to swap his briefcase to his other hand. He regards me as I hop out. "You're home late."

"I was about to say the same thing to you." I raise my voice to be heard as the rain falls harder outside, pounding against the concrete.

"I wasn't supposed to be, until Samuel called me into the warehouse this morning. Those new hockey sticks came off the assembly line with a bug, which pushed back my entire day. I had to play catch-up." He glances at me from the corner of his eye as he opens the door into the house. "You left in quite the rush."

He doesn't need to ask any questions. I know what he's implying, except I don't know how to answer without cracking open a can of worms.

"Sorry, I would've run it by you, but it was an emergency. Clarity called. I had to bring her home from the hospital—she had a freak accident during practice with her partner. Do you remember Victor?" I slide my shoes off next to his, then pick both pairs up and move them onto the shoe rack as he walks into the kitchen.

"No."

Not surprising. He loves Clarity, but hates the fact that she didn't follow in mine and Cole's footsteps and play hockey. Especially since she's in the same sport that my mother was before she left him alone with me as a baby. He shocks me by asking, "Is she okay?"

There's that weight on my chest again. I might as well rip the bandaid off now.

I watch as he pulls two Tupperware containers labeled *Wednesday* out of the fridge, thanks to our chef that preps every meal for us. He sets one in the microwave. I roll my shoulders back to brace for impact. "Yeah, she's totally fine. Walked away with a few bruises, but Victor broke his wrist. He'll be out for the rest of the season."

"During her senior season? That's too bad." His tone implies otherwise.

"Yeah. I talked with them and their coach. I'm taking Victor's place."

Dad laughs. I don't.

He goes silent and leans against the counter as he meets my eyes, running a hand over his cropped blond hair. "You're kidding." It's not a question.

"I'm not."

"That's quite the opportunity," Dad mocks. "You're really going to put on a sparkly dress and follow in your mother's footsteps, huh?"

An embarrassed—no, a frustrated—blush bursts over my cheeks. "Not the dress part, but actually, yeah. You got it. Her memory lives on with me."

His eye twitches. "You're going to tell them no."

I swallow to wet my dry throat. "I've already made up my mind."

He sighs and turns away to rip open the drawer closest to him. Silverware rattles once, then again as he pulls out a fork and tries to slam it shut. The soft-close hinges catch it at the last second.

I chew on my cheek so hard that I draw blood as the microwave beeps. He pulls out his dinner and stirs it aggressively. Silently.

It's the silence that sends my heart racing. The last time this happened, he was driving us home after the semi-finals game. There wasn't much to say after I fought that referee, drawing blood and the eternal disappointment of my father. Although, it wasn't quiet for long before he blew up at me.

"If I can't talk you down, then I'm going to tell you this." He stabs his fork into a cubed potato and turns to face me, using a hard stare to pin me to the spot. "Be smart about it. Skate and do whatever you have to do on the weekends, and do the internship during the week."

According to Clarity, there's two months until this big Invitational competition, which gives me approximately eight weeks to match her standard, or at least try to meet it. That would only be sixteen practices, maximum.

I clench my hands. "I don't have time for both. I need more practice time than that."

"You already proved yourself by messing up on the ice. I gave you a second chance with this internship, and you would be an idiot to throw away your future again."

I rear my head back when he uses those words with me. Idiot. Throw away. *Again.*

"Dad, I'm using my skills to help out a friend. This is the Janskys' we're talking about. The least I can do is skate with Clarity until Victor is healed. I'll finish out my internship in the spring," I say with conviction as I lay my hands flat on the edge of the kitchen island.

"How many hours do you clock in a week?" He lifts the fork and takes a bite.

I run the numbers in my head. "About twenty, twenty-five." I could get more skating practice accomplished in one week than eight, if he would just let this go.

"What time does practice start?" he asks around another mouthful.

The only reason why I showed up to hockey early every day for three years is because I could catch the first few minutes of Clarity's practice before Coach Lloyd started working us like machines. She hasn't changed the timing of her schedule since high school started, so I answer his question confidently. "6:30, sharp."

"I'll tell you what. If you leave school, come to work for a few hours, then leave at six, you'll make it to practice on time. This is the only way this is going to work," he says as he walks across the kitchen toward the dining room.

I inhale, slowly. I didn't expect any part of this conversation. Knowing my dad the way I do, the only answer I was expecting was a solid, unshakeable *no*. I'm definitely not going to start jumping up and down because of this conclusion, but it's better than a screaming fight.

And, I don't admit this often, he's right. I can do both and prove that I'm not a failure. I can work with Clarity, win the Invitational, and fill the gap between us. I can learn how to run SporTech while doing it. If I pull this off, maybe Dad will actually smile and regard me with pride as he introduces me to his colleagues, not as his NHL-bound son that unfortunately stepped away from the game, so, well, *here we are.*

"Okay." I clear my throat and try again. "Fine. That's fine. I can do it."

"I'll let you reach out to Paul and share your new schedule with him. Do that tomorrow, don't bother him tonight. You'll probably have to rush that Vantix proposal that's due next Friday. And make sure you eat. I left your container on the counter." His words are muffled as he rounds the corner into the dining room.

"Will do," I mutter as I stalk around the island and grab the forgotten container, tossing it right back into the fridge. There's no chance that I'll be able to keep that down right now.

I walk past the living room that received the touch of a soulless interior designer over the summer, and go up the perfectly vacuumed stairs that the housecleaner must've spent all day on.

Dad used to do things around the house after Mom left us. Over the years, he's added helping hands. He now has someone for everything, but there's not a single person he can hire to parent me. I know that if he could, he would. It's moments like this that make me understand why Mom never came home.

As I enter my bedroom, I refuse to acknowledge the gleaming shelves on the opposite side of my bed, showing off every award, trophy, certificate, and medal I've won from hockey over the years. I kept all of that stuff up as a reminder that, somewhere deep inside of me, I've always had what it takes to be successful. Even if nobody around me is saying that I'm doing a good job, these things are a visual reminder that I am.

Tonight, seeing them is like a slap to the face. They're glimmering reminders of my past, who I used to be.

I was sharpening my hockey skills in middle school, and by high school, I was good. Really good. I was the best center that the team had ever seen. My sense of the game was amazing, and by junior year, I was becoming a sensation across the Midwest.

I had it all. Scholarships lining up for senior year. Dad only gave me compliments, never complaints. Coach Lloyd was finally viewing me with respect, not like another brainless teenager.

Until the semi-finals game against our long-time rivals, the Edina Hornets. We were two minutes away from making the road to finals and securing another trophy for the third year in a row. The end of the game was in sight when Willie, my good friend and teammate, took the puck down hot and fast to the net. Edina's defenseman cut in, made contact with his head, snagged the puck, and got a shot past our goalie and into the net.

It didn't matter, though. At least, it shouldn't have mattered. It was *illegal contact to the head*. Willie had a bruise for weeks after that tournament.

The refs were stubborn toward us the entire game, but I insisted on a challenge, a replay review. The referee turned me down. I asked again, with a little more force and a few more curse words. He ignored me.

I had already bottled up a lot of anger from Clarity and Cole's seventeenth birthday party from the weekend prior, and the string that was holding me together snapped. I couldn't stand seeing another friend get pushed around.

So, I saw red, and punched the ref down on the ice. And gave him a few extra hits for good measure.

That was the last time I saw the ice.

I haven't had the heart to go near it again, especially since Edina went on to the finals and won the game.

I turn away from the shelves, my stomach rolling as I start to unbutton my shirt. Who am I to think I can step back on the ice after an entire summer off and become this skating star? To shape myself back into the person Clarity used to rely on?

My phone vibrates in my pocket and jolts me out of my misery. I take it out to scan the notification, until my eyes lock onto a different one that I missed.

Off the Ice with Clarity Jansky
New Video: "Mastering the Midline:
Twizzles & Timing in Ice Dance"

Clarity's latest blog post is live. When I click the notification, I'm not surprised to see that she already has thousands of views and hundreds of likes. Let's add that to my list of issues tonight: how am I supposed to fill Victor's shoes when thousands of her followers are expecting the dream team to sweep the ice dancing competition circuit?

What was once a silly endeavor to pass the time in middle school has turned her into a national sensation. Every figure skater in the country knows that she is the It Girl when it comes to skating commentary, tips, tricks, and even the occasional interview when she has the chance to meet other famous athletes. She has always wanted to go into sports broadcasting after she wins a few Olympic medals. I think she could settle for being a content creator.

Clarity's voice pours out of the speakers as the video automatically starts to play, paired with her cheery smile on the screen. She makes me forget where I am when those beautiful brown eyes latch onto mine, her dark hair brushing against the same neck that I was lucky enough to kiss as she turns to introduce Victor.

Another notification drops down, momentarily pausing the video and shaking me out of the memory.

> *Heyyy are you home yet?? Can you plz call me?? I miss youuu*

That's right. I never texted Tiffany back. Of course it's Clarity who distracted me from answering—it's *always* Clarity.

Why do my problems always come back to her?

May 2010 - Age 11
Clarity

The bus rolls over a curb as it turns the corner, disrupting the hardcover book balanced on my right knee that is covered with my history homework. My hand jolts and scrapes a sharp pencil line through question number six. Another piece of paper was resting on my left knee, but now it's slipping to the floor.

I curse, using one of the words that dad said to the lawnmower Saturday morning.

Was that only two days ago?

Jason reacts faster than me, launching forward, slapping his hand down on my knee right where the skin is still torn up from yesterday. He catches the homework before it can fall, and I inhale sharply as pain shoots up my leg. "Sorry, I'm so sorry. I got it."

"Thanks," I mutter, and glance at him from underneath my eyelashes as I slide the paper back in place.

He's sheepish, tan cheeks turning pink, his eyes apologetic.

I should be the one apologizing since I'm copying his history home-work. Cole laughed at me when I asked to copy his, and now he's distracted in the seat across the aisle, reenacting a moment from his latest practice with one of his friends.

Seriously, I never do this, but all my late nights at the rink combined with yesterday...

My stomach twists.

Tiffany.

Squeezing my eyes shut, bile and tears rise to the surface. Will I get sick first, or burst into tears? I can't turn in my homework if it's unrecognizable.

Jason bumps his knee against mine, making me look up. The apologies have left his face and are replaced with questions. His eyebrows draw together. "Hey, are you okay?"

I'm never going to be okay again.

I nod. "Yeah. I just feel bad."

"For what?"

"Relying on you."

Jason's mouth curves into a lopsided smile, and a little bit of the weight lifts off my chest.

"Don't worry about it. You can always rely on me."

Chapter 5
Clarity

T he worst time of day is lunch, without a shadow of doubt. There's nothing I hate more than sitting down in front of a crowd of people, choking down my perfectly portioned and weighed serving of food. I spend every Sunday, my only day off, meal prepping lunches to hit one-thousand calories—no more, usually less.

At least I can eat my breakfast and dinners in peace. I wake up too early to run into anyone in my family, and everyone is almost always in bed by the time I get home. That's the way I prefer it.

My hatred for this hour is only amplified by the fact that I've already had three people stop me on the way to the cafeteria to say how much they loved yesterday's video, and how excited they are to watch Victor and I dominate at the Invitational.

They seemed thrown by the fact that my smile didn't reach my eyes, and that my words of thanks rang hollow.

What else am I supposed to tell them? I can't explain that I panicked last night and dragged Victor down with me, along with every good chance at standing on the podium. I can't say that I stayed up all night because every time I closed my eyes, I could hear his wrist bone crack like a gunshot and feel the blade of my skate sink into his thigh. I'm definitely not going to admit that my coach is currently emailing application paperwork to Jason Forbes, the hockey team's ex-golden boy.

It's hard to breathe as I inflict more pain on myself by scrolling through the comments of the video I posted yesterday while slowly walking toward the cafeteria. Each word is a paper cut, a sharp reminder that Victor is sitting in a hospital across town.

@icedance_obsessed
Are you KIDDING me?! That twizzle sequence was smoother than melted butter. Can't wait to see you guys at the Classic!!

@icecole_jansky
real talk, I've never seen anyone on your team move this in sync. you two are terrifying. go win this damn thing

@annabellelloyd67
SCREAMING!!! Give them the win now. I said what I said!

@cutwithgrace
This the girl everyone's hyping up? Okay...

@offtheicestans
wait no bc if this is just practice footage i'm scared to see what they're cooking for the invitational

@d.is.for.darika
unreal. top five moment of the season already

@bladesandbeauty
THIS is senior level elegance. Can't believe you're still in high school, girl!!!

@swatt2011

WOW how does that move look so effortless? I watched it a few times and realized how exquisite your guys' skating is because of the difficulty of these elements and then their delivery... PURE MAGIC and ART

"Basking in the glory of your fame?"

My phone slides through my hands, and I catch it before it can hit the floor.

Sterling grins sheepishly and tilts his head, the same brown curls I used to run my hands through flopping to the side. "Sorry, Claire. I thought you heard me say hi. You left calculus in a rush."

"I'm sorry, I was distracted." I pretend that his old nickname for me doesn't land like a punch to the gut as I put my phone back in my pocket.

"I see that. Here, I don't want this. I figured you could eat it before practice later." He sidesteps closer to me as our peers bottleneck at the entrance of the cafeteria, bathing me in the familiar scent of his sandalwood cologne as he presses a protein bar into my hands.

My skin prickles, and I hold my breath until he puts space between us again. I barely glance at the wrapper. Both of us know that this will end up in the trash before the day is over, but I humor him by sliding it in the side pocket of my lunch bag. "Thanks."

"Of course. Somebody has to keep the school's most famous celebrity fueled." He pauses for a moment. "You looked really good in your video. It's cool to watch you grow the more serious you get about your training."

As if he isn't one of the many people that I've been working hard to prove wrong. We got in a fight after Willie, my brother's friend, stumbled across him cheating on me with someone from the girls hockey team. The night of my seventeenth birthday party a few months ago, may I add. He told me that I didn't stand a chance making it to a regional show down the street, much less the Olympics.

"Thank you," I coolly repeat myself. I'm *really* going to have to get serious without Victor, but he doesn't need to know that. "We've been working hard."

"You always have." Sterling raises his voice to be heard over the clamor as we move toward the sea of lunch tables. His gaze darts to a spot over my shoulder, and another smile pulls at his cheeks as he regards me one more time. "I'll catch you later. Good luck at practice tonight."

He doesn't give me the chance to say anything as he slips into the crowd and weaves toward his table of friends.

The reason for his quick disappearance is answered immediately as Annabelle comes up alongside me, a lunch tray balanced in her hands. Her eyebrows are tight as she stares after Sterling. "What is his problem? I swear to God, I will—"

"You'll what?" I interrupt with a laugh. "Scare him off for a week, just so he can come crawling back?" I continue toward our lunch table. She stays hot on my heels.

"Actually, I was going to say that I will talk to my dad and get him kicked off the hockey team. Give him a taste of his own medicine."

"That won't fix anything. Just leave it be." That's what I've done in the time following our breakup. We kept our space from each other for a while, until he started to slowly wiggle back into my life. Besides, he doesn't say or do anything to rekindle the relationship. I think he's trying to mend our friendship.

Annabelle scoffs and thankfully drops it as we approach our lunch table. Cole, Nick, and Willie would certainly have plenty to add to that subject.

Willie spots us first, and he brightens.

"'Sup, losers," he greets us, leaning around Cole to give us a fist bump, which we return.

He's sporting a crooked smile thanks to a broken jaw that never healed correctly—courtesy of his freshman year hockey tournament—and the same sweater he wore yesterday. The only difference is his hair, neatly braided in cornrows. I know hockey season is around the corner when Willie gives up the afro and gets his hair done.

"Nice hair, you look sharp." I set down my lunch bag and take the seat next to Annabelle as she sits next to Willie.

"Oh, lord. Don't get him started," Nick says around a mouthful of pork chop. That's classic Nick behavior. Nothing about the kid is classy.

"Too late." Cole sighs as Willie slaps his hands down on the table and starts to talk over him.

"Funny story, actually. I gave up on James and started talking to this chick who reads tea leaves on the bottom of mugs and whatever, and I thought the only things she could do with her hands was shuffle out tarot cards and touch this—"

Cole raises his hand. "Don't want to hear it."

Willie casts him a sideways look. "Turns out that she's pretty good at doing hair."

Nick waves his fork in the air. "I preferred the body builder you hooked up with last month. If you're not careful, Hazel is going to give you a potion one of these days that will make your hair fall out, or some other crazy shit. She's weird."

"Trust me, the only potion making that's going on is when I take my—"

Cole slams his apple juice down on the table. "Can we please not talk about sex for one day? Please? What is wrong with you?"

"I wish I could say 'lots of things', but Hazel has been saging me, so…" Willie shrugs. "My conscience is clear as glass."

"Your conscience is locked in a box, tied to an anchor, and currently sitting at the bottom of a muddy lake." Annabelle side-eyes him.

He sticks out his bottom lip and pretends to trace a tear down his cheek. She flicks a broccoli floret into the puddle of barbecue sauce on his tray, and he curses as he digs it out.

Nick shifts his tray further away from Annabelle before turning to me. "When do you leave for Colorado? Tonight, right?"

I pull an orange out of my lunchbox, using it as an excuse to avoid eye contact. I push my fingernail through the rind. "Yeah, so, there was a small change of plans."

Annabelle snorts and echoes, "*Small.*"

I shoot her a quick glare. Cole pauses while holding his spoon in mid-air.

Nick scans the table, brows raised as he catches Willie's eye. "Should I ask Hazel to make me a mind-reader?"

"C'mon, bro. Be respectful."

"Sorry, okay, maybe it's not small." I peel off a small chunk of rind and rehash the story for the millionth time. By the end, Nick and Willie's jaws are on the table.

"Damn, girl," Willie finally says. "That's tough."

"I don't think I heard you right." Nick digs his finger in his ear, pretending to swab out earwax. "Did you say *Jason* is going to be stepping in? Jason Forbes? The hockey player?"

"He hasn't been a hockey player in months," Annabelle says. "That's the whole point."

"Well, I'm sorry that I have a hard time picturing the man wearing tights and dancing around like a ballerina. The last time I saw him on the ice, he punched a full-grown man so many times that blood was pouring out of his mouth. That's not exactly a picture of beauty and grace, is it?" Nick challenges her. He spins to Cole. "Back me up here?"

Cole stares from underneath his eyelashes, his expression ice cold. He doesn't need to say a word. Nick points at him. "Exactly. Cole gets it."

I split open the orange, refusing to let their opinions punch holes in my plan. They might make good points, but they weren't standing in the room with me when Jason agreed. They didn't see the determination on his face. At least, that's what I keep telling myself. He'll shape up, because if he doesn't, I'll be stuck on the practice ice until the next competition season rolls around.

"Hey, man! What's good? We were just talking about you!" Willie jumps to his feet as Jason walks over. He pulls him into a hug and slaps his back so hard that the sound carries over the clamor of the lunchroom.

Our entire table turns to watch. If I wasn't hungry before, I'm definitely not now.

Jason turns to smile at us. He's wearing a sage green sweatshirt that compliments his eyes so well that it should be illegal. Honestly, it should be illegal that thought just crossed my mind.

"Hi. Sorry to budge in. I'll only stay for a minute," Jason explains as he walks around the table and takes the empty seat next to me. My stomach backflips. I slide onto the edge of my seat, pressing my shoulder into Annabelle to put as much space between us as possible.

"Look who decided to grace us with his presence." Cole slides his tray closer to Jason. "Do you want half of my sandwich?"

"No, thank you. I should go back to Tiffany in a minute."

I exhale. At least he's not rejoining our group.

"She let you off her leash? I'm shocked," Nick deadpans.

Willie grimaces. "Ouch."

I lift my gaze to meet Cole's, and he rolls his eyes. I know he's thinking the same thing I am.

Jason brushes off Nick as he spins to face me. "How's Victor today?"

"Back in one piece. He texted me this morning to say his wrist surgery went well. They'll send him home tonight, assuming his recovery goes smoothly." I was happy to hear he's alive and well, except it was a face-slapping reminder that yesterday's events were all too real.

"That's good. Speaking of, I came over here about this." He pulls out his phone and hands it over. I recognize the online paperwork. Ortiz didn't waste any time sending it over.

"What about it?" I scroll further down and scan the empty boxes.

"There." Jason leans over, and the back of my neck prickles when he enters my bubble to point at a question under Section One. "What's the difference between 'pairs' and 'ice dance'? We can't be doing both. It says to select one."

"Are you kidding?" Annabelle laughs. "You've been around for how long, and you still don't know what she does?"

"Even I know that she ice dances," Nick adds.

Something sharp flashes across Jason's eyes. He covers it fast. "Okay, I guess I missed that part."

"It's fine. We're ice dancing." I check the box for him, even when my heart pulls. He had to have known that. Right?

"What about the one further down? That one. Do I check the box that says 'traveling alone?' Technically, I'm with you. But not *with you*, with you." He bites his cheek.

Cole pauses mid-chew. "Please never phrase it like that again."

I pretend Cole didn't just say that. "No, leave it. We travel in association with Ortiz Stars, we're not independent." I keep scrolling, until a flicker of movement catches my eye. Heat floods my face.

Tiffany is cutting across the cafeteria like a human asteroid. She looks five seconds and one small inconvenience away from tearing this school apart with her bare hands.

Cole senses my shame and glances over his shoulder, then groans. "I do *not* have the patience for this today."

All of us are bristling as Tiffany swoops in, her red hair swept back in a claw clip. Her eyes are still flaming, yet she graces us with a smile as she takes the empty seat next to Jason. "What are you doing, baby?"

Annabelle audibly gags. I stick my elbow in her ribs and wrestle a nonchalant expression on my face.

"I had to ask them something." Jason plucks his phone from my hand. Tiffany tracks the movement. Her eyes snap to mine, and narrow.

I shrug. It's not like I told him to come sit with us.

"You could've googled those questions and saved yourself the time," Willie says.

Tiffany turns to him. "What questions?"

"About skating. It seemed simple to me." Willie swabs his carrot stick through a puddle of ranch.

Nick hisses, "*Willie.*"

"No, please. I'd love to know what's going on." She faces Jason, her eyebrows lifting with surprise. "Skating? They're letting you back on the hockey team?"

Cole scoffs. "Not that team."

Jason shoots him a look that could wither crops, and I close my eyes for a moment. Seriously, what are the odds he didn't mention to his girlfriend that he's stepping up to the plate for me?

Tiffany stays silent, expectant, as Jason sighs. "I was going to talk to you later, but sure, let's do this now. Victor got in an accident last night, and Clarity doesn't have a partner. I'm filling the spot until he recovers."

This time, when Tiffany turns toward me, I recognize the hatred on her face. She wore that same expression in fifth grade when she told me we would never be friends again, ever.

"You're joking. You don't have *any* backups?" She asks me.

"If I did, do you think I would've reached out to him?" I flourish my hand at Jason. His eyebrows snap together.

"I just think it's interesting that you have access to the entire hockey team, yet you go out of your way to capture the one guy you can't have."

"You said it yourself: *they're on the hockey team*," I reiterate, my frustration growing. I gesture to the boys at my table. "Nick, Willie, would either of you guys like to skate with me?"

Willie shakes his head, *no*. Nick replies, "I would, but I don't wear tights."

I nod, my point proven.

"Maybe you should ask Sterling then," Tiffany says mockingly and tilts her head to the side. A scoff slips out of me before I can catch it.

"Absolutely not." Cole steals the words right out of my mouth.

"Hello, I'm right here!" Jason waves his hands. "There is no need to fight about this. Everything's going to be fine. Tiff, I'll be skating at the same time you have practice. I'm keeping my internship. Nothing is changing, okay?"

Flames dance in her eyes as she gets to her feet. "We're talking about this later."

"Great idea." Jason mirrors her and glances around our table. His face softens when he lands on me. "Thanks for your help."

"Any time." I watch as they walk away, Tiffany's spine straight like a sergeant's, Jason's shoulders curved like a prisoner of war. Despite myself, my heart hurts for him.

"That was awkward." Willie returns his attention to his lunch.

"No thanks to you, dumbass." Cole reaches around Nick to smack the back of Willie's head.

"Remember what I said yesterday?" Annabelle murmurs to me. "Monster."

"She'll be fine." I pick up my forgotten orange.

She will have to be, because I can't do this without Jason.

Chapter 6

Clarity

S mooth jazz flows out of the speakers in the restaurant. Candles flicker at the center of every table, reflecting against the empty chairs and booths.

Friday nights are usually hopping, but this one might as well be bottled up in molasses thanks to the road construction that shut down the entire street.

Picking up the spray bottle that I left on a nearby chair, I spray a weak stream of cleaner in the general direction of the tabletop and use the rag in my other hand to wipe slow circles. My eyes are trained on one of the TVs that's mounted on the wall. Since it's so slow, I managed to sweet-talk Stella into live streaming the Fall Classic that is currently happening fourteen hours away in Colorado. Where all of my teammates are. And I'm not.

Look, I'm trying to count my blessings. At least Stella allowed me to turn the program on. Our other manager, Maureen, is off today.

"I'm pretty sure that you've wiped that table, like, four times, yet you've still managed to miss the alfredo every time," Cole says from the table behind me where he's stacking silverware inside of cloth napkins.

I jolt back to life and tear my attention away from the TV to scrub the white puddle of sauce. "Thanks."

"Wow, no biting words of sarcasm? No complaint that I'm folding these napkins wrong?"

"All of my brain power is in Colorado Springs right now." I shove the last chair back into its spot before moving on to the next table.

Cole snorts, and I glance at him as I pass. He has his dark hair brushed back for work to control the hockey flow he's starting to grow, but a few strands escape the hold of his hairspray and brush over his eyes. He blows a stream of air to get them to move as he uses both hands to roll the silverware.

"You should put more of that brain power into cleaning tables," he fires back, then yelps when I spray a jet line of table cleaner in his direction.

Smirking, I make sure to face his direction as I spray the new table and refold the rag. If I keep my back to him, he'll probably get his revenge by throwing a fork at me or something.

Just as I lean over to begin wiping, the phone in my apron vibrates. I toss the rag over the back of a chair, then pull out my phone to see who's texting. Victor.

"No phones out on the job."

"Do you ever shut up?" I cast Cole a cool glare as I unlock my phone and pull up the message.

He points a knife at me. "Four times a day, for your information. Breakfast, lunch, dinner, and sleeping. Who's texting you? Your secret boyfriend?" He wiggles his eyebrows.

"Yeah, actually. His name is Ben."

He sets the knife down on a napkin, then pauses to scrutinize me. "Ben? Do I know him? What's his last name?"

"Ben Dover." I grin.

Cole bunches up a napkin and throws it at my head. I pick it up and begin to set up my arm to throw it back at him, until I notice Stella walking out of the kitchen with a water pitcher. She heads over to the only four customers in the restaurant that are finishing dinner. I resort to tossing it back on his table.

"You're an idiot. And now I've wasted a perfectly good napkin."

"It's not like I made you throw it." I click on Victor's message. Cole mutters under his breath.

Are u watching the Classic??

Umm yeah! Of course

I've got it streaming at work

Slow night

Juliette & Monty are up next. Fingers crossed that they mess up or trip or something

Lol dude we're on the same team as them

Don't care. I would have the same energy if we were competing. They need a low score so you and Jason don't feel threatened at the Invitational

As far as I know, Jason hasn't turned in his paper-work yet

He's probably going to text this weekend and say that he changed his mind.

I'm sure Tiffany is keeping him off the ice. Jules and Monty can take the win. My career is over, anyway

I chew on my lip as I watch Victor's text bubble appear and disappear a few times. It's bad enough that people are already speculating in my comment section, asking why I haven't posted in two days, and why I haven't been sharing content in Colorado. I've had some really cool opportunities over the years thanks to my blog, but I swear, my fans take it too seriously. I'm already dreading the messages I'll get tonight when Victor and I don't perform.

As I wait for a response, I glance up at the TV. The reporters are finishing up with their spiel, and the cameras change to an overhead shot of the entire ice rink.

The stadium is full, and all eyes are on Juliette and Montgomery as they take their warm-up lap. Juliette is wearing a gorgeous navy blue dress, glittery beads tracing the bodice like it was sewn by hand. Montgomery is perfectly matching in a sleek suit. My gut twists with jealousy. Or maybe it's disappointment.

I bought a brand new performance dress over the winter to wear specifically for this competition. It's breathtaking, and currently collecting dust in my closet.

My phone vibrates again.

> *Ur wrong. Don't listen to the idiots on your page*

After a moment, Victor sends another long text.

> *Ur also pretty dumb if u genuinely believe that Jason has written you off. I heard from Darika that Tiffany hasn't looked in his direction since Wednesday. What do you think has her so riled up?*

Another texting bubble appears, and he sends a third message much faster this time.

> *Your career isn't over. Once Jason comes around, it'll just be beginning.*

I hold my breath as I read his words. It feels like spiders are crawling up my intestines, considering the way my entire body shivers.

> *Love you & miss you.*

> *Thanks for the vote of confidence. I'm gonna focus on this performance, but I'll text you in a few!*

Victor replies with a thumbs up emoji, so I turn my phone off and slide it back in my pocket. I pick up my rag and return to lazy circles on the tabletop as I watch Juliette and Montgomery settle into position.

There's never been any volume on these TVs, so as to not disturb the dining atmosphere. Instead, my brain fills in the blanks since I've heard their performance music when entering the rink for my own practices.

They begin their number by pushing off the centerline, immediately mirroring each other's movements. It's neat to see from an outsider's point of view as they set up for their first maneuver, a spin combination.

The thing is, they simply lack... *something*. Chemistry, maybe? A spark? They both appear borderline bored as they go about their routine. I'm shocked that Ortiz hasn't beaten passionate expressions onto Juliette's face by now. She probably lets her get away with it because her skills are truly remarkable.

I observe how her feet fall, the way her arms reach out, how Montgomery lifts her. I search for weaknesses while planning how I can do better. It's a nice distraction against the disappointment that keeps threatening to take over my body.

While they are on the ice pulling sub-titled comments out of the reporters' mouths like, *"Stunning!" "Wow, watch their synchronization right there!" "This is a spectacular pairing!"* I'm scraping rock-hard spaghetti noodles that are stuck to the table with my thumb nail.

The bells attached to the front door of the restaurant jingle, and I glance away from the performance for a moment to check on that table of customers. They're still chatting, cleaning off their plates.

"Hey, Cole?" I ask as I turn my eyes back to Juliette. Like, come on. It wouldn't kill her to smile. "Would you mind checking the stand?"

"You got it, boss. You just keep standing there, watching TV. You're killing it," Cole says sarcastically as he stacks his rolled napkins in the bin and stands up. He dusts his hands off as he walks to the front.

I stick my tongue out at him before wiping away the remnants of the noodles and refocusing my attention on the ice. Juliette's dress flies in the breeze as Montgomery balances her on his shoulders, spinning in a fast circle. Hopefully the judges catch how she keeps fighting to regain her balance.

Cole's voice floats over the empty restaurant as he reaches the front of the store. "Good evening, welcome to Fratelli's. How many—Oh, hey. What's up, bro?"

The pair on the ice becomes a lot less interesting as I catch Jason's voice.

"Not much, man. Good to see you." His voice is distorted from being around the corner on the other side of the restaurant, but I'd recognize it anywhere. "Is Clarity working tonight?"

The blood chills in my veins.

"Good question." Cole's tone immediately becomes defensive. "Why do you ask?"

"I need to talk to her...?"

"About what?"

I hear Jason sigh. "Cole. Please."

They're both silent for a moment, then Cole speaks again. "I don't know where she is."

"I'll find her."

"You can't just—" He groans in frustration.

Jason comes striding around the corner. I startle, eyes darting down, pretending that I've been buffing this table all along. Completely oblivious to their conversation. Dumb, naïve Clarity.

"Hey, C.J." Jason raises his hand in greeting. He's wearing black sweatpants and that sage green sweatshirt again, which is totally appropriate attire since it's started to become consistently cold every night.

What shouldn't be appropriate is the way that sweatshirt brings out the color of his eyes. His hair is tousled, like he didn't stop dragging his hand anxiously through it once on the way here.

I paste a smile on my face, despite the nerves that are starting to snowball through my body.

"Jason." I set the rag down on the table. "To what do I owe the pleasure?"

"I'd like to talk to you, if you're not busy." His gaze flashes away from me to the empty tables of the restaurant. Even the group at the front has paid their bill and are starting to get up.

"Sure, I have time." I pull out a chair at the table closest to us and take a seat. He does the same, fiddling with the strings of his sweatshirt.

It's weird having him in front of me, all alone, excluding the wordless reporters droning on about skating sponsors behind my back. I'm used to seeing him in school with other students around as distractions, or next to Cole. Even the times he's been here, it's always been with his friends, packing in the carbs after a long practice.

Jason catches his anxious habit and drops his hands before locking eyes with me. "I just got done signing the paperwork to join the team. I emailed it back to your coach, and she's filing it now. It's done."

I've been trying to prepare myself for this moment the last few days, although I didn't do a very good job because I don't have to fake the shock that reverberates through my soul. Both of my eyebrows shoot up into my hairline. "Seriously? You're not pulling my leg?"

"Not your leg, not your arm. I'm serious." He straightens up. "I've taken some time to make sure this is going to work, so I don't think there is anything else to consider."

"What about your internship?" I blurt. My hands start shaking with adrenaline, so I fold them together.

Jason reaches for the strings again, then immediately resorts to folding his hands together. "That's one of the things I had to figure out. I talked to my dad, and I'm going to go in for a few hours every day before practice."

"What?" I can't even think about handling waitressing on top of skating practice. There's a reason why I only help out when completely necessary. "You can't do that. That's *way* too much to juggle."

A haze drifts over Jason's eyes. It's gone as fast as it came on. "It's only three hours. I'll be fine." He pauses to scuff out a spot that I missed. "I want to do this. I miss..." He fades out and bites his tongue for a moment. "I miss the ice. Things are different now, and I'm ready for a change. I want to learn something new."

"What did Tiffany say?" I lean forward, resting my forearms on the table as I search his eyes. "You talked to her, right?"

His jaw twitches and a small blush paints his cheeks as he nods. "I did, a few times. She..." He searches for the right words. I don't think it's a good sign that he even needs to find the right words to explain her actions.

He leans back in the seat and takes the opportunity to adjust the sleeves over his wrists. "She was able to hear me out. I'll be honest, she isn't very happy about this."

I can't help it; I snort. Loudly. "Trust me, I didn't expect her to start doing somersaults at the news. I'm surprised she didn't hit me yesterday, actually."

Jason laughs unexpectedly, and my pulse jumps at the sound of it.

"She wouldn't go that far. But she did ask for boundaries and curfews, which I'll have to abide by."

Boundaries? *Curfews?*

I want to tell Jason that it sounds like he's dating a parole officer, but decide to leave well enough alone.

"Whatever you need to do to keep her happy," I say with a shrug. "You have a few more days to sit on this, anyway. The team won't be back from Colorado until Sunday, but Ortiz wants to start practice on Monday so we're ready for the Invitational. If I were you, I'd start doing research and watching videos to prepare yourself for her terminology. Maybe scroll through my content."

As I speak, it hits me that this is really happening. I actually have a new partner. One that could potentially be worthy of bringing us all the way to Nationals in January.

"Research?" Jason tilts his head. "Why can't we start practicing on our own tonight?"

"*Tonight?*"

"Look what the cat dragged in! Jason, honey! I haven't seen you in forever!" My mom crows as she walks around the corner, holding a new bin of cloth napkins.

A smile splits Jason's face. He jumps up and lets Mom set the bin on the table before giving her a hug. "Hey, Lauren. It's good to see you."

"You too." She lets him go, but not before giving his shoulders a shake. "You kids grow up so fast! What have you been up to lately?"

He shrugs. I recognize the look on his face. It's this expression of *life is kinda awful but we don't have all night to discuss it*. Instead, he sums it up in one sentence. "Not a whole lot."

"Well, I don't know if I believe that. We hardly see you around anymore! Must be that girlfriend of yours." Mom smiles warmly, though I don't miss the way her eyes harden. She's hears plenty from Cole and I, yet she still asks the polite question of, "How is Tiffany?"

A different expression crosses Jason's face, and his easy smile fades. He acts fast to pick it up. "She's good."

Mom quirks her eyebrow. When Jason doesn't provide any more information, she nods. "That's good to hear."

He rubs his wrist. "While I've got you here, what are the odds I could take Clarity off of your hands a little early?"

If it were any other young man, Mom would never let this slide. However, this is Jason we're talking about.

She flourishes her hands. "By all means! I don't think she's missing out on any tips." She winks and gives the barren dining room a pointed look. "I'll let you two hit the road. Don't be a stranger, sweetheart."

She gives him another hug before meeting my eyes for a moment, her smile growing. I don't like the weird energy she's exerting into the world as she nearly skips away. Who knows what her problem is.

Jason peers down at me, a goofy grin on his face. "To answer your question, yes, tonight."

I hate the twinkle that reaches his eyes. I hate his perfectly straight teeth. I hate that he's beating me at my own game.

But I don't hate his idea.

I get to my feet and untie the apron behind my back. His eyes track the movement as I slip it off and throw it over my arm.

"Alright," I say. "Let's go see what you're made of."

August 2011 - Age 12

Jason

S eagull's cry overhead and loop in slow circles as they keep an eye out for some sorry suckers spilled lunch. The waves of the lake lap at the shoreline, stretching toward the canopy tent that Lauren and Aaron are wrestling with, their curse words swept away by the breeze. Spruces, pines, and oaks stand watch around the edge of the lake, enjoying this hot August day as much as we are.

Cole stumbles as we step off the sidewalk and into the sand, jostling the heavy cooler. I grunt as it knocks into my shins. "Dude, watch where you're going."

"Says the one who isn't walking backwards." Cole readjusts his grip on the handle before continuing our way to the tent.

Aaron steps out of the way as we duck under the shade. Lauren points at the corner. "Right there, boys. Wonderful. Thanks so much for bringing that down."

"What else is left?" Aaron unsticks his t-shirt from his chest.

"Chairs and the food," Cole replies and brushes off his hands.

"We can grab it. You guys have already done a lot to help, and we appreciate it. Go have fun." Lauren waves her hand toward the lake where people are already enjoying the water, soaking up this last leg of the summer.

"Don't have to tell me twice." Cole grabs the back of his shirt and rips it off, immediately followed by his sandals.

"Thanks," I call after his parents as they begin to walk away. As I slip my shoes off, I glance toward the parking lot. Annabelle and Clarity hung back to change in the public restrooms, except that was probably ten minutes ago.

Worry begins to scratch at me. I don't want to think that Clarity got kidnapped. There's no way. Not when Annabelle is with her. With the amount of talking she does, the kidnapper would bring them back within minutes.

I start to turn to Cole to voice my concern until someone starts shrieking at the top of the hill. Annabelle comes running down the sidewalk, her curly hair tied back in a ponytail. She's the one making the noise while reaching back to whack Clarity with her shirt.

Clarity.

She spent the morning in the back of the van, curled up with a blanket against the window. Aside from that, I haven't seen her in a week because she's been spending every day practicing at the rink, then going over to Annabelle's house.

I don't know what she's done over the summer since I've actually seen her last, but seeing her now is a shock, thousands of volts straight to the heart. Her long legs flash, overtaking Annabelle. Her body is perfectly molded, the bright shades in her swimsuit drawing out the deep tan in her skin. I forget how to breathe as she runs under the tent. Her eyes are brighter than her smile as she throws down her clothes.

"Hi. Bye," she says breathlessly, holding eye contact with me for one blessed second. She starts to smile before continuing her sprint down to the water. My hands shake and my vision tunnels. Annabelle and Cole could be gnats for all the attention that I give them as I watch Clarity dive under a wave.

I don't know who just ran by me, but that definitely wasn't the same girl that I've spent the last eight years hanging out with.

Cole says something while shaking his head. I don't hear him. My ears are buzzing, and the only thing that I can even think to say is, "Um, when did Clarity turn so... gorgeous?"

The shock of those words falling out of my mouth is what snaps me back to reality.

Oh, no. I admitted that to the wrong person.

Cole turns toward me so fast I nearly trip over the cooler trying to back away. His face twists like I just said something disgusting.

"Dude! That's my sister." He shoves my shoulder. Not hard, but enough to make his point. "You can't—just—no. Gross. Don't even think about it."

His nose wrinkles, and he waves his hands like he's literally shooing the thought away. "She's off-limits, okay? Got it? Like, forever. I don't care if every other girl on the planet disappears, because you're not allowed."

He gives me one last shove before storming off toward the water, muttering something under his breath about throwing up.

I should probably laugh it off, but I can't. Something's different now, and I'm kind of terrified there's no going back.

Chapter 7

Clarity

It feels wrong to be at the rink past 9:00 p.m. The janitor recognized us as he was leaving and was happy to leave us alone to skate, but it took everything in me to not beg the man to stay, just so I wouldn't be left alone with Jason.

The drive over here was awkward enough. This entire situation is making me rethink this master plan of ours.

The locker room is eerily quiet without the constant flow of foot traffic, so I make quick work of throwing on the cheap leggings that I keep in my locker. I also keep a backup pair of skates here in case of last-minute practices like this, and I grimace as I pull them out. The white leather has definitely seen better days, but the laces are good and they fit like a glove.

I hurry back out in my socked feet, skates in hand.

Jason is on the floor of the staging area as I come around the corner, deep in a pigeon stretch, his sweatshirt in a pile in the corner. He wore a black t-shirt underneath, and it's currently clinging to his chest and arm muscles. He must be keeping up at the gym. I recall sliding my hands over those biceps—

Focus.

I push the memory far away, deep in the recesses of my brain where it belongs.

He tilts his head up and grins. "I thought you ran away already."

"No way. I have too much on the line." I sit on the bench across from him and pull on the first skate. "So, no Tiffany tonight, huh?"

"Nope." He pushes himself up and rustles through his bag. "She's at a pre-season meeting. Well, not for much longer, but she's going home after."

"I've got to say, I'm surprised that she gave you permission to be out this late," I tease as I tighten my laces.

"She thinks that I'm out with my hockey friends, so it wasn't a big deal. That will keep her off my case if she ever catches wind that I was here at the rink." He settles beside me on the bench and pulls on the tongue of his skate.

I bite my tongue to force a mask of neutrality on my face.

He lied to his girlfriend about his whereabouts. I don't care that his girlfriend is Tiffany. I've seen this play out before, and that's because I was on the receiving end in my past relationship.

Jason has told me multiple times over the years that I could trust him, and I'm sure he tells Tiffany the same thing. He can say the right thing all he wants, because the truth of the matter is that he's doing the wrong thing behind a closed door. He might have his reasons, but so did Sterling.

"Seriously? You lied to her?" I laugh in disbelief to keep the frustration out of my voice. "I really don't want to be a part of your guys' drama if she decides to show up on a whim."

"Trust me, she won't." He glances up at me. Pieces of hair shield his eyes and make it hard to read his expression. "Besides, this is fine. She would understand." He looks away, biting his lip. "Eventually."

That definitely doesn't ease the bad feeling in my stomach. I felt this way the entire way here, and it's what I heard in Cole's tone earlier. Yes, he was defensive when questioning Jason, and that was because he also knew that this was a terrible idea.

Except I need Jason to reach my goals. Leave the drama out of it.

I stay silent as we finish tying on our skates. If there's one thing he's good for, it's taking a hint. He doesn't say anything else as I lead the way onto the ice. My legs move independently as I reach up to retie my hair into a ponytail, capturing the loose strands.

He stays in stride with me, and I glance at his feet out of habit. Of course he's wearing Bauer Vapor Hyperlites. They're great skates if a person feels like dropping a grand and wants to play hockey.

"Jason?"

"Yeah?" His head snaps in my direction. I can't stand how he always regards me like I'm the only person in the room. A blush crawls over his face despite the fact it's cold enough out here to literally make water freeze.

"I'm going to point out the obvious here." I incline my head toward his feet. "If you're serious about this, you better get some figure skates. Especially before Monday. Ortiz will cut your fingers off if you step on her ice wearing those."

"What?" Jason gasps and lifts up his foot, effortlessly skating on one leg. "What's wrong with my skates? I spent good money on these things!"

I open my mouth to tell him exactly what's wrong with his skates and why they'd never work for what we need to do. That's until I catch the devilish grin that's growing on his face, so I shove him. He stumbles with a loud laugh.

I bite back a smile as the sound echoes. "Money can't teach balance, it seems."

"Balance schmalance." Jason waves his hand to swat away my comment. "I can hold my own in that department."

I push off my outside leg to skate a circle around him, making the shape into a warmup stretch by doing progressive leg swings, staying grounded with my left leg while swinging my right leg higher and higher.

"I don't care if you can hold your own." I stretch my right leg into the air in a perfect split, then wrap my arm around the calf to hold the stretch. Jason's eyes widen in surprise, or maybe fear at the contortion. "I'm more worried about whether you'll also be able to hold *me*."

Dropping my leg down, I change directions swiftly and repeat the stretch on the other side. "I want to remind you that the type of skating we will be doing is still a team sport. The difference is, if you let your hockey buddies down, it's because you have to sit in the penalty box."

I fold my leg back down to the ice, then spin around to skate backward in front of him while matching the fast pace that he has already set.

"You know what happens when you let me down? You drop me on my head, all because your talents stop at 'holding your own.'" I use his words against him and smile. "No pressure."

"Wow. If you're trying to talk me into skating with you, you're not doing a very good job right now." Jason laughs again, though his glimmering eyes remain stoic, trained on mine.

"I apologize. You'll do great." I skip around to face forward again. "Are you ready to attempt your first figure skating move?"

"Born ready." Jason skates alongside me. His arm brushes against mine. Goosebumps race across my skin. "What are you thinking, Coach?"

I intentionally press my elbow into his ribs in response to the nickname. "A basic upright one-foot spin."

"A whoey-whatey?" His face pinches together.

"You know when the Olympic skaters start spinning really fast and everyone in the room gasps and asks how on earth are they not getting dizzy?"

"Oh. That one, yes."

"That's what we're looking for."

Jason nods. "I'm more of a visual learner, actually."

I give him a heartbeat before his face turns scarlet and his eyes go wide with recognition.

"Oh, God. I didn't mean—it's not like—well—"

"Stop. It's fine." My own cheeks turn pink, but the moment loses its humor when I remember what he told Tiffany. "Watch my technique, okay?"

Pushing off the blades of the skates, I gain speed around a quarter of the rink before cutting down the middle. I am more at home in this arena than my own house. I know where to begin to slow down before lifting my right leg off the ice and spreading my arms back, transitioning into a comfortable spin.

After three solid revolutions, I straighten my spine and bring my arms out directly to either side, moving my right leg in front of my body. To finish off the move, I tuck my right leg close to my left and bring my arms above my head. The inertia of my body changes and causes my body to begin a rapid-fire spin.

Jason is a blur of color. The walls of the arena fly past. It's a habit to count the revolutions. When I hit five, I lower the heel of my right skate and push that same leg back out, instantly slamming into a clean stop. My heart hammers, and a few black dots pop over my vision.

Applause bounces over the ice. I'm pulled back into the moment as Jason skates over, his face split apart with wonder. "Okay, that was amazing."

"Thank you. I appreciate it, I really do, but you haven't seen anything if you're impressed by a simple spin."

"How do you do it?"

He copies me, except it's more like a small oval shape.

"It's all physics," I begin to explain. "The ice has very little friction to slow a skater down when they're in motion. Spinning like that is angular momentum, which is dependent on angular velocity and the moment of inertia. Angular velocity is a measure of how fast an object is spinning—"

"Okay, Bill Nye the Science Guy. Slow down." Jason raises his hands. "I don't need the physics lecture, I just want to know how."

My jaw drops in horror. "The physics is the best part!"

"I disagree. I skate to forget about school, not be thrown back into it head first."

"You're not being thrown." I blink at him. "The angular momentum is carrying you right into it."

"Clarity." Jason skates right up into my space and presses his pointer finger into my shoulder. "I dare you to say *angular momentum* one more time."

I'm tempted to say it to see what he has up his sleeve. Unfortunately, all of my thoughts are carried out of my head with more angular momentum the moment his finger touches me.

I trace his finger with my gaze, then his hand, moving slowly all the way up his arm to his face.

Jason has a light splash of freckles across his strong, straight nose. They are a visual reminder of the summer season that we are leaving behind. He only has them after being out in the sunshine.

There's still a small scar near the corner of his right eye. It's barely visible, but I notice it because I was the one who accidentally gave it to him in fourth grade when we were playing with crab legs at dinner and the sharp edge of mine scratched his face. I kissed that scar last year.

I've been staring at his face for an awkward amount of time now.

Warmth floods my cheeks as I quickly backpedal and clear my throat. "Um, sorry. The spin."

"Right. You're right." Jason's voice is thick as he gives me plenty of space, his hand falling down to his side. "I'm all ears."

"Okay, follow my lead." I begin to skate away while forcing my heart to return to any speed except for Mach-1.

"Start with a two-foot spin. Put your left arm in front of you and keep your right arm off to the right. Look to the left and bend your left leg." I perform the exercise as I explain it. Glancing over my shoulder, I confirm that Jason is following directions. The awkward energy he was emitting a moment ago has been replaced with a professional amount of concentration.

"Use a pivot to spin on two feet. Stay stable, breathe, and feel the center of the spin. Start to pull your arms to the left." I draw my arms in, and another swift glance confirms he's still staying with me.

"Okay, good. Don't drop your hips, but try to lift your right foot up once you feel centered. It doesn't have to be very high. Cross your arms over your chest." Finally, I ease out of my own spin so I can watch Jason.

He does well—he is successfully performing a spin. His left knee is wobbling, his eyebrows are tight with fear, and a talented toddler could probably run faster than the speed he's spinning at, but a win is a win.

"Perfect! You're doing great." I clap my hands together.

In the back of my brain, I see Victor flying up alongside me before performing a double-axel, finishing the move off with a spin that's so fast—

No, I remind myself. A win is a win.

"Puke, dizzy, stop," Jason throws out those three words in a rapid fire.

"What—Oh! Put your right foot down and lift your—or not."

Before I can get the words out of my mouth, he collapses onto the ice, causing it to shake under my feet.

I can't help it: I laugh. It's not the polite laugh that I reserve for conversational purposes. It's a hunched-over, snorting, *what the hell was that* type of laugh.

Jason joins in as he rolls over onto his side. Blond hair flops over his eyes as he motions down at his body.

"Here's your professional skating champion. Right here in the flesh," Jason exclaims between giggles as he tries to catch his breath.

I pull myself together as I glide over and offer him my hand. "When was the last time you fell over?"

"By myself, without being body slammed?" He accepts the help. His callouses scratch against my palm before I let go. "Probably fourteen years ago."

"You're welcome for the reality check."

"Thanks for keeping me on my toes." He beams, overly happy for a boy who ate ice a few seconds ago.

For the second time tonight, I find myself at a strange lack for words. Nothing that I want to say feels right.

Something about the way Jason watches me every time I talk zaps the voice out of my throat. He's always done that. He will turn to put his entire focus on me, dialed in to hear every word that I say. A small indent will appear between his eyebrows, and his jaw tends to tick like he's making a serious effort to simply listen.

Not even Tiffany—

Oh, God.

Tiffany.

She's probably at home by now, absorbed in the *Bachelor* and painting her toenails red while glancing at her phone, waiting to hear from Jason and how his day was.

She should be the one witnessing these micro-emotions on his face, not me. She should be the one noticing how the lights catch his eyes. She should be memorizing the freckles running across his cheeks before they disappear for the winter. Not me.

This behavior is not me.

"I'm going to take a water break," I announce suddenly, and point off to the side. "Keep practicing those spins, okay?"

A similar haze breaks around Jason. He nods and slowly glides backward, his attention on me. Always on me. "Okay. Whatever you say—"

"Don't—"

"—Coach." He winks before turning away.

The wink was casual, playful. At least, that's what I tell myself when my stomach somersaults.

I skate over to the edge of the rink as fast as possible without looking like I'm running away before unlatching the door and jumping out onto the mat. Waddling over to where I left my phone, I snatch it and pull up my messages. I click on Cole and shoot off a text.

Come get me please????

I realize that sounds too desperate, so I quickly follow it up.

I'm at the ice rink with Jason. We are done. I don't want him to bring me home in case that psychopath is stalking us

I don't want to die tonight

Mom told me that you guys went there. You're dumb AF

I'm omw loser

Relief deflates my body. I shut my eyes for a moment and send up a prayer of gratitude. It's a miracle that Cole saw my text right away, and that I got a hold of him before he got home from work. If he was in his pajamas at home right now, not even a house fire could get him out of bed until tomorrow morning.

I shuffle back over to the door of the rink. Sticking my head through the doorway, I begin to open my mouth, then pause.

At some point, Jason decided to mimic my move from earlier. His hands are over his head, and his body is an impressive blur as he spins in a beautiful pivot. Then he sticks out his leg, continuing to follow my lead. It's a little shaky, but he manages to come to a complete stop without tipping over.

Visual learner, indeed. Hope for our future begins to swell in my chest until guilt washes it back down to the bottom.

I can't get attached. I refuse to be played for a fool ever again.

Chapter 8

Jason

There's only one person in the world who can get me out of bed at five in the morning, and that person is Clarity. Always has been.

When I used to sleepover at the Janskys' house, back when I could tolerate sleeping on Cole's bedroom floor, I would wake up at the sound of Clarity's door creaking open, her bare feet thudding over the hardwood.

I don't have any siblings, and Dad has always been quiet as a mouse, so any noise out of the ordinary would wake me up. The thing is, I'd count the seconds until they added up to five minutes, then I'd get up and slip out of Cole's room while leaving him to sleep.

That was always my chance to float downstairs and catch her in the living room, turning on her favorite show as she finished waking up. I never got the obsession with *Teen Wolf*. At least it gave me an excuse to settle into the sofa next to her armchair and ask what episode she was on, opening up the doorway for conversation.

Clarity probably caught on to me, especially because I did that for nearly every sleepover during middle school, but that's one of the things I've always admired about her: she never makes anyone feel stupid or embarrassed. Even to this day, when someone leaves a comment on her blog posts that sends *my* blood pressure through the roof, she replies in a way that's so graceful it makes me believe she was born with a heart of gold.

I yawn for the millionth time as I enter the rink on Monday morning. The sound of blades striking the ice echoes down the hallway from the South Rink. Someone from the girls' hockey team is already on the ice.

I've never understood the die-hard athletes that squeeze in extra time in the weight room or on the ice before school, so maybe this is the universes way of making me understand.

My sneakers squeak on the tile as I take the staircase that leads down to the training wing. A boy bursts around the corner as I take the final step down.

I nearly fall over my feet to keep from running into Cole. "Good morning to you, too."

"Well, I must still be dreaming." He pulls me into a half-hug and slaps my back. "I never thought I'd run into you here again."

"I have a feeling I'll be hearing that a lot. You're here early." I mean it literally and figuratively. Cole could never keep up with Clarity's schedule, either. He always preferred to hit the gym with me after school.

He shrugs. "Since it's senior year, I wanted to start the season on a high note. Besides, according to Annabelle, Coach Lloyd has been considering making me captain."

"Seriously?" I smile. That is the one perk of Clarity's best friend being the hockey coach's daughter and assistant coach: we always get the headline news first. "You've had that upgrade coming for a long time."

"Yeah, only because you're not around to take it." He punches me in the arm as we continue to walk down the hall, and the glimmer in his eyes fades. "I still can't believe you've switched sides."

"Me either. I'm only doing this to help Clarity." Maybe the more I say it, the more I'll believe it.

"Hey." Cole's forehead furrows. "All I ask is that you keep your distance from her."

The corner of my mouth lifts. "That'll be hard. From what she's said, I'm pretty sure we're supposed to dance—"

"You know what I mean." He shakes his head. "This is weird enough. Don't make it weirder."

As far as I know, Clarity never told him about the kiss we shared before junior year. I sure as hell didn't. But it's the little jabs like this that make me wonder if he knows more than he lets on.

"I won't. She's safe with me."

"She better be, because if you hurt her, I hope you don't expect me to keep standing by you after everything."

I don't think he's talking about dropping her. A shiver runs down my spine. The three of us have been together since kindergarten, and I can't imagine life any other way.

That makes it easy to say, "I promise, I'll keep her safe."

Cole stays silent for a beat before nodding his head toward the yoga room. "Alright, well, good luck."

"Thanks. See you later." We split directions. He continues toward the gym without me, and I go to the yoga room.

I've spent four years in this facility, but this is the first time I've ever stepped foot in this room. There's three people in here, and Clarity is the first to shift her gaze. Her smile grows, something I could never do if my leg was literally vertical in the air like that, pressed against the furthest wall. I was almost in tears just watching her do it the other night. On skates, nonetheless.

"Good morning," she greets me warmly and unravels her leg. "Welcome to day one of training."

"Hi, C.J. Happy to be here." I eye the blonde girl, who looks vaguely familiar, and the dark-haired guy. They're on their yoga mats, folded into positions that look more like contortions than stretches. The pair stops chatting to watch me walk over to her.

I don't know what to do. Should I hug her? Dap her up? Fist bump? Kissing is definitely off the table.

She breezes past me to grab two mats from a pile in the corner and brings them to the front of the room, closest to the wall of mirrors.

Alright, then.

"Jason, this is Juliette and Montgomery. They're new on our team. I'm sure you'll see them around because they book the practice slot before us." Clarity flourishes her hand at the two other people in the room.

Montgomery pushes himself onto his feet. Dark waves of hair threaten to fall over his eyes as he holds out his hand, which I shake. A smile cracks his stony face. "Nice to meet you."

Juliette does the same, and I'm surprised once she finds her feet. She's the shortest one in the room by quite a few inches. "It's very kind of you to step up to be her partner. We were horrified to hear that Victor got hurt, but I think you'll enjoy being back on the ice. Figure skating is a good change of pace."

"Thanks. Yeah, we're trying to make the most of this situation." I glance at Clarity. Her smile has tightened, unconvinced.

"We'll leave you guys to get acclimated. A bit of extra ice time won't hurt us." Juliette rolls up her mat as Montgomery grabs their bags off the bench in the back.

"Alright. See you later." Clarity waves as they leave the room.

I follow her over to our mats. "Team mates, huh? Are you three friends?"

"I wouldn't call them friends, exactly." She turns to face me and tucks loose pieces of hair into her bun.

"Good, then I can say this without feeling guilty. They seem like Grade-A assholes."

"Jason!" Clarity gasps and whacks my chest. "That is not nice. They're good people, and phenomenal athletes. They won the overall senior class at the Fall Classic over the weekend."

"They wouldn't have if you were there." I cross my arms.

She rolls her eyes, which makes my heart skitter. "That doesn't matter. Pay attention to them if you can, you might learn a thing or two. They were mine and Victor's competitors for a long time, until Montgomery moved here last month for college. We're lucky to have them on the team."

"Where does Juliette go to school?" I watch as she leans into a forward lunge and follow her lead. My hamstring immediately reminds me that I haven't stretched in weeks.

"Here. Her entire family moved so she could keep skating with Montgomery." She steps into a lateral lunge. I do the same and grimace. She catches my expression in the mirror and grins. "You're in for a treat if this is already bothering you."

"I don't know what you're talking about. I'm as fresh as a daisy. I thought I recognized her when I walked in."

"You've seen her around, I'm sure." Clarity switches legs.

I keep leaning into my current leg, giving my hip the chance to unlock as I glance at her in the mirror. She wears every emotion so beautifully, and aside from happiness, my second favorite of hers is concentration. There's something about the pull of her brows, the press of her lips, and the dedicated look in her eye that leaves me breathless. She draws her eyes upward, and I quickly avert mine.

"How's Victor holding up?" I ask to break the silence.

"Good. We talked last night. He's been resting after his surgery, and he's giving the stitches on his thigh a chance to heal." She watches me as I switch sides, and the weight of her full attention nearly knocks me over.

My knee wavers. I press my foot harder into the ground. "And how are you doing?"

"Me?" She scoffs. "Honestly, I don't know. This sucks."

My gut twists. She catches my hesitation before I can act fast enough to shove it down. She backpedals quickly.

"Not you! You don't suck. I'm happy to have you here. It's just... Victor and I were so close to having a perfect season, you know?" She sighs and settles on the floor, brushing a speck of dust off her mat. "I haven't had the heart to tell my followers that he's injured. Everyone loves him, but I think that's the worst part. They're not going to understand, and it's going to fall back on me."

"It wasn't your fault." I settle onto the mat and lean into a pigeon stretch as I watch the memory from Thursday night flit across her face.

"I'm the one who panicked. Even when he told me to take a break..."

"Clarity." Her eyes snap to mine. "You're talking like you haven't been under pressure to be perfect for the last eleven years."

"Perfection is what puts athletes in history books. Otherwise there would be no use for Nationals, or the Olympics, dare I even say the other sports leagues like the NHL?" Her tone sharpens and her nostrils flare. "There's no room for me to fail."

For one second, I catch a glimpse of a different girl next to me, and it sends a genuine shock through my bones.

This is the version of Clarity that I walked away from when I left my heart at her feet, shattered and bleeding. It was hard enough to deal with her detachment then, and it's not any easier to see a hint of that same coldness in her again.

She realizes her mistake at the same time. "I'm so sorry. I shouldn't talk to you like that. I'm not mad at you, seriously. This whole thing is already so frustrating with the media expecting me to knock this season out of the park. And now I'm scared to drop your name on my blog because people are going to do FBI-levels of stalking you. They can be ruthless."

"They're the ones who should be scared. I dare them to come at me." I attempt to lighten the mood.

Clarity gives me the side eye. "Please don't get kicked off the team before we even start."

"Who says they're going to catch me this time?"

She reaches over to shove me, knocking me off balance but putting a smile on my face. "You better play nice. My audience is half the reason why I have the USFSA development career team scouting me this year."

"*You* are one hundred percent the reason why." I retaliate by getting on my knees and shoving her back. She's all giggles as she falls onto her side, and it's hard to be serious as I point down at her. "Don't you dare give the credit of your hard work to a bunch of strangers. You need to be nicer to yourself."

"And you need to keep stretching, because if you can't touch your toes by the end of the week, Ortiz will make your life hell." Clarity settles back into her stretch and shoots me a quick grin, her signature one that turns my organs into goop.

"I'm pretty sure she will either way." I swing both legs in front of me.

She starts to respond, until I hear something vibrate. Unzipping the pocket on the side of her leggings, she slides out her phone to read the notification. I glance over as her screen lights up, and regret it instantly.

I wish I could trick my brain into thinking I read the name Sophie, Scarlett, or even Samuel, but no. There's no mistaking Sterling Mayer. That spineless, no-good waste of space. He doesn't even deserve to be called a man, and the fact he's still bothering to text Clarity after ruining his relationship with her—by cheating, out of all things—makes me see red. This is just my luck. I finally get to where I want to be, and of course he's still in the picture.

She quickly pales and turns off her phone to put it back in her pocket without responding. It doesn't matter. The damage is already done. She might be able to overlook what he did, except I never will.

September 2012 - Age 13
Clarity

I can't drink Pepsi. There's something in it where the second it hits my stomach, it's resurfacing and bringing everything with it. I've been keeping this secret from Victor for the last few years, so he doesn't question it when I ask for a few dollars so I can go to the vending machine and buy one, forcing myself to suck it down while being well-aware of what fate will bring a few minutes later.

What I didn't plan was for him to be holding my hair in the back hallway as I stay bent over the trash can. My time prediction was off and I couldn't make it to the bathroom in time. Other competitors pass in the background, muttering worriedly, but no one has the time to stop and check in. Out on the ice, the announcer starts to rattle off the upcoming list for our age group.

Victor pats my back as I finish choking up last nights dinner. I spit out saliva as I finish, my heart hammering, stomach empty. His nose is crinkled as I turn around.

"Do you need me to get your mom? Are you okay to compete?" Victor tilts his head in concern. He looks a little green, himself.

I rest a hand over my stomach and gently press down. The little hump that was built over my abdomen a few minutes ago is gone. Completely flat. Nothing left. I try not to look too happy as I shake my head.

"I'm fine. Pre-comp jitters got to me. I'll be okay."

"You don't get nervous." He frowns. "I've got some peanut butter crackers if you—"

"No!" I inhale sharply as he flinches and repeat myself. "No, thank you. I'll be fine without."

"Okay..." he drawls out the word and eyes me, unconvinced, as he fixes the strap of my dress. I turn away and tighten my ponytail, swiping at my mouth.

Now I can focus on winning.

Chapter 9

Clarity

C alculus is my least favorite class for two reasons. Firstly, it's the only subject where I'm holding onto a passing grade with white knuckles and clenched teeth. Secondly, I have to perfectly time my arrival and departure to make sure I don't give Sterling the chance to intervene.

He's been getting to class early over the last few weeks, so I've been slipping into the bathroom that's down the hall to waste time touching up my makeup until the bell rings. Mr. Rhodes looks at me sideways every time I slip into the classroom right as he's shutting the door, although he never says anything. Technically I'm never late.

I push open the bathroom door, and the last thing I expect to see is a clump of girls standing in front of every mirror, laughing and jostling each other around. They're all wearing the same embroidered Speech and Debate team jackets. Every stall door is shut, however the girls inside are still adding to the conversation.

Letting out a long, slow exhale, I spin around and walk right back out. The universe must really be against me today because Sterling is walking down the hall in my direction. His eyes lock on me and he brightens. My stomach drops to my shoes as he reroutes his path.

"Hi, Claire." He falls into step alongside me. My skin crawls with that stupid nickname. "Did you get my text this morning?"

"Text?" I recall the way my body reacted like I was falling out of a rollercoaster. It was ironic because I had just given Jason a lecture about how involved my audience is in my life, and moments later, Sterling sent me a screenshot from an online forum that's already spreading rumors about my change in partners. "I haven't checked."

"Well, according to *Ice Wire Weekly*" —Sterling pulls out his phone and opens the internet— "Clarity Jansky, the dark horse favorite going into the U.S. International Ice Dance Invitational, might be a lot more interesting to watch this year. Not because of her talent, but because she'll be in the arms of someone new." He stops reading from the article. "You didn't go out west with your team, and I heard that Victor went to the hospital. You used to come to me about everything, but it seems like that's changed."

"What?" I scoff, even when guilt turns my gut. "There's nothing to tell. It was a freak accident, and Victor is fine now."

Sterling's jaw tightens subtly. He always does that when he's stuffing down his temper. "You could've at least said something about skating with Forbes. I thought you were done pretending to entertain him."

My head lightens as I forget how to breathe. I haven't told a single person outside of my personal family and friends about partnering with him. "Where did you hear about that?"

"People had a lot to say in the comments."

Of course they did.

I pull the sleeves of my sweater further down my wrists. "I had no other option. Jason has the time and talent—"

He snorts. "To be a figure skater?"

I forgot how much I hated it when he cut me off. I keep talking as we step into the classroom. "And I know he will do great. I'm going to make a post about the switch later today."

"You'll need to be careful. People won't be happy." Sterling walks past his assigned seat and follows me to mine at the front of the room.

"Tell me something I don't know." I set my books on my desk and face him. I regret my word choice as hurt flashes across his eyes.

"It's not just changing partners. Jason has a reputation too, but it's not a good one. Try looking him up right now, and let's see what videos and articles come up." He motions at my phone. "Come on. Do it."

My breath catches as he brushes against me. "He's my friend."

"He's going to drag you down," he fights back.

Juliette clears her throat as she comes to a stop behind Sterling. I never expected to find comfort in her presence, but here we are. She raises an eyebrow.

Sterling glances back at her, more words dying on his tongue as he shuffles out of the way of her desk. "My bad."

"Thank you." She places her books down and glances at me, her blonde eyebrows tightening.

He starts to walk away, then doubles back to rest his hand on my chair.

"Just so you know," he starts, undeterred when I shift away from him, "I'm glad you still get to skate. But with him? You're asking for trouble."

"Thank you for your concern," I reply bitterly.

He stares at me for a moment longer. When I don't say anything else, he shakes his head and walks off, all the way to his desk this time.

"Jackass," Juliette mutters. She's only been around for a few weeks, however she's not an idiot. Someone would have to be blind and deaf to not pick up on the fact that me and that boy have history.

"You're preaching to the choir," I whisper in reply as Mr. Rhodes walks into the room. He's nursing a fresh cup of coffee, dressed like he just finished helping the first moon landing. He shuts the door behind him and doesn't even greet us before directing everyone to open their textbooks to page ninety-eight. Thudding books and shuffling pages ensue.

We fall into silence as he begins to teach. It's hard enough trying to understand derivatives and integrals, but it's nearly impossible to focus with Sterling staring lasers at the back of my head the rest of class.

Anxiety is still rolling through my body like thunderstorm clouds and I haven't even stepped a foot inside of the ice rink yet.

I wave at Cole as he drives away. He honks the horn in response. As he follows the curb out of the parking lot, it puts the view of Jason's Range Rover directly in my sight.

Lightning strikes inside of my heart.

There's no way I can face Ortiz in this state of mind. She will smell the nerves on me like a bloodhound. That woman is not just a retired, highly decorated figure skater. Back in her day, she trained under international coaches. Now she trains her students all the way to the top before passing them over to Olympic trainers, if they are talented enough to handle the pressure.

It's my goal to go international in the spring so I can get on the road to the Olympics. If I can secure a few gold medals, I'll be credible enough to follow my dream of being the figurehead for figure skating broadcasting. I've been chasing that dream my entire life, and I thought Victor was going to be the one that would help me achieve it.

As much as Victor loves to skate, I don't know if he'll ever be able to reach the same level again, even after his wrist heals. My entire world is balancing on Jason right now.

Team edits closed last night. The only stone that's left to turn starts now, and that stone has a question written on it: Does Jason have what it takes?

There's only one way to find out.

I remind myself to breathe as I pull the strap of my bag higher up onto my shoulder and push open the doors of the rink, icy air causing my cheeks to tingle. If I don't get my emotions under control, it might give Ortiz a reason to believe that I can't handle the stress of high-level competitions. I can't take on any more setbacks right now. So, I paste on a smile and decide to act confident until the real confidence seeps in.

I pass through the lobby, blissfully quiet for one more week until hockey practices start. As I head down the stairs toward the North Rink, I get a bird's-eye view of the ice below. A few lone skaters are dotted near the boards, and Ortiz is skating on the outskirts of a male and female pair. Juliette and Montgomery. I recognize them from early yesterday morning when I came for extra ice time and borrowed Juliette an extra pair of gloves out of my locker.

I watch the two perform a beautiful set of twizzles, a series of rotations on one foot as they move across the ice. It's imperative that a pair stay in sync for twizzles, and it's like they're a mirror of each other.

Envy stirs in my chest. I shake it off as I finish my descent down the stairs and round the corner, entering the staging box next to the rink.

Jason raises his head from where he's currently stretching on the bench. His smile is instant.

"C.J." He leans into the stretch. "I could've picked you up when I left work, you know."

I drop my bag on the other side of him. "I don't want to add fuel to your girlfriend's fire."

He sits up, his smile slipping. "She'll get over it." He says the words as a statement. No room for argument.

I unzip my jacket and stuff it in my bag before joining him in a quick succession of stretches. "I'm sorry if this is creating an issue in your relationship. Seriously, I have no intention of putting a wall between you guys."

"It's okay, we've argued over less. You don't need to apologize. I'm the one who made the choice, so I have to deal with it." He sits next to his bag and pulls out fresh, black figure skates.

I incline my head toward him. "Nice skates. Where'd you get them?"

"I had Jordan at All Star hook him up yesterday," Victor cuts in as he walks around the corner, favoring his injured leg. His jacket is pulled tight over his shoulders, the sleeve bunched over his right arm where a cast is holding his wrist together.

"Hey, Vick." I grin and stop stretching to meet him halfway, pulling him into a sideways hug on his good side. "It's good to see you."

"I wasn't about to miss this big moment." Victor squeezes me, then slaps Jason's shoulder as he passes.

Jason crinkles his nose. "It's not my first day on the ice."

"Once you get out there, it'll feel like it."

Jason doesn't argue with that. He keeps tightening his laces, and Victor leans on the boards to watch the ice. I finish stretching, shaking off the nerves, feeling much better as I unzip my bag and pull out my skates. That's until I sit next to Jason and begin to pull the first one on. The moment I grab the ties and give them a tug, the lace snaps in half.

"Oh, you've *got* to be kidding me." I hold up the loose string.

Jason inhales sharply. "That's great."

"What happened?" Victor cranes his neck and scowls. "Didn't you just get those a few months ago?"

"For my birthday. They're practically new." I hold up the second skate and inspect it. That lace is also starting to fray under one of the top hooks. One sharp yank and it'll suffer the same fate. "Seriously? We go on the ice any minute!"

"Don't you keep backup equipment here?" Jason offers and takes the skates from me to inspect them. Victor wanders over to see for himself.

"I do!" My old, busted up skates are down in the locker room. "Hang on, I'll be right back."

"Better hurry," Victor says.

Racing down the hallway on my socked feet, I barge into the locker room, spooking a girl who's packing up her bag. I round the corner to my locker and curse. The door is cracked open, the lock gone. Grabbing the edge, I fling it open and curse again. Everything has been stolen. It's completely empty.

Panic threatens to choke me. I beat it away. There's no time for games. If I'm not on the ice in a few minutes, Ortiz will have my head.

I spin on my heel and start out of the locker room, nearly scaring the poor girl again when I ask, "Hey, did you see anyone break into locker thirty-seven back there? Or take anything out?"

She shakes her head, eyes wide. "No, I'm sorry. It's been a quiet night. I haven't seen anyone come back here until now."

"Thanks anyway," I grumble and continue my mad dash back to the ice.

The boys watch me expectantly as I return, and Jason's gaze flashes to my empty hands. "Did you get lost?"

"Everything is gone. My locker was broken into."

"What?" Victor's eyebrows draw together. "Who would do that?"

"I don't know." I look at Jason. "We're so screwed."

He scratches his jaw. "I still have my hockey blades in my car. These figure skates will be huge on you, but you could borrow them and I can wear my old ones."

I scrunch my face at the thought. "No way in hell. I'd rather..." I fade off. Darika is approaching the gate. She was one of the single skaters I saw practicing a few minutes ago.

"Victor! You're back!" Darika shrieks and jumps off the ice as her attention falls on Jason. She immediately slows down, her eyes widening. "And Jason. Hi, Jason."

I roll my eyes at the lavender haze in her gaze. Jason raises an eyebrow. He glances between her and me like he's trying to place how he knows her.

Victor is doing a terrible job at hiding his smirk, but he humors her by giving her a one-armed side hug. "It's good to see you, girl."

"I'm so sorry," I cut into their conversation, "but we don't have time for small talk. Are you done practicing?"

"Yeah." She shakes off that puppy love look when she focuses on me. Her lips quirk when she notices my feet. "Where are your skates?"

"Right here." Jason holds them up, the frayed laces holding on by a thread.

Darika gasps. "What happened?"

"Great question. I haven't touched them since yesterday. The thing is, I don't have any other skates here. What size are your feet?"

"Eight." Darika holds up her foot. "Sometimes eight and a half."

Perfect.

"I'm begging you, can I please borrow your skates tonight? I will return them to you tomorrow. I promise."

Darika brightens and bounces over to the bench. "Of course!" She makes a point of sitting next to Jason. He scoots away.

"Thank you, thank you, thank you." I put as much gratitude in my tone as possible. I sit down and snatch the first skate out of her hands, forcing it on my foot.

Juliette and Montgomery come skating over to the door and stumble onto the mat. They collapse on the nearby benches with heaving chests and tired yet gleaming eyes. Juliette scans the bench, her mouth hardening when she notices Victor.

"Hi, everybody," she greets as she loosens her skates. "Victor, I didn't think you'd be back so soon."

He shrugs. "I'm not here to skate, just overseeing practice."

Juliette nods. Montgomery eyes me, and he's the first to notice I'm wearing Darika's tan skates, unlike my white ones.

"Are you all good, Clarity?" he asks as he unscrews his water bottle.

Juliette follows his gaze and blinks. "God, what happened? Where are your skates?"

"Well, that's just the question of the night, isn't it?" I finish tying them on. Jason gets to his feet and steps around Darika to offer me his hand. I take it and let him help me up while wiggling my toes. The skates are a little tight, but they'll do. "Sorry, but we really need to go."

"No problem. Good luck, you two," Juliette says with a controlled smile.

"See you on the other side." Victor moves back to his place on the boards.

"Thanks. Thank you again, Darika." I throw the words over my shoulder then nod at Jason when he opens the arena door for me. Victor latches it behind us. It's weird having Jason skating alongside me as we make a beeline for Ortiz, who's waiting in the middle of the arena.

She watches us approach, arms crossed. "Forbes. I'm glad you made it."

"I'm happy to be here, ma'am," Jason says as he reaches up to rub his neck, then catches himself. At least he's listening to my two biggest words of advice: don't let her see that you're nervous, and always address her as *ma'am*.

Ortiz glances between him and me, and a flicker of amusement crosses her face. "I'm sure that you are. Let me set the record straight. I know who you are. You may have been a star on the hockey rink, however you're in my arena now. Figure skating is a completely different game and I expect nothing but your best effort."

Please don't scare him off.

Jason tilts his chin down. "I hear you."

"Do you? There's no room for mistakes here. Any weakness in you becomes a weakness in her." She points at me, and despite the long-sleeved shirt I'm wearing, goosebumps crawl over my skin. "You better be able to prove why Kerr and Jansky are so set on having you here."

"Yes ma'am." Jason rolls his shoulders back and continues to meet her eyes, seemingly unphased. I'm impressed with his composure, because I'd be shaking in my skates if I were him.

She continues to regard him for a moment, sharpening those steel eyes on him before skating backward and motioning at the rink. "This is going to be your guys' home base nearly every night for the next month and a half. There are forty-eight days until the Invitational, and if we want to get Forbes in any sort of shape to keep up with you, Jansky, and to even think about competing against those athletes, you guys will probably want to practice alone on the evenings you don't spend with me. The Invitational isn't going to be a stage, it's a microscope. You two will have everyone's attention."

I glance at Jason from the corner of my eye. Nothing betrays his emotions. If he's feeling anxious, scared, or any trepidation about this commitment, I'm none the wiser. If anything, he appears exactly like he said he was a moment ago: just happy to be here.

Ortiz pauses. She must be thinking the same thing because she clears her throat and continues. "Most practices start with basic skating skills to get you two warmed up and in sync, then we'll work on teaching individual moves. Choreography will follow for the short program and the freestyle. I'm assuming she filled you in on those terms, Forbes?"

"Yes, ma'am."

I resist the urge to snort. So stoic. At least he's listening to my advice.

We spoke a bit this morning, and I gave him more details about what figure skating—or ice dancing, in our case—entails.

Ice dancing competitions consist of two parts: a rhythm dance and a free dance. The rhythm dance has required elements, like lifts or step sequences, performed to a specific rhythm of music within a required tempo range that the judges choose.

The free dance also needs a wide selection of skating skills, although we get to choose the music we skate to, with a goal of pulling off an entertaining performance that appears effortless. It takes innovative choreography, timing, and cadence to win.

After both dances are finished, the scores are added together to determine the overall placement. This year, I'm going to clean house again at these competitions. I just know it.

Ortiz finishes explaining, "After choreography, we will focus on technical elements. In a few weeks, we'll be able to do run-throughs of each performance and I'll break you two down before I build you back up. Understood?"

We nod simultaneously. I've heard this lecture many times.

"Good. Forbes, stroke off on the wall so I can watch your technique. Jansky, go with him and stick to the outside edge. Find his rhythm."

"Sure thing. Let's go." I buzz toward the edge of the arena. Jason sweeps next to me as we reach the wall. Despite the height advantage that he has over me, I find it easy to match his tempo. There's a good chance that Victor helped with this transition since he is almost six feet tall, only a few inches shorter than Jason. I've learned how to hustle without making it seem like that's what I'm doing.

The ice passes in a blur beneath us. That familiar feeling of freedom fills my lungs, despite the tight leather around my toes. Until Jason opens his mouth and says quietly, "Your coach is a treat."

The corner of my mouth quirks. "She's *our* coach now."

He chuckles, then his toe pick catches the ice, causing him to stumble.

I dive forward to grab him, but he's already re-centered and blushing a furious red. He waves his hand dismissively at Ortiz in a silent apology.

"What was that?" I question. I've seen this boy skate my entire life, and he *skates*. Never stumbles.

"Goddamn figure skates. I forgot about the toe picks." He frowns. "Sorry. I haven't had the chance to get used to them."

"Will you be okay to practice tonight?"

"I'll be fine." Jason sets his jaw determinedly. "We're on a timeline for this competition, and it sounds like I have a lot of catching up to do."

There's no room for me to argue, especially when Ortiz shouts, "Are you two done talking or can we begin practice now?"

"Sorry, ma'am! We're ready!" I respond, embarrassment crawling up my collar. At least, I'd like to think that we are.

Nearly two hours later, I feel like I've begun to climb up a steep mountain only to stumble and slide all the way back down to the bottom, hitting every branch and rock along the way.

Jason is a fantastic, accomplished skater. He's amazing in every respect: his balance, strength, and ability. He is a natural at looking out for me.

The thing is, in Ortiz's words, he moves like an oaf. Stiff, like a board, like he's expecting some two-hundred-pound guy to come flying up at any moment and try taking him off his feet.

I understand that it's his first day, but I didn't realize how hard it was going to be going from being *this* close to a perfect routine with Victor to being thrust back to square one with Jason. He knows the basics, he just needs to learn all the aspects of becoming a figure skater and a dancer.

Needless to say, the idea of us skating together suddenly seems really, really dumb.

The two of us are sweating like a glass of iced tea sitting on the porch in the middle of summer as we return to Ortiz after practicing our synchronized spin for the hundredth time. The poor guy was starting to turn green before she finally called us over.

Considering the expression on her face, it seems like she's thinking the same thing I am: we came so close, only to fall so far. I risk a glance behind her shoulders to check in with Victor. We make eye contact, and he pretends to choke himself. I bite my cheek and flash my attention back to Ortiz.

"Okay... we will give that a break for tonight," she says. That's how I know this situation is dire. There's no biting insults or words to make us better. She's given up. "The last thing I want to see you guys try is a simple lift so I know where we need to start tomorrow."

"A lift?" Jason laughs in disbelief.

"Yes." Ortiz taps the toe pick of her skate against the ice, impatient. "You agreed to skate, and that means hopefully one day you will be able to hold Jansky on your shoulders. Are you strong enough to do that?"

All humor drains out of his body. "Of course I am."

"Then yes, you will perform a lift. It's a simple beginner move. Hand-to-armpit hold. Jansky, here." Ortiz waves me over.

I oblige. She proceeds to show Jason where to hold me and explains how to enter and exit the lift, poking me around all the while.

Finally, she turns to him. "Capiche?"

He seems a little pale, his eyes wide as he stares at Ortiz. "Uh..."

"Great. Just don't drop my star athlete." She moves out of the way. "You will never hear me say this again, but I am not expecting perfection. Just get the girl off the ice. If you don't get this over with tonight, it'll just get harder. And we need you spinning her around your head by the end of the week."

"Right. Right, okay," Jason stammers and skates up to me, his eyes wild like a raging ocean. They raze over my body, and suddenly I'm struck with the question, *what if he's nervous about touching me?*

I come close to shaking my head. No, it's not like he's never touched me before. He'll be fine.

"Alright, Forbes, start by getting momentum backward and Jansky will put herself in position alongside you. You'll grab her right hand with your left and put your right hand under her armpit. She will balance herself on your left hand, you'll spin around in a circle, and let her down," Ortiz says slowly, as if the slower she talks, the more the words will stick, like a quality superglue.

Jason visibly swallows as he pushes off his skates and begins to move backward.

"Breathe. You've got this." I glance at his feet and take bigger strides to move alongside him. In the back of my mind, my knees hit the ice and blood soaks into my leggings.

Not now.

"My palms are so sweaty," he curses quietly.

"It's okay," I soothe. Only one of us can be a wreck at a time. I reach out. "Give me your left hand. Prepare yourself to look over my left leg so you can keep an eye on the ice."

Jason reaches his hands out, and I grab onto his left. This isn't the first time we've held hands tonight, but he's right. His are damp with perspiration. I grimace.

"There you go. One, two, three." I prepare myself as his right hand goes under my armpit. I push off the ice at the same time he swoops me up.

Fear and hope battle in my chest. Fear, because the last time I was in the air, I fell out of it. Hope, because as much as I have my doubts, this moment makes me realize that Jason can be a worthy partner.

Until, suddenly, the wind catches my hair and I hear him curse again. Loudly. His hand slips out of mine. He makes a wild grab for me. It's too late.

The side of my head hits the ice first, and abrupt pain races down my neck. My hip follows, and I yelp in shock.

It takes a moment for me to remember how to breathe. The ice didn't seem this solid when I was a kid.

"Shit! Clarity, are you alright?!" Jason drops onto his knees next to me. His hands shake as they hover over me like he doesn't know where to touch first.

"I'm fine, it's okay. I'm fine." My voice wavers between gasps. The ice bites against the palms of my hands as I push myself up. Even the air feels colder against my lungs as I refill them.

Jason swoops in to the rescue, engulfing my hands with his as our fingers tangle together. With one smooth movement, he pulls me to my feet. I squeak at the brute strength, at the ease he handles me with.

He's still trembling, eyes filled to the rim with fear. He's still holding my hands. I haven't let go of his yet, either.

Victor is on the edge of my vision, the rink door flung open, his feet positioned to race over the ice. He reminds me that he's okay, Jason's okay, I'm okay. The ache in my head and my hip are already beginning to subside—it really wasn't an awful tumble—and the remaining pain is soaked up as Jason keeps his palms pressed against mine.

Ortiz skates over, frowning. "Are you alright, Jansky?"

I spook and drop his hands like they're on fire. That same heat crawls over my body as I face our coach. "Yeah, I'm fine. Just knocked the breath out of me."

"Thank God." Ortiz turns on Jason. He immediately recoils. "What did I say about dropping her? This is a prime example of why we get these maneuvers over with. You're lucky that she didn't have far to fall, that you weren't going any faster, and that you could slow down her descent. Now you know what not to do tomorrow."

"I know. That was completely my mistake," Jason says.

"Yes, it was." Ortiz lets her words hang in the air. "I think that's enough for tonight. I'll see you both tomorrow."

We thank her and Jason skates alongside me as we head for the exit together.

"That was the most horrific thing I've ever done in my life." He avoids my gaze.

"Everyone needs to get their first failure over with," I say with more conviction than I feel and wave my hand dismissively.

"Next time I would like it if it weren't at your expense. I'm never going to get that damn sound of you hitting the ice out of my head." He shudders.

I slow to a stop. "Jason, look at me." I wait for him to turn around and meet my gaze. "I'm *fine*. That won't be the last time it happens. Victor dropped me plenty of times before we got the hang of things, just ask him. Believe me, I knew what I was getting into with you. You'll be better off by moving on and getting over it before tomorrow's practice."

Jason hesitates, then nods. "You're right. Sorry."

"Don't turn into a weenie on me," I tease. "Your confidence from earlier was better."

"That was before I dropped you. Besides, I was watching everyone while you were in the locker room, and it's no wonder this team swept up the competition in Colorado that you've talked about. Everyone else is amazing."

My stomach drops at the mention of the Fall Classic. The competition that Victor and I were supposed to dominate, but Juliette and Montgomery did, instead.

I turn away and continue to the exit, my toes pleading to be released. "You'll get there. Besides, I really don't feel like talking about that stupid competition."

"It didn't seem stupid to you when you mentioned it on your blog last month." He bumps me with his elbow.

I shift away from him, putting plenty of room between us.

"Things were different a month ago." I hurry to meet Victor at the door, his face pinched with unspoken questions.

Yes, they were different, and I'm starting to wonder if I would've been better off cutting my losses and coming back stronger next year.

Chapter 10

Jason

It's been one week since I started practicing with Clarity. I never expected switching over to figure skating to be a walk in the park, obviously, but I've never been this sore in my life. I've been spending each morning learning how to dance properly, collapsing either face first or ass first on the ice multiple times during each practice, and then passing out in bed every night with bags of ice tied around my hips and ankles and knees. And I thought my problems would stop there.

That was until Tiffany texted me last night, asking if I could start picking her up on my way to these early morning workouts. We don't usually meet outside of school anyway, so the request felt weirdly domestic, like she suddenly remembered we're dating.

I shouldn't care—hell, I should probably be happy that my girlfriend wants to see me—except this is *my* time with Clarity. I don't know what exactly tore the two apart back in middle school, but I do know that every time they're in the same room together, the tension is palpable. I can already feel it pressing against my skin as I open the gym door for Tiffany. She breezes inside, her red hair swishing in a ponytail.

My attention flies past the other skaters who have already claimed equipment and land on Clarity, who's near the back wall. She's rolling out mats in front of the mirror, next to five-pound weights on the floor. This ought to be good. Although, I'll take anything over the foxtrot training she put me through on Saturday.

"I'm surprised that more people aren't here since hockey starts tonight," Tiffany says as we walk toward the back of the room.

"Everyone is probably enjoying their last morning of freedom until Coach Vines and Lloyd assign a training schedule." I glance at her as she unzips her jacket, showing off her workout outfit. "I know that I would be."

"Don't complain about a situation that you put yourself in. You didn't have to agree to this." She casts me the same icy glare that she does every time we're on this subject.

Irritation makes my skin crawl. I scratch my wrist. "That wasn't my point."

Clarity catches our voices and turns around. A controlled smile builds on her face, except it doesn't reach her eyes. "Good morning." She tugs down the sleeves on her thin long-sleeve shirt.

Tiffany throws down her jacket next to Clarity's bag. "What's on your guys' agenda for today?"

That itch starts to grow, making me rub the side of my neck. Tiffany doesn't even bother to hide the displeasure on her face.

"Pilates." Clarity crosses her arms.

"Pilates?" Tiffany snorts. "Shouldn't he be lifting weights so he can actually pick you up?"

My stomach clenches as shock flashes across Clarity's face. As if I haven't been bench-pressing her body weight since freshmen year.

"The weight isn't the problem." I add my bag to the pile. "It isn't Clarity's fault that I don't have full flexibility in my shoulders."

"This is a good way to start the week." She flourishes her hand at the weights. "Balance, joint stability, and alignment are all—"

"I know what pilates is." Tiffany's eyes darken.

Cole walks around me to grab a water bottle out of Clarity's gym bag and pitches in, "Do you? Because I saw the way you were playing by the end of last season, and I think you could benefit from some balance training." He raises an eyebrow as he takes a long, slow drink, driving his point home.

Tiffany's cheeks turn red. "You wouldn't know proper form if it hit you across the face."

Their dynamic has been like this since elementary school; Cole gets under her skin, Tiffany lashes out at him. I once hoped that when she and I started dating they would be civil, but that hope died a long time ago.

"Okay." I wave my hands. Man, I knew I shouldn't have left my bed this morning. "That's enough. I deal with enough problems every day. Let's not make another one, alright?"

Cole shrugs and sets down the bottle. "I don't have a problem."

"Me either." Tiffany sniffs.

"I'm about to if we're not on the mats in the next five minutes," Clarity says sharply, and my chest swells in agreement. Leave it to her to set the record straight.

Tiffany doesn't hide her eye roll as she steps away. "I'm going to go lift."

Cole wiggles his fingers dismissively, but once her back is turned, he pretends to poke his eyes out. Clarity smacks him in the chest, which makes me cough to hide my laugh.

"I won't ever understand it," he says.

"Understand what?" I pull my phone out of my pocket, and as I go to set it on my bag, I catch a text notification from Dad that I must've missed on the way here.

> Meeting got pushed back. Your presence is expected at 5pm...

The rest of the message is cut off. It takes everything in me to not pitch my phone at the wall. Of course he scheduled a meeting to start one hour before I'm supposed to leave work.

"...which I get, but she's not it, man," Cole finishes his sentence. I have no idea what he said. Considering the horror in Clarity's eyes, I can't imagine it was very nice.

"Cole Aaron Jansky." She pushes him away. "Take your bad attitude somewhere else, would you? I don't need your negative energy rubbing off on us."

He stumbles with a loud laugh, and holds up his hands in the shape of a heart. "You guys don't count. You're already winners in my heart."

I return the heart. "Love you, man."

"Don't instigate." Clarity grabs my bicep and spins me away. She lets go just as fast, but it's too late. My heart is already in my throat. "Remember what Ortiz said about wanting to see more out of your core? That's where we're going to start today. You need to strengthen those deep core muscles."

"I have a core already." My gaze catches on her stomach as she lays down flat on her mat. She's gotten so skinny over the last few years. I've been meaning to ask her about it. The problem is, I don't know how to approach the subject without sounding like a jerk.

"You have a surface core." Clarity watches me lie down next to her, making my skin prickle with the full weight of her attention. "Those are superficial muscles that make you look strong. A deep core is what helps you stay balanced and stable. That's why you wobble on one foot."

"I wobble because I'm trying to keep up with you." I flash her a smile.

"If you strengthened your core, you wouldn't have to try. It would come naturally." I laugh, which makes her smile, but she's not done humbling me. "Okay, let's do some leg circles. Lift one leg and draw small circles in the air."

She grounds her body against the floor and elegantly traces perfect circles, her foot pointed toward the ceiling.

"This is supposed to help?" I follow her lead and grimace as my hamstring retaliates. It still hasn't forgiven me for the extra ice time I took yesterday.

"Only when you're doing it right. Seriously, are you trying to kick soccer balls or make circles?" Clarity pushes herself up onto her knees. I inhale sharply when she grabs my leg, sending a pleasant wave of shock through my body. The moment is ruined when she takes me by the ankle. A high-pitched shriek slips out of me.

"Hey! You know my feet are ticklish." I try to jolt my shoe out of her grasp. The last thing I need is for her to rub my ankles the wrong way and send me into a laughing fit, catching unwanted attention from Tiffany.

"Oh, don't be a baby." Clarity tries to keep a straight face, but I don't miss the smile that she's wrestling with as she yanks my leg higher.

I hiss as she bends my foot to point like a dancer. Electricity jolts through my muscles again, and it's not just because my body doesn't naturally move like that. My brain starts short circuiting. I almost miss her next words.

"Hold that position. Notice the difference?" She lets go, leaving me to take over control as I rotate my foot around.

"Sort of." I feel extremely stupid for roughly five seconds, until I start to notice heat building in the middle of my abdomen. My face bends in concentration. She grins, way too proud with herself.

"Very nice. Now, go counter-clockwise."

"Are you trying to kill me?" I ask through gritted teeth as I do what she says.

"I just want to see you succeed." She returns to her mat. The timing is perfect because she misses the way I flinch at her words.

The last time I heard those words, Dad was driving me home after that last hockey game. I was brushing dried blood off my knuckles as he screamed at me, beating the wheel, the dashboard. I couldn't get a word in while he was reminding me of how deeply I messed up, how stupid I looked, how much time and energy he had wasted on me. I ruined that career path, and if I don't stay for his meeting later, I might ruin this one, too. But if I don't make it to practice on time later, I'll also ruin Clarity's.

Every time I try to do the right thing, it's like it comes back to bite me in the ass. The universe loves to remind me who's in charge.

I fall silent, partially to concentrate, mostly because I have nothing to say to that. I pretend that I don't notice her glancing at me out of the corner of her eye. My chest loosens with gratitude as she keeps quiet, only speaking to instruct me on the next movement.

Finally, after another series of movements that make me believe my abs are seconds away from lighting on fire, Clarity calls for a break. She pops onto her feet, seemingly unaffected as she rearranges her sleeves and gets herself water.

It takes everything in me to not tear up as I push myself into a sitting position. My core reminds me that it has officially clocked out for the day.

I nudge the five-pound weight that's next to my knees as far away as possible. "I never thought I'd say this, but that weight nearly took my life."

Clarity grabs my water bottle out of the side pocket of my bag and passes it over to me. I can't get the cap off fast enough.

"Size doesn't matter now, does it? Controlling it is the hard part."

I sputter and spray water all over my shoes. "Excuse me?"

"Get your mind out of the gutter, Forbes. You know what I mean." She kicks the bottom of my shoe as she passes me on her way to the nearest paper towel dispenser, which makes me smile.

I take another pull of water when a loud laugh gets my attention. Tiffany is at the squat rack, taking plates off the bar as she says something to the brunette boy beside her. He's a hockey player, judging by the logo on his shirt, but I don't recognize him. He must be new on the team this year.

She tosses her ponytail over her shoulder as she straightens, casting him a confident smile despite his gaze flickering toward Clarity. My stomach clenches as I watch his eyes raze over her body.

Cole finishes wiping down his leg press machine and wanders over, a smirk growing on his face. "Your girlfriend seems to have made friends with Johnny."

"And Johnny is about to make friends with Clarity." I push myself onto my feet. The boy walks away from Tiffany and trails across the room. Her jaw slackens.

"At ease, soldier. Don't go break somebody else's nose." Cole eyes me. I know he's not referring to the referee. He still hasn't forgotten the time I punched our goalie's nose in eighth grade when I found out he made a competition out of who could talk to Clarity the most out of five other boys.

Clarity is on her way back with a handful of paper towels when Johnny stops her. He's all smiles and easy charm, but satisfaction swells through my body when all she offers him is a guarded lift of her lips.

"Hey, Clarity, right? You run that skating blog. I love—I mean, my sister loves your stuff. Could I get a picture with you?" he stutters, his cheeks turning pink.

"You're kidding me," I seethe as Clarity says something that makes him brighten again, and he pulls out his phone.

"Better get used to it." Cole swirls his water bottle and wiggles his eyebrows. "She's like a C-list celebrity around here. Hi, Tiffany."

Tiffany ignores him. She knocks against my shoulder as she passes, her nostrils flaring. "I'm ready to go."

I tear my eyes away from Clarity to watch Tiffany fight with her jacket. "But we're not done."

She spins around. "I am."

Cole watches us like a tennis match, chewing his bottom lip, fighting a smile.

"Then you can sit in the lobby or out in my car." I point at my bag. "The keys are in there. I'll be out in fifteen."

The words fall out before I can stop them, and I don't even believe they came from my mouth.

Even Tiffany stares at me for a moment, and it's terrifying to watch the emotion leave her face. It must take her off guard as well, because she heeds my words without a question, snatching the keys out of my bag. Cole salutes as she walks past.

Clarity comes up and passes me the paper towels as she watches Tiffany leave. "Do you need to go?"

"Absolutely not." I wipe the water drops off my legs and allow myself to exhale. "What's next?"

April 2014 - Age 15

Jason

The familiar sound of drums pours out of the Bluetooth speaker. Lauren gasps and spins around from where she's standing at the kitchen counter, putting her back to the cheese ravioli she was just filling. "Oh, my god! This is my favorite song!"

"You say that every time anything by Fleetwood Mac comes on," Aaron says from where he's feeding dough into the pasta machine, a role that he doesn't trust any of us kids to do yet. He flicks his fingers at his wife as Lauren shimmies over to him.

Cole looks up from across the table. "Don't let her start. Clarity, skip this song." He nods his head at his mom's phone, his hands coated with egg and flour.

I press the ravioli mold into the next section of dough and glance up to watch Clarity. Her back is to me as she stirs the sauce on the stove, her hair swept back in a messy bun. She bobs her head in time with the beat, swinging her hips back and forth.

Instead of indicating that she heard her brother, she starts to sing along with Stevie Nicks to the first line of *Dreams*. Cole rolls his head back and groans.

Lauren joins Clarity in singing and takes Aaron's hands, pulling him to his feet. He's the complete opposite of my dad—not just because he has a full beard and a head full of black hair that's starting to pepper with age, but because he actually stands up with a huge smile on his face and sways his hips. Lauren lifts their arms up, not missing a beat as she slides her hands down his wrists.

Cole holds his arm over his eyes. "You guys are *so* embarrassing."

I don't know what he's talking about because I've been a part of every bi-annual Jansky pasta-and-sauce making party for the last several years, and it never fails to turn into an actual party. Their parents are hard-working people, and these are the only days of the year where they seem to actually let loose.

Aaron sweeps Lauren into his arms, and the two of them continue to dance as she keeps singing along, their pasta forgotten.

My hands slow to a stop as Clarity continues moving with the beat, sidestepping with her feet at her station. I set the mold down all together when the chorus crashes and she whirls around, strands of her hair tumbling loose as she sings into the spoon she was just stirring with, sending splatters of red sauce down onto the tile.

Cole gripes about the mess. I'm swept up in their performance as Lauren jumps to her daughter, grabbing her arm and pulling her into the fray. The three of them continue to dance, completely immersed in their performance.

I want to laugh, and a small part of me even wants to get up and join them. To sweep Clarity in my arms as easily as Aaron does, twirling her around and around.

Instead, the weirdest moment of melancholy chokes me, pressing tears against the back of my eyes. This is the closest I'll ever get to having a complete family, witnessing them laugh and stumble and sing in the kitchen. Cole is lucky to complain, sick of the exposure to moments like this.

I'm afraid that I'll never be able to fully soak it in.

I don't know who my mom is and where she's at. I don't know whether she dances around the kitchen, or if she prefers to sit off to the side and laugh. I can't even remember the sound of her laugh. Dad won't ever hold her in his arms, smiling so hard that his eyes are nearly closed. We don't have these memories to look back on. Instead, when tonight is over, I'll be returning to an empty house. The only sound of life will be my footsteps echoing down the halls.

But, for now, this is enough.

Chapter 11

Clarity

J ason has been around my family since kindergarten, and this is the first time that he's ever been late for anything.

I check the time on my phone for what feels like the millionth time as I finish stretching near the boards, bypassing the hundreds of notifications that have built up over the last thirty minutes. The latest one makes my stomach twist.

> **@skategirlz_unite** commented on your post:
> i mean no shade but are you sure jason's really in this?? isn't he the hockey guy who got benched for punching a ref?? bold move putting your whole season in his hands...

Swallowing, I set my phone down on the bench and start to pace. He was so confident that he could balance all of his responsibilities on top of practice. If he were to ask me, I'd tell him that he needs to grow a spine and start saying no to some people in his life. Except for me. I desperately need him here, like, *right now*. Juliette and Montgomery's performance music ended a few minutes ago. We're due to trade places at any moment.

The sound of shoes pounding down the stairs causes me to turn, and I nearly cry in relief seeing Jason. He's not in any better of a mood than I am. Actually, he looks extremely pissed off for a guy who's decked out in brand name business attire. Considering how much he does in a day, he must have to change outfits at least five times. Good thing his daddy hires a dry cleaner to pick up and drop off their laundry every week.

I grit my teeth the second that thought flashes across my mind. He's doing the best he can, even if I wish he could've done better by being here ten minutes earlier.

He disappears in the direction of the locker room at the same time the gate rattles behind me. Juliette steps off the ice first, followed by Montgomery. Both of them are drenched in sweat, and they're wearing matching smiles as they take the nearest bench.

Ortiz trails behind them to say to me, "I know they're done early. I need to run over to the speakers and restart them. The Bluetooth keeps disconnecting." She holds up her phone. "Be on the ice at 6:30 sharp, alright?"

"Yes, ma'am." I watch as she skates to the opposite side of the rink before regarding the other two. "How was practice?"

"Great. We're finally getting that damn step sequence nailed down." Montgomery unwinds his laces and glances around the box. "Where's Victor?"

"I think the better question is, where's Jason?" Juliette straightens once she finishes pushing on her blade guards. I don't know how she isn't freezing in that t-shirt. I'm cold enough as it is without sweat cooling on my skin.

"Victor's running late. Jason... is also running late." I hesitate as the sound of loud laughter echoes from the lobby. Now the hockey boys are showing up for their first practice of the season, and they're probably going to pin Jason to the wall with questions.

"Must be nice having a life that doesn't revolve around the rink." Montgomery finishes pulling off his skates, his dark eyebrows pulling together.

"I wouldn't know." I take the bench across from them and feel Juliette's eyes on me as I pull the skates out of my bag. That's when I notice the sleeves on my shirt have started to ride up. I quickly yank them down, covering the yellowing bruises. "Jason wouldn't either. He spent more time on the ice than I did as a kid."

"I doubt that," Juliette says and drops her gaze. "Both of you are great skaters. I saw you guys practice last week."

"Jason has always been a natural. Ortiz practically beat me into the athlete I am today." I tug the first skate on. The effort takes the air out of my lungs. "Her training methods are relentless."

"You must be doing something right. I thought I saw online that Kovalenko is watching your season." Montgomery brushes the hair off his forehead.

Yeah, her and thousands of other people across the country. I can hear the opinions of all those voices in my head, droning like a hornet's nest. Maybe it is bold of me to balance my future on an ex-hockey player.

"I'm sure she'd be scouting us too if we followed Coach Ortiz's advice to a T." Juliette casts him a look that I can't quite read as she pulls gloves out of her bag. "Darika was talking to me while we were in Colorado, and she said that Ortiz gave her a meal plan so she could lose a few pounds by the Invitational."

My hands freeze on my laces.

I was nine years old the first time Ortiz poked my stomach. I was in a situation like Darika, only a few weeks out from my first real ice dancing competition. She told me that there was no way I could go out and perform looking like *that*.

It wasn't a meal plan, exactly, although I didn't need one. I knew what she meant. That same night, when Mom offered dessert, I gave Cole my serving. I haven't had zeppoles since.

"Oh." I resume tying the skate. "Yeah, Ortiz can be a lot, but she means well. Besides, I feel much better when I watch what I eat. Less weighed down." I cringe at how the words sound coming out. Why not write *I cry about what I've eaten in a day every night!* on my forehead with a Sharpie?

"I get that. I don't think I've eaten breakfast in months," Juliette says with a laugh.

Something deep in my chest loosens, even when Montgomery eyes us. "That's not cool."

"Relax. Not like that." She nudges him as she stands. "If I eat too early, I'm super bloated for the rest of the day. You know what I mean? Makes it hard to be comfortable for practice."

"I understand." My cheeks flush as the words tumble out before she's done talking.

Montgomery shakes his head as he finds his feet and grabs his bag. "You guys are crazy, and this conversation is making me hungry. Let's go eat, Jules. Clarity, it's been a pleasure, as always. Good luck."

"Thanks. Bye guys." I tuck in the loose ends of my laces as they walk off, and I finally relax as a shadow comes around the corner. "It's about time—I'm sorry, what are you doing here?"

Sterling smiles sheepishly, his hockey skates tucked under one arm, and a Vitamin Water in the other. "Figured I'd come say hi before hitting the ice. The golden boy is cornered in the locker room, so I knew I had a minute to see you. Here, I brought this. The vending machine spit out an extra, and I know it's the one you like."

He holds out the Vitamin Water, the reddish liquid sloshing inside. My stomach twists. This flavor is my least favorite, and it has sugar, and one hundred extra calories that I wasn't counting on consuming. I hope Victor or Jason like pomegranate.

I paste on a smile as I take it. "That's kind of you. Thanks. You could've done me a solid and brought Jason with you, too."

Sterling's smile slips, but he quickly catches it. "I'm sure he's not far behind. I can't wait to see him from the other side of the windows. It'll be a big change."

Considering his tone, I can't tell if he means that positively or negatively. I scramble for the right words to say. Thankfully I'm saved from replying as Victor finishes descending the stairs and limps over, his lips twisted in a scowl. "If you're spending your time the right way, you shouldn't be looking over here at all."

"How can I not when I share the same rink as a big star?" Sterling nudges my arm in one of the same spots that Jason grabbed too hard last week when we fell, leaving another baseball-sized bruise. I wince and step away, then immediately regret it when his eyes narrow.

Victor bristles. He never liked Sterling, even before we started to date. The only reason why he tolerates him is because I've begged him to leave Sterling's antics to me. He shouldn't be anyone's problem but my own.

"Alright Jansky, where's Forbes?" Ortiz's question rings over the ice.

I curse and turn away from the boys to face the ice as she comes across the centerline, hands on her hips.

"Uhh..."

"Coming! I'm here." Jason comes jogging around the corner in socked feet, his skates in hand, his training clothes wrinkled. His eyes flash dangerously when he sees Sterling.

Sterling grins and nudges me with his elbow. "See you on the ice. Have fun, Forbes."

"Don't fall your first day back on the ice. Wouldn't want to see that fragile ego bruised." Jason cuts him a cold glare as he passes and lifts his arm as he approaches, herding me away.

"Cut the bullshit. Both of you have practices to attend." Victor plucks the drink out of my hand. He raises an eyebrow at the label. "You hate pomegranate."

"I hate a lot of things right now." I cross my arms and watch Jason fly through the motions of putting on his skates. "Thanks for joining us tonight."

"You can thank my dad." He stands in front of me. We're inches apart. I take a step back, and my heart leaps in my throat as he tilts his head down, his green eyes locking onto mine. He was simmering with anger, but I watch the emotion melt away. "I wasn't the one who scheduled a five o'clock meeting. I got here as fast as I could."

"Well, make it faster next time," I blurt in my panic to say something. Anything. He recoils, and his expression hardens again.

Damn it, maybe not that.

It's too late to take it back. I whirl around and go out onto the ice, allowing the clacking of the blades to fill the awkward silence. The sound is doubled as Jason joins me, and I can feel his irritation like it's my own. Maybe it is my own.

Ortiz whirls her finger in the air. "Don't come to me. Start your laps."

"Alright." Jason backtracks toward the boards. There's a sure sign that something is bothering him—the second he stops regarding Ortiz as *ma'am*, something's wrong.

At least he slows down long enough for me to catch up. I don't know how to apologize for my outburst, so I try to make it up by quietly asking, "How was work?"

He scoffs. "Stupid. I'm over the nitpicking. I didn't realize there was a right and wrong way to hole punch papers."

"That's frustrating. I'm sorry that happened."

"It's fine. You think I'd know that about my dad by now."

We stay silent for another lap. I finally dare to speak when I don't think Ortiz can hear. "I made a blog post about you today."

That gets his attention. The side of his mouth pulls up. "Oh, yeah? What did the famous Clarity Jansky have to say about me?"

I feel the warmest I've been all day when he says my name like that. "I figured it was time to settle the rumors and introduce you as my teammate."

He brightens, and I realize how much I miss this version of him. "I'll check it out later. I'm sure your followers are just *ecstatic*." He says that last bit with so much sarcasm that it almost makes me laugh.

"You'll be pleasantly surprised. Most of the feedback is positive."

"Most?"

"Forbes!" Ortiz calls out. "Reverse skate! Lead with your arms, watch your core. Match his pace, Jansky."

Jason immediately jumps around, transitioning into a beautiful backward skate directly in front of me.

I adjust my strides so I won't kick out too far and trip him as I reach up to tighten my ponytail. "Yeah, a few people are bummed to hear that Victor—" I cut myself off with a loud yelp as he trips over his feet, landing flat on his back, shaking the ice. My life flashes before my eyes as I pick up my feet like I'm walking barefoot on hot coals, doing everything in my power to avoid sinking my blades into another person's flesh.

Ortiz is likely calling out profanities from across the arena. I can't hear her over the blood rushing in my ears as I make a tight circle and rush to his side, holding out my hand to pull him up. "Are you okay? What was that?"

Jason sits up, his face pale as he grabs my wrist. I expect him to brace against my weight and stand up, so he takes me off guard by using his other hand to push up my sleeve.

The overhead lights reflect against the yellow and purple bruises scattered on my arm. My gaze cuts to his, colliding in the middle.

His chest rises and falls in panicked succession.

"Clarity." Jason's voice wavers. "What is this?"

"Nothing." I yank my arm away and slam the sleeve back down.

He jumps to his feet. "Please don't lie to me. Who did that to you?"

You.

No, *me.*

I swallow. "Jason, I'm fine. This happened after practice on Saturday, after we slipped. I landed wrong."

"That's not just from—" He cuts himself off and inhales sharply, curling his shaking hands into fists.

"Should we continue today or tomorrow?" Ortiz skates between us and turns to Jason. "I'd like to offer today, since you're obviously fine."

"Sounds great to me. Sorry. C'mon." I grab Jason's hand and pull him away. He squeezes my palm before I let go. It's the only time he squeezes me for the rest of the night; otherwise, he keeps his touch lighter than a feather.

Chapter 12

Jason

My head has been aching nonstop for the last month since I've started figure skating, and I'm starting to think the only time I'll find relief again is when I'm six feet under the dirt.

I settle back in the chair at my cubicle, rubbing my knuckles against my temple as I glance away from the spreadsheet on the computer screen that I haven't touched in the last twenty minutes. I should be applying the final details so the information is ready to go for the press conference tomorrow. I reach for my phone, instead.

Clarity posted on her blog last night, voicing how excited she is for the Invitational next week. She shared a picture of herself standing in front of the rink boards with her hands on her hips, smiling, alone. Victor must've taken it for her before I arrived. The thing is, neither of them asked me to jump in a photo. Not that it matters. It's her platform, after all. It's the comments that gut me, and the latest ones from a few minutes ago twist the knife.

@annabellelloyd67
Been rooting for you since day one. Don't stop now, Clarity. You were born for this!

@laceemacee
umm... homegirl looks like a wind gust could take her out. better eat a burger or you'll snap in half

> **@l8trsk8tr**
> Where's Jason?? Did he already flake or get kicked off this team too? Can't wait to see who the next lucky guy is LOL

Gritting my teeth, I swipe past carbon copies of similar comments other people have already posted. I couldn't get paid enough to say what some of these people are saying. What's worse is that some of them are butting up against the truth.

I'm obviously not the only one who noticed that Clarity has lost weight. At least the world can't hear her panting every time we start a routine, and they can't see the bruises she's hiding behind long sleeved shirts and high waisted leggings. But at least they have the balls to say something. I still can't find the right words to urge her to find help.

Besides, maybe I am on the cusp of getting kicked off the team, because I'll be the first to say that I'm terribly unprepared for this competition. Clarity is nice enough to keep her mouth shut about it, however I don't miss the way her eyebrows tighten every time I stumble out of a transition, or the way she holds her breath every time I pick her up for a half-assed lift.

Not that it's entirely my fault. I don't know what's wrong with her, but every time we approach a lift in our choreography, she jams up. If she's not stiffer than a board, then she's rag dolling. It's impossible to know what's going on, because every time I ask about the bruises or the hesitation during the lifts or the fact she's gotten impossibly lighter over the last few weeks, she stone-walls me. I always get the same answer she gave me last year when I told her that I loved her:

It doesn't matter.

It does. It always has, and I will tell her that every day for the rest of my life if it means she will wake up one day and just talk to me.

"Hey, do you have a minute?"

Paul, the product and development manager, pokes his head into my cubicle. The fluorescent lights reflect off his bald head, and the crazed look in his eye sends a jolt of alarm down my spine. I've been working alongside this man since I started my internship, and the only time I've seen an ounce of panic on his face is when his wife called to yell at him for not taking the chicken out of the freezer.

"Um." I glance at the time. If I'm not out the door soon, Ortiz and Clarity will be racing to see who gets to skin me first. "I've got ten minutes."

"Perfect. Your father and I need to talk to you." He starts to walk away, leaving me to scramble after him, the chair spinning in my wake.

"That doesn't sound good. Am I fired?" My chest unclenches at the thought. It would be a nice change of pace if I had a few hours to breathe every day. Between this, school, skating, and appeasing Tiffany's emotions in my precious free time, I barely have the chance to eat and shower.

"No." Paul chuckles, breaking into the smile that I'm used to seeing him wear. "No, absolutely not. Although, I can't say the same for the folks down at the warehouse."

That's not reassuring. I lengthen my strides to keep up with him as we curve around the bullpen. For being such a short man, he sure can move.

We pass the conference room and the offices that are starting to empty as everyone else is trickling out for the day. I expect Dad to be alone in his office, so it catches me off guard to see Kristie, the head software architect, and Jada, our product marketing manager, standing near his desk. They should've gone home already.

Both of them look like they've seen ghosts. That doesn't stop Jada from offering us a taut smile as we walk in. Dad gets on his feet and grabs the binder closest to him. I recognize it as the same one I put together the other week. His eyebrows are wound together so tight that I start to wonder if I accidentally printed out the product report in Chinese.

"Jason, when were those HyperShot Pros supposed to be delivered?" He asks.

"On the eighth." I hesitate. "Today."

The delivery date is practically carved into my brain. I'm the one who helped Paul finalize the order a few months ago. Those HyperShot Pros are going to change the game of hockey. They're going to be the first AI-enhanced hockey sticks available on the market.

Dad deals Kristie a sharp glare, and she flinches.

"I swear, FedEx had no idea what I was talking about. I don't know where the boxes went but they're not on any delivery trucks." Kristie twists the rings on her fingers.

"What happened?" I glance past Jada and Dad to search Pauls face. "Did someone steal the shipment?"

"Hard to say. They left the warehouse—Tony confirmed that—but they didn't go on the right truck." Paul scrubs a hand over his face.

"Where could they have gone?" Kristie's voice raises an octave. "It's not like someone can take a massive, hundred-pound box and hide it under a blanket."

"We need them by tomorrow for the PowerShift press event," Jada says, winding her fingers through her long braids. "I've already got the Aether Dynamics PR manager up my ass. If we don't show up tomorrow, we're forfeiting STRYDE next weekend. They've already got their panties in a wad because I couldn't present a solid presentation deck beforehand for their itinerary."

Paul tuts. "Did you tell them that this design barely has one foot out of development—"

Dad talks over them, using a tone that causes me to flinch. "We're going tomorrow, and we're keeping our spot next weekend."

Everyone snaps their mouths shut and straightens their spine. "Paul, you need to check inventory logs at our warehouse. Find out if we have any spare sticks, even if they're demos. I don't care if they're unfinished, because Kristie will make sure the sticks that we *do* have can pass with the press tomorrow. Even if we have to spoof a full network simulation."

He turns to Jada. "Prep a backup press script tonight. If we can't get the real sticks in time, we need to spin this as a teaser launch, or a limited reveal. You need to stall for time and make it look intentional. Everyone understand?"

"Yes, sir," Paul answers in a way that reminds me of talking to Ortiz—Oh, man.

I need to leave for skating practice any minute.

"Now!" Dad claps his hands together. Kristie and Jada scatter like birds. He points at me next. "You need to call our warehouse and find out where in the hell they sent those boxes. Coordinate with the shipping carrier, and if they don't know, file a missing claim."

"I think he should go to the warehouse and make sure the shipment hasn't been misplaced," Paul adds.

"They're not *at* the warehouse." Dad slams the binder down on his desk. I lock my knees, afraid to break eye contact, except I risk it to glance at the time on my phone screen. I can't do everything they're asking within the next few minutes.

"Not ours." Paul shakes his head. He's the only one who can get away with talking back to Dad. "The shipping carrier, once he finds out. Go look before they close."

"I can't."

Both of them turn to look at me like I'm the one who purposely went behind their backs and caused this mess.

"Excuse me?" Dad rests a hand on the back of his chair.

"I need to leave for practice."

"Jason, for the love of all things." He slams his chair into his desk, making the old oak rattle. "You can cut the shit for one night. This is more important than putting on a tutu."

Paul coughs. My cheeks flame, yet I don't back down. "The Invitational is next weekend. These next few practices will make or break how we perform." And whether or not Clarity can make it to Nationals.

His eye twitches. "You didn't tell me that. The STRYDE conference is next weekend. You're expected to be there."

"Dad, I told you two weeks ago!" I laugh to keep from screaming. "I put in time off. This isn't new information."

"With everything that goes on around here, did you really expect me to keep track of where you spend your time?" He rearranges papers on his desk. "Find my goddamn sticks, then we can talk about where you'll be next weekend."

I step forward and curl my shaking hands into fists. "You're lucky that I'm even staying tonight."

"Watch your tone, mister." He stares at me. "There are kids out there begging for an opportunity like this, and I placed it in your hands."

"I don't want to be here. I *never* asked to be here!"

"Go call the warehouse!" Dad yells back in my face, spittle flying from his mouth. "Go! Jesus! You are on my payroll, and you are a part of this team, so start acting like it!"

I slap my hands down on the desk to keep from leaping over it and strangling his throat before turning away and kicking the chair closest to me. Paul shrinks back against the wall like a cornered animal, his eyes shining with fear. I don't acknowledge him as I storm out.

Blood rushes to my head. Rage makes me shake. I check the time on my phone again. It's two minutes past six. I should've been on the road two minutes ago.

If this were happening at any other time in my life, I wouldn't care less. Hell, I could probably use a moment like this to prove to Dad that I'm the son he deserves.

But the second that Clarity is involved, the cards are off the table. It isn't fair that her future is caught in the middle of a mess I didn't create. It's not her fault that our employees lost nearly a-quarter-of-a-million dollars' worth of equipment.

It's a toss-up whether I'm going to puke or shit my pants first as I stop at my desk and pull up her contact in my phone with trembling hands. I can almost see the comments under her post next week. "*Who are Jason and Clarity again? Doesn't matter. It's not like they won anything at the Invitational, anyway.*"

I squeeze my eyes shut as the phone starts to ring, and choke down bile.

"Hey." Her voice cuts through the line, laced with concern. "What's going on?"

"C.J." My voice shakes. *Mercy.* I swallow as I press my thumb and pointer fingers against my eyes. "I'm fine. Everything's fine. Well, actually, it's not fine."

"Did you get in an accident?" Panic overrides her concern.

"No. I've still got all of my limbs. Look, I'm so sorry, but I need to cancel practice tonight." I can't breathe, can't catch my breath.

She's silent for a moment. A long moment. "Seriously?"

"Something happened at work." I start to ramble. "It's not my fault, but an expensive box of equipment got lost in delivery, and we need it for a press event tomorrow. If we don't get it by tomorrow, we might not be able to go to our conference next weekend. Which I don't even care about, because we have the Invitational, but my dad forgot that I'll be at—"

"Jason."

I stop in my tracks. My chest heaves as I wipe my eyes. There's a shift in her tone. Every time she throws her walls up, she shifts her tone.

I don't need to be standing in front of Clarity to see the haze drift over her eyes, the same haze that I've been trying so hard to wipe clear.

"Go figure it out. Seriously, your dad needs you, and I need to get ready for practice. I'll see you tomorrow, okay? Don't worry about it." Her and her stupid kindness. I wish she would curse, or scream, or treat me the way I deserve to be treated.

"I'm so sorry." She's done everything for me, and I can't even be there when it matters the most.

"Good luck." The line disconnects.

The silence hurts just as much as it did the first time.

June 2015 - Age 16

Jason

The radio is low, cutting in and out of reality. I'm half asleep. The cold window soaks through my pillow, and the hum of the tires against the highway starts to pull me back under. Cole is snoring lightly against the opposite window, knocked out cold after a long week spent in Connecticut. Lauren mutters under her breath as her pencil scratches against the sudoku book she's been working on.

All of the sounds are so comforting that I don't realize I've fully drifted off until the car bumps over a bridge. A soft weight falls against me, jolting me awake.

I freeze and risk glancing over.

Clarity.

Her blanket is wrapped around her torso. Her book has slipped from her hands and landed near her feet, the pages bent. She kept herself contained on the middle seat for the first few hours of the roadtrip, and now, she's leaning against me. Her head is on my shoulder. Her breath is slow, even. She doesn't stir.

My chest tightens, like my heart is being wrung out by invisible hands. She's so close I can smell her shampoo—light and sweet, like flowers. My pulse starts to hammer in my ears. I've been alive for 16 years, yet I completely forget how to sit, act, and breathe.

I turn my head forward and stare at the back of the drivers seat, willing her parents to not turn around. She's sleeping. That's all. It wouldn't be a big deal to them.

But to me, this is everything.

My right arm begins to go numb with the pressure. I shut my eyes for a moment, hoping and praying that I won't disturb her as I slowly, carefully, shift my arm out from underneath her. She inhales sleepily, and I pause.

Don't move away. Please.

She doesn't. I'm stuck pressing my arm against the back of the seat. I can't sit like this until she wakes up, so instead, I let it fall right around her shoulders, my hand resting on her blanket.

Clarity nestles into me without waking, and presses her nose into my shirt. She fits against my side so naturally that all of my theories from the last few years are confirmed: she was made for me.

I bite back a laugh that's half panicked and half disbelieving. My whole body is fire and ice all at once, and I don't dare move. I don't even take in a full breath in case it'll disturb her.

If anyone looked back right now, I'd be screwed. Cole would never let me live it down. Her parents would probably wonder how my arm ended up around her. Thank God no one looks. The car keeps rolling steadily, as if the universe itself is in on my secret.

So I sit perfectly still and pretend this doesn't mean what it does. Like my arm didn't want to be here. As if it isn't the only thing I'll think about for weeks.

I could watch her sleep next to me for the rest of the drive, but I will my eyelids to close, memorizing the feeling of her chest rising and falling against my ribs.

Chapter 13

Clarity

I miss the end call button the first time because my hands are shaking so hard. My fingers are ice cold. I flex them, trying to will blood back into my veins.

This is the last thing that needs to be happening right now.

Jason has already cut way too many practices to close for comfort. I never miss the look in Ortiz's eye each time it happens, like she's weighing whether it's worth having a conversation with him about his timing. Technically he's never been *actually* late, so there hasn't been anything to reprimand him for. Now she's going to have a field day with this, and I'm pretty sure I'm going to have an aneurysm.

The metal locker is cold against my skin as I press my forehead into it. I want to scream, but there are two girls giggling around the corner as they pack their bags.

I should've known that this entire charade was too good to be true. Jason's commitment, his easygoing attitude, the spark that made all of this work in the first place, has started to vanish. He hasn't been laughing off mistakes anymore.

Every time I think that a boy can be different, they prove that they're exactly who I thought they were in the first place.

At least he's been nice enough to continue to treat me with a level of gentleness that's reserved for fragile dishes, even when his hands are shaking with fury as Ortiz yells across the ice, *"At this point, Clarity should've skated solo!"*

I open my eyes and push away from the locker. It'll only be a matter of time before that comes true. I start to pace.

This is how it started with Sterling. We had spoken over the years at hockey games, until we had our first real conversation at the same party where I kissed Jason for the first time. Sterling's timing was spot on, because he texted the morning after the party.

I was desperate for a distraction, and Sterling was perfect... for maybe three months.

That's when he started to flake. He pushed off plans, then cancelled them all together. He bought me things and took me on dates to make up for it. Then, at mine and Cole's birthday party, Willie caught him with another girl. As much as it hurt in the moment, I think our breakup was the best birthday present he could've ever given me.

I rake my hands through my hair. I should've known better, then and now. My gut was trying to tell me this from the beginning, and now it's too late. Jason and I are locked into this partnership.

Fine wisps of hair tangle between my fingers. Truthfully, I'm not doing any better than Jason is.

I've been trying to juggle school, skating, training, and the blog. If I can't keep up with everything, Anya Kovalenko is never going to look in my direction again.

My body has been revolting also, with my stomach constantly growling and blood spotting in my underwear for the past two weeks. I can't remember the last time I wasn't cold. Even now, I shiver through my sweater.

The girls' chatter fades, silenced by the door shutting behind them. Since Jason isn't showing tonight, we're never going to get our lifts ready in time.

My heartbeat is pulsing in my throat. That malicious forum that tagged me last night is going to tear me apart even more, and I don't know what to do about it.

I don't know what to do anymore.

My shoes squeak as I rush over to the bathroom stalls, my stomach aching. The stall door bangs against the wall as I shove it open, and the tile bites my knees as I drop to the floor. I barely get my hair out of the way as the vomit rushes up, hot and fast. I choke it out, spitting and coughing, relishing the silence that comes with the buzzing in my ears. Flushing away the contents, I shut my eyes for a moment.

If I slow down now, I'm afraid that I'll never be able to get back up to speed again. I can do this by myself for one night.

Jason's problems aren't my problems, just like Sterling's choice wasn't something that I made him do. I need to focus on myself.

I push myself onto my feet, wipe the tears from my eyes, and return to my bag. I pull out the tin of mints and pop two in my mouth for good measure. Not that I need to worry about sour breath without a partner to get close to.

The reminder makes me flinch, and I hate the way my heart skitters. Jason doesn't deserve to get that sort of reaction out of me. But the second *that* thought crosses my mind, more tears press against the back of my eyes, because I know that's not true. Seriously, could I be any more pathetic?

I finish pulling my hair back into a ponytail and throw the bag over my shoulder before heading out of the locker room. The sound of blades scraping over ice echoes down the hallway, and I follow the noise around the bend.

Juliette and Montgomery are the ones making all the racket, cutting diagonally across the ice in mismatched twizzles. Montgomery is almost a full rotation ahead of Juliette, and Ortiz's face is twisted in disappointment as she reprimands them.

The pressure must be getting to everyone, because they've been off the last few weeks, too. They come off the ice arguing more often than not, and if it weren't for the fact that they can still nail their lifts, I'd like to think that Jason and I might actually have a shot next weekend—despite the problems we're having.

Victor is leaning against the boards, a wool cap pulled over his hair, scowling as he reads something on his phone. He looks up and his expression doesn't change. "Jason's running late again. Imagine that."

"He's not coming at all, actually." I dump my bag onto the bench and take a seat, slipping off my shoes.

"Excuse me?" He straightens and walks over. He lost his limp once his leg healed, although his wrist is still bound in a cast. "Where the hell is he?"

"Work." The familiar motion of pulling on and tying my skates grounds me. "He called and said they lost a ton of equipment. He got roped into helping play detective."

"So what? Tough luck. Does he remember that the Invitational is next weekend?" Victor crosses his arms.

I scoff and a bitter comment builds on my tongue, until I recall the genuine panic in his tone. He sounded just as caught off-guard as I feel, and guilt pricks my skin.

"Yeah. He feels really bad. But if you knew his dad, you'd know that he can't exactly walk out," I say as I adjust the tongue on my skate.

"Well, he should've, because you two need all the practice you can get." He raises his hands defensively when I throw him a sharp glare. "Just saying. I was reading something that *Skate Snaps* posted a few hours ago, and they were saying that you two are the ones to watch. A lot of people are curious to see how you'll perform with a hockey player."

"Me included," I grumble under my breath as I roll out my ankle.

"Seriously, Clarity. If you won't tell Jason that this can't happen again, then I will." His eyes sharpen. "Don't let his inability to say no be the reason why you can't chase your dream."

"It was his willingness to say yes that saved my dream." A spark of defiance ignites in my chest, and it takes me off guard.

I finish tying my first skate and straighten to look Victor in the eye. "Everyone is expecting us to pull off this massive miracle. Before Jason, I only had Anya's attention. People knew you and I would win together, and that's not guaranteed anymore. I've been gaining thousands of followers every week because everyone is curious to see what he and I will do. Now, I have these brands messaging me that I've never even heard of. The manager of Overtime, that sports podcast, reached out to me begging for an interview."

My chest heaves as I watch his face fall into stoicism, except I'm not done. "I don't know what the hell is going to come out of this competition, and as scared as I am that he and I will have worked so hard for nothing, I can't sit here and say that it's all been a complete waste of time."

Victor watches me as I begin to tie on my second skate, analyzing the cracks in my armor. "The only thing worse than being talked about is not being talked about." He uses the quote that we always used to say when I first started my blog. "Until you get bashed for not making the podium."

"I don't care if I have to drag him through the routine by the back of his neck. We're making the damn podium." I get to my feet as Juliette and Montgomery approach the gate.

Victor steps forward to undo the latch, and he puts his hand on top of the gate to push it open at the same time Montgomery puts his hand down to pull it. Their hands touch, and I don't know whose cheeks burn faster as they both retract their hands like they were bitten by a snake.

Juliette's frown deepens as she reaches around her partner to whip the door open, nearly catching Montgomery's side. His blades clack as he jumps out of the way, and I don't miss the way Victor's eyes flare.

"Where's Jason?" Juliette casts a brief glance at the empty benches.

"He's busy. How was practice?" I ask coyly.

"Fantastic," Montgomery bites out in a tone that suggests otherwise as he steps past. If it weren't for the skates on his feet, I'd assume he would keep right on walking out the door and straight to his car.

"Let's go, Jansky! Forbes!" Ortiz yells. My already upset stomach aches worse when she says Jason's name. Great. I'm so glad they left her in a good mood for me today. This is going to be fun to explain.

"Good luck, soldier," Victor mutters as I step onto the ice. The click of the lock behind me makes me feel like I'm being locked in an arena with a hungry lion.

Her eyebrows draw together even further as I skate across the ice, alone. "Where is he?"

If it weren't for the fact I have nothing to puke up, I would probably be sick. I swallow. "He had an emergency at work."

"The only emergency he should be concerned about is the one where he can't seem to lift you over his shoulders, and we perform in seven days," Ortiz says angrily.

My head starts to spin even thinking about being lifted over his shoulders, and I blink away the black dots. "I understand, but it's not like I told him to skip practice."

"That's just the problem, isn't it? This is your only shot at reaching Nationals to land a spot on Team USA, and your partner barely has one foot in the door. I can't bring you two to the top if both parties aren't willing." She shakes her head. "He's lucky that there are no other options for you, otherwise I wouldn't let him back in the door."

I dig my blades into the ice to keep my knees from shaking. What am I supposed to say to that? I could tell her to send me home, instead. The thing is, I can practically see that Skate Snaps headline Victor was talking about in my head: "*Top 5 Pairings to Watch at the Upcoming Ice Dance Invitational!*" Mine and Jason's names are probably in a bold, fiery font at the top of the list.

"I'm here, aren't I?" The words are sharp coming out.

Ortiz eyes me, then flourishes her hand toward the rink. "Warm up, then come back so we can build on your bracket turns and counters."

"Yes, ma'am." I spin on my heel and push off. The cold air feels good on my cheeks that are warm with embarrassment. Habit makes me reach out for Jason's hand, and I stumble when I'm met with open air. My face gets hotter.

As much as Jason irks me sometimes, I wish he were here. Only because he always knows what to say to fill the silence, and he always answers the questions in my head before I even have to ask them. He's always known how to do that.

Movement catches my eye as I round the corner near the West Rink, where the hockey boys are stepping onto the ice in their gear, taking their warmup lap on the other side of the glass. I notice Annabelle first, thanks to her neon orange sweatshirt. She's got a clipboard in her hands as she skates toward a clump of boys, and their helmets bob as they nod at whatever she's saying. They turn and race off, putting me in her line of sight.

She starts to smile, but it immediately turns into a confused frown as she cocks her head to the side. We've been friends for so long that we don't need words. I know what she's asking: *Where is he?*

I subtly shake my head. She presses her lips together.

Cole and Willie skate up to her, and Cole watches our interaction as Willie asks her a question. She turns to answer him, and Cole makes sure I'm watching before he slices a finger across his neck. Yeah, Jason is going to be getting an earful from more than just me.

I chew on my lip and continue to follow the bend of the rink, and my attention skitters across the rest of the boys. Sterling's presence is like a magnet, and I despise the way my breath catches when I notice him staring at me. His pace has slowed to a crawl, and his mouth is twisted in a smirk.

He's the one who told me not to trust Jason, and now he gets to watch me skate without him.

My feet are on fire as I bound away, desperate to move away from the window, as if Sterling will materialize beside me and give me another reminder of how dumb I was to put my future in the hands of someone who couldn't even respect their own.

As if I need the reminder.

Chapter 14

Jason

L iterally the only silver lining to this morning is the fact that Tiffany woke up with a migraine, so I get to be alone with Clarity. Guilt kept shaking me awake last night, and I'm going to take this chance to apologize for leaving her high and dry.

I glance at the text thread between Tiffany and me as I take the stairs down to the training wing, and I hover my thumbs over the keyboard, contemplating sending her a message to feel better.

Our conversation from last night taunts me, sitting above the update on her migraine. I sent her a long text explaining that I was going to have a late night and wouldn't be around to talk because of work, and all she sent in reply was a thumbs up emoji.

It's not like our relationship has ever been the blueprint for good communication, although there's definitely been a disconnect over the last few months. Actually, come to think of it, I don't think we even fully connected in the first place. I don't know.

I was hoping to catch her sometime this week to talk about our relationship, or lack thereof in this case. It's not fair of me to keep leading her on like this.

I tell myself that I'll deal with it later as I slip the phone into my pocket and continue down the hall toward the yoga room. The door is cracked open, and I grab the handle to go in, but hearing Sterling's voice makes me stop in my tracks.

"...looking good, especially in that outfit. Is that what you're wearing next week?"

The hairs stand on the back of my neck like I'm in the presence of a wild animal. I let go of the door handle and hold my breath. Clarity makes a sound like a scoff and a laugh combined, and I want to throttle Sterling for having the balls to be in the same room as her, much less make her laugh.

"Absolutely not. I don't fit in that dress anymore."

"How? Girl, you've always been like a double zero," Juliette's voice floats out next.

"More like a size four. It's not that the dress is too small, it's actually too big." Clarity pauses. She's probably readjusting her stretching leg, however, my mind jumps to conclusions. What if she's looking to Sterling for validation, or he's spotting one of her moves? "I've lost some weight since my last competition."

"Well, whatever you're doing, don't stop. You've never looked better," Sterling replies.

Fury surges through my veins, turning every blood cell into a live wire. His words spur me forward, and I nearly take the door off the hinges I fling it open so hard.

Juliette and Clarity startle from their places on their mats. Sterling just turns and smiles. If I didn't know better, I'd assume he knew I was listening the entire time.

"Morning," Sterling says. "Glad to see you could make it today."

"I missed one practice." I walk across the otherwise empty room, making a beeline straight for him. His smile falls as I approach, and he jumps out of the way to keep from getting ran over. "Doesn't mean you get to crawl out from under your rock."

"Jason." Clarity uses the same voice with me that she does on Cole when he says something inappropriate. It makes my breath hitch, although I don't regret it. My bag lands on the floor with a loud thud.

"If you're stretched so thin, I can always step in. I can't imagine it's that hard if you're doing it. Besides, Clarity already knows I've got stamina."

I whirl around, and Sterling's eyes glint. This time, his grin is devilish. I'm one breath away from crossing the room and painting my knuckles red with his blood when Clarity jumps to her feet. Juliette stays bent over her legs and watches our exchange with an amused expression.

"Boys, it's too early for this. Be nice or leave." Clarity levels a cold glare on both of us. As much as I hate to go against her word, I clench my jaw and stand my ground, not willing to be the first to back down.

Sterling shrugs and turns away. "Whatever. I need to go workout, anyway. Good seeing you ladies. Jason." Nodding his head, he scratches his neck with his middle finger as he passes. He can be petty all he wants, because at the end of the day, I'm the one who gets to stay with Clarity.

"Some things don't change," I mutter under my breath as I grab a mat from the corner of the room. Laying it down next to Clarity's mat hurts—this is the first time she hasn't had it ready to go for our warmup, almost like she wasn't expecting me to come again.

Clarity rolls her eyes and turns to Juliette. "Anyway. The dress is cute, but Ortiz wants to put Jason in silver. The beading wouldn't match."

I crinkle my nose at the reminder as I bend into a forward fold. When Ortiz sent me the link for the costume to buy, I forwarded it to Clarity to make sure it wasn't a joke. She knows I'm an easy-going guy, except there are two things I wouldn't be caught dead wearing: silver and sequins. I immediately got a phone call from her, and it was only so she could laugh in my face. We both agreed that Ortiz must really have it out for me.

Juliette steps off her mat and begins to roll it up. "So, change the beading."

"I'm not Cinderella's godmother. I can't perform miracles." Clarity joins me on her mat, and the smell of her perfume nearly knocks me flat on my back. She's wearing the same scent she did on the night of that Fourth of July party when she kissed me for the first and last time. *She* kissed *me*.

"Does that make me your fairy godmother?" Juliette smiles and straightens, tucking the mat under her arm. "I'd be happy to do it for you. I can bring in the sides to fit you again, especially if it's Lycra. I wouldn't even have to redesign the embellishments."

"You can sew?" I ask, desperate to get my mind off of that memory before it consumes me. I thought the only thing Juliette did in her free time was build her army of flying monkeys.

She proves my point by eyeing me, her smile tightening. "Yes, I can sew."

"I always wondered about that. Your performance outfits are so unique. What do I owe you?" Clarity pauses her calf stretch to ask.

"Nothing." Juliette puts her mat away and grabs her backpack. "I'd be happy to do it for a friend. Just bring it with you to practice later and I'll get it done by the end of next week."

Clarity's shoulders crumple in relief. "You are saving my life. Seriously. I was going to drain my savings tonight to order a new outfit."

I bite my tongue.

"It's what I'm here for." She brightens and waves as she heads toward the door. "See you guys later."

"Wow." Clarity tucks a loose piece of hair behind her ear and turns to me. "That was nice of her."

I want to tell her that I could be nicer and buy a new dress so she wouldn't have to worry about Juliette sewing razors blades into the hems. I'm pretty sure that conversation would end with her rolling up her mat and beating me over the head with it. Neither she nor Cole has ever accepted handouts from me or my dad in the past, and I can't imagine that's changed.

"Definitely." The silence is thick as I roll up my spine and glance at Clarity.

She's visibly chewing on her cheek as she uses her foot to slide the mat toward the back wall. "We should probably run through the choreography for the routine." *Since we didn't get to last night.* She doesn't have to say it. The words are loud, even unspoken.

"I wanted to apologize for last night. I'm sorry. I didn't have a choice, Dad made me cancel." I keep myself busy by clearing my mat out of the way so I don't have to watch the disappointment cross her face.

Instead, it's heavy in her tone as she asks, "Did you get it figured out?"

The way she skirts around the apology makes my lungs ache. I tug at the collar of my shirt. "Yeah, I went to the shipping company's headquarters and they found the boxes. Everything worked out."

"Then that's all that matters. You don't need to apologize."

"I let you down."

She stills, and I know I've hit a soft spot. Her eyelashes flutter the same way they did when I poured my heart at her feet, begging, *"Don't tell me this is impossible."*

I press my fingernails into my palms and continue. "I know the timing was terrible, but I couldn't get out of it. I promise you, I tried."

"Ortiz threatened to take you off the team." Her eyes flash between mine as I walk toward her.

"I'm sure she did." I stop in front of her and search the depths of her brown eyes, watching the frustration grow there. "Can you please forgive me?"

My gaze slips down the gentle curve of her nose. I can't stand how it crinkles when she's irritated, and how badly I want to brush away the stress lines on her face. I hate that I'm probably the reason for one or two of those lines.

She inhales slowly, and the hum of the central air conditioning reminds me of the cicadas buzzing when she responded, *"This is impossible."*

"People notice everything. Everyone is talking about us," Clarity says quietly, but sternly.

My stomach plummets. There's no way she's referring to that same moment from where we—she—decided to never talk about a potential relationship again.

I thought that I'd buried those emotions so deep that not even a tsunami could wash up the grave. That's the curse that comes with being near her again: everything has come crawling back to the surface. I wouldn't be shocked if people are putting together the pieces that we were once... *something*. Too close to be friends, too guarded to be lovers.

"About what?" I cross my arms to keep from touching her.

"The fact that I haven't been posting anything." I blink. Of course this is about her blog. "They want to see videos. They're rooting for us to clean house at the Invitational."

"We will."

"Jason, I'm working with a ghost of you." Clarity mirrors me, crossing her arms as she steps closer, tilting her head back to hold my gaze. "You are everywhere at once, yet it feels like you are nowhere at all. Fine, yes, I'm pissed that you cancelled last minute. But it hurt worse because I've been holding my breath, waiting for that to happen."

I rear my head back as indignation flares in my chest. "That isn't fair. I am doing the absolute best I can to show up for you every single day."

"And for your dad. Tiffany. Your friends. Should I go on?" Clarity sounds exasperated. "What are you even doing here?"

The air becomes stale, and it's hard to breathe when she's staring at me like this. I'm shocked that she doesn't know the answer, or maybe she does and she wants to hear it come out of my mouth.

I'm here because, despite everything and everyone else in my life, she will always be my true north. No matter where life brings me or who tries to control me, my bones know which way to turn. I will never be too far gone to find my way back to her.

I don't know how to tell her this without repeating myself from our last argument.

"It's always been you."

I can't control my gaze as it drops to her lips.

My phone starts to ring. Loudly.

We jump away from each other, and I realize how close we actually were. Clarity runs her hands over her hair, and I nearly drop my phone as I pull it out of my pocket. Amid the chaos last night, I forgot that I turned my phone off silent so I could hear any updated phone calls that might've come through. I never fixed it, so now I have to stare at my dad's name on the caller ID and wonder why the hell he's calling when he knows I'm training.

I decline his call, and my cheeks burn. "Sorry. That was my dad."

Clarity snorts. "Figures."

Embarrassment crawls down my neck, and I shiver as I swipe down on the screen and turn on Do Not Disturb. I go back to the bench and set my phone down before returning to her. "I'm all yours."

"That's just the problem, isn't it?" She bites out and strides over to the mirrors.

"What? What's the problem?" I follow her.

Shaking her head, she comes to a stop and turns out her left foot, pointing her toe. She lifts her arms and rolls back her shoulders, getting in frame for the start of our short program. "Nothing. We're wasting time."

My chest heaves as I take up position behind her, raising my arms to shadow her. She stares at my left elbow in the mirror, and I straighten my arm until she nods curtly with approval, no words needed.

I like to think that I know her well enough that there's no need to speak in these moments, but I've always had a hard time seeing past her poker face. She won't even glance in my direction. The worst part is, I'm starting to wonder if I even deserve her attention.

July 2015 - Age 16

Clarity

When I was in elementary school, I wanted nothing more than to be included in everything that Cole and Jason did. They were a part of the boys, and girls were rarely allowed.

I wasn't included at certain birthday parties, or bike rides around the neighborhood, or master plans at lunch. Becoming friends with Annabelle and Tiffany lessened that sting, and by third grade, I really couldn't care any less. I was content.

But that little girl deep inside of me was pleasantly surprised to be included in the 4th of July plans this year. Archie, one of the senior boys on the hockey team, got permission to host a party at his parent's lake house.

Jason picked up Cole and I since the car we share is in the shop. Annabelle would've come with, unti she got stuck at home nursing a first-degree sunburn. I kept reminding her to wear sunscreen at the beach yesterday, but what do I know?

I'm left alone to walk out of the house and down the garage stairs, protecting my freshly refilled drink that a senior girl handed me. Firecrackers pop in the distance, barely discernible over the music bumping out of the speakers in the garage.

Cole scrabbles near the bottom of the steps with one of his other senior teammates—a big, burly, defenseman that I can't remember the name of. He comes up victorious, holding the ping-pong ball above his head.

"Got it!" Cole shouts and elbows the big guy. "You're forfeiting your turn for foul play. Finder's keepers."

"That's not how this works," Willie says from where he's standing on the other side of the folding table, his hands on his hips, his chest gleaming with sweat from the heat.

It's just the three of them. Jason isn't at the table.

I search the boys who are gathered near the walls, laughing and talking with their friends as they watch the cup pong game. Some girls on the far wall part like the Red Sea, giggling as they let somebody through. There he is.

"Yes, it is, especially when somebody smacks the ball out of the air." Cole gives the senior boy a pointed look before returning to his side of the table, giving the ball in his hands a good luck kiss.

One of the brave girls steps away from her friends to grab Jason's hand as he passes, whispering something in his ear that makes him blush. I quickly look away and finish descending, heat building in my chest. It burns my heart, my lungs.

"Don't hate the player, hate the game." The senior boy goes to stand next to Willie. Cole waves his hand, shooing him further away. The senior puts his hands in the air and takes two strides backward.

"Forbes! Yo, leave the ladies alone. We're about to be back in business." Willie waves him over.

Jason strides over to Cole, running a hand over his hair. "Sorry, I didn't think they were going to find the ball. I grabbed a new one from the bucket." He holds it up.

"Put that away, big dog. That's got bad vibes. I've been spending the entire game powering up this little guy." Cole shows off the ball in his hands, then points at the single cup left on the other side of the table. "And we're going to win."

Shrugging, Jason pockets the ball into his swim trunks. He's one of the few guys who hasn't ditched his shirt yet, although it almost feels worse seeing that thin fabric stretching around the new curves of his biceps and clinging to the ridges of his abdomen. He looks so good that I can't even watch. I refuse to be another starry-eyed, giggling girl. There's nothing to be flustered about because he's my friend. That's it.

I head for the opening of the garage, desperate for a breeze to cool my prickling skin. Sipping at my drink doesn't help. I wanted a soda water, until the older girl pouring drinks insisted on making me drink a vodka cranberry. I didn't seem to have a choice, so I asked her to measure out the vodka at least—there's 97 calories in 1.5 ounces—yet I feel every drop absorbing into my bloodstream. The alcohol makes me feel warmer, like the inside of a popcorn seed expanding, absorbing heat, waiting to burst.

As I dodge around a loitering group of people, one of the boys steps out, running right into me.

I gasp as the liquid inside of my cup sloshes out, splattering against my stomach. Thankfully, I came prepared wearing my swim suit, and I left my cover-up inside.

The boy curses and shoots his hands out, steadying me. "I'm sorry. That was my bad. I didn't see—Oh, Clarity?"

I look up into the eyes of Sterling Mayer, the right defense on the boys' hockey team. He occasionally hangs out with Jason, Cole, and their buddies. Last school year he was in my history class, constantly flashing me hidden smiles. He gives me another smile now, putting the dimple on the right side of his mouth on full display.

"Hi, Sterling. Sorry, I didn't mean to run into you." I shuffle backward, and his hand lingers on my elbow.

"I'm the one who ran into you." He glances at my stomach where I'm wearing a quarter of my drink, and a look of resolve crosses his face. "Hang on, let me grab you a napkin."

"It's... okay." I purse my lips. He's already slipping away, but he makes his way back just as quickly. I hold my breath as he settles one hand on my waist, dabbing at my stomach with the other.

"Nobody told me that you were here," Sterling says casually. A curl falls over his eyes. "And I haven't seen your friends."

"I came with Cole and Jason. Annabelle is at home. She got a nasty sunburn yesterday." I nibble at the inside of my cheek as he passes me the napkin. I use it to wipe my hand off. He keeps his other hand on me, running his thumb over my skin. My heart kick starts, and I find the decency to say, "Thank you."

Sterling smiles. "You're welcome."

Screaming and clapping breaks out behind us, making me flinch. Cole and Jason must've won because Cole has his hands in the air like he just won the state tournament, motioning with his hands to keep the praise coming. Jason fist bumps his buddies, laughing as he accepts back slaps and hair ruffles. His eyes bounce around the garage as he turns in a circle, until, finally, he finds me.

I step away from Sterling's hand at the same time Jason notices, and that beautiful smile slips off his face.

Sterling is saying something to me. I don't notice because that same group of girls cuts mine and Jason's invisible string, hovering around him. He deserves the attention, although I refuse to watch.

I turn and walk away from Sterling.

Away from Jason.

Chapter 15

Clarity

Look, it's time that I face the truth. Despite spending every night practicing on the ice and every morning refining in the training room, winning this competition seems as attainable as driving a car to the moon.

Case in point: the reverse rotational lift with an upside-down position. Otherwise known as the current bane of my existence.

We're trying to reincorporate it into the program, and I swear, we're never going to nail the move again. I've fallen more over the past two weeks than I have in the last ten years trying to get thrown over Jason's shoulder. My knees are already bruising from five failed attempts tonight.

Who knows, maybe the sixth time is the charm, as long as Jason doesn't distract himself by glancing over at the hockey practice again and I don't think about hanging upside down over the ice, my skull waiting to be cracked open like a coconut.

"Brace your core," Victor reminds me from behind the boards as I fly past, his phone trained on me as he records.

He says that as if a weak core is the real problem here. If I brace myself any more, my joints are going to fuse together. Even my jaw is clenched, bracing for impact. My heart jackrabbits as Jason swoops in and reaches out his arms.

"Breathe! Breathe!" Ortiz shouts.

Despite her advice, I hold my breath and my vision swims. Fear suddenly paralyzes me. The crack of bone echoes across the ice, and my blade catches on something tender, tearing, slicing.

Jason's hands are on me, warm and solid, sweeping me out of the memory as fast as he gets me off my feet. He registers the panic on my face a moment too late and he curses as he throws me over his shoulder, reining in his strength and momentum.

I squeak as I collide against his shoulder like a sack of potatoes, knocking him off balance in the process. The ice rushes toward my face. Suddenly, the air whooshes out of my lungs as he twists his arm back, grabbing the first thing he can get a hold on—my neck—and sacrifices himself in the process. He lands hard and heavy on the ice, his entire backside banging down. I collapse on him, barely feeling the impact as his arm absorbs the shock.

I roll off of him, the bile in my guts threatening to make an appearance. He groans. I sit up and whirl around, expecting to see blood. There's nothing, but I still crawl over to him, tears pricking the back of my eyes as he cradles his arm to his chest.

Ortiz flies over, her blades scratching the ice. "What the hell was that? Are you trying to give each other a concussion? One more bad landing like that is all it would take to end your careers."

"We're fine, thanks for asking," Jason says bitterly as he slowly sits up and tests his arm, rolling it in the socket. He makes eye contact with me and his gaze softens just for a heartbeat as he tells me, "I'm fine."

"Next time, just drop me, would you?" The terror I'm experiencing sounds a lot like anger coming out.

It takes him off guard. He flinches. "I'm not going to let you get hurt."

We glower at each other, chests heaving, until he ruins the moment by glancing at my mouth for the second time today. It was bad enough when he did it this morning in the yoga room. That alone almost makes me slap him, which is crazy because five seconds ago I was nearly in tears over him.

"Let's thank our lucky stars that everyone's okay, shall we? One injury was enough." Ortiz points at Victor, who's white-knuckling the boards. I don't know when he put his phone away. Hopefully it was before Jason and I ate shit.

He shifts, pressing a palm to the ice to push himself up to his knees, and winces.

"Are you seriously hurt?" I demand, my stomach twisting. That's the last thing we need.

He exhales through his nose, jaw tight. "I said I'm fine." His blades clack against the ice as he stands and glides over, offering out his hand. "Come on."

I smack it away. "I don't need your help."

His eyes flash, unreadable, as he pulls his hand back and straightens. I get onto my feet, my knees shaking as I lift my chin and look him square in the eye. "You're not supposed to throw me like a football."

Jason shakes out his arm. "It'd be a lot easier if you'd stop freezing up. I can't exactly follow the rules of being graceful and delicate if I'm working with a two-by-four."

Shame scorches through me. I beat it away and reply through gritted teeth, "I didn't *freeze*."

Not for more than a moment, at least.

"Well, you sure didn't relax, either." He tilts his head defiantly.

That urge to smack him again makes my hands twitch, and I cross my arms. "It's not my fault you can't handle the pressure."

Jason lets out a humorless laugh. "*I* can't handle it? That's rich, coming from you."

Ortiz lifts her hand. "Alright, that's enough."

He keeps going. "You push yourself until you're running on fumes, but that won't make you stronger. It means you make mistakes that could cost us the entire routine."

"Oh, you want to talk about mistakes?" I take a step forward, my blade striking the ice. "What was that back there? Throwing yourself under me like that? It would be a pretty big problem if you broke your arm because there wouldn't be a routine to perform. What would happen if you hurt yourself?"

Jason throws his hands in the air. "Then I get hurt. That's how this works. I'm not letting you break a bone on the ice, so get used to it." His voice is rough, and something inside of me wavers. He's breathing hard, his eyes darting between mine, searching my face.

Ortiz pinches the bridge of her nose. "Forbes—"

I speak at the same time, "You don't have to—"

"Yes, I do!" Jason raises his voice, ignoring Ortiz. He drifts closer to me, his warmth pushing into me. "I'm your partner. It's my job."

My pulse spikes, and I lean into his face to say, "I didn't ask you to be my partner."

I immediately regret my choice of words when Jason flinches, his expression shuttering. He turns his face away. My chest tightens, collapsing onto my lungs.

"That's it!" Ortiz's voice cracks like a whip, cutting through the tension. "You're not accomplishing a damn thing standing here, yelling at each other. Practice is over. You two need to figure this" —she moves her hands in circles— "out, and I'm not talking about the lift. I don't know what happened to my Jason and Clarity, but this isn't them."

Jason slowly lets out air between his lips. I blink rapidly as she slams this door shut in our faces.

Ortiz points at both of us. "One week. That's all we've got, and we already had to throw last night in the trash. Let's take the weekend, then start acting like we have a competition to win at practice on Monday. If you two want to implode, do it after the Invitational." She shoots us a cold, disapproving look before turning and skating off, leaving us alone.

"Great. This is just great." I mirror her by spinning around and making a beeline to the exit as fast as my skates will take me. Jason follows in my wake, the scratching of his blades echoing across the empty rink.

Victor is already holding open the door, his lips pressed in a thin line. I point at him as I pass. "Not a word from you."

"I wasn't going to say anything." Victor swings the door shut as Jason steps onto the mats behind me, clicking the lock in place.

"I already know we're royally screwed. This was so stupid, we're never going to meet competition standards," I grumble as I collapse onto the bench and yank off one skate so harshly that my ankle twinges.

Undeterred, I do the same with the other. I'm left panting with the effort.

Jason stops short, a wounded look flashing across his face. "How can I live up to your standards when you're constantly changing them on me?" His tone is sharp and disbelieving.

"Be honest. This isn't about skating. You're using me." I hook my thumb through the rabbit ear of my lace and yank it out so fast that it whips against my hand. "You're here to prove to everyone that you didn't blow your shot, and that your dad was wrong. This is your redemption arc."

His expression twists. "Redemption? You really think that I came back to the ice for anyone but you? For myself?"

"I think it's easier for you to pretend this is just about skating rather than admit you don't know what you want anymore."

"Right. You've got me all figured out," Jason says sarcastically, then his voice drops. "I know exactly why I'm here. So remind me, why did you say yes when Victor offered me up? You had the chance to say no."

"Can I be honest? I don't know. Talk to me in six days after you prove whether or not this was a good idea." I shove my skates into my bag. Victor shuffles backward, rubbing a hand over his hair.

"It's way too late for that." Jason slices his hand through the air. "I don't know if this matters to you, but I don't think this idea was stupid. I don't think we're wasting time. I've already sacrificed as much as you have, and I've been busting my ass to make sure you're skating with someone worthy enough to take you to the end of this season."

My breath hitches, and my throat burns. I shake my head to throw his words off, refusing to look at him.

He's unphased. "You can be mad at me all week long, and yell, and even throw things if it makes you feel better. But you don't get to shut down and shut me out every time something doesn't go the way you planned. We're going to get through the weekend. After that, if you want to take Ortiz's words and be done, fine. At least we can walk away knowing we tried. Goddamn it, Clarity. Just please don't talk like none of this matters."

"I can't do this right now." I stand, slide my feet into my sandals and grab my bag. If I stay here any longer looking into his soul-crushed eyes, listening to the desperation in his voice, he's going to break me again.

Jason takes a step after me as I fly out of the box. Victor catches his elbow, though I can't hear what he says. I'm already gone, taking the stairs up to the lobby two at a time, rushing to put as much distance between us as I can.

I don't stop at the lobby. My feet carry me down the hallway, twisting through the building until I stagger out onto the balcony that overlooks all the arenas. Jason was supposed to bring me home, but if I'm next to him for one more second, there's no saying what I might do.

Instead, I sink down in the seat closest to the railing overlooking the West Rink. I'll go home with Cole once he's done with practice, and this is the best spot to wait. I haven't been up here in so long that I almost feel like a kid again, using this vantage point to understand what's going on down there.

Twelve kids are on the ice, and six of them are sporting flimsy neon jerseys. Must be a mock game, since the rest of the team are hovering behind the boards, chatting among themselves as they watch the puck flash from stick to stick.

It's easy to pick Cole out of the crowd because he's the only one that seems to be watching the game seriously. Willie and Nick are standing next to him, clutching their bellies in laughter, sticking out like the sore thumbs that they are.

Willie straightens and wipes his eyes, looking up to blink back his tears. His eyes draw to me like a magnet, the only body sitting way up here in the bleachers. He rubs his eyes again, does a double take, then glances over toward the empty North Rink. He nudges Cole with his elbow, ducking his head toward his ear. Cole follows his gaze, frowns, and begins pushing his way through his teammates.

Wonderful. Looks like I'm ruining everybody's practice today.

I track his path to Annabelle, who's standing on the edge of the crowd, her curls poking out from under her hat in every direction, clipboard in hand as she watches the ice. She looks up as Cole approaches and scowls at whatever he says.

I slouch down further when she also looks up here, shaking her head before walking away, disappearing toward the staircase. I make sure Cole is glancing up before giving him the finger. He gives me a thumbs up in return, which makes me feel even worse.

I hear footsteps a moment later, and I startle. There's no way she got up here that fast.

"Wow," Victor deadpans as he sits next to me. "Nothing like dealing with the consequences of your own actions."

"You sure know how to make a girl feel better."

"I'm sorry, but let's be real. You might as well have kicked the guy while he was down."

Leaning forward, I rest my elbows on my knees and bury my head in my hands. "This was supposed to be easy, Vick. All I want to do is knock some common sense into him."

"I could say the same thing to you. I've been on the sidelines every night, and he's not the sole problem here. When did you stop believing in yourself?"

I drop my hands to glare at him. "Do you know who you're talking to? I'm not saying I'm perfect, but at least I can stay on my skates."

"At least Jason doesn't look like he's going to wet his pants every time you guys go into a lift." He tilts his head. "You and I worked together our entire careers, and I've never seen you look so scared. What are you so afraid of?"

"This!" I motion at his cast wrist. "Getting in the air and hurting another person that I care about." I've done enough damage to Jason in the past. He doesn't need broken bones to match.

Victor rests his good arm on the armrest and leans forward. "Accidents happen. That's life. If you can't get over the fear, you might as well quit while you're ahead."

"I can't quit. This is my life." And the pipeline into my future. My head aches just thinking about what my audience would think if they heard that argument between Jason and me.

"Then accept the shit that comes with it. Including looking into Forbes eyes, saying "I trust you," and letting him pick you up. First, you need to extend the man a little bit of grace because you expect just as much out of him as Ortiz does at every practice." Victor quirks an eyebrow.

I stare at him, fighting back tears.

"Sitting here is a terrible way to practice skating." Annabelle comes walking down the aisle. Seeing her immediately breaks the dam, making my vision hazy as she takes the open spot on the other side of me.

"That's the theme for tonight, because practice *was* terrible," Victor says.

I brush my thumb against a tear that escapes. "You didn't have to come up here. The boys need you."

"So do you, and fortunately, you take precedence. What happened?" She clasps her hands together. Victor stays quiet to let me answer.

More tears fall, faster than I can swipe them away. "Everything. Nothing. And that's just the issue. It's one step forward, two steps back. Here's the cherry on top: Jason officially hates me."

Victor scoffs. Annabelle laughs, loud. "That's impossible."

"After tonight, after he comes to his senses, he will."

"Clarity, I love you, and so does he."

I ignore that. "I told him to stop treating me like a baby, and that he's not cut out for competition, and that he's been wasting my time."

She stops laughing. "Wow, okay. Ruthless."

"That's what I said." Victor shrugs.

"I know." I drag both hands down my cheeks, wiping away the wet tracks. "I messed up everything."

"Don't give yourself so much credit. Seriously. Do you even know who you're talking about? This is the same boy that taught himself Italian to talk with your grandparents at Christmas. You'll come up with a way to make it up to him, and when you do, he'll be fine. You'll be fine," Annabelle clarifies.

Her saying that brings me back onto the ice, Jason putting himself under me so he was in harm's way. Not me.

"I'm fine."

"What he needs is reassurance." Victor shifts onto the edge of his seat. "You need to trust him."

Unfortunately, I always have. That's also the problem.

Annabelle mistakes my silence as a loss for words and says, "Text him tomorrow and see if he has the time to meet up for a solo practice. That might help take the stress off."

"That's a good idea." Victor nods.

"I don't know." I drag my fingernails over my thigh. "Sometimes I wonder if we made a mistake by forging forward with Jason. Maybe I should've skated alone."

"Don't say that." Victor shakes his head. "Besides, I was the one to suggest him in the first place, and I don't make mistakes."

His arrogance, as sarcastic as it is, causes me to roll my eyes. "I can definitely name a time or two when you have, smart ass."

Annabelle frowns at him. "What about when you dated that football player during sophomore year?"

His lips twist. "I'm not talking about that. Give Jason time." He meets my eyes, and the sudden intensity written on his face takes me off guard. "I've been watching you two for over a month, and I can confidently say that he would take a bullet for you. I don't think it's beyond his power to buckle down and to pull himself together by next weekend. He has the talent and the drive to go far, but if he finds out that you're going around saying you made a mistake choosing to skate with him, that would affect him more than falling on the ice a few times."

He ducks down to keep eye contact when I try to look away, grief weighing me down. "He doesn't need to hear that you're nervous for the Invitational, or that you don't think he has what it takes. If he's anything like me, he already knows those things. Tell him something he doesn't know, girl."

His words don't just drive the message home. They pull into the garage, park, and bring the groceries inside.

It makes me cry again, and Annabelle reaches over to rub my shoulder. I don't know what to do, because if I were Jason, I'd find a better way to spend my time.

Chapter 16

Jason

I ce hisses underneath the metal blades of my figure skates. Cold air stings the exposed parts of my body as I gain momentum. The breeze turns into a whipping wind. Determination keeps me warm as I fly down the center length of the rink.

Five hundred empty seats watch me with a critical eye as I launch off my front skate, rotate one and a half rounds in a single axel jump, and land on my opposite foot. I spread my arms out wide as the blade reconnects with the ice, guiding my body in a wide arc, keeping my center of balance. I let myself believe for a moment that, if Ortiz were here, she would finally have something nice to say about my jump.

For the majority of my hockey career, I practiced with other people. In the rare moments I got to practice alone, I soaked up the peace. When I'm by myself, I get the chance to focus on me, on the ice. There's no one to influence me. No one to tell me what I'm doing right or wrong.

But Clarity has ruined me.

I transition into a one-footed spin, the same move that Clarity showed me one short month ago. This time, I don't fall flat on my butt. The border of the arena turns into a blur, even when I choose a focal point to keep my balance.

Since we've come back together, her presence has become my force of gravity, keeping me tethered to the surface of the earth. Her dark hair can be found in the shadows beyond the lights. The echoing of my skates could be mistaken for her following behind me. As I envision the next move, I can practically feel her hands slipping into mine.

It's impossible to not sense her all around me on the ice when she's the one who has unintentionally motivated me to keep skating all of these years.

I didn't realize how fast I'd come to rely on her again. Late night practices followed up with even later night texts, laughing myself to sleep with her jokes about Ortiz. Early mornings practicing choreography in the yoga room in front of the mirrors, watching how perfectly our bodies synchronize. I've been spending more time with her in the cafeteria at school, our knees brushing and our heads bent together as we scrutinize the videos that Victor captured the night before.

The silence that followed last night made me feel like I lost her all over again. It's the longest we've gone without talking since we started skating together.

After our fight last night, I took the morning to wallow in my bedroom. It gave me the chance to really sit and think about my actions, like a kid in timeout. I was caught between calling Tiffany to finally end things, or texting Clarity to apologize for yesterday. I was in the middle of crafting an apology text when she messaged me first, asking if we could practice alone today.

Of course I said yes.

I decided to get to the rink an hour earlier than she asked to meet, desperate for a little more ice time. We're on the home stretch, and if I don't practice every day, I don't know if I'll become the partner she needs me to be by the Invitational.

The last thing I want to do is let Clarity down. Figuratively and literally. I'm sick enough of dropping her as it is.

As I move down the ice, I set myself up for a line of twizzles. This is the one movement that her and I nail almost every time, and I perform them with confidence.

I straighten my line at the end of the move and twist my body around, jumping into a half rotation and skating backward. I lift my gaze to find another focal point.

Instead, I find Clarity. In the flesh. Not an illusion. I nearly fall over.

She grins as she skates over. The overhead lights seem to dim in comparison. It's so nice to see her smile.

"Hey, I hope I didn't scare you."

"C.J. Not at all," I lie happily and shift my momentum to move toward her. That force of gravity is overwhelming.

Her blades hiss across the ice until she comes to a stop, nodding at the centerline. "Your spin was beautiful. It looks like you've been figure skating forever."

"Thanks, I happen to have a pretty good teacher." I cut off my sentence awkwardly, the words, *and she's cute, too,* dying on my tongue. Even thinking them in the privacy of my mind makes my cheeks heat.

"Ortiz is the best," Clarity agrees, although that's not who I meant. I let it go as she looks down and scuffs her toe pick against the ice. "Speaking of, I want to apologize for last night."

My heart skips like a rock bouncing against the surface of a lake. "You don't need to apologize for anything."

She meets my eyes again as she laces her hands together, pulling at her fingers. "Yes, I do. I've been taking out my frustration on you."

"Because I can handle it."

"But it's not fair. I need to control myself. Besides, you were right. The fear I have about that stupid lift paralyzes me. I'm sorry because I trust you, but I don't trust myself, and I'm ruining everything."

"No, you're not." I put my hands on my hips. I hide my smile when she mirrors the movement. "You're not the only one who's afraid. I'm trying to be the partner that you deserve, but I'm not doing you any favors by letting the pressure get to me."

She watches me closely, and I scratch my neck. "I know I can skate. That's not the problem. My problem is you."

Her eyebrows lift. I press on.

"All I'm worried about is if you're happy with me."

There. That's the truth, and I hate how naked it feels. Clarity wasn't expecting to hear it either, given the way she suddenly looks like someone poured a bucket of cold water on her head.

"I'm happy," she says, her voice carrying over the empty rink. "I don't regret doing this with you at all."

"That makes two of us." I offer her a smile and hold out my hand, feeling a lot lighter than I did five minutes ago. "Would you like to practice our rhythm dance now, or do we have more grievances to air out?"

She looks down at my palm, and just as I begin to assume she'll skate past and leave me hanging, she reaches out and takes it. I swallow in an attempt to moisturize my dry throat.

"Yes, that would be lovely. I didn't come all of this way to stand on the sidelines and scream at you."

Her hand is soft and warm. My palm is so big it nearly swallows hers, yet in my mind, it's the perfect fit. I can feel the shapely lines and the bones that make up the shape of her hand.

"I hope not. I pay people to do that, and I don't remember paying you," I answer dumbly. My head is starting to get light.

Clarity laughs. Every inch of my heart swells again.

I use our connected hands to pull her alongside me before using extra force to whip her forward and let go, which makes her laugh harder as she glides forward like a toddler learning how to skate.

"Hey!"

"We're burning daylight here!" I say in an exaggerated imitation of Ortiz, going as far as clapping my hands aggressively. "No time for messing around."

"There's all sorts of time for messing around." Clarity glances at me over her shoulder, capturing my gaze with a quick grin.

It's hard to say whether she's flirting with me. It doesn't matter either way because I may as well be a kangaroo for how quickly I jump to conclusions.

Clarity keeps talking as she settles into her starting position on the ice. "Alright, I'll count us down whenever you're ready."

I do the only thing that I trust myself to do right now, which is nodding.

She is already in position, her left leg cocked as she keeps her chin inclined toward the ice, her arms delicately raised. I come to a stop behind her hips, heat radiating off my body as I place my left hand on her elbow and arc my right arm behind me, mirroring the angle of her head and training my eyes on the ice.

Clarity inhales slowly. I mimic her breathing pattern, even as she exhales. My chest loosens and my head clears. Sometimes getting close to her is all I need to recenter.

"Go on my count," she says quietly. With our heads tucked together like this, her hushed tone causes a shiver to run down my spine. "Three, two, one, and go!"

She breaks away from me in a flash of movement, dramatically singing the first few notes of the song as she waves her arms with a dancer's flourish.

The singing catches me off guard, making me laugh as I backpedal away. "What are you doing?"

"Filling in!" Clarity exclaims before singing more notes, her voice carrying over the ice. "Don't stop!"

Grinning like an idiot, I launch off my blades in a simple 180-degree spin as she does a full rotation. I pause before taking off after her, my heart soaring with the chase.

She begins to sing the first few lyrics in short bursts around her panting breath as she slows down, her arms positioned with the poise of a ballerina. I spin on the toes of my skates and fly backward in a wide arc until I meet her right in the middle of my path. She's facing me with an equally as stupid smile on her face. It must've been too much work to keep belting out the lyrics, however she's still humming the song.

My favorite parts of the routine are when she's in my arms, and this time is no different as I grab her waist and pick her up for a moment, pulling her toward me to guide us in a spinning circle. She rests her hands on my forearms. I squeeze my hands so she has some muscle to hold on to.

We lift our left legs simultaneously, and her physics comes into play as our circle gets faster. She stops humming to count our rotations out loud. "One, two, three, four. Catch me!"

"Always," I respond between huffs of breath, guiding her into another series of rotational spins. I don't need to see her face to know that she's painting the perfect picture of passion and intimacy. She doesn't just skate; she lives and breathes the emotion that comes with every movement.

We transition into a catchfoot spin—I'm very proud that I'm starting to remember the names of these moves—and I keep my hands steady on her for guidance as I stay in a sit spin.

Her dark hair flies. She's back to singing the song. My lungs could burst with joy.

For as quickly as we went through those moves, we break out of them. My hands are empty and cold without her there to fill them as she turns away from me and hustles down the ice. I'm right behind her, antagonizing this cat-and-mouse chase. This is nothing new. In my world, I've been chasing her for years.

As we continue to dance through our routine, I count down each movement as we approach the lift.

"Clarity," I say between panting breaths, cutting off her happy vocalization, "the lift. Let's try it."

"Huh?" We skate alongside each other for the next move, and I'm so close that I can see the shock rimming her eyes. "Are you sure?"

"No questioning, just reacting," I reply in what I wish wasn't another imitation of Ortiz.

A bright smile cracks across Clarity's face, like the sun peeking through the clouds. We're rapidly approaching the part where, in the past, I've grabbed her rib cage and simply spun her to fill the time so Ortiz could plan a different move instead.

This time, I'm hoping and praying and wishing on stars that I won't mess it up.

There's a glimmer of fear on her face, which makes me refuse to show my own anxiety for her sake. She can trust me. I push out the sensation of her slipping through my fingers. I kick out every thought that tells me I can't do this, that I'm not capable. I know I am an amazing skater. If I stop at amazing, Clarity doesn't even have a word that she stops at. I refuse to be the one who holds her back from her full potential.

That's why, when she swoops into my arms, I catch her with confidence.

Grabbing her abdomen with one hand and bracing my other between her shoulder blades, I forget about all of our failed attempts as I flip her upside down.

Clarity keeps herself balanced perfectly in my arms as she splits her legs. She's steady, and way too light for my liking. So light that she hardly affects my center of balance as I try my hand at a few rotations.

She giggles giddily, echoing the same sound my entire soul is making. We've been a team for a while, but tonight, we are one body. I don't want to let her down. I don't want to let go.

Exhaling, I carefully lower her down. She exits the move with grace. Her body doesn't even jostle as her blades reconnect with the ice and she softly glides away as if she wasn't airborne a moment ago.

She whirls around and shrieks, pointing both hands at me. "Jason Carter Forbes! Are you kidding me right now?! You were perfect!"

I laugh and bound forward, whisking Clarity up in my arms. She is shining as she grins down at me, her arms resting behind my neck for balance as I spin us in a circle, excitement coursing through my veins. Her hair gets in my mouth. I don't care. It's bliss.

I set her down on the ice. Her eyes are lit bright with delight. Both arms are still wrapped around my neck. Her chest is heaving with exertion. My hands are still on her waist. They're pulling her closer. Goosebumps overtake my skin. I am fire and ice as my fingers twine into her waistband.

I tilt my head down, and in the heat of the moment, I do something that I've been wanting to do since the last time it happened.

I kiss Clarity.

She is overpowering. Her mouth is soft against mine, and she makes a noise of exclamation—

No. A noise of disgust.

My eyes fly open as she pulls away, fast.

Her exhales are fast and ragged as she brings both hands to my shoulders and pushes me away so hard that she almost knocks herself over in the process.

I stumble, my blades clacking against the ice as I fight to hold my balance against the force. Her eyes are wide with panic this time, like a cornered dog. It's a drastic difference from the singing girl a minute ago.

She reaches up and brushes her fingers against her lips, blinking as she looks down at her hand. "Oh, my God."

"Clarity—" I reach out and take a step forward.

Her eyes snap up to mine and she backpedals, pointing at me for a very different reason this time. "Don't. Don't come near me."

The tone of her voice is like a gunshot, loud and sudden and stinging. I recoil as she spins around and skates off so fast that she leaves ice chunks where she was standing a moment ago.

I just kissed her.

It doesn't matter that we finally performed a successful lift. After tonight, there's a good chance that I've ruined all of our chances at ever skating together again.

July 2015 - Age 16

Clarity

Annabelle hasn't missed much at this 4th of July party, besides me talking to Sterling earlier. Nothing exciting has happened. Everyone was hanging out in the garage when we got here, which turned into multiple rounds of cup pong, then swimming in the lake, eating pizza and gossiping by the fire, lighting off illegal fireworks over the lake, and now everyone is gone.

At least it seems that way as I step outside the sliding door onto the patio, the rough stone digging into my bare feet. Moths and beetles bump against the light fixture by the door, their little bodies occasionally clinking against the glass in their desperation to navigate the dark night. All of the chairs around the bonfire are vacant, made obvious by the light of the flames reflecting against bare plastic. Empty beer bottles and cans of seltzers that were smuggled in by underage teenagers litter the patio. It's the stamp of approval of a good night.

I'm proven to not be alone when people start yelling and laughing a couple hundred yards away at the bottom of the hill by the lake shore, accompanied by the sound of loud splashing.

I stepped inside a few moments ago to use the restroom, clean the kitchen, and refill my drink, so it seems hard to believe that everyone swarmed down to the water so quickly. At least, I think it was a moment ago. There's a good chance it could've been an hour.

I patter around the side of the fire, setting my drink down on the arm of a chair that isn't in the line of smoke. I throw another log on the fire before collapsing down next to my cup, my knees weak with too much alcohol and not nearly enough food.

My brain feels deliriously heavy as I tip my head back to marvel at the stars. It's a perfect Minnesota summer night. I'm comfortable in my bright floral bikini, and the sweatpants I just put on over my bottoms help keep me warm. There are no clouds in the sky. The light pollution isn't bad tonight, showcasing the bright prickholes of heaven that can be seen beyond the black nothingness. Frogs and crickets chatter in the long grass. Every few minutes, a firework booms way off in the distance.

"Hey, C.J."

Now I'm *really* not alone.

I raise my head and smile at Jason as he walks through the backyard covered in shadows. "What's up?"

"Not a whole lot." He shrugs. "I was worried about you when I noticed you were missing."

I want to laugh. He has nothing to worry about up here. Not while his buddies are three sheets to the wind, messing around by the water. The sound dies in my throat when he steps into the light cast by the fire.

I've spent almost my whole life dancing on the outskirts of Jason's reach. Figuratively speaking, considering he has never touched me except for accidental touches here and there. Once I dreamt that I fell asleep in his arms in the back of my parent's car, except that wasn't real. He is my brother's best friend, and I refuse to regard him as anything else. Not a distant neighbor, not a schoolmate, and certainly not a crush—even if he has been all of those things at one time or another. But never for very long.

All of those other titles pave the way for *feelings*. Emotions beyond compliance or airbrushed happiness.

Treating Jason as Cole's best friend leaves no room for games. It's a simple reminder that he's not even supposed to be in my circle. That's why I've been avoiding him all night. I don't want to face the reality of my situation.

Yet, as the golden firelight ignites his honeyed skin, casting slivers of shadows over his abs and biceps and all of the other important male muscular groups, that circle suddenly has a corral door that's being swung open. I don't know if it's the vodka talking, years of repressed energy, or both. I'm suddenly acutely aware of the damp blond waves draping over those sweet, bright green eyes. We might live in the Midwest, but this boy just stepped off the front page of a Hollister catalogue.

Jason clears his throat as he chooses a chaise lounge chair and drags it closer to me. The sound of the legs scraping over stone breaks the awkward silence as I realize I never answered him. I was too caught up in his uncanny beauty.

"How are you holding up?" He sits down, folding his left ankle over his right knee.

"Just peachy." I grab my cup, taking a small sip, letting the alcohol sting the back of my throat. I take a moment to scramble for the right words now that we're alone for the first time all day. "I cleaned up the kitchen, and everyone was gone when I came back outside. I thought about joining you guys by the lake, but I'm enjoying the peace and quiet."

A girl down at the lake screams and immediately starts laughing, causing the frogs to go quiet for a moment. Loud splashing quickly ensues. I quirk my lips up. "I *was* enjoying the quiet."

Jason laughs, the sound warming my chest faster than this drink ever could. He runs a hand over his hair. "Yeah, same. I needed a break from the circus."

I gasp teasingly and lean forward, holding a hand over my chest. "You? Needing a break? Don't tell me that Jason Carter Forbes is willingly skipping out on the fun."

I expect him to laugh again and play along. Instead, he looks up from the fire to my eyes. "Maybe the circus wasn't as fun without you there. Besides." He glances at the firelight again. "I mostly came to get away from my dad."

I lean back and slowly nod along. Jesse has always been the gift that keeps on giving. Especially when he's making sure Jason gets ice time every day, even in the off season. He even hired a special private chef to make sure Jason gets all the right nutrition. This is the first night in a while I've seen him eat something other than his perfectly weighed and proportioned meals. Pizza and soda doesn't exactly fit the bill.

We don't talk about his dad very often since it's such a sore subject, so I don't know how to approach the topic. Jason saves me by continuing to speak. "Cole is definitely letting loose, though. He's having a great time down there."

"He always does. He deserves it after the way that girl from Hopkins led him on all summer just to ghost him. If you were to ask me, I don't even think she exists. Some old man probably catfished him."

Jason nods and shrugs simultaneously, showing his agreement without actually saying anything. He's studying me again, and my skin prickles with his gaze. "Are you sure you're okay? You've been off tonight."

"Off?" I echo and meet his gaze again. "How so?"

Other than the fact I planted roots in the wall like a wallflower when the pizza got delivered, haven't looked in Jason's direction more than twice all day out of insecurity and jealousy while all of the other girls had no problem walking up to him, and stayed out of nearly every drinking game. And disappeared to clean the kitchen, when I refuse to do the dishes at my family's restaurant where I actually get paid to do it.

Jason tilts his chin down and raises his eyebrows at me like he's making the same checklist. I huff and hesitate. "I'm fine. I just... have a lot on my mind."

"Like what?"

"Nothing. It's stupid." I take another sip of my drink and advert my gaze.

"I doubt it. Stupid isn't a part of your vocabulary. I like to know what you're thinking."

A strong blush rushes over my cheeks as I watch the flames dance, letting his words find a home in my heart. I glance at him from the corner of my eye, admiring the way the firelight catches his profile. The blood begins to gallop through my veins. It's not like I can admit that he is the one thing that has been taking up nearly every inch in my brain, snuffing out every other thought.

I speak quietly, almost to myself, "You shouldn't be up here."

Jason frowns. "Why not?"

I find the bravery to face him head-on, sitting up in my chair and setting my drink down. "Because you're Cole's best friend."

He holds my gaze, unwavering. "And? He doesn't control me. I wanted to see you, Clarity."

The breath hitches in my lungs when my name leaves his mouth. "It's complicated."

Every drink I've had tonight has gone straight to my head. I don't know how to tell him that I can't be alone with him because I start thinking about things like his muscles and infuriatingly messy hair and the beauty of his gaze. It's complicated because he's one of the only boys that admires me like priceless art, like he wants to memorize every line. Never like he's picturing me with my clothes off, like some of Cole's other friends.

Jason unfolds his legs and leans closer as he repeats himself, "I came back to find *you*. I don't care about Willie and Nick and the others. I don't care what Cole thinks. Complicated doesn't mean wrong."

I laugh nervously, but the intensity in Jason's eyes makes me go quiet. Frankly, it makes it impossible to think clearly. He's viewing his artwork closer than he ever has before.

"You're not supposed to say stuff like that."

Jason's mouth tilts in a smile, and he keeps his voice low to ask again, "Why not?"

His eyes flicker between mine, searching, waiting, and the weight of his gaze feels like a slow-burning fire warming me from the inside out. I'm caught in the push and pull of every reason I should stop this and every reason I don't want to.

"Clarity?" Jason murmurs, his voice low and uncertain, like he's afraid that he's crossing some invisible line with all of these questions.

I should put space between us. Remind him—remind *myself*—that he's Cole's friend and this shouldn't happen. However, the world feels hazy. The only thing that's clear is him, lingering so close that I can feel the heat of his skin.

Every cell in my body is screaming. He smells woodsy and faintly spicy, an afterthought of his cologne since the lake washed most of it off. It's intoxicating. He shifts closer. His lips part slightly, and I can nearly hear the last thread of my resolve snapping.

"I can't..." I start. The words die on my tongue because I know they're a lie.

I can't breathe.

Can't think.

Can't stop myself.

Instead of answering, I close the space between us, launching off my chair to grab both sides of his face as I press my lips to his.

The second we connect, the world tilts. His lips are soft but insistent, and everything else I've ever dreamed of. He inhales sharply like he's been holding his breath as long as I have. One of his hands slides to the small of my back, his callouses rough on my bare skin, lighting me on fire, pulling me closer. His other cups my face and he tilts my head, deepening the kiss.

It's electric. It's like my first time stepping in the skating rink, my head spinning with the sheer rightness of it... even though I know how wrong this particular moment should be. My hands move on their own, tangling in his hair as his thumb brushes my cheek. A shiver races down my spine.

I tip my head back to let out a shuddering sigh, bordering on a groan as he trails his lips down my neck. His teeth nip at my throat. This time, there's no hiding the sound that I make. I trace my hands down his warm, solid chest and settle on his biceps. Maybe I'm crazy, but I swear that he flexes his muscles under my palms.

Cracking my eyes open, my gaze lands on the side of his face, right on the scar I gave him a few years ago. I can't help it as I lean forward and press my lips against it.

He lays a hand on my jaw and gently redirects my mouth back to his. The fire crackles somewhere behind us, drowned out by the pounding in my ears. The entire world dissolves around us until it's just him.

We finally break apart, my lips tingling, and I'm breathless. He rests his forehead against mine, his eyes still closed, and his hand lingering on my face like he's afraid to let go.

"That..." Jason starts, his voice barely breaking a whisper, "was not what I expected tonight."

I laugh softly, though it comes out shaky. My heart feels like it's about to burst. My thoughts are a chaotic mess of everything I should say, and everything I want to say.

Unfortunately, one rises above the rest, taking the spotlight.

I just kissed him.

Suddenly, I launch backwards like I've been stung. As if I didn't initiate the kiss.

He inhales sharply, his hands falling without me in them. "Hey—"

"I know." I stumble backwards, running into my chair. My cup topples, spilling on the ground. "I know that was wrong."

"It's not wrong." Jason shakes his head. "It's just..."

"Complicated," I firmly finish his sentence. "I know. Look, this can't ever happen again. We can't mention this to anyone. Ever."

The passion in his eyes is gone, evaporated with my outburst. I know he loves me because he doesn't argue, even when it's blatantly obvious that he wants to. Instead, he slowly nods like a robot.

"Okay. It never happened." His voice cracks.

I cross my arms. We sit in silence for a moment, the fire crackling between us. Jason chews his cheek, continuing to bite down words.

I finally turn away before I can change my mind. "We should get back to the party."

He stands. "Okay."

I hurry away from him, down the path toward the lake. The cool night feels like a splash of ice water on my face. My thoughts race, tangling into a knot of regret and exhilaration that make my chest tighten.

What was I thinking?

I quicken my pace, my bare feet scuffing against the dirt. He's Cole's best friend. I know better. I'm supposed to know better.

Until my mind drifts back to a few moments ago. The way his hands steadied me, and the press of his lips like he wanted it more than I did. My stomach flips despite itself, and the weight of reality crashes down just as quickly.

This was a mistake. A massive, universe-sized mistake.

I glance over my shoulder, pretending to swat my hair back as I catch a glimpse of Jason. He's trailing a few steps behind, hands shoved in the pockets of his swim trunks. He's quiet, expression unreadable, and that only makes my racing questions worse. Why didn't he stop me? He's always been the responsible one.

Another flush crawls up my neck as I stumble on the path. What if he actually tells Cole? What if he doesn't? Are we expected to pretend this didn't happen and take the secret to our graves? That thought sends a pang that I can't explain through my heart.

The sound of laughter and music grows louder as we approach the lakeshore, and I force myself to swallow the lump in my throat. All I have to do is act normal. As if I didn't just make everything a hundred times more complicated.

I try to steady my breathing and straighten my shoulders. My lips are still tingling from where his had been, and the memory of his touch lingers like a flame I can't quite put out.

Chapter 17

Clarity

The first time I kissed Jason, it felt unavoidable. It happened in the heat of the moment at a party, and I regretted it immediately. Not because it was necessarily wrong, but because it felt so terribly right that I couldn't bear to face the truth.

Nothing's changed, because I still refuse to face him. If the Invitational wasn't in four days, I probably would've cancelled practice tonight, but no. I plastered on a smile and I held his hands and I danced in his arms. I acted like I hadn't felt the warm press of his lips, the exhale of his breath in this exact spot not even twenty-four hours ago.

My act wavers the moment Ortiz ends practice. I let go of his hands like they've electrocuted me and race toward the gate, leaving Jason behind.

Victor raises his eyebrows and opens the gate for me. "You need to piss that badly?"

"I'm just so excited to see you." I hop off the ice and collapse on the closest bench.

He rolls his eyes. "I'm really feeling the love. What's up with the awkward tension out there?"

"What tension?" Jason steps off the ice.

My hands start to tremble as I unwind my laces.

"I felt like I was watching a middle school dance." Victor holds out his arms like a tin man and begins to sway. "Mrs. Schlanger would've loved you guys. There was *plenty* of room for Jesus."

I almost throw my skate at Victor's head.

Jason does the smartest thing he's done all weekend and takes the bench across from me. "I don't know what you're talking about."

Oh, yes he does. We didn't say one goddamn word to each other all practice long, except we didn't have to. He was the one that kept tightening his grip on my waist or squeezing my hand in an attempt to get me to move closer. I didn't give in unless Ortiz snapped at me. I couldn't even look him in the eye. I still can't.

"Let's start with this." He motions his good hand between the spots we've chosen. "What happened to smoothing out the tension yesterday?"

"What, we can't have one off day?" I ask sharply as I yank off a skate.

"You two have been having an off week, actually." Victor pauses and pulls his phone out of his pocket. I glance up as he turns away, and scowl when I catch the name *Monty* at the top of his screen. He steps back to answer the text, leaving my eyes to fall on Jason.

He's already glancing at me from under his eyelashes. Making eye contact infuriates me further, and I all but kick off my other skate and leap to my feet. The quick movement sends black dots over my vision. "I'm going to grab my stuff."

"Okay." Jason's cheeks redden as he ducks his head.

Victor waves dismissively. His voice follows me around the corner as he asks Jason, "Seriously, what happened?"

I walk faster to avoid hearing his reply. I'm sick of hearing his lies, and there's no way he'll tell Victor the truth. Hell, I don't even know if he's told Tiffany yet, or if he will. Knowing her, she's probably going to wait for the right time to get her revenge. My chest aches thinking about it.

I could barely look at myself in the mirror in the weeks that followed uncovering the truth of Sterling's infidelity. There was something about me that wasn't good enough to satisfy him, and it killed me knowing that he had to find that quality in someone else. I guess all of that time spent trying to figure out why he did that manifested into this mess; now *I'm* the home-wrecker.

I'm out of breath as I enter the locker room. It's blissfully quiet for the next few minutes, until the girls' hockey team wraps up practice. I plan on being long gone by the time they come around, so I hurry back to my locker to take out my sweatpants and sweatshirt. Tucking the clothes under my arm, I grab my phone next and scowl as it buzzes over and over.

There's no reason for anyone to be calling me. I still flip it around to check. Maybe something happened at the restaurant and my parents—

"Holy shit," I curse.

Over one thousand notifications have piled up on my phone, and they're still rolling in. Instagram comments and DMs, Twitter tags, comments and activity from my blog. I haven't posted in days. There's no way *this* many people have suddenly found my page.

A new comment on something I'm tagged in pops up.

@skateordietwinsies
Can confirm. I heard from a friend on the team that she's passed out during training before. I hope someone gets her help before it's too late.

Passed out?

I click the comment and my stomach sinks when I'm brought to the Skate Snaps page. My knees wobble as I read the headline, and I grab the locker door to keep from collapsing.

Exclusive: Are Minnesota's Invitational Favorites Already Falling Apart?
Submitted Anonymously to *Skate Snaps Midwest*
Published: November 10th — 7:03 PM CST

With the U.S. International Ice Dance Invitational just around the corner, eyes have been locked on Clarity Jansky and her new partner, former hockey golden boy Jason Forbes. After an abrupt partnership switch earlier this season due to Victor Kerr's injury, many fans were skeptical about whether a hockey player could pull off the grace and timing of high-level ice dancing.

Now, we may have our answer.

Two videos submitted to *Skate Snaps* show the duo in practice at the Greater Midwest Ice Complex. While the footage is grainy, what's clear is this: the program is unpolished, full of missed connections and shaky lifts. At one point, Forbes appears to lose his grip on Jansky entirely... forcing her to catch herself mid-air. A moment that could've ended in serious injury.

But what has fans most concerned isn't the choreography. It's Clarity.

"She looks thinner than ever," wrote this anonymous contributor. "You can always see her shaking, and Jason's constantly adjusting to compensate. It's obvious he's trying, but what's more obvious is the fact that she's not eating."

Sources close to the team suggest the pressure of being the "ice princess" has finally caught up to Clarity Jansky. Some believe she's leaning into the aesthetic: fragile, angelic, untouchable. Others think it's all about control, earning sympathy, praise, or a headline during her rising stardom (thanks to *@Off The Ice*) even if it costs her her health.

One thing is for certain: If this is what they look like going into the weekend, they're going to fall harder than she already has.

Skaters and fans alike: do better. We love this sport, but not at the cost of someone's safety.

We'll be watching.

— *Skate Snaps Midwest*

Rating: 309 comments | 2.3k likes | 376 shares

Horror begins to stir deep inside of my body. It starts as a simmering heat deep inside of my chest and quickly burns out of control. I feel like I'm going to roast alive. I can't get my jacket off fast enough, especially when my fingers fumble the zipper three times. It falls to the floor in a heap as I scroll down and click the first video.

Someone must've hidden in the seating on the second level and zoomed in as far as they could because the quality is grainy, but it's definitely us. The video was taken early last week because I remember Jason wearing that damn green sweatshirt for the first time since we started to skate together. Ortiz was drilling us on the curve lift. I don't need to watch the video to know what happens. I do anyway.

I watch myself skate backward into Jason's arms as we set up for the lift. My head spins with the memory as he bends to take my weight, locking his arms around my hips. He starts to lift, and I wince as I watch my body tremble. My arms flinch, not posing, but bracing. I wish I could go back in time and rearrange my weight, except it's too late. I'm already leaning too far to the side.

The arc of the lift falters as my chest begins to dip and my right skate nearly drags on the ice. Jason strains to correct course. Tears prick in my eyes because he's giving it everything he has and it looks like he's going to recover, until my left arm instinctively curls. My body folds, and even now my gut lurches as I slip out of his arms.

Jason acts fast, tightening his grip and grabbing me to keep me from crashing down. His face is tight with the effort as I throw my weight backward, completely reliant on him. The video ends the moment he sets me safely back on the ice, catching the terrified sheen in my eyes.

"I'm not letting you break a bone on the ice, so get used to it."

His words from the other night ring in my ears.

I know from experience that I shouldn't look at the comments. Unfortunately, my fingers move of their own accord. It will haunt me if I don't see what people have to say.

@spinwithsasha
Not gonna lie, watching that video broke my heart. This is what pressure in the sport looks like when coaches, parents, and fans care more about gold than mental and physical health. Clarity's not the problem, we are.
↳ **@amygazukskates**
Then say that, but don't ignore the fact she's glamorizing starving herself for the aesthetic
↳ **@icequeenevie**
What proof do you ACTUALLY have she's starving herself? A blurry video and a blog post without an actual source? Be so for real
↳ **@skatesnapsmidwest**
Some people actually know what's happening behind the scenes.
↳ **@rebafan88**
tbh it's giving 'bitter I didn't make the team.'

@icequeenevie
Everyone needs to calm down. Jason literally started ice dancing, what, like two months ago?? They're doing fine considering that. Stop tearing down kids for clicks
↳ **@skatesnapsmidwest**
Nobody's tearing anyone down. But pretending they're ready for the Invitational when their basic lifts are collapsing isn't supportive... it's delusional.

@cutieontheice24
claritys been my idol since she posted that how to land your lutz breakdown in 8th grade you're all sick if you think she's faking it for sympathy

@minneskategirl112
You know what's wild? Everyone expected C and V to make Nationals and now that she's with Jason suddenly everyone wants to drag her down. I see what's happening here...

@skatemomn_ci
This is why we don't let our daughter read skating blogs anymore. Toxic gossip disguised as concern. Shame on you all.

@icedout999
I don't even care about the drama, I just wanna know where Jason has been my entire life. He skates like a brick but looks like a whole Hollister model

Words. They're just words.

This is something I've been telling myself since middle school when I got my first hate comment. These people don't know me. They don't know my favorite color, what's on my bucket list, or what jokes make me laugh. But if that's the case, then how are they seeing right through me?

I watch the video again to look at myself through their eyes. I have no idea why they think I'm starving myself. My stomach was so bloated that day that it's a wonder I even squeezed into that shirt. Those leggings add five pounds to my thighs. I'm shocked Ortiz didn't say anything. No wonder Jason couldn't lift me. He *still* can barely lift me.

The Invitational is in four days. The article got one thing right: if I can't control myself, we're going to fail.

I can't fail now, even if I deserve to.

My phone buzzes with another new comment.

This time, when the bile rises again, there's no swallowing it down.

I barely make it to the nearest trashcan in time, dry heaving on the air that comes up. How ironic is it that I haven't eaten all day because

I've been so worked up about Jason kissing me? Thinking about that again makes me shudder, and I spit out bitter saliva right as the locker room door flies open. Twenty sweaty, chattering, laughing girls come stumbling in.

Most of them ignore me the same way I ignore them as I slink toward the clothes I dropped on the floor sometime between reading that article and sticking my face in the trash. I wipe away the tears under my eyes as I pick them up, and my attention flashes to the front of the room as Tiffany walks in.

Her red hair is a blazing mess as she pulls out her ponytail, and our eyes clash in the middle. I'm dizzy with the blood flow that suddenly pours into my head, sending a frustrated blush over my cheeks as her expression hardens. That's when the pieces click.

The sabotage article, the anonymous sender, the sneaky videos. Her discontent, the snide comments during school, the frustrated updates from Jason.

Tiffany. Tiffany snuck those videos and sent them in to ruin us.

She peels off her gloves as I stride across the room. "Did you have time to sneak a video before practice, or did you send it in after you skated your laps?"

Tiffany twists her lips as she throws her gloves on the bench. "What are you talking about?"

"You were there, so you tell me. The angle of the video was from your side of the rink." My heart leaps into my throat as one of her teammates leans in and whispers something in her ear, triggering a smirk on her face. I'm still not done. "You've been waiting for this, haven't you? Since the day I paired with Jason, you've been wanting me to fail."

"Please. You can do that on your own. Some people must finally see what I've known all along." She shrugs. One of the other girls slams her locker closed a little too hard and spins around to eye me, and the one who whispered in her ear grins.

"Enlighten me," I bite out. My hands tremble as more girls pop their heads around the corner. I probably should've found a different place to confront her—I'm like a rabbit in a foxhole.

"You're a mess. People think you're this delicate dancer, but you've always been made out of paper. Why would I ever waste my time recording you?"

The unfairness of this situation, her accusations, make me want to throttle her. "Because you can't stand that he's better off with someone else."

Finally, Tiffany stiffens. I recognize the warning in her tone as she says, "Watch it."

"No, let's talk about it. I'm sure everyone knows by now." I flourish my hand toward the girls who are starting to creep closer, the same girls who haven't been afraid to glare daggers at me every day for the past eight weeks in school. The locker room door bangs open somewhere behind them. "You think I want him? Do you seriously believe that I chased him when he kissed me last night—"

Both of us freeze. The girls gasp. My breath hitches as her eyes widen with realization. A pin could pop the tension like a balloon. Instead, she closes the space between us and slaps me so hard that I bite the inside of my cheek. Blood rushes over my tongue.

"You whore!" Tiffany shouts, her voice echoing off the cement walls. "I should've known!"

I spit out blood and it splatters on the tile. She descends on me again. I flinch, preparing myself for another blow.

Her hands hit skin again. It's not mine. Annabelle is here, and she jumped in front of me. She received her fury.

"Who are you calling a whore?" Annabelle yells and shoves her backward. Another girl jumps forward, and Annabelle smacks her away.

Tiffany stumbles, only to step right back up to the plate. "She kissed my boyfriend!"

"I did not kiss him." The words stutter out of my mouth.

"Right, he tripped and his mouth landed on yours. You're so full of shit." She points at me over Annabelle's shoulder, and Annabelle makes her step back as she continues, "You've been waiting for this, using skating as your excuse, but I see you. I've always seen you, you attention-seeking *bitch*."

"That's enough." Annabelle risks her life by putting her back to Tiffany and grabbing my arm, leading me away. I don't expect the girls to make a hole in their circle, but they do, shooting us various glares of disgust and humor. "We're leaving."

"That's right, Clarity. Keep playing the victim like you're not the problem!" Tiffany shouts.

I grab my stuff as Annabelle claps her hand on my back and nearly pushes me out. She herds me into a side hallway with the vending machines and grabs me by the shoulders. Her brown eyes glisten with shock.

"I'm sorry. What the hell was that back there?" Her voice shakes with adrenaline.

"Jason kissed me yesterday." I swipe away the blood that has started to trickle down my lip. "I swear, Annabelle. It was an accident. We followed your guys advice and practiced alone, and it went really well. He got excited and kissed me."

"You're kidding." She squeezes her eyes shut for a moment. "I've heard that one before."

"It was!"

"He knows better." She lets go of me. "Tiffany should be hitting *him*, not you."

"I'm sure she will. He has a big storm coming."

"He deserves it for being an idiot." She digs car keys out of her pocket.

I press my tongue gingerly against the side of my mouth, testing the wound. "I'm just as guilty. I should've kept my mouth shut."

"She had to find out at some point. It's not your fault she's mentally unstable." She shrugs. "I can take you home."

"Jason was going to." I fall in stride with her as she starts toward the back exit. "Although I was hoping to wait around and catch a ride with Cole, after everything yesterday."

"Absolutely not. Cole was going to find Jason to ask him about something for hockey, and you don't need to be near either of them when Tiffany comes raining down."

I wince. "Do you think Jason is going to be okay? I just ruined his relationship."

That fact weighs heavily on my heart, now that I have a moment to process it, tears well behind my eyes again. As much as I don't like Tiffany, no girl deserves to find out information like this.

"Trust me, he'll be fine. Don't worry about that, you didn't have to do a thing. He ruined that relationship before it even began." She swings the car keys around on her finger, and they jingle a little too happily considering the circumstances.

I refuse to believe that. I swallow hard, fighting down more tears.

I should've listened to my gut from day one.

Chapter 18

Jason

Practice absolutely sucked. This was the first time where I didn't want to touch Clarity and practice our choreography. Not because she did anything wrong. It's actually the opposite: *I did everything wrong.*

I knew I should've broken up with Tiffany last week. I should've put a lid on my feelings for Clarity, but I let the heat of the moment get to me yesterday. I didn't sleep at all last night. I probably should've taken the chance to call Tiffany and finally tell her...

Tell her *what?*

That I didn't have the balls to be a man and end things when the time was right? That I'm too scared to admit that what I did yesterday was unforgivable, and I can't handle it when people are genuinely angry with me?

Now, to make matters worse, I need to follow through with my original plans and drive Clarity home. I don't even want to take her anymore. Maybe I should text Cole and ask if he can bring her home after practice so I can go wallow in my misery, alone.

Footsteps thump up the stairs.

And now it's too late.

I grimace as I turn to face Clarity. *Shit.*

"Hey. I thought you snuck past..." I fade out. That's definitely not her.

Tiffany practically flies across the lobby, appearing in front of my face with her fists swinging. I duck and dodge her other hand as it whizzes past my ear, and catch her other fist with my lip. The shock hurts more than the pain, and as much as I know I deserve this, I grab her before she can hit me again.

"You *kissed her?!*" She shrieks and resorts to jamming her knee at my crotch.

I let go and jump backward. My skin crawls.

She knows.

Tiffany stops trying to attack me to watch the realization dawn across my face. Her shoulders rise and fall in time with her breathing, and she shakes a finger at me.

"When were you going to tell me? Huh? You probably weren't going to say a goddamn word." Her fingers twitch as she steps forward. "No wonder you've been avoiding me."

"I was going to tell you."

Tiffany laughs, devoid of humor. "Well, I had to find out the truth from your new side piece! Why is she the one telling me, Jason?"

My heart skips a beat.

Clarity told Tiffany?

I'm not mad at her for letting the cat out of the bag. Seriously, I only wish that I would've broken up with Tiffany first. There's no one to blame here except me, and that's exactly what I say. "Don't blame Clarity for this. I'm the one who initiated it."

Tiffany lurches.

"Initiated what?" Cole shrugs the strap of his bag higher as he steps off the stairs, his face pinched in concern as he glances between us.

I clench my jaw. He's the last person who needs to be here right now.

She spins to face him and smiles like the Joker. "Your best friend kissed your sister."

Disbelief flutters across Cole's face, followed by annoyance. "Again?"

"Again?" Tiffany echoes him and turns to stare daggers at me.

I had no idea that Cole knew about that first time. He never mentioned it, or even hinted that he knew. Clarity is surprising me left and right tonight.

"So, this isn't the first time she's sought you out. She came back for seconds." Her hands curl into fists again.

"That's not true."

"Yes it is. She's never been able to leave you alone, or take no for an answer. You know why?" She tilts her head. "She's jealous of me. Always has been."

Cole's sticks clack together as he sets his bag on the floor. "That's definitely not true."

"Tiffany—"

She ignores us. "I told you to stop practicing with her. I said this was a bad idea. I should've listened to my gut, but I was a good girlfriend and encouraged you to follow your dreams, even at the expense of my sanity. Look where that got me." She's panting with rage. "I don't know how we're going to fix this, but we're starting with you telling that bitch you're done."

She's got this all wrong. Clarity isn't the one I'm done with.

"Tiffany, I'm sorry, but I can't do this anymore. We're over."

Cole inhales sharply. Tiffany physically recoils. "Excuse me?"

"I'm done with this—your" —I stammer and wave my hands in the air— "your bullshit! I'm *done*."

Her jaw drops, and I watch the last few ounces of love she had for me evaporate. That shock and sadness is the flint against the stone of anger. "You son of a—"

"I don't care! Keep calling me names and hitting me, but it won't change the fact that I'm breaking up with you. I'm done!" I throw my hands in the air. "No more!"

During our entire relationship, I can't recall a single moment when I've yelled at Tiffany until now. That's probably because our relationship is so beyond over that there's no more room for argument. No more competing with her impossible standards. No more wondering if what comes out of my mouth is going to start a fight that lasts for days on end.

Honestly, part of me is so relieved that I want to pick her up and carry her one more time, right out to the curb.

"I hate you!" Tiffany screams, her voice echoing down the halls. "I *hate* you!"

"Great!" I yell and point toward the doors. "Then go hate me somewhere else!"

Half of me expects her to throw her pacifier on the floor and keep screaming her fool head off. She shocks me by storming past, forcing me to jump out of the way, filling the hallway with the sound of her stomping toward the exit. A moment later, the doors slam shut. Silence follows. It's so loud that it makes my ears ring.

I rest my hands behind my head as I turn in a circle. My body is reacting like I narrowly missed a bear attack, and I take a second to regroup. Calm my heartbeat, get feeling back in my fingers and toes. Swallow. Close my eyes. Breathe.

I don't know what I expected our breakup to be like, but it wasn't that. The only thing that matters is that it's done. I can move on from one of the worst mistakes I've ever made in my life, and the freedom that fills my lungs is intoxicating.

Cole clears his throat. "I don't know if I should congratulate you, or slap you."

"Let's start with a congratulations." I shake my head. "I'm sorry you had to see that."

"I'm not. That's the best thing I've witnessed since me and Clarity... Hold up. Where is Clarity?" The spark in his eye gets snuffed out with alarm.

He's right. She was already taking a long time, and she's still not here.

"I have no idea. She was grabbing her stuff from the locker room." I start to pull out my phone to text her. Cole is already on it. He calls her, and frowns a moment later when she doesn't pick up.

"That's weird. She practically lives on her phone," he grumbles.

"Call her again." I step forward to look over his shoulder, and he smacks me away. "Text her. Leave a voicemail, or I will."

"Relax, Monica Geller. Her battery probably died or something." Cole pulls up Annabelle's number, and chews his cheek as the phone rings. Then, his shoulders sag with relief. "Have you seen Clarity?"

I incline my head to catch her reply. He waves me off again.

"Thank god. We—" he cuts off, then his eyes widen and he whips around to stare at me. "She *what?*"

"You already knew about that," I whisper as my cheeks heat up.

"She *slapped* her?"

I freeze. If Clarity actually laid hands on someone, then I'm going to keep an eye out for flying pigs on the way home. Cole stays silent, letting Annabelle talk on the other end as I dig out my car keys. He does the same, fetching his gear bag from the floor before heading toward the exit.

"Yeah, I'll be there soon. Okay. Bye." He hangs up and shakes his head. "Your girlfriend—"

"Ex."

"—is insane. She hit Clarity. Annabelle is bringing her home." Cole pushes open the first set of doors.

The cold November air is the perfect offset to the shock, the anger, that suddenly flares through my veins. "Excuse me? There's... What?"

As much as I want to say there's no way, I believe that, unfortunately, there *is* a way.

Tiffany never hid her disdain for Clarity. Even five minutes ago, I was the one who almost got beat up when she came at me swinging her fists. Except those two were best friends growing up. Me and Cole have definitely had our moments, however if push came to shove, I could never lay a hand on him.

Sure, the girls haven't been close since fifth grade, but still. The idea of slapping Clarity is like throwing a puppy in a river. Just thinking about it makes me want to cry.

"Tiffany is lucky that I don't go and wipe the floor with her ass right now. I'm going to deal with my sister." Cole starts off toward his car.

"I'll be right behind you." I click the unlock button on the keys, and my Range Rover chirps.

He stops to look at me, his eyebrow raising. "I don't know if that's a good idea."

"See you at the house." I keep walking and jump into the driver's seat. The engine barely has a chance to turn over before I hit the gas.

It's bad enough that I couldn't be there to protect her from Tiffany's wrath. The least I can do is help pick up the pieces this time around.

Annabelle's old car is already parked in the driveway, so I park on the street to let Cole have the last open spot beside her. My breath fogs in the air as I hurry toward the house, and Cole falls in with my footsteps.

"Nice job obeying the law at that four way stop." His shoes crunch over brittle leaves that have gathered on the sidewalk.

"What the cops don't know won't kill them." I grab the door handle and shove my shoulder against the door, unsticking it from the frame as it swings open with a loud groan.

Everything about the Janskys' house is the complete opposite of mine, yet this place is what I consider home, from the people who occupy it to the mismatched furniture that fills it.

"Hi, Cole," Lauren says from the kitchen.

"Close enough." I kick off my shoes and glance at Clarity's sneakers. The relief is as sweet as the smell in the air.

"Jason, sweetie, is that you?" Lauren pops her head around the corner. She wipes her hands on a towel and smiles, although it doesn't quite reach her eyes. Like mother, like daughter. "Sorry. I thought you were my son. Well, you still are. You know."

"*Ciao.*" Cole wags his fingers before throwing his gear bag into the corner of the foyer.

"Can you please put that nasty thing in the garage?"

He grumbles and turns back around to oblige.

"It's okay, I know you like me better." I smirk when Cole gives me the finger. The joy is lost as I notice the empty living room. "Where's Clarity?"

"Upstairs. She's with Annabelle. They're cleaning up." She hesitates. "Were you...?"

"No, I wasn't there. If I was, I would've turned Tiffany inside out. I broke up with her, by the way."

Lauren's shoulders collapse with relief. "Oh!" She clears her throat and wrangles her face into submission. "Oh. I'm sorry."

"Don't apologize. It's about time he banished the Wicked Witch of the West." Cole slips into the kitchen and swipes his finger through a bowl on the counter. Lauren reaches back to pop him with her towel, and he shrieks.

"It's okay. I'm going to run upstairs." I turn the corner and bound up the stairs, taking them two at a time in pursuit of Clarity. I crane my head as I approach the end of the hall, mustering the bravery I didn't have back in the spring when something similar happened after Sterling and she broke up.

There's a light under the bathroom door. Quiet, muffled voices seep through the crack, and they come to a screeching halt when I raise my fist and rap on the door.

Soft footsteps pad closer, followed by Annabelle asking, "What's up?"

"Please let me in."

"Oh, it's you." The door opens, and Annabelle rests both hands on the doorframe like a bouncer as she looks me up and down. "If you're going to look me in the eye and say that you're still with her, I'm going to push you right back down the stairs."

"No, I broke up with her. We're done. Please let me in," I plead.

Satisfaction crosses Annabelle's face as she drops her hands, then glances over her shoulder for approval.

"It's okay," Clarity says softly.

Annabelle steps toward me, forcing me to move backward. She uses this moment to get up in my face, her eyes flashing between mine as she lowers her voice. "It's bad enough that you laid your dirty hands on her. If you hurt her again, I'm going to make your life a living hell and make sure that you don't ever get the mercy of a quick death."

I nod as guilt chews at me. "Understood."

She scowls as she steps away, muttering something about hockey boys as she walks toward the staircase.

Clarity's eyes cut to mine in the mirror as I step into the bathroom. She lowers the washcloth from her face before turning around, settling the backs of her legs against the cabinets. "Hi."

"Hey." I pause for a moment to digest how relieved I am to see her. Her hair is frizzy, she's in the middle of wiping makeup off her face, and her right cheek is swollen, but the damage isn't as bad as I feared.

"So." She glances down and pulls at a loose thread in the wash cloth. "I'm sorry for my big mouth and... telling Tiffany."

"I should be the one apologizing for not telling her immediately." I try to will my feet to move closer, except I'm rooted in place.

Clarity shakes her head and keeps her eyes trained down. "That's just the thing. It wasn't my place to tell her. I was overwhelmed after that stupid— after practice, and it just slipped out."

"It's okay. Well, it's not okay that she hit you in response." That anger from earlier resurfaces, and I redirect the emotion by swinging the door shut behind me and walking over to her, taking the washcloth out of her hands. She sidesteps out of the way as I turn on the sink, dunking the cloth under.

"It was warranted. I was so angry when I found out that Sterling was cheating on me that I probably could have punched him in that moment. I just feel so gross being on the other side of the problem. Now I'm the problem."

Something checks deep in my soul, like a jockey correcting their mount.

"Don't talk about yourself like that. You and I both know that you've never been the problem." I shut off the sink.

Clarity snorts and watches my hands. "The way I remember it, I always have been."

"Why's that?" I turn to her and cup her face in my hand, using the other to swab the cloth under her eyes, catching the final smears of mascara.

I realize what I'm doing at the same time a bright blush bursts over her cheeks—embarrassment, probably—and my hands tingle as I pull away, passing the cloth over as fast as I grabbed it.

She takes it. "Let's start with me forcing you into a contract to skate with me."

"*I* signed the contract."

"I could've gone solo."

"No, you wouldn't have."

She purses her lips. "Okay, well, you guys have been doing just fine over the last year until I got involved."

"Wrong again. We've never been fine, because I never wanted Tiffany." The words fall out before I can stop them, and my alarm is mirrored on her face. I already know how she's going to respond because this isn't the first time we've had a conversation like this. I've got my walls built and fortified, so whatever she's about to say can't hurt me.

To my surprise, Clarity stays silent. She twists the cloth in her hands. For a moment, I think that's the end of the conversation, until she finally glances up at me and furrows her eyebrows. She's staring at my mouth, and my heart jackrabbits.

"Seems like I'm not the only one who received Tiffany's wrath." She takes the initiative to reach out this time, swiping at the cut on my lip.

I wince at the burn and let her finish before asking, "Speaking of, what happened between you two?"

Clarity eyes widen. Her shock is palpable enough to make me backpedal.

"Not that it matters now," I hurry to add, "but I never understood why you guys were best friends one day, then enemies the next. Nothing has been the same since, and nobody knows why."

"She never told you?" She folds the cloth before setting it down.

"Never. I can imagine this is a surprise, but she didn't like to talk about you." I try to lighten the mood. Unfortunately, my joke falls flat.

She manages to give me a half smile. "No one except my parents and Annabelle knows what happened. Cole put the pieces together. Tiffany swore me to secrecy, and I think we've both got too embarrassed to ever try talking about it."

I cross my arms and stay quiet, letting her choose whether she wants to say anything. Given the look on her face, she's obviously trying to come up with an answer for that herself. After a moment she keeps talking.

"It was a few weeks before fifth grade ended. Annabelle and I were going to spend the night at Tiffany's. Her parents left for the afternoon, and she wanted to go in the pool." Clarity's eyes become hazy with the memory. "We weren't supposed to swim without an adult home, but Tiffany kept saying it was fine. She told us we would be in and out before they got back."

Her voice wavers. My chest pulls tight with dread.

Cole almost never wanted to hang out with the girls when Tiffany was around, so it's not like I had the chance to analyze that trio's relationship. But I do remember when Annabelle and Tiffany would come over to the Jansky's house, Tiffany was always the ring leader. Not that either of the other girls ever fought against her.

"She started climbing up onto the pool house roof," Clarity continues. "Which we were also sworn from doing, but she jumped off even when we told her no. She did it over and over. We begged her to stop, except she wouldn't listen."

I can picture Tiffany's backyard from the handful of times I've been over there, and her words make me wince. That pool house is a few yards away from the pool, and it's not like the roofline is close to the ground. One wrong move and a person could easily splat on the concrete.

Clarity runs a hand over the ends of her hair, twisting them around her fingers. "She dragged me up there next. I told her I didn't want to, and she got frustrated and told me I was being dramatic, and boring, and that I should try it once."

I can barely catch my breath. "What did you do?"

"I tried to move around her to go back down the ladder, but she pushed me."

My stomach plummets.

"I slipped, and my knees hit the shingles first." Her voice tremors. "I rolled off the edge and barely made it into the water. I hit the edge of the pool on the way down, which knocked the breath out of me. I had a hard time kicking because my knees were raw, but I came up choking on the chlorine and my cuts were bleeding, and Tiffany was screaming at me. Calling me stupid for not jumping, and a dumb klutz."

"Jesus. That's..." I fade out, unsure how to finish the sentence.

That's terrifying, and twenty different shades of messed up. The imagery of Clarity getting shoved off that roof nearly makes me sick. Tiffany should be counting her lucky stars that she didn't immobilize her friend. If I would've known about this, I never would've gotten together with her.

Her eyes drop to the tile, blinking quickly as if she can't believe she's finally saying this out loud. "Annabelle ran over to the neighbors, and they came racing over. They called her parents, so they got home and called my parents. And it was just a mess."

Clarity exhales shakily.

"Tiffany got in a *lot* of trouble, and she blamed me, saying that I just wanted the attention. She said that I made everything harder for her at school, and I guess I ruined her summer because she wasn't allowed in the pool at all for the rest of the year. My parents didn't want me to be alone with her again, and her parents grounded her from seeing her friends for a while. And I... I don't know. It was easier to avoid her than deal with all of that."

She looks down at her hands. "We never talked again. I think there's always been a part of me that didn't want to know if she actually meant harm or if it was a stupid accident. Sometimes I wonder if things would be different if I would've found the spine to just jump."

Her voice cracks on the last word. I step closer without thinking and wrap my arms around her. She quietly sinks into me.

I bury my face in Clarity's hair as she presses her face into my shoulder, a few of her tears soaking through the fabric of my shirt. She's trembling as her body lets go of the emotion.

My own eyes sting, and my chest aches with the reality.

She fell off a roof, almost drowned, and thinks she deserves the fallout. I never knew, and never thought to ask or push the subject.

As much as I want to, there's nothing I can do to go back and fix the past. Not for myself, Tiffany, or Clarity.

Instead, I do what I can now. I stay with her.

July 2015 - Age 16
Clarity

I t's a wonder I get any sleep the night Cole and I get home from the 4th of July party. My conscious is so guilty when I wake up the next morning that it literally makes me sick. Or maybe that's the alcohol finally fighting back.

My entire bedroom spins as I pace back and forth like a kenneled dog. No, I *should* be kenneled. Brought straight to jail, because what was I thinking? That kissing Jason would fix everything that's been going on between us? If anything, it's made our dynamic ten times worse. I was supposed to keep my crush on him buried forever.

I can't go downstairs. If I go down there, my mom will take one good look at me and *know*.

I can't find solace in Cole—hell, if he found out, he'd kill me before going out and killing Jason. I can't tell Annabelle or Victor. And I definitely can't reach out to Jason one final time to warn him again that if he tells anyone, I'll kill him, first.

My life is ruined.

I flop facedown on my bed. My stomach gurgles, giving me a warning that I have sixty seconds until—

The entire mattress vibrates as my phone buzzes.

I pull a muscle in my neck I move so fast to grab my phone off the pillow where I left it. Someone took a picture of us kissing and now it's circulating on social media, staining my blog. Annabelle had a fortune teller tell her the truth. The cops are after me—

1 new Instagram notification!
@ster_it_up (1 DM):
Hey Claire, it was good to see you at the party yesterday.
Have any other plans for the week?

Sterling Mayer. That's why I can be nervous after yesterday. We hung out, he reached out to me, and he wants to see me again. He's cool, cute, and he's always been nice to me.

Forget about Jason. I don't need him when the obvious option has been in front of me all along.

That thought makes me want to sob the second it crosses my mind.

I need to distract myself.

Inhaling slowly, I tap on the notification.

Chapter 19

Clarity

"Now what are people saying?"

I turn off my phone and lay it facedown in my lap. "Nothing."

Cole casts me a cold, sideways look before turning into the school parking lot. "The comments I saw this morning beg to differ. They had a *lot* to say then."

"Nothing *new*," I repeat with the same sass that we, unfortunately, share as twins. I snatch up the lunch bag resting between my feet. "I'm handling it."

"The same way you handled Tiffany?"

"Let me out of the goddamn car." I unbuckle and grab the lock, pulling it up before he comes to a complete stop in the parking spot. The tires are still rolling as I jump out.

"Hey! You—"

I slam the door shut. I don't need to listen to his whining about safety. The only person I should've listened to was my mom.

After everyone left last night, she was the one who put a steaming mug of peppermint tea in my hands and told me that I should stay home from school for a day or two to let the drama die down. She gets nervous about the audience I entertain on my tiny corner of the internet as it is, and she's seen enough movies to know what kind of bullying happens following a situation like this.

But I know what would happen if I stay home. I might as well roll over and show my belly while I'm at it. Mom has her opinions, except Dad didn't raise a quitter. That's why I dragged myself out of bed this morning, hid the dark bags under my eyes with an ungodly amount of concealer, bypassed most of the Instagram stories I was tagged in and the hate comments that were left on my blog overnight, and got in the car with Cole to go to school.

Regret is already making my feet heavy as I walk toward the entrance. Other kids are getting out of their cars, staring at me, pointing, whispering. A group of girls walk down the sidewalk. I recognize them from the hockey team at the same time they notice me, and the words of the blonde girl in the back float to me on the breeze.

"I can't wait to read her blog post tonight: 'How to ruin your reputation in ten easy steps.'" She grins as her friends laugh.

Cole catches up with me as embarrassment crawls over my skin.

"Funny," he raises his voice as he adjusts the collar on his jacket. "I thought of a better title: 'How to stay bitter when no one wants you, part one: run your mouth and hope it distracts from your ugly personality that matches your face.'"

"Don't start." I smack his arm. He keeps his attention trained on the blonde, and even quirks an eyebrow as her group comes to a stop. She spins around, her smile falling.

"Relax, Cole. If your sister didn't want people talking, maybe she shouldn't be throwing herself at taken guys."

Those words don't settle well in my already-upset stomach.

"You're just pissed no one's ever looked at you long enough to even think about being with you, Marcy. The only thing my team ever has to say about you is how they wish you'd get out of the way of the vending machine. You should stop worrying about those Nutty Buddy's and start thinking about how you can defend the ice better. You've got all that mouth and no trophies to show for it. You want to talk about something embarrassing? Let's start with your hockey career."

"Dude!" I hiss. No matter what people say about me, there's no need to attack the accomplishments of other people—or lack thereof. I'd be the first to know how that feels, and I recognize the hurt that flashes across Marcy's face.

Okay, maybe it's a *little* satisfying considering the situation, but still. There's no need for Cole to rip into her like that.

"You're such a dick," one of her friends says angrily and puts her hand on Marcy's shoulder, shoving her forward as their group walks away.

Marcy shoots us one last glare. "You two are cut from the same cloth."

"Tell Tiffany I said hi." Cole waves at their retreating backs.

I grab his elbow as we step up on the sidewalk, forcing him to stop and look at me. "You need to knock it off."

"What I should've done is knocked some sense into her."

"Thank you for standing up for me, but I'm a big girl." I let go of him. "I can take care of myself."

His lips twist. I know he wants to argue, because I do the same thing when sharp words are on the tip of my tongue. Surprisingly, he raises his hands up in surrender. "Sue me for looking after my younger sister."

"Hardly." I continue toward the school entrance. "By two whole minutes."

"That was the best two minutes of my life." He grins, then yelps when I punch his arm. "Ow!"

"Stop being so dramatic." I put space between us when he squares up. My phone vibrates in my pocket, and I take it out at the same time he drops the act and takes out his phone, too.

"An all-team meeting? What the hell?" Cole lifts his head. "Did you get the email, too?"

"Yeah." I skim through the email that Coach Ortiz, Coach Lloyd, and Coach Vines sent over, explicitly stating that all practices are pushed back tonight for a mandatory meeting. "Why not put me on a pedestal in front of everyone and make me juggle while we're at it? People are already talking about me, so let's make it worse." I huff and slide my phone back in my jeans.

"What are you talking about? Maybe someone messed with the hockey equipment again. Don't assume that everything is about you." Cole grabs the entrance door before I can shut it in his face. If it weren't for the smirk on his face, I'd assume he's being serious.

"That girl was right. You are a dick."

He points at himself. "Pot." He points at me. "Kettle. Don't forget we share the same genes."

"I try my best to forget every day. See you later." I split off to the left toward the locker bay while he goes to the right. He salutes in response and gets swept away by the morning rush.

I keep my head down and use the same method that I used to when me, Jason, Cole, and Annabelle would play hide and seek as kids. If I can't see anyone else, they can't see me.

Except I'm not seven years old anymore, and this isn't my parent's living room. The stares itch against my skin like sand burrs, and their words buzz like flies.

"Did you see Gloria's selfie in the locker room after Clarity left?"

"I heard there was blood on the floor."

"The comments on her blog are more entertaining than any of her posts ever were."

"*I saw a Tumblr post that said Clarity told Tiffany about the kiss. Isn't that crazy?*"

"*I'm team Tiffany.*"

"Are you okay?"

I nearly startle out of my shoes and whirl around, pressing my back against my locker.

Sterling's eyes widen. "Jesus, I'm sorry. I didn't mean to scare you."

"You always... Never mind." I bite my cheek and turn back around to twist the combination into the lock. "What's up?"

"Just doing damage control again." He shrugs his backpack off one shoulder and digs in the front pocket, coming up successfully with a candy bar. "I thought I'd give you this to help you feel better. You've been getting into a lot of pickles lately."

I eye the Snickers like it's a venomous snake, and I handle it like one. I glance at the nutrition label. These 280 calories are the last thing I need to feel better, and the cheery label definitely doesn't help either. *You're not you when you're hungry.* "It's like my dad always says, it could be worse."

Sterling leans next to my locker. "How could it be worse?"

"I could be homeless, parentless, and left with no money." The candy bar lands with a heavy thud beside my lunch bag. Two things that probably won't be touched for the rest of the day.

"I'd let you live with me." He tilts his head. The way he looks at me makes me feel dirty.

"Let me count my small blessings." I start to gather my textbooks.

"C'mon, Claire." I grimace as he keeps talking. "I tried to warn you from the start. You're putting your trust into the wrong guy."

I set the books back down and stare at him for a moment. "You think so, huh? I always thought I had a good read on my partners."

I watch my words fly right over Sterling's head.

"Did you really let him kiss you?"

"*Let* is a stretch," I say. My lips tingle with the memory.

His eyebrows pull together. "So, it wasn't consensual? Wow. He's a winner."

"It wasn't like—"

"Do you remember when I told you that he was going to let you down? Look where you're at now, thanks to him. Guess your little boyfriend can't protect you after all."

A scream bubbles up in my throat. I probably would've agreed with Sterling a few nights ago after I got into that fight with Jason, but things have changed since then. I don't know what changed, exactly, except it's hard to be mad at him when he keeps showing up for me, even when it's hard. *Especially* when it's hard. And that's one thing Sterling could never do.

"What do you want me to say, Sterling?" I throw my hands in the air helplessly. "Obviously I'm not saying what you want to hear."

If we've had this argument once, then we've had it at least ninety other times in the past.

Sterling shrugs. "I heard that you still talk about me."

My jaw almost falls open.

The only time I talk about him is to tell Annabelle that he's still being a thorn in my side. Jason caught us in the training room the other week, and that's only because Sterling was already there with Juliette when I arrived. And the likelihood of Jason spreading rumors about Sterling and me is the same as my hair suddenly turning green.

He mistakes my shocked silence for admittance, and smiles. "If I were Jason, I'd at least defend you."

"Who told you that I talk about you?"

"People." He scratches his wrist as a few guys walk past. "Does it matter?"

"It does, actually. Because unless you heard it from my mouth, I'd stop being so concerned about it." I tuck both sides of my hair behind my ears as Sterling reels backward, smile fading.

His eyes jump behind my back and his expression darkens further. "I thought the janitors already took the trash out this morning."

I sense Jason before I see him. Something in the air shifts, like building electricity before lightning strikes. The hairs on the back of my neck stand on end.

"Funny." He walks around me, his chin lifted. But the real threat is sitting behind his eyes. "I was starting to think this day couldn't get any worse, and then I saw you."

Being in the same vicinity as these two is miserable. Especially when Jason tries to subtly place himself between me and Sterling. I'm not the one who needs protecting, because if one more person tries to fight my battles for me, I'm going to lose my mind.

"Can I help you?" Sterling asks lazily.

"You can start by walking that direction" —Jason points down the hallway— "take a left, then your first right. That's where you'll find the one person who asked for your opinion."

The counselor's office. If he were talking to anyone else, I'd probably laugh.

Sterling turns to me. "What did I tell you earlier? A real winner, huh?"

"You're not talking to her anymore." Jason steps in front of him, slicing Sterling out of my line of sight. My breath catches. "You're talking to me now."

I dismiss him. "Bye, Sterling." Better to get rid of him now before things escalate.

"See you later." He leans around Jason to get one last look at me. Jason steps toward him, and he scurries off. It reminds me of a stray dog being chased away from scraps.

Jason faces me, and the rage etched across his face makes me flinch. Between the article from Skate Snaps and this situation with Tiffany, old videos of him have been resurfacing as strangers on the internet scramble for content to hold against us.

That means the video of him tearing into that referee is recirculating, and I forgot how terrifying he is when he's angry.

Whatever he sees on my face makes him deflate, and he turns away for a moment to rub his face with both hands. "I'm so sorry. I was already pissed off, and seeing him didn't help."

"Really? Gosh, I just thought you didn't like my shirt."

He drops his hands to give me an unamused look. "You should've told me about that blog post last night. The one tearing you down."

I lower my gaze to the floor and inspect the scuff marks on my sneakers. "It was bad enough that you had to deal with my sob story."

Thinking about the way he held onto me while I clung to him makes my cheeks hot with embarrassment. That situation with Tiffany happened years ago. I know better than to let it take over me. I thought I had moved past that.

"Clarity."

I snap my head back up. I also know that I'll never move past the sound of my name coming out of his mouth.

"I want to hear about this stuff. I can't help you if I don't know."

"It's not your problem to carry."

He exhales hard through his nose. "I'm not asking you to dump every feeling you've ever had in my lap. But you don't have to pretend everything is fine to make it easier on me." He takes a step closer, and even though he doesn't touch me, I feel the warmth of his presence pulling something loose in my chest.

I want to tell him that I didn't say anything because telling him would make it real. I'd have to explain to him that some stranger out there in the world is affirming my biggest fear, that we're not ready for the competition. I refuse to do that, for his sake.

He stays quiet, giving me the opportunity to speak. I'm wrestling for the right words when the warning bell rings.

"We should get to class." I put space between us again, taking my textbooks out of the locker, shutting the door, and giving the lock a courtesy spin.

His eyebrows knot together, yet he smiles softly. "Way to change the subject."

I wave him off. "I appreciate you. You are my knight in shining armor, and I'd be nothing without you. Is that better?"

This time, his smile is very real. "I've been waiting for you to say that my whole life."

"You're so full of it." I shove his shoulder. He laughs, and follows me out of the locker bay. Frowning, I add, "What are you doing? Your English class is that way."

"I'm not leaving you to walk to class alone. When I signed that contract, the fine print said that I had to double as your bodyguard." He dramatically squares his shoulders as we enter the main hallway. Heads swivel as we pass.

I eye him, even as my heart swells. "Oh, really? I don't know if that's true."

"It is. I've gotten really good at reading contracts during my internship. C'mon, you don't need a tardy slip on top of everything else you have going on." He lengthens his stride, and I do the same.

I know I should probably turn him away. We've got to be quite the sight; the boy and girl whose names were run through the mud not even twenty-four hours ago. He's not doing anything to help those rumors, and obviously he doesn't care.

Truthfully, I'm just grateful he hasn't given up on me.

Chapter 20

Jason

I tap my foot as I watch each floor tick by on the elevator.

10.

I can't believe I'm about to do this.

11.

But I'm doing it for Clarity. That's reason enough for me to inhale, slowly.

12.

Gather my thoughts. My reasons.

13.

It's hard to find thoughts to hold onto when I've been thinking about everyone else but myself for the last few years.

14.

I'm going to shit my pants.

15.

The elevator dings and swooshes open. My heart jumps into my throat as I step out and curve around the hallway to the entrance of the office. I pull open the door and the sounds that follow are oddly comforting—end of day chatter, that noisy old printer my dad refuses to get rid of spitting out papers, acoustic music softly playing from the receptionist's desk.

I shove my hands into my pockets to keep from shaking as I walk past all the other empty offices. Kristie must be in a meeting, Jada always hangs out at the desks of her marketing team this time of day, and who knows where Paul has disappeared to.

The only office light that's on is at the end of the hall, and I don't know whether to be relieved or absolutely terrified.

Dad is on the phone as I walk in, pacing along the windows at the back wall. He barely gives me a passing glance. "I don't care. We have the bandwidth to move forward." He pauses to listen.

Great. I could be waiting another five minutes, or five hours. A quick glance at the clock on the wall confirms my fear: I need to be on the road to the rink in thirty minutes, otherwise I'll miss this team meeting. And I'm not missing *anything* this time around.

My attention strays to the hockey photos hung on the wall behind his desk. The ones of him when he was in college, and the ones of me when I was en route to my future in the NHL. My favorite is the one where the photographer captured me cracking a clean shot into the net. I remember that game. That's when I got the winning score at state finals in overtime during sophomore year.

I expect my chest to clench at the sight. Instead, it loosens with the memory.

There's a new path for me to focus on now.

I wasn't brave enough to break up with Tiffany when my gut was telling me it was time. The least I can do is not make the same mistake with this internship.

"Okay, great. Thank you." Dad lowers his phone and hangs up. He doesn't look up as he asks, "What's going on, Jason?"

"I wanted to let you know that I won't be coming into work tomorrow." Yeah. Real slick.

That gets his attention. "Why not? Don't tell me that you're getting roped into helping Cole with something now, too."

"I'm resigning from my position. It's not where I'm supposed to be right now."

He stares at me for a moment. I resist the urge to wiggle under the pressure, until he finally looks away to walk over to his office door. He shuts it. "You've got some nerve telling me what you will and won't be doing. Do you know how many people would kill for an opportunity like this? How many doors this opens for you?"

"I didn't ask for any of this. I want to focus on skating." I clench my hands together as he comes back over to stand behind his desk.

"Remember, you're the one who made that decision. You're the one who ran off to play ice princess instead of focusing on the real world."

Heat flares through my veins. "We're not playing around—"

"This isn't a game." He raises his voice over mine. "This is your future. Right here." He points at his desk, and my stomach twists.

"That's not fair," I whisper.

"What was that? Speak to me like a grown man."

My gaze slices to his. "That's not fair. I'm not saying I *don't* want to take over one day, I'm just not ready."

"Then when will you be? When will you learn?" His eyes are ablaze, reflecting my own.

"One day, Dad! I don't know! I haven't even graduated high school yet. There are other people who need me more right now." And I'm not helping her one bit when half of my brain, my energy, is spent here.

"Clarity doesn't need you," he snaps. I recoil from the sharp sting. "She's using you. The second she gets what she wants, she's going to drop you, and you'll have nothing to show for it. She isn't going to stick around when you're broke and jobless."

Tears prick the back of my eyes. I cross my arms, and use my right hand to pinch my bicep. Hard.

He's still not done.

"You're chasing someone else's dream and dragging yourself down for what? A childhood crush? You think *that's* stability?"

"She's one of my best friends. She cares for me; she wouldn't use me." I say that for myself as much as for him.

"I'm your father. I'm the only one left that actually cares about you!" he yells, and I flinch. "One day, you'll thank me. When you finally grow up and realize you need someone in your corner who will help you handle your life, not derail it."

As much as I was hoping we could have a civil conversation this time around, I shouldn't be so disappointed that this is how it's ending. Yet I'm shocked into silence.

This is how it's always gone in my life: I try to help around the kitchen, or cut the grass, or do the laundry. But when I accidentally drop a plate, or get one line crooked, or miss that one red sock, the hammer comes down and the opportunity is snatched away.

It's the same thing with Clarity. I try to prove—to her *and* myself—that we can be more. Yet something about me isn't enough, and she always finds someone else. If I were to walk away after this weekend, she would find someone else for the next season.

"Maybe you're right," I reply through gritted teeth and whirl around.

"I know I am." He scoffs and his chair groans as he sinks into it. "Use your brain for once, would you?"

Something deep inside of my chest feels like it's cracking as I grab the door handle, and I freeze.

Actually, we're both wrong.

When I wasn't needed in the kitchen, I helped in the yard. When I was banned from touching the grass, I ran into the laundry room. I've always played this stupid game of trying to be useful around the house, in the rink, at the business. Since Clarity told me to go find myself last summer, I went and found someone who could tell me who I needed to be for them. I molded myself into that guy to please Tiffany, to make things easier. Except it wasn't easier.

All I ever wanted was for my friends and family to be happy with me. But if I go to bed tonight thinking that I've made dad happy by keeping this job, I won't sleep another night for the rest of my life.

I've spent the better part of seventeen years being who everyone else wanted. I didn't lose myself because I tried to help around the house, or played hockey, or got this stupid internship.

I stopped choosing who I wanted to be. Until today.

If I don't get my ass in my car and go support my teammate, *my Clarity*, not the fake version dad is trying to sell me, I'm going to lose my fucking mind.

So, I turn back around.

"You know what? You're right. I need to start using my brain, so here are the facts: I was chasing someone else's dream. Yours."

Dad's head whips up, and he gets on his feet. "You—"

"*I'm* talking. I've spent my entire life doing every miserable thing you told me to do because I thought maybe if I just stuck it out, it would click. Except nothing ever did."

He raises his voice again. "Because you don't have what it takes!"

I raise mine to match. "Because I didn't want it!"

"Don't you yell at me, son."

"You're yelling at me!" I throw my hands in the air. "I want to skate. Not because of Clarity. *Me*. I want it for me."

"Dammit, Jason! Help me out here!" He slams his fists down on his desk. "You're throwing everything away!"

"Help me!" I step forward and jam my finger into my chest. "Help *me*, Dad! I'd rather do what I love and learn as I go than get handed success while hating every second of my life. I'm going to practice, and I'm not coming back here until the season is over."

Dad's chest is heaving, and his eyes are dark. "If you walk out that door, you aren't walking back in anytime soon."

"I wasn't planning on it. See you at home." I relish the way his nostrils flare as I retrace my steps out the door. My heart races, threatening to jump out of my throat and sprint laps around the building.

Pressing my palms against my eyes, I pause in the hallway for a moment and take a moment to recoup. I can't remember the last time I stood up to him.

A door creaks open. I drop my hands and watch as Paul creeps out of his office, his face forlorn.

"I'm sorry," I say. "I didn't realize you were still here. Hopefully we..." I fade out. The entire office probably heard us screaming at each other.

Paul walks over without a word and pulls me into a hug.

I make it to the rink in the nick of time. I'm getting out of the car when I notice the Jansky twins cutting across the parking lot. They might've shared a womb, however the only thing that's similar about them is their dark brown hair and the way they walk.

I jog to catch up with them, my breath vaporizing in the air, and they turn their heads in unison when they hear me approach. I aim for the space between them and throw my arms around their shoulders.

"How is my favorite pair of twins doing this afternoon?" I smile at the way Clarity's face turns pink. As if we aren't nose to nose during practice every night.

"Horrendous," Clarity says.

"Amazing, now that I've seen your beautiful face." Cole pats my cheek.

I drop the arm that's around him first, letting my other linger on Clarity's shoulder for another moment before letting her go. "My beautiful face isn't making your day too, huh?"

"Your ego is big enough without me adding to it." She elbows my side, though I don't miss the way her eyes flit from mine to my lips and back up again. Heat expands through my body. "You're in a good mood. Work must've gone well."

"It was great, actually." I try to be sarcastic, but it comes out genuine. "I got sick of the hoops that my dad was making me jump through, so I told him where to put it. I'm done with my internship for the season."

Clarity's neck nearly snaps as she whips to look at me, her eyes wide with shock and pride.

Cole laughs and lifts his hand. "Atta boy, Forbes! I'm proud of you."

I return the high five. "I feel like a whole new man."

"You look like a whole new man." Clarity wraps her arm around my waist and pulls me into a side hug as we walk. Butterflies let loose in my stomach. I'd fight with my dad a million times over if it meant she'd touch me like this again. "That must've been difficult."

"It needed to be done." I resist the urge to kiss her head. I don't know where to put my hands. Do I hug her back?

It's too late. She's retreating. Cole is watching. I don't know what to do. I'm not paying attention, and my foot catches the lip of the curb. He grabs my elbow before I can go down, and now he's smirking. I shove him away, and he shoves me back.

"Behave, boys." Clarity rearranges her scarf as we approach the doors. I rush forward and hold it open for her.

Cole blows me a kiss as he walks past, until I abruptly cut in front of him and flick him the bird since she isn't watching. He lifts his leg and kicks me in the ass.

I bite back my smile as I take my place as Clarity's shadow, although my face drops the second we begin to descend the stairs of the North Rink. Most of the other teams are already here, and heads are bent together as boys and girls murmur and laugh and hypothesize. The ones near the aisle look up as we pass and nudge each other, pointing at her and me as we pass.

She rolls back her shoulders, and I can feel the embarrassment radiating off her. I glare at the kids who raise their eyebrows, daring them to say something. I've started fights over much less, and I'm not afraid to get dirty again.

Behind me, Cole taps my shoulder. "There's Nick and Willie. Let's sit with them."

I relay the message to Clarity just as Nick glances over his shoulder, then does a double take when he sees us coming. He waves, then elbows Willie so he'll move over and make room on the bleacher.

Willie leans around Nick and grins at us as we pass between the bleachers. "There's the three musketeers. Clarity, you had me fooled. I thought you weren't going to show up to your own presentation."

"*My* presentation? I'm not the one who started this." Clarity sits next to Nick, and I sit next to her as Cole files in behind me.

The blonde ponytail that's in front of us turns around, revealing Juliette. Her eyes are heavy with concern. "Hey, guys. What an absolute mess. How are you doing, girl?" She reaches out and shakes Clarity's knee.

Montgomery spins and offers her a tight-lipped smile. "Do we need to beat somebody up for you?"

"Let's start with Tiffany," Cole cuts in. "Then whoever submitted those videos to that forum. You guys can start by taking a baseball bat to their cars, with extra ass-whooping on top. I'm willing to pay the extra charge."

"And some arson for dessert," Willie adds.

I roll my eyes before glancing across the aisle, over to where the girls' hockey team is gathered, to make sure nobody heard that. Of course they didn't. They're all gossiping like a bunch of old ladies at the nursing home, huddled around Tiffany. Her eyes cut to mine, and the look she gives me is lethal. A few of her team members notice, and one of them even flips me off. Guilt makes me look away, along with a strange sense of relief.

As much as I still wish I had handled our breakup sooner, I'm so glad that we're not together anymore.

"We're not stooping to their level," Clarity says, regaining my attention. "I'm doing fine. Fine enough. Too late to do anything about it now."

Nick shrugs. "Doesn't mean it doesn't suck."

A boy leans down from the row above us and taps Clarity's shoulder. I bristle and turn around first, and my stomach tightens. It's the same kid from the gym a few weeks ago.

Clarity glances back at him. "Hey?"

"Hi, sorry to bother you." His cheeks go pink, and I picture myself throwing him down the stairs. "Mayer said you dropped this." He holds out a lavender scrunchie. She didn't have that when we were walking in.

Clarity and I lift our gazes at the same time, a few rows back to where Sterling is sitting. He smiles and wiggles his fingers at us.

Oh, we're not doing this again. I already let him get away Scot-free in the locker bay.

She snatches the scrunchie out of Johnny's hand at the same time she grabs the back of my jacket, hauling me back down into my seat. My vision is fuzzy with rage.

"Thanks." Clarity turns back around and puts her hand on my knee. "Relax, Jason."

"I'm going to kick his ass," I mutter quietly.

"Whose ass are we kicking?" Darika sidles into the bleachers in front of us, forcing Juliette to shift closer to Montgomery. I must've not been as quiet as I thought.

"Yours," Nick says. "Nobody invited you over here." It's always hard to decipher from his tone when he's joking and when he's not. Considering the way Darika laughs, she takes it as a joke.

"That's not nice." Juliette glares at him.

"Yeah, Nick. Didn't you know we're at an anti-bully presentation?" Willie flicks the back of Nick's head. A few of the guys start mumbling behind us.

"Speaking of, when are we getting this show on the road? We're cutting into practice time." Nick cranes his neck to look down in the box where Ortiz, Lloyd, and the girls' hockey coach, Tracy Vines, are huddled together, talking in low voices.

"Any second, actually," Annabelle says from behind us, making me flinch. Nick nearly jumps out of his skin.

"God, don't do that!" Nick shakes his finger at her angrily. "Next time, I'm going to slap you."

"Anti-bullying presentation," Willie reminds him.

"Careful, Morris, your wimp is showing. Move over." Annabelle pushes Nick into Willie, which makes both of them complain loudly. I move closer to Cole, and Clarity presses into me as Annabelle ends up halfway on her lap.

We situate ourselves quickly as Coach Vines leads the small processional out of the box. Vines is the only woman that could give Ortiz a run for her money. She means business, and her blonde hair is always tied up in a ponytail, threaded through her baseball cap.

Down near the ice, Lloyd blows sharply into his whistle and silence immediately settles over the arena. He jumps into his monologue, thanking everyone for gathering together on short notice before Ortiz takes over.

"All three of us have been receiving more complaints because of this latest... turn of events. Many more complaints than we ever have, actually," she says. "This is everyone's reminder that bullying is not acceptable and will not be tolerated. All of us are on the same page for managing these matters."

Vines steps in and holds up her finger. "Which includes immediate termination from your team."

Worried chatter immediately bursts over the rink. I set my jaw. Annabelle and Cole look at Clarity, and she looks at me. I lock eyes with her, and I see right through the panic on her face.

I mouth, *breathe.* Her shoulders collapse.

Lloyd raises his whistle and gives it another ear-piercing blow, silencing every conversation.

Vines clears her throat. "Thank you. We will continue to keep a close eye on team relations, and if the situation calls for it, we will get rid of any problems. Please, everyone. Give each other some grace."

"I want to give Tiffany a beating that'll bring her an inch within her life," Annabelle grumbles. Clarity and I share another look. Nick snorts so loud that the sound echoes.

Ortiz shoots a glare in our direction before wrapping up and sending us all on our way to practice. She makes eye contact with me and beckons with her finger, making my gut twinge. I should've known that we wouldn't get away that easily.

Everyone gets up and makes a break for the exit at once. The two hockey teams split toward their respective hallways, probably itching to change and get on the ice. The back of my neck prickles, and I'm sure Tiffany is dishing out another glare. I refuse to look and find out.

A handful of the figure skaters head toward the lobby. I expect Juliette and Montgomery to be a part of that group since it's past their practice time. Much to my surprise, they step onto the staircase and turn to go downstairs, toward the locker room.

Juliette pauses once she's out of the way as Montgomery continues down the stairs. She gives us a small smile. "Keep proving everyone wrong, guys. Both of you are an asset to the team. Don't forget it."

Clarity returns her smile as she gets up, while I search her for a lie.

"We'd be nothing without you." Darika pumps her fist in the air. "We're stronger as a team!"

"How? You don't even skate with a partner, Darika." Nick stands and cracks his back.

"As if you'd know what a team feels like," Annabelle shoots back at him. "You might as well be skating alone for all the good you do."

Willie and Cole laugh. Nick looks like he wants to shove her, but refrains.

"Thanks, guys." Clarity waves at Darika and Juliette as they walk away, then turns to the boys. "Good luck at practice."

Nick raises his fist for a bump, which both of us oblige. "You too."

Willie pulls us in for a group hug. "Later, Jansky. Love you, Forbes. I respect both of you."

"Thanks." My mouth tugs up and I gingerly pat his back. I take this moment to glance up at the bleachers. Sterling is watching as he steps out of his seat, and I make sure to lay my hand on Clarity's back. His eyes tighten, and I look away as Willie lets us go to catch up with Nick and Cole. Clarity and I continue down the stairs.

Vines and Lloyd have already disappeared in the direction of their rinks. Ortiz is waiting around the corner with her arms crossed. We're the only ones left near the bleachers, yet she keeps her voice low. "Jansky, do you need to tell me something?"

Clarity comes to a stop, and I glance at her. At this point, I thought her secrets were Ortiz's secrets. She looks equally as confused. "What?"

"Do you have an eating disorder?"

I inhale sharply. Clarity looks like she's been punched in the gut.

Out of everything Ortiz could've brought up, this is the last thing I was expecting. I've been dancing around that question for a long time, and she's throwing it out like she's asking for a traffic update.

Clarity squeaks out a half-hearted, "I'm sorry. Excuse me?" The look on her face is the exact reason why I've been avoiding this conversation for the last two months. My anger quickly comes back to the surface.

"I saw the article. We've talked about staying on a strict diet, but not so restrictive that you lose weight. I've been watching your physical condition decline over the last few months. It's no wonder you can't keep your focus on the ice. What's really going on?"

Clarity stares at her, shocked into silence.

I'm not. I step forward. "She can handle herself."

"I never said she couldn't. As your coach, I'm only concerned." Her lips tighten into a thin line.

I roll my eyes. "I'm sure you are."

Defiance flashes over Ortiz's face, and she faces Clarity. "For the sake of your well-being, I believe that it's in our best interest to cancel practice again tonight."

"Cancel?" She lets out an exasperated laugh. "We perform in a few days!"

"If I let you two on my ice after the events of the last few days—especially after that article about you, Clarity—I fear that you two won't even make it through the door at the Invitational." Ortiz glances at her watch. "I'd much rather that you two go home, rest, eat, and regroup. Come back stronger tomorrow. I already rebooked your ice time tonight."

I don't miss her dig at Clarity's eating habits, and I don't forget watching Juliette and Montgomery head for the locker room. Yeah, rebooked out our ice time right under our noses. Clarity casts me a look, confirming that we're thinking the same thing.

"A warning would've been nice," I say bitterly.

"I could've said the same thing when Kerr got injured, and maybe we would have found a different partner for Jansky so we wouldn't be in this mess right now." Ortiz eyes me. I should punch that smug look right off her face. "Don't tell me how to run my team, Forbes. Go home. I'll see you both tomorrow." She weaves around us and walks away. There's no room for argument.

I start after her to give her the same speech I gave my father, except with more colorful language. Clarity grabs my elbow and stops me in my tracks.

"Don't listen to her. I wouldn't have skated with anyone else."

"How dare she pull the rug out from under our feet like that?" I turn to face her, and the sadness that's rippling in her eyes almost sends me right down the hallway again. "We're not the problem. *She* is. Dress rehearsal is tomorrow!"

"I know." She inhales shakily. "I don't know what we're going to do." Saying that tips her over the edge, and tears swell in her eyes as she says, "I don't know *what* to do."

"Hey. Look at me." I bend down to her eyeline and reach out for her hand. She grabs it, her palm trembling. "We've got this. *You've* got this. Do you remember what your dad always used to tell us?"

"Don't touch the thermostat."

"Okay, not that one."

She shakes her head.

"It'll be alright in the end, and if it's not alright, it's not the end." I search her eyes. "This isn't the end, C.J. Alright?"

"Right," she whispers. Then she turns around and starts toward the stairs. I hesitate for a moment before following.

God, I really hope this isn't the end.

July 2015 - Age 16
Clarity

I 've never liked Sunday's very much because they're my one day off skating, and they're the one day that both of my parents work the lunch rush at the restaurant. So, the chores at home fall on us kids.

Cole went with them to help wash dishes, but I'm not faring much better outside, kneeling over our little garden, pulling up weeds.

The screen door to the townhouse is open since today shaped up to be a beautiful, balmy day, and I wanted to let fresh air into the house. What I don't expect is to hear the garage door open and close. Not when I glance at the time on my phone and notice that it's only noon. Nobody should be home for another four hours.

I scowl and stand. Pulling off my gardening gloves and brushing the dirt off my thighs, I step onto the patio and call out, "Hello?"

I think my dad has a shotgun in his closet, except I've never seen it before. I have no idea how to handle intruders. Rather than the burglar wearing a black ski mask that I was expecting, Jason pops around the corner.

I nearly fall over in relief. "Jason? What are you doing here?"

"Hi. I biked over. Sorry I didn't text," he says in rapid fire as he walks over and lets himself out the screen door. I step backward and try so hard not to notice the way his t-shirt is clinging onto his shoulders.

There's a lot of things I've been trying hard not to notice over the last few months, and the kiss we shared two weeks ago has not helped. I've been distracting myself with Sterling, instead. Him and I have seen each other almost every day since then, and he's been perfect to keep Jason off my mind.

"No problem. Cole must've not told you that he's working—"

"I'm not here for Cole."

I stare at him, tongue frozen mid-sentence. I recollect myself. "My dad—"

"I'm here for you, Clarity."

The way he says my name takes the breath from my lungs.

"What's going on?"

Considering the way he's looking at me, my gut clenches like he's going to kiss me again. That scares me because the part of me that I've been trying to bottle up doesn't know if that's a good or bad thing.

"I don't know." Jason throws his hands in the air. "Actually, I do. Goddamn it. I can't keep pretending that we didn't kiss. It's killing me because it's all I can think about."

"Then... don't?"

He laughs, loud, but there's no humor. "I can't! I can't do this anymore! You've always been the center of my world, and lately every time I see you, I want to kiss you. I want to be the one who makes you laugh and buys you shit. I can't be just friends anymore. This is killing me, and I know you don't want to hear it, but I've been thinking about this speech for two weeks and if I don't say something, I'll die. I want *you*."

I flinch.

"Jason..."

He points at me. "Don't tell me it's impossible."

I inhale to keep from crying as he affirms every single word I've been dreaming to hear for months. Years, even. "This is impossible."

"God—" he cusses and spins around, putting his hands on his head.

"It's not about you as a person. That's not it." I follow him as I explain, throwing my gloves to the ground. "It's the situation. I can't date Cole's best friend. I refuse to be the one who drives a wedge between all of us and ruins everything. It can't be me—"

Jason whirls around and shouts, "It's *always* been you!"

"It was a mistake!" I shout back. "I was drunk! It's not love." My voice cracks on the word, and goddamn it, I start to cry. "I'm sorry, but we can't be together. It'll never work."

His face shutters as he steps forward. "I'll make it work. You can't tell me what I feel." He lays a hand over his heart.

"That doesn't matter. I'm seeing someone else. I've been talking to Sterling since the party."

Finally, he stops. His shoulders fall, and I see every stripped emotion in his eyes as he stares at me in disbelief.

"No."

"Yes." I sob. "I'm sorry, Jason. I'm so sorry. I can't be with you. I won't let myself. You need to find someone else. It'll never work. It'll..."

He strides forward and cuts me off, wrapping me in his arms so tight that it feels like I've left earth and been absorbed by his universe. He smells like cologne and feels like home, and I fucking hate him for kissing my forehead. I hate him so much that I pound my fist against his chest until he pulls away, tears streaming down his face.

"You're sure?" He whispers.

"Go home."

He nods and bites his bottom lip but stops arguing as he turns around and walks away.

I leave my gloves on the patio as I run inside, sprint to my room, press my cheek against the carpet, and sob as my heart shatters.

Chapter 21

Clarity

@cutieontheice24
this is the longest Clarity's gone without posting... does anyone know if she's okay after everything that happened?? are her and jason still competing tomorrow??

↳ **@icedancelover**
She's probably embarrassed. If my "partner" kissed me and blew me up online I'd go ghost too lol

↳ **@oliviasblades**
Y'all really still blaming HER when JASON was the one cheating?? Tiffany's reaction was uncalled for but let's not pretend Jasons innocent

↳ **@iceduo**
can't believe they're still allowed to compete. the judges better not go easy on them just because of the drama

↳ **@skatewatcher88**
Not to be rude but jason's been nothing but a problem since he showed up. Deadass tanked her career in like 3 weeks lol

↳ **@amygazukskates**
Tiffany ate her up and I stand by it... Clarity's not a victim, she just plays one

↳ **@annabellelloyd67**
Okay, but you're all so loud for people who WISH you had their chemistry. They've been through hell and they're still skating. THAT's talent.

ꞁ **@tanyastrinkets**
@annabellelloyd67 Girl chemistry can't fix scores
ꞁ **@ice_tea_babe**
honestly hope they bomb tomorrow. this whole stunt has been so messy. it's bad for the sport.
ꞁ **@twincitytwizzles**
They're literally TRAINING right now why are you guys acting like she owes you a daily update???
ꞁ **@d.is.for.darika**
just wait until they come in first and all of you switch up. bookmarking this thread

"Alright!" Ortiz claps her hands together, the sound echoing over the ice. "Places, you two. Let's see where we're at."

We'd probably be feeling a lot better if she hadn't screwed us over last night and actually let us practice. In twenty-four hours, we'll have completed our rhythm dance and we'll be preparing for our freestyle. I swear, if we fail to step on that podium, I'm never going to let Ortiz hear the end of it.

Not saying that we're going to lose. I've never *not* been on the podium before.

Seriously, I think those hate comments I've been reading the last few days are starting to rot my brain.

I slide my teeth over my bottom lip as I take a wide arc toward the center of the rink. Jason meets me there, his eyes darting over me. Despite his little speech yesterday, he's been edgy all practice. And, given the circles under his eyes, exhausted.

I'm in the same boat. It's been a long time since nightmares have plagued me, except the combination of reliving that terrible memory with Tiffany, the recent internet comments, and the stress of tomorrow's competition has stolen my peaceful sleep.

"Ready?" He puts his hands on his hips.

"As I'll ever be." I come to a stop and roll out my shoulders before lifting my arms, holding my position. My heart begins to race. We need to make this perfect and prove that we're ready to compete. My stomach grumbles in disagreement.

Jason's blades scratch over the ice as he moves in, taking guard behind me, mirroring my position. I'm already breathless, and my lungs ache as I try to regain control.

"Breathe, C.J.," Jason murmurs. His low voice does nothing for the pounding of my heart.

"You got this!" Victor's voice rings out from the sidelines. I squeeze my eyes shut, which doesn't do anything but send black spots over my vision when I open them.

Ortiz starts the music, and it flows out of the speakers, signaling for me to break away. I nearly fall over in my desperation to get away from the sensation of his breath tickling the back of my neck.

My legs move of their own accord without any help from my brain, taking over the wheel when I'm still mentally three steps behind. Our routine is like clockwork: the chase, the capture.

Jason grabs my waist for the first spinning circle and pulls me so close that my breath hitches. I grab his forearms like I'm supposed to, however this time I genuinely have to use him for balance to keep from toppling over.

This catches him by surprise. I can hear it in the way he grunts and falters to keep upright. I hope no one is recording this mistake, too.

We're both fighting for our center of gravity by the time we're done rotating; Jason physically, me mentally. My brain is swimming. My eyes are heavy. I blink, my skates stutter, and suddenly, my knees are headed straight for the ice.

Jason takes over to wrap his arms around my waist and yank me up so quickly that I'm sure he's going to leave another bruise. He spins me around and grabs my shoulder with one hand, using the other to cup around my face. He leans down to my eye level, filling my vision with a perfect view of his green eyes, flooded with panic. He doesn't have to say a word. My tears are already answering his questions and tracing lines down my cheeks.

The sound of Ortiz skating over is scarier than being yelled at. I'd much rather take the anger of her words than the simmering disappointment of her silence.

Jason doesn't flinch when I bat away his hand and wipe my tears. He searches my eyes in a way that makes my skin prickle. It's like he can see right through the surface of my emotions, straight down to what's broken inside of me. I can't believe that he's still choosing to stand beside me after seeing it. Sterling would've never.

"That's not the way I wanted to start this practice." Ortiz crosses her arms. "Is this really the way you guys want to kick off the night?"

Jason spins around, his blades scratching the ice. "She stumbled. Give her a break, would you?"

"Neither of you can stumble in front of the judges tomorrow, or flail around like a chicken with your head cut off. You two know what you're doing, so start acting like it." Her eyes flash to mine, and her scowl deepens.

"Yes, ma'am," I whisper. My empty stomach turns again, and this time the pain spreads down to my toes and up to my lungs. Jason senses the shift before I do. He wraps his arm around my back like it's meant to be protective. He's holding me up.

"We're going to start by getting some water. We'll be back in a minute." Jason all but drags me away, and instinct makes me pick up my feet to move forward.

"You two have wasted enough time. We need every minute to prepare!"

He slams to a stop and faces Ortiz. "No thanks to you for cancelling our practice last night. All I'm asking for is one minute. Please, and thank you."

She blanches, shocked into silence. Anger quickly shadows her face. She doesn't get the chance to say anything. Jason is already herding me toward the boards again, his jaw clenched. My heart aches from racing so fast.

"Who are you and what did you do with Jason Forbes?" I mutter. I hardly recognize this opinionated boy.

He scoffs, and rubs my back. "I've been right here all along."

Victor quirks his eyebrow as we approach. I'm surprised to see Montgomery standing next to him, wearing a matching expression.

"I'm afraid to ask what that was about," Victor says.

"She needs water. Grab mine. Please. It's the green bottle." Jason points at the bench. I rest my forearms on top of the gate. My vision blurs at the edges, like a camera trying to gain focus. I feel like I've run through our routine thirty times in a row.

Victor starts to turn. Montgomery acts faster, twisting off the lid since he has two good hands. I glance up at him. "What are you doing here?"

"I wanted to catch your routine before the big day, but it looks like I'm a bad luck charm." He holds out the bottle, and I take it.

"You're not a bad luck charm. They've been riding the struggle bus for a while." Victor shrugs when Jason glares at him.

I raise the water to my lips, then bend over the boards and spit it out next to Victor's shoes.

He yelps and jumps away, banging his cast on the boards. "Dude, what is wrong with you?"

"That is *not* water!"

"It's raspberry lemonade flavored," Jason says.

"You could've warned me." The extra flavor sticks to my tongue. It's so sweet.

I should've known—this is the same kid that used to eat his entire bucket of Halloween candy in one night and never got sick.

"It's from an electrolyte packet. It'll make you feel better than regular water right now. Kerr, do you have any snacks on you?"

It takes Victor a second to realize Jason is talking to him. He still seems spooked about the puddle near his shoes. "Getting hangry, are you?" He digs into his pocket and comes up with a granola bar. I take another sip of this hummingbird food and wince.

"Stick your face over the boards and find out." Jason snatches it out of his hand, ignoring the look that Montgomery dishes out to him. "Thank you. Here, I'll trade with you." He softens his tone for me as he takes the water bottle from me and presses the granola bar into my hand.

"Absolutely not. Not right now." I try and give it back.

He wraps his hand around mine in defiance. "You need something. Your blood sugar is tanking again, and I'm not going to sit around and let it happen."

"No. I can't."

"C.J." He drops his voice. "You almost collapsed."

I look down at the wrapper. That's 250 calories I didn't work into my diet for the day. If I slipped that many extra calories into every day, that's 1,750 after a week.

"I can't have anything until after practice." My voice catches. "I'm supposed to watch what I eat."

Victor sighs.

Jason's expression shifts. I expect to see irritation or anger written on his face. The heartbreak that's there instead takes me off guard.

"You're supposed to compete," he says gently, searching my eyes, "and you're supposed to live."

And I can't do either of those things without doing this.

My eyes sting as the tears come again, hot, silent, and heavy. The wrapper crinkles as I tear it open.

If my stress levels during that practice were high, Ortiz looked one small inconvenience away from having an aneurysm by the time practice ended. Once I pulled myself together, she unleashed her wrath on us, making us run through the routine an extra time to make up for my mistake. Then again because she wasn't satisfied. Then again, because Jason rolled his eyes when she said that. Then we had to practice our freestyle and start all over again.

By the time I limp into the locker room and peel off my sweat-soaked training clothes, I'm completely, totally spent. I don't even notice that I walked straight past Juliette until I exit the bathroom stall in my sweater, my sweat-soaked hair thrown in a ponytail, windbreaker draped over my arm.

She looks up from where she's sitting at a high-top table pushed against the wall, bent over a black dress with a container of beads near her elbow. "How'd rehearsal go?"

"Ortiz is on one today. If we weren't ready to compete before, we definitely are now."

"She was the same way with us. I thought Monty was going to punch her when she asked for one more go." Juliette straightens her spine.

"Don't let Jason hear that, otherwise he'll ask Montgomery to hold her down so he can throw the first punch." I feel a little better knowing we aren't the only ones getting nit-picked, even if it's totally overkill. I float closer to the table. "Is that mine?"

"Yes. I got busy last week and fell behind, but all that's left is tightening up the beading. I wanted to finish it so I could send it home with you tonight. What do you think?"

"Oh, wow." I step forward and run my finger down the silver gems. My throat tightens. "Juliette, this is... Wow."

I don't know what else to say. The beads were red before, to match Victor's red pantsuit. Now there are different shapes and sizes of little gems that sparkle in the light. She didn't touch the deep V neck or flowy skirt, but I can tell the sides are tighter, as she promised.

"Thanks. It was a fun project. If skating fails me, I'd love to go to fashion school and become a designer." She passes the dress over, and I run my hand down the bodice.

"I'd definitely hire you to design my costumes," I reply, then feel a blush heat my cheeks. "Oh, my god. I'm sorry. I'm not saying that you're not cut out for skating. That's not what I meant."

Juliette drops her needle into the bead container before closing the lid. "Girl, stop. I know what you mean, and I take it as a compliment. Trust me, the way you skate, you'll be going pro before I do."

"Don't say that." Guilt washes over me. Thousands of people online would disagree. "You and Montgomery are phenomenal. You've always been the pair to beat."

"And so have you. Do you remember during freshmen year, when you and Victor swept the Junior Nationals? I'm pretty sure our coach referred to your program for months afterward." She laughs, and I crack a smile. We did have an amazing season that year.

She continues, "You've always performed with a different energy than everyone else. It's like you rub off on everyone around you. Even Jason has come leaps and bounds during his short amount of time on the team. Of course, everyone had high hopes for him, but it was hard to tell whether or not anything was going to come out of it. He's become a fantastic skater."

"He's always been amazing. An amazing skater." I catch myself.

Juliette shrugs. "Figure skating is different from hockey. You know that. You should be proud and relieved. Your luck has been awful lately, so I'm glad he's a good fit."

He is a great fit, and I am proud. I've been rooting for that boy since his first hockey game when he shot his first goal, and nothing has changed since.

"Thank you." I scratch my fingernail over one of the gems near the neckline. "And thanks again for doing this for me. You're saving my bank account." Along with my sanity.

"You're welcome. I'm happy to." Juliette gets up and pushes her chair in, then tucks her container of beads away in her bag. "See you in the morning?"

"See you then." I wave as she finishes grabbing her things and leaves the locker room.

I use this moment to look at the dress—really look at it—and I smile. Getting this dress back is one of the best things that's happened to me in weeks. I'll take this as my sign that everything is finally starting to look up.

Chapter 22
Clarity

I cast a sideways glance at Jason as we walk up the sidewalk toward the entry doors for the Bloomington Ice Garden, my breath drifting away in the cold air. This arena is where all of my dreams started, just twenty minutes south of Minneapolis. It's a funny twist of fate that I ended up here again all of these years later with the one person I kept convincing myself I didn't need.

He's been quiet most of the morning, sporting his usual game day expression: head down, furrowed eyebrows, blinders on. He always got this way before hockey games, too.

I've always loved to skate, but I never had an interest in getting rough like him and Cole. Mom surprised me with figure skating lessons when my brother and I turned six. While he was busy trying on his new hockey gear, she packed me up in the car and inadvertently gave me a lifelong dream: becoming a famous, world-renowned figure skater.

I took lessons by myself for a year, until I found out about ice dancing and begged for a partner. When I got matched with Victor, him and I worked together diligently for two more years. Finally, we were ready for our first competition, and it was a big one. My entire life felt like it had led up to that moment, and I left my heart out on the ice. All the late practices, swollen ankles, and time spent crying in the locker room were distant memories the moment we wrapped our hands around that first-place trophy.

Nothing else mattered. We didn't just win; I was proving to everyone, including myself, that I was good enough. To this day, nothing else matters. As long as I make it to practice on time, watch my food intake, and don't let Ortiz see my tears, I can be a winner. *We* can be winners.

Jason leads the way through the fray, carrying each of our bags in his hands. He uses them as bumper guards as he cuts through a thick crowd of French Canadians, given their blue competition jackets with the Quebec flag stitched on the back. They shoot him a look, and I hurry to catch up. They mutter to each other in French as I brush past, and I catch one of them say *"Off the Ice."* They all start to laugh. My cheeks burn.

"Wow, this feels like déjà vu." Dad falls into step beside me, craning his head back to take in the exterior of the arena. "Wasn't it yesterday that we were helping you pin your hair back and shooing you onto the ice?"

"Funny you mention that. I was just thinking the same thing." I reach up to fiddle with my earrings.

"Time flies, that's for sure." Mom steps around to walk on my other side. My shoulders loosen with the wall of protection, guarding me from the people who are starting to stare.

Mom reaches back to twist her hair in a knot, holding it at the nape of her neck as Dad opens the doors for us. We all show our nerves differently; Dad chatters like a broken record, Mom overheats, Jason turns stony, and I refuse to eat, completely nixing my already-meager appetite.

My stomach pinches at the reminder, mirrored by the tremor in my legs. I tried on my dress when I got home last night, and it was perfect, aside from a few loose threads that I pulled out of the bodice.

It's great that I can wear it again, thanks to Juliette. Yet when I went to bed, all I could think about was that damn granola bar Jason made me eat and how it would swell me like a balloon. I ate a bowl of fruit this morning, and that's going to have to be good enough to get me through the day.

"What time are you guys hitting the ice?" Dad stops in the lobby, scratching his peppered beard. People swerve around us like we're a car that pulled over on a busy highway.

"Senior rhythm dance starts at noon. We're the fourth pair to go." I glance at Jason when he sets his bag down on the floor to fish his phone out of his pocket.

"We have a little over an hour," he says as he checks the time.

"Do you want Dad and me to get you guys registered?" Mom's eyebrows draw together.

"No need. Ortiz had us pre-register. We should probably go get ready," I remind her.

She inhales sharply and steps forward, nearly sweeping me off my feet with a hug. "Go knock their socks off, honey. You guys have worked *so* hard for this. I know it won't go unnoticed. We'll be right in the front row."

"Something would be wrong if you guys weren't," I manage to eke out since she is squeezing all the air out of my lungs. I pat her back, and she finally lets go, her eyes damp with tears.

"I'm so proud of you kids." Mom pulls Jason into a hug next. He finally cracks a smile and pats her back. "It will be so cool seeing you two work together. It's sweet enough that we got to watch you guys grow up together, so this is just..."

"Mom," I cut her off as she scrambles to find the right word. "I love you, but we're on a time crunch."

"We'll put on a good show for you, don't worry." Jason picks up the bags again when she lets go.

"I'll distract her while you run." Dad winks and pulls me into a quick hug. "Love you, kiddo."

"I love you guys, too." I shut my eyes for a moment before stepping back.

Dad reaches out and slaps Jason's shoulder, since his hands are too full for a hug. "Don't drop my daughter, now."

Jason chuckles good-naturally and dips his chin. "I would never." Neither of us has the heart to tell him that he actually has, multiple times, even if only by accident.

"Just so you guys know, Victor and Annabelle are running late," I say as I take my bag from Jason. He begrudgingly lets go. "Do you mind keeping an eye out for them?"

"Of course not. We need to wait for Cole too, so we will all be there to greet you guys on the other side. Go get 'em!" Dad shakes his fist before grabbing Mom's wrist and pulling her away. She waves happily with her free hand as they disappear into the crowd.

I return her wave before letting my smile fall as I turn away, Jason on my heels.

"See you on the practice ice?" he asks.

"For sure. Stay out of trouble," I try to say lightheartedly, except it comes out more serious than I mean it to.

"You're one to talk, Miss Drama Magnet." He nudges me with his elbow. I knock my elbow against his ribs in reply, which makes him laugh as we split off.

I get caught up for a moment by event volunteers that are separating the show spectators from athletes. A quick confirmation keeps me going down the correct hallway.

Pushing the locker room door open, I stop in my tracks. It's a flurry of activity here. Athletes are buzzing around, changing and powdering and adjusting last minute things. Coaches run around, calling out for their team members.

I chew my cheek as I slip back to the bathroom stalls, choosing the closest empty one. Setting my bag on the floor, I dig out the dress and change. My fingers find the zipper in the back, and I grimace as I start to yank it up. I might be paranoid, but the fabric feels tighter today, pulling taunt over my stomach. I hold my breath as I try it again. Seriously, it zipped last night—

The seams start to split down the bodice, popping like kernels, one after another.

Oh, my god.

"No," I mutter and drop the zipper to run my hands over the holes. "No, no, *no*."

My fat ass just ripped the dress open.

I can't breathe, and I can't get it off fast enough. My skin crawls with goosebumps, exposed to the cold air as I wiggle my fingers through the open holes.

I shouldn't have listened to Jason and taken that damn granola bar. I could've taken smaller portions of dinner over the last few months. Or maybe I should've listened to those trolls a few years ago when they left nasty comments on my blog, telling me to quit and do better things with my time, like taking a weight loss course.

It's too late for any of that. What I really need to do is find Juliette. She fixed this dress once, and maybe she can do it again. I just need to find her. Now.

I go through the motions of putting my practice clothes back on, and I stumble out of the stall. A few girls look at me in the mirror, and the one in the middle spins around.

"Hey, are you Clarity? The one performing with that hockey player?" She pauses. "Um, I think your shirt is on backwards."

I stare at her. Her smile falters.

"Clarity!"

Darika dodges and weaves around the other girls, her dark hair swept back in a low bun, her eyes rimmed with kohl and gold eyeshadow. Her eyebrows pinch together. "Is everything okay?"

I don't trust myself to speak. Instead, I hold up what's left of my dress.

She gasps and throws her bag on the ground to grab it out of my hands, sticking her fingers through the holes. "This isn't good. What happened? Do you have an open pocket knife rolling around your bag?"

"No, I have no idea." My throat tightens. "This has never happened to me before. I don't know what to do."

"You skate in less than an hour!"

"I know!" I snap, then regather myself. "I know I do. I don't..."

Slowly, my sentence sputters out as my gaze traces down to the floor, crawling over her bag. A ridiculous idea dawns on me like the first sunrise after a long, dark winter.

"What time do you perform?" I ask.

Darika looks up from inspecting the ripped threads. "Later this afternoon, around three."

"What are the odds that I can borrow your performance dress for our first dance? I can sweet talk Annabelle into running home for me later and grabbing a different dress for my freestyle, so I don't need your outfit all day."

"The odds are very high!" Darika shrieks and throws my sorry excuse for a dress in my arms before finding the nearest bench to set her bag on. "I always pack a backup dress. Ortiz wants me in my red one, so you can take the purple."

"Smart. I forgot mine." Lately, I'm lucky if I even remember to floss my teeth.

"That's okay. Here. Hopefully it fits." Darika holds out the dress.

"Either way I need to squeeze in that damn thing. My career depends on it." I take it before whisking her in a brief hug. "Thank you so much. You're saving me."

"It's what friends do." Darika beams as she lets go. "Break a leg!"

Gratitude makes my spirits perk up as I hightail it back to the stalls.

Darika is also petite, especially since she's only a freshman. It's still a tight squeeze into this outfit since she's shorter than me. The fabric is taut over my shoulders and around my hips, constricting my stomach. I'm afraid to move in case I rip the seams on this dress, too, as I finish preparing myself in the locker room and rush out to the staging rink.

I turn the corner and scan the benches that are teeming with all colors of the rainbow as different pairs prepare for their performance. One guy stands out from the rest, his blond waves styled handsomely compared to the last time I saw him. His eyes cut through me like a blade.

Jason rushes over dressed in his silver costume. He grabs my shoulders and searches my face. "God, you scared me! Where were you?" His attention dips to the dress. "And what are you wearing?"

"I'm so sorry. My dress is in pieces. I had to borrow one of Darika's."

"What?" He rears back. He raises his voice to be heard as a voice over the loudspeaker announces the ice dancing performances coming up. "Pieces? How—?"

"I don't know. We need to focus. Right now, the competition is more important."

"Right." The scowl on his face makes me think that I'm actually not right.

"C'mon, let's warm up." I walk over to an open chair and sit down, tying on my skates as fast as possible. I've already wasted enough time this morning.

Jason follows suit, and I catch him periodically glancing at me out of the corner of his eye. The worried look never leaves his eyes, even as we join the masses on the ice and begin to stretch out.

I do my best to ignore the pairs that nudge each other and nod their heads in our direction, whispering in each other's ears. I know they're talking about us, and that knowledge doesn't do anything to ease my mind. I never thought I'd miss the days when I couldn't make a full lap around the rink without people stopping me to chat, talking about how much they love my content and how cool it is to finally meet me. I'm pretty sure everyone here is basking in my misery.

Jason must notice as well, considering he's looking at every person we pass like he's entering a boxing ring with them. He's not going to do any good for the rumors that are already going around about him still being a danger. He sticks close to me, his fingers occasionally grazing my waist.

I wish I could say it's comforting, but every touch feels wrong. That's because it probably is. I made him break up with Tiffany only a few days ago, and now he's out here skating with me because I pressured him into it.

Ortiz leans over the barrier of the staging rink as we approach, waving her hands. "Let's go, you two! You're coming up!"

"Time to shine," Jason grumbles under his breath. I don't answer. I have no words to comfort him. If I had anything left in my stomach to puke up, I would. I haven't been this nervous to perform since I was ten.

Ortiz falls in step beside us as we head down to the main arena, spewing last minute advice.

Juliette and Montgomery are stretching outside the boards of the rink with a handful of other upcoming skaters. Juliette looks up first, her eyes lit with apprehension as she checks out my outfit. Her lips twist. "Good luck, team."

"Thanks," Jason says for the both of us when I don't respond. He puts a hand on my back to keep me moving when I begin to slow down. Ortiz keeps going with her pep-talk, although it sounds like she's speaking above water while I'm being held under.

Beyond the boards, the crowd cheers as the announcer's voice echoes over the ice. "Next we have a fan favorite, Clarity Jansky! She is partnered with a new face for the rest of the season, Jason Forbes…"

A small whimper escapes my throat. If Victor was here, he would be taking my hand and leading me on the ice with a Broadway smile.

Ortiz pushes us. "Go! Head in the game! Make me proud!" Jason shoots her a vicious glare.

My ears ring as he and I split off, a practiced smile on his face, a taunt one on mine.

I try to look for my parents and friends. I can't find them. Instead, my eyes land on four people wearing white jackets, sitting next to the judges booth. My fingertips immediately lose feeling as they make eye contact with me and smile. USFSA officials. They can put in a good word with Team USA, even open doors to Four Continents or World's.

I'm so caught up in them that I almost get away with lapping Jason. He's already settling in place. Embarrassment causes my cheeks to flush as I hurry over.

He tucks his face down into mine, and my heart skitters when I realize he's about to kiss me. No, not a kiss. His smile has fallen, overtaken with fret. "Clarity, I don't think we—"

"It's time." I put my back to him. My arms shake as I raise them, settling in my position. An ocean roars in my head, the strength of the tide pulling on my neurons, threatening to wash away everything and take it out to sea.

Jason huffs as he mirrors me. The announcer says something that's lost on me. Lovely music starts to play.

Damn it. *My* music.

Jason is already wheeling away in a show of power. I'm lost as I bound forward, the bright lights above slicing across my line of sight.

I almost forget to slow down, slamming my heels down as he flies around my side, flying backward in an arc to face me. My path and momentum barely take me into his arms. Another second and I would've been out of his reach.

He grabs my waist and picks me up for a moment, pulling me toward his body, his abdomen against my back. I grab his forearms as he lets me back down and keeps his hold on me, guiding us in a spinning circle.

I raise my left leg at the same time Jason does with his, and our circle gains speed. We hold the move. Actually, he holds me in the move. I'm already dizzy. I feel like my brain stem is gone, leaving my brain to clunk around in my empty head. The officials are going to watch it roll across the ice and end my career forever.

That would give the internet something to talk about.

He lets go so we can move on.

I stumble. I don't know what I'm doing here. I can barely breathe, barely catch my breath as I glide toward the wall. I can't focus as Jason presses me into the next move.

He shouldn't be here, either. I made him end his internship. I broke up his relationship. I am the home wrecker. I am a body wrecker, too. Useless. I need something sweet so I can taste it again as I let it resurface, regaining control.

I am in control of my body.

I am so wildly out of control that I can't do anything but cling to Jason as he swoops me off my feet, preparing to flip me over in the reverse rotational lift. I've always trusted him more than anyone else, even my brother. He will always take care of me.

Jason tosses me over his shoulder, and I rag doll, my body screaming, *enough!*

The ice sure is white today. It's the last thing I see before my vision goes black, my head connecting with the ground.

October 2015 - Age 16

Jason

I don't usually wake up early on Saturday mornings to go to the rink, but Coach Lloyd keeps telling me that this is going to be *my year*.

He's been hearing through the grapevine that different scouts from colleges in the area are planning to attend different games over the season, so I need to be dutifully prepared to keep my title as the best center in the midwest for high school hockey. Getting extra time on the ice without any other distractions will be my golden ticket to a full ride, despite being in my junior year.

There's only one other car in the lot—the janitor—so I park my car near the building. The brittle October wind tries shutting the car door for me and I shiver as I grab my bag out of the backseat before hustling up the sidewalk. Walking into the cold rink is a relief. At least there's no breeze in here, and the janitor remembered to keep the door unlocked for the early birds.

Following the hallway through the main lobby, I'm not surprised that most of the other walkways that split off the lobby are still dark. The only one that's lit is the one that leads to the North Rink. I follow the lights because the light switches that I need are down this direction, anyway.

The wheels on my bag clack so loud over the floor that I almost miss the loud *bang!* of blades hitting hard ice. I guess I'm not the only one who had the idea of getting here early. Curiosity gets the better of me, and I creep forward until the wall breaks, transitioning into a steel railing.

Immediately, I can't breathe.

I should've known that Clarity would be here. Surprisingly, she's not with Victor.

She's alone.

Only a few lone lights ignite the ice, keeping a watchful eye as she flies around the curve of the far boards and cuts diagonally across the arena, pushing off her feet and flying into the air, spinning like a top. I hold my breath until she lands, but, impossibly, she lifts off again. Her black hair whips through the air, her face bent in concentration.

It's so good to see her that it almost sends me to tears.

Lately, the only time I've seen her are in glimpses beyond the Plexiglass at practice before she leaves for the night or in passing at school. Now that I think about it, we haven't spoken in months. *Months.*

I curse and wipe at a pesky tear that slips out of my eye, my heart breaking with the reality of how close yet how far away I am from her. My feet ache to walk down there and tell her how beautiful she looks, but I listen to my brain, instead.

I turn around, whisk away more tears, and go home.

Chapter 23

Jason

Looking back, I realize that my life has been built around a series of lies.

It started before I was even born, when a woman I don't know had a baby with my dad.

I never questioned growing up alone with Dad until I started going to school. When I finally found the courage to ask him where Mom was, he said that she didn't care enough about either of us to stick around more than a few months after I was born. She left for work one day and never came home. Their love was the first lie.

Dad is the second lie. Everyone at his company worships the ground he walks on because of his supposed integrity, his ability to get shit done, and his no-nonsense attitude that gets expensive deals turned over fast.

At home, when it's just me and him, I see that integrity for the lie it is. He loves to tell me exactly what I'm doing wrong. I've been pushed to be good, better, and best, especially when it comes to sports. Except for figure skating, I guess. He couldn't be bothered to step away from work to come watch our competition—not that it matters now.

The third lie is the way I used to act around Clarity.

I pretended not to care that she shared crayons with Daniel Owens in kindergarten. I pretended not to pay attention to her skating alone on the lake as Cole and I played hockey. She fell and stumbled and tripped day after day, and I've tried to forget how perfectly clear and blue the sky was when she managed to spin. I didn't notice when she wasn't around anymore because of her skating lessons.

Middle school was no different. I acted like I had no idea that she'd turned into a stunning teenager overnight. I definitely didn't lose all sense of my vocabulary for a few months every time I tried to talk to her. It was no big deal when the hockey team was keeping tabs on who could talk to her for the longest. Although, my resolve finally snapped that day and I broke the nose of our goalie. After that, everyone left Clarity alone.

In high school, I found the courage to approach her alone one night. I couldn't keep lying to myself. I had been doing it since the day we met. The truth led to the greatest moment, the greatest kiss, of my life. Until reality crashed back down and Clarity reminded me that we could never go there again.

After that, I kept lying to myself to keep my heart safe.

Yes, I was okay dating Tiffany to frost over the pain. Yes, I was fine pretending Clarity didn't exist for an entire year. Yes, I could overlook the life draining out of her eyes and the fact that Cole scooted around every conversation that got close to talking about her personal life.

A series of lies, indeed.

If I had been honest with myself as a young kid, maybe I wouldn't be pacing in the lobby of the hospital, replaying the image of Clarity crashing to the ground, scarlet blood pooling over the white ice.

The taste of iron fills my mouth. I let go of my tongue and blink myself back to reality.

Big, fluffy snowflakes are floating down outside the window, catching the light of the setting sun. It's a sick reminder of how beautiful life is in the midst of such an awful situation. Outside of these walls, life continues to go on.

Victor huffs from the chair in the corner. "You're going to wear a hole through the floor."

I turn and regard him. The pinched look of fear on his face gives away the real reason for his snarky comment.

Annabelle is curled up on the floor beside him, asleep, using her jacket as a pillow. We've been waiting for hours.

"I feel so useless." I run both hands over my hair.

The most I've done to help today is kneeling next to Clarity on the ice, taking off my stupid vest to hold it against the wound on her head as the EMTs rushed over. After that, her mom went on the ambulance ride to the hospital while her dad, Cole, and I followed.

When we arrived, only the immediate family was allowed back in the room with her. Leaving Victor to steam, Annabelle to spiral herself into exhaustion, and me to wear a hole through the floor.

"I understand the feeling." Victor picks at a hangnail. "Doesn't get any easier, does it?"

"No, but at least the last time this happened, I was *with* Clarity. No offense."

"None taken. I'd rather be with her right now, too."

He's being sincere, except that makes me scrunch my nose. If anyone out of the three of us should be at her bedside, it's me. Especially if we're going by seniority. I'd fight both of them at the same time if it meant getting to her first.

Before I can say something dumb like that, the doors leading back to the emergency rooms click open. A male nurse walks out, his scrubs wrinkled from a long shift, yet an easy smile crosses his face when he looks at us. "Annabelle? Victor? Jason?"

"Yes." I nearly trip over my feet in my haste to approach the nurse. "I'm Jason."

"You got the right group." Victor is a little slower as he uses his good arm to push up from the chair. He nudges Annabelle with his foot and she groans. "Wake up, sleeping beauty. Time to go."

"My back." Annabelle winces as she pushes herself up and blinks at the bright lights.

"Pop an ibuprofen. Let's go." I try not to sound pushy since she's Clarity's best friend. From the look Annabelle gives me as she gets up, I didn't do a good job. She gathers her things off the floor and joins us.

"I'm Walt, and I assisted Doctor Carlson with Clarity's head trauma. She is awake and doing much better. I was sent to take one of you guys back to see her," Walt explains.

"Seriously? One of us?" Annabelle's eyebrows furrow.

I begin to open my mouth to tell her that I'll fight her for the right to go back there, but Walt beats me to it. "I'm sorry, but that's protocol. Only four visitors at a time. Three people are already with her."

"I'll go," I blurt out, cutting off the end of his sentence.

Annabelle and Victor give me matching glares.

"What makes you think you can go first?" Victor asks. "I was her partner first, and I've been injured before."

"I'm her best friend!" Annabelle complains.

"She's been my entire life since kindergarten," I say firmly and take a step toward Walt.

He stares at us, checks his watch, and sighs. "Look, my charge nurse is running behind. If we make this quick, I can take all three of you back there. Just please mind your P's and Q's, otherwise all of us will get in trouble."

"I'll dot your I's and cross your T's if it makes you feel better." Annabelle flourishes her hand. "Lead the way."

"Thank you." I could kiss Walt's feet as he leads us through the doors and back into the eerie hallway. Somewhere down the corridor, the wheels squeak on a cart.

"Don't mention it." He tucks his keycard back into his shirt pocket. "You've known her since kindergarten, huh? How long have you guys been dating then?"

"Spiritually or emotionally?" Victor raises an eyebrow. Annabelle laughs.

I ignore them, although there's no hiding the way my cheeks flame. "We're not dating. Just friends."

"Hm." Walt gives me a sideways look that I can't decipher.

I'm about to change the subject when Annabelle asks, "How is she? Is she going to be okay?"

"She's doing much better," Walt repeats himself from a minute ago. "We addressed the head wound, with the help of a few staples. She has a mild concussion, but she will recover in a week or two. The wound might take a little longer to heal, but she will be fine."

I can finally breathe.

"Her body's condition is a different story." Walt slows his stride as we approach a room near the end of the hall. "It will take longer to address that, but I'll let the doctor explain everything. Here we go." He opens the door for us, making Lauren, Aaron, and Cole look over.

I nearly mow over Walt in my rush to enter. I falter as I step inside.

The first thing I notice is how pale Clarity looks in the hospital bed, eyes closed. Her face, her olive skin, usually glows with determination. Now, her skin appears thin and pale as paper. Her black hair is braided back to keep the hair off the wound. A white bandage is wrapped around her forehead, protecting the side of her temple that hit the ice.

The room smells faintly of antiseptic, a sharp contrast to the floral perfume I've come to associate with her. Machines beep softly alongside the bed. They're unnervingly loud in the silence. An IV is taped to her elbow, and my chest tightens at her slender wrists—too slender.

I swallow hard, forcing down the lump in my throat as I gingerly shuffle forward, like any sudden movement might shatter her entirely.

"Jason. Thank you for waiting for so long." Lauren comes over, wrapping me in a hug that steals the breath from my lungs.

I close my eyes until she lets go. "You don't need to thank me."

I'd spend the rest of my life waiting for Clarity, but Lauren doesn't need to know that right now. She moves on to hug Victor and Annabelle. Cole reaches out, fist raised. I return the fist bump.

Clarity's eyelashes flutter as she blinks her eyes open and slowly turns her head at the sound of my name coming out of her mom's mouth. She smiles tiredly. "Hi, J.C."

I chuckle at the irony of the nickname and crouch at her bedside, reaching forward to tuck a stray hair around the bandage. "You stole my line."

"I know." Her smile falls, and her sweet brown eyes immediately fill with tears. This poor girl has cried more in the last few weeks than I've ever seen in my life. "I'm so sorry for scaring you."

"Do not apologize." I swipe at a loose tear that rolls down her cheek. "You're okay. You're safe. That's all that I care—all that matters." I manage to catch myself before I spill out my feelings in front of everyone. That same tired smile crosses her lips but doesn't reach her eyes.

Annabelle steps up next to me and I startle.

"Forget about Jason. You scared the shit out of me." Annabelle reaches out to shake her leg.

Victor crosses to the other side of the bed. "And me. I thought you were going to be the next one in a cast."

"No more surprise trust falls, that's for sure." Lauren comes to my other side, her gaze raking over her daughter. That loving yet worried look on her face is likely mirroring mine.

"You got it. I'll let Jason know the next time I'm about to pass out," Clarity jokes, her voice weak.

Cole shrugs. "I thought it was part of the routine." Annabelle looks at him like he's crazy.

The door opens again, and another doctor enters the room. Her mousy hair is greying and pulled back in a tight bun, her face reflecting the tension that comes with a high-pressure job. But her eyes are kind as she surveys the packed room. My attention drifts to her name tag. Doctor Carlson.

"Wow, you have quite the support system, Miss Jansky." Carlson shuts the door behind her, clipboard in hand.

"Only the best," Cole replies and steps back to join his dad in the corner, who's watching his daughter closely as if she's about to vanish into the sheets at any moment.

"I have diagnostics and a treatment plan for you here." Carlson holds up her clipboard. "Shall I have anyone step out in the hall?"

"No. I need everyone here." Clarity sits up.

"Alright. Well." Carlson grabs a vacant chair, pulling it closer to the bedside before sitting down. "I'll start with the obvious injury. You have a grade one concussion from the impact of falling on ice. Since you lost consciousness for a few seconds, your symptoms may take longer to resolve. But given the CT scans, I don't foresee any long-term issues."

Lauren, Annabelle, and I deflate simultaneously, grateful for the confirmation of the good news. Aaron steps closer, not looking as convinced.

"As for the not so obvious... You understand why you lost consciousness in the first place, correct?"

Clarity blinks slowly. "I was under a lot of stress."

Victor snorts, calling out her bullshit.

Carlson shakes her head. "Considering your height and frame, you're severely underweight. Clarity, you're way below where you need to be."

The tension in the air thickens quickly, like cheap oatmeal. Clarity goes so still that if it weren't for the heart rate monitor tracking the beats, I'd assume she just died.

"I take eating disorders very seriously." Carlson leans forward. "During the few short hours you've been hooked to a machine, you've given us reason to also diagnose you with bradycardia—having a heart rate, on average, of less than sixty beats per minute. Which will explain the fatigue and lack of energy.

"Dehydration is another common symptom of these issues, and is noted in your chart. I'm not saying all of this to shame you. But I need you to understand the severity of this situation. It is impossible for you to show up for your people" —she waves her hand around the room— "and yourself with this kind of lifestyle."

I reach over and lay my hand on Clarity's. More silent tears stream down her face. Aaron puts his arm around Lauren's shoulders, offering his support as she cries, too.

Carlson clears her throat. "We are making cognitive-behavioral therapy a must for your treatment plan. I have a few fantastic people to refer you to. Given your current state, you'll need weekly sessions for up to forty weeks. Your therapist will help you understand where these eating habits stemmed from, how to cope with them, and how to make better nutritional choices."

Clarity nods, as if she could respond any other way. She tries to speak, except tears clog her throat. All she can do is shakily inhale and exhale. I squeeze her hand, and she squeezes mine back. Cole continues to stand guard in the corner, unreadable. Victor and Annabelle are silent.

"I'll be back tomorrow once you've rested," Carlson says as she stands, "to check in and answer any questions you may have. For now, I will let you spend some time with your family."

"Thank you," Cole says quietly, speaking for all of us.

Carlson nods, resetting the chair she was in before exiting the room. Lauren and Aaron follow the doctor out, and Lauren bursts into tears.

"This isn't your fault, Lauren..." I catch the front of Carlson's sentence before the door clicks shut, cutting off their conversation.

"I'm so stupid," Clarity whispers, her voice strained. I let go of her to grab a Kleenex out of the nearby box, then pass it to her. She wipes her tears away. "What am I going to do?"

"You're going to get the help you need and figure your shit out." Cole joins us again, walking to the other side of the bed, next to Victor. He crosses his arms. "I tried to tell you that you couldn't get away with this forever."

Annabelle and I cast him matching glares. He throws me a look that asks, "*What?*" I roll my eyes at him before turning to Clarity.

"You're going to do what the doctor said and find a therapist. We'll help you recover, and everything will be fine," I say as soothingly as I can, attempting to convince myself as much as her.

Clarity laughs, and the sound is jarring given the situation. She balls the tissue up in her hand. "Nothing has been fine in a long time."

I can't argue with that. Nobody can.

Annabelle throws her jacket over one of the empty chairs. "We'll make the most of this situation. You can rest and recoup before hitting the ice again, and come back even stronger."

"We have Nationals in two months." Clarity looks at me. "Oh, my gosh. Where did we fall in the lineup?"

"I don't know." I was so preoccupied with her fall that I forgot to check the scores from today. All the attention turns to Victor.

The look on his face makes my stomach drop.

"The top ten pairs with the highest scores from the season are moving on." Victor takes his hat off and runs a hand over his hair. "We were in the top five, but since you guys didn't earn any points today, you dropped to number eleven."

Cole curses. I grab the edge of the hospital bed as the realization hits Clarity, and she deflates.

We worked so hard, woke up so early, and stayed up so late, to just barely fall short.

Barely.

She looks at me, and the heartbreak written on her face brings tears to my eyes. I don't know what to say. There isn't anything *to* say.

Our season is over.

Chapter 24

Jason

The weekend passes fast, even though it's the first time since I started skating that I've had two full days to myself. Okay, maybe not exactly *to* myself.

It's been even longer since I've hung out with Cole and Clarity like we were little kids. But that's exactly what we did, down to solving crosswords in the living room and working on puzzles in the kitchen since Clarity couldn't do anything else, thanks to her concussion.

Annabelle, Victor, Darika, Nick, and Willie came by for a few hours yesterday to play a board game since she was feeling better. It was a nice change of pace to slow down and enjoy the company of our friends. Take our minds off the results of the Invitational.

The downside is Monday comes too quickly. I don't care that it's Monday—Tuesday is arguably the worst day of the week, anyway—although I do care that all eyes are on me as I walk into school. Everyone must have heard about the skating accident.

Guilt has already been eating me alive without outside influence because of how deeply I messed up. Victor tried easing my mind yesterday, reminding me that Clarity was the one who blacked out. I told him that I'm the one who hesitated, and that by the time I dove to catch her, it was too late.

I let her dad down; I dropped his daughter.

My phone buzzes as I close the door of my locker, and I shake off the memory as I open Cole's text.

I just told off some chick that said you purposely dropped Clarity on her head to get back on the witch's good side. LMAO.

These people are rotting their brains online. Like go touch grass tf

If there's ever a day when I try to get back together with Tiffany, someone better check under my bed to make sure the real version of me isn't tied and gagged while my brainless clone is running rampant.

I start to reply, and glance up as I turn the corner into the hallway. It's almost like I manifested her.

Tiffany is coming down the hall from the opposite direction, and her eyes latch onto mine.

She's been avoiding me for the last week, and it's been the greatest week of the year. That's why I'm shocked when she weaves through the crowd like a fish going upstream to meet me.

"Hi?" I don't mean to sound rude—okay, yes I do.

"Hey. Can we talk?" Tiffany stands in front of me, forcing me to stop. I sigh. People turn their heads as they walk past, ogling us.

"Isn't that what we're doing?"

"I'm serious, Jason."

The things that Clarity shared with me last week cross my mind, and a strange mix of sadness and anger makes me consider ignoring her and continuing to class. Instead, I cross my arms. "We can talk here."

She glances at everyone passing by, and I cross my fingers behind my bicep that she'll reconsider. "Fine."

Damn it. I uncross my fingers.

"I was sorry to hear what happened at the competition. That had to be hard to watch."

"You mean hard to live through?"

She bites her lip. "That's what I meant." She reaches out to touch my arm. I step back. "I wanted to tell you that I know we didn't end things on the best note. I was hurt. I'm sorry."

"Were you hurt before or after you hit Clarity in the locker room?"

Tiffany blinks. "Okay, I didn't handle that well, but can you blame me? She was always getting between us. And look where that got her. She's not even skating. I just figured..." she fades off.

"You figured what?" I tilt my head and squeeze my fingertips into my arms, hoping the sensation will distract me from the anger coursing through my veins.

"Let's be honest. She couldn't handle the pressure. She's not who you thought she was." She flicks her ponytail over her shoulder.

Anger pokes me like a hot iron. I drop my voice to say, "You don't get to talk about her like that."

"Come on. You're all alone now." Tiffany flourishes her hand around the hallway to prove her point.

Little does she know I've spent more time with my friends over the past two days than I have in the past year.

"I really hope you don't think I'm done with Clarity just because she fell."

"I thought you'd realize I was right about her all along."

"You thought wrong."

People slow down as I raise my voice over hers. Some pretend not to listen, others are blatantly eavesdropping. That doesn't deter me. They're going to gossip and spread rumors anyway, so I might as well give them the facts.

"I'm not alone." I flick my eyes between hers. "And I don't want your sympathy. Actually, I don't want *anything* from you."

Her lips tighten. "I'm trying to be *nice*."

"Don't let me be the one to stop you from your journey of enlightenment." I step past her.

Tiffany's eyes narrow. "You always did love broken things." She keeps walking in the other direction.

I spin on my heel and take a few strides backward as I call out, "Why do you think I stayed with you so long?"

A few people gasp. Someone mutters, "Holy shit."

She doesn't stop, but she goes rigid like I shot her in the back. I continue to class.

Though Tiffany claimed she wasn't the one who snuck those videos and chopped Clarity down at the knees, sometimes I wonder if she paid someone on her team to do it for her. If looks could kill, I'd be minced into little cubes by the girls hockey team. I can feel knifepoints on my back as I approach my lunch table.

Cole smirks as I take the seat next to Nick. "First it was everything online, now it's arguing with Tiffany? You're becoming a real magnet for trouble, Forbes."

"Tell me about it." I lean over to look past Nick and acknowledge Willie. "I'm sorry for all of the times I've teased you about seeing Hazel. I think I need to be cleansed or something."

Willie nods solemnly. "I forgive you, bro. Got some demons that need to be cast out?"

"Yeah, you could say that." I notice Clarity as I speak, following Annabelle across the lunch room.

There's a small strip of gauze taped over her staples and the right side of her face is still pretty banged up, though it doesn't lessen her beauty. It's so good to see her that I want to jump up, sprint across the room and sweep her into my arms. I settle for catching her eye and smiling at her. My heart tugs when she offers one back.

Nick glances at Clarity over his shoulder, then over at me, and rolls his eyes. "Right. You'll be just fine, big dog."

Willie waves his hands as the girls arrive. "Welcome, everybody! Five dollars a seat! The money goes to a good cause."

Annabelle sits. "Children with cancer?"

"My empty bank account, actually. What's up, Patchy the Pirate? How are you feeling today?" Willie asks Clarity.

"I'd feel much better if I hadn't gained over a thousand haters on my blog overnight. If these people wanted to see me fail me so much, why bother following me? Have you seen this?" Clarity takes the seat next to me and passes me her phone. She leans over my shoulder to read along, and I'm so overtaken by her nearness that I fumble the phone for a second. Nick reads over my other shoulder, and Willie jumps up to look over my head.

@sophiaskates05
So sorry this happened... but also... This was your ONE shot. You and Jason blew it. It's almost like you can't replace Victor and expect the same results

---

@saul.ontherocks
This whole "miracle comeback" duo was a PR stunt from day one. Finally exposed!

@ozzy.bear
imagine skating for YEARS just to get taken out by your partner
↳ **@rochesterfigureskater**
It was an accident!!
↳ **@amygazukskates**
"Accident" is generous. Look at that lift frame-by-frame. He lets go

---

Nick scoffs. "This is just rage bait. Don't listen to them."

"Who names a bear Ozzy?" Willie frowns, and yelps when Annabelle pinches his arm.

The fury makes it hard to see straight as I pass her phone back. "I bet all of those people still use a skate aid. Nobody has the right to leave comments like that." Especially not when her fall could've ended so much worse. My gaze flashes to the bandage on her head. She's lucky to have walked away with just a concussion and a minor cut. Why rub salt in the wound?

"They kind of do." Clarity nibbles her lip as she scrolls down further. "Some people saw the USFSA officials talking to Juliette and Montgomery after placings. Rumor has it that they're overshadowing us on the radar."

"Yeah, *rumors*." Cole sets down his apple juice. "Maybe they were asking after you to make sure you were okay."

"Don't stroke my ego. We all know that's not the case." Clarity sets her phone facedown before rubbing her hands over her face. "This is it. I'm accepting defeat."

"That sucks, because I'm not." I shrug when she casts me a side eye, although I don't miss the way she softens.

"Juliette can kiss it. They would be idiots to go after her and her boy toy. They all know there's no one who can out skate you—" Annabelle cuts off when Cole picks a noodle off his tray and throws it at her. "Hey!"

He cuts her a pointed glare. I glance over my shoulder and my stomach slips. Darika is walking over with Juliette in tow. Hopefully she didn't hear any of that.

Darika is quick to take the empty seat next to Cole. "Hey, guys." She slaps her tray down. He launches forward when her uncapped water bottle starts to tip toward him, and he rights it again.

"Hey, D," Clarity greets her warmly, then turns to Juliette. "Care to join us?"

Juliette shuffles her weight between her feet. "Sorry, I don't think I can today. I just wanted to stop by and check in with you. See how you're doing." Her words are short, and she looks like she's being force-fed a lemon.

Clarity is eyeing her like a wild animal, and some alarm rings deep in my chest. There's no way she's going to confront Juliette about those USFSA members. Then again, she's been doing and saying a lot of things I didn't expect lately.

Cole has a similar calculating expression on his face as he watches their conversation. Annabelle tilts her head, her eyebrows furrowed. Willie slowly slurps his pasta off his fork.

"I'm doing better now. The doctor said I should be healed and ready for the ice again in a week or two," Clarity says.

Juliette nods and gives a small smile. "That's great. I'm really glad to hear that. The vibe was totally off at the competition after they took you to the hospital, so I'm glad that you're not following in Victor's footsteps and getting benched for the season."

"Can't tie the Janskys down for long," Nick comments. Cole raises his drink to that.

Clarity chuckles. "Thanks, me too. And thank you for checking in."

"It's the least I can do. See you guys later." Juliette flutters her fingers at us and walks toward the opposite side of the cafeteria.

Annabelle picks up her fork. "That was weird."

"Bro, *she's* weird." Willie stabs another noodle.

"That's not nice," Darika surprises me by saying. It's a comment I'd expect out of Clarity first. I glance over at her to get a read on what she's thinking. Her expression is guarded as she opens her lunchbox. I try to play it cool as usual, like I'm not watching what she's eating.

"You should've said something to her," Nick says to Clarity.

"It's none of my business." Her phone buzzes on the table at the exact moment mine does in my pocket. She picks it up at the same time I slide mine out.

"What kind of weird stuff is going on over there? Secret group chat?" Annabelle cranes her head to read over Clarity's shoulder. She goes pale. "Or not."

"You've got to be kidding me." Clarity's shoulders collapse.

"What? Who died?" Cole cranes his neck. The rest of his questions fall on my deaf ears as I pull up my email inbox. Ortiz put me and Clarity in an email, and I'm afraid to read past the opening line. *Termination of contract.*

Ortiz Stars Skating
Termination of contract

To Mr. Jason Forbes and Ms. Clarity Jansky,
I regret to inform you that after careful consideration, I have made the decision to terminate our coaching relationship, effective immediately. This decision is not one I make lightly, but I believe it is in the best interest of all parties involved.

Over the past few months, I have observed patterns that suggest our work together is no longer yielding the results necessary to compete at the highest level. Ms. Jansky, your recent behavior—frequent arguments with other skaters and an inability to maintain focus—has disrupted the training environment I strive to uphold. Additionally, Mr. Forbes, your progress has plateaued despite the intensive coaching and resources I have provided.

I must prioritize the development of skaters who demonstrate both exceptional talent and unwavering discipline. Since the rest of the athletes are in the thick of the competition season, my focus needs to be on individuals whose potential and commitment align with the goals of this team.

While this marks the end of our professional relationship, I encourage you to reflect on your aspirations and consider a coaching environment that may better suit your needs. I wish you both the best in your future endeavors.
Sincerely,

Alanna Ortiz

Head Coach, Ortiz Stars Skating

"Well, are you going to share with the class?" Darika pushes.

Clarity either ignores her or doesn't hear her. She looks up at me, my shock mirrored on her face.

"Now can we accept defeat?" she whispers.

"Absolutely not. We're going to go to her office and demand an explanation after school," I say with finality. "This isn't going to fly."

I refuse to let it.

Ortiz is still in her office when we reach the skating complex, and from the looks of it through the glass door, sifting through paperwork now that she has a free moment before practices start up again.

Clarity's footsteps land harder, like she's convincing herself to not turn tail and run.

I reach out and brush my fingertips over her back. I mean to be reassuring, but the small touch sends sizzles up my arm. "We got this. All we're doing is having a conversation."

"With the devil herself," Clarity grumbles. "But I'd be lying if I said that without her, I would still be stuck in the novice classes."

"I don't think that's true. Without her, you probably wouldn't have been in the hospital for twenty-four hours."

I'm sort of joking, until Clarity shrugs in a way that makes me wonder if Ortiz was more involved with that accident than she's letting on.

Ortiz looks up from her papers, her grey eyes hardening when she notices us. I almost expect her to pretend she didn't see us. Surprisingly, she gets to her feet and walks around her desk to open the office door. "I was wondering if you two would show up."

I bite back a sharp retort. *Clarity's doing much better after a night in the hospital and a wicked head injury. Thanks for asking, though.* It's the cleanest of the ones that run through my mind. The rest are full of curse words.

Clarity beats me to answering, saving everyone's ears from my creative language. "Do you have a minute?"

"I don't think I have a choice." Her eyes flash to the bandage on Clarity's head. No remorse crosses her face as she walks back over to her desk and takes a seat. At least she finally finds the decency to say, "I am glad to see you on your feet. That was a nasty landing."

"We're not here to talk about how terrible that performance was," Clarity shoots back with the most vigor that I've ever heard her use with Ortiz. "I have given you literally everything since I was six years old. You've watched me grow up and helped me become the skater I am today. I have put my blood, sweat, and tears into that ice." She points in the direction of the rink, her voice shaking on the last word. "Jason has done the same, improving more in two months than Victor did. I don't understand how you could drop us so easily, like none of that matters."

"Of course it matters." Ortiz leans forward, splaying her hands on her desk. "It has been an honor watching you grow up out there, and I appreciate Jason's flexibility. I am not in the business of looking in the past. I look into the future. When you were a young girl, I could see your future here. Now?" She shrugs passively, like we're discussing the weather. "You've always appreciated my honesty, so I'll be honest one more time. I don't see you thriving here anymore. Either of you."

I cross my arms to refrain from grabbing the glittery glass shelves on the wall closest to me and tearing them down so I can watch the gold, silver, and bronze awards shatter on the ground. I actually do a double take when I notice one trophy near the top of the wall.

Ortiz Stars Skating - Clarity Jansky & Victor Kerr - Junior National Ice Dancers - 1st

The irony of Clarity's name being on the wall of champions almost makes me laugh. I bet that if I looked harder, her name would be recurring. She is part of the reason why Ortiz has a waiting list a mile long of skaters wanting to join her program.

On the contrary, Clarity is chewing her lip, cheeks red. I remember that look from when Annabelle accidentally popped the head off her favorite Barbie doll in elementary school. She's fighting back tears.

"That's all there is, then? That's it?" I snap, breaking the silence.

Ortiz's attention flashes over to me. "I made it very clear in my email why I am terminating this contract."

"Did you? All I saw was piss-poor excuses rattling off how disappointed you are that Clarity isn't the same impressionable child that she was eleven years ago and how you want to pour all of your energy into Juliette and Montgomery. You encouraged us to *reflect on our aspirations*," I quote the email, "but I'm going to encourage you to take your head out of your ass."

Clarity gasps. "*Jason.*"

"What is she going to do?" I laugh exasperatedly. "Kick us off the team? Checked that box already."

"This decision is final." Ortiz sets her jaw as she stands and motions to the door. "Good luck, Mr. Forbes and Ms. Jansky. You need it."

This time, I actually flip her off. Clarity grabs my hand and drags me out of the office, shutting the door behind us. Her chest is heaving and her eyes are wild like a spooked horse. She waits to speak until we turn down the hallway.

"You shouldn't have done that," Clarity scolds, though there's no venom in her tone. "I was getting her to come around."

"I must've not been a part of the same conversation, because that's not what I heard. Her mind was made up. I'm proud of you for trying, but we're done here."

Her eyes well with tears. "All those years..."

"Hey. Hey, hey, hey, look at me." I come to a stop at the bottom of the staircase that leads up to the lobby and grab her hand, turning her to face me. She looks away, and I gently rest my hand on her cheek. "Look at me, please."

She exhales and obeys, searching my eyes, her own wet with tears. I wipe them away with my thumb.

"Ortiz said it herself. Don't look at the past with guilt, okay? You had good memories here, and you learned what you needed to learn. Take that knowledge and move forward. I don't care what that woman says." I pause and crouch down to meet her eyes. She tries to glance away again. "I don't want to stop. Not because of her, or this."

The tears run faster down Clarity's face. She exhales bitterly. "It doesn't matter if we keep going. Nationals is off the table."

"Then we find another table."

"Jason." Her voice cracks. "You don't get it. There *is* no next step. We don't have a coach, or a team. God, we don't even have a rink! No one wants us."

I shake my head. "That's not true. I want us." She scoffs and starts to turn away. I snag her arm. "They can shut every door they want, because I'll kick in a damn window. Just—" I scramble for the right words. "Tell me you're still in this with me, even if we have to start from square one."

Clarity looks at my hand, then up at me, eyes wet and rimmed red. I quickly let go. For a long second, she says nothing. Then, she says, "I don't know what I want anymore. I'm so tired of pretending like every closed door is a secret detour to something better. You know? Like if we work hard enough, or wish hard enough, it'll all just come back."

"Clarity..."

"I'm not asking you to give up. But you need to stop acting like this just didn't happen."

I recoil, my skin prickling. She continues, "Like we didn't get kicked off the team we gave everything to, or like I didn't just—" She cuts herself off and swallows hard, her eyelashes fluttering. "I don't want to talk about this right now. I can't."

She turns and starts up the stairs, wiping her face with her sleeve.

The last thing I want to do is stay silent, but I choose to do so for her sake.

November 2015 - Age 16

Clarity

I throw my duffel bag over my shoulder and hurry out of the locker room so I can find Sterling to say hi before he starts hockey practice. Then I need to go home and soak my aching hips in the bathtub.

Hockey players are filtering down the halls, and when I turn the corner to meet him by the vending machines, I'm more surprised to see Tiffany grabbing a drink out of the dispenser.

It's so shocking to see her this close that I genuinely short circuit, my feet skittering to a stop, the smile slipping off my face. I quickly pick it up and paste it back on as she turns to me, her eyebrows drawing together.

"Hi," I say breathlessly.

"What do you want?" Tiffany cracks the seal on the cap.

"Nothing. Waiting for Sterling." I bite my lip. "So, you and Jason, huh?"

I try to sound happy for her, but my enthusiasm falls flat. I've been stuffing down so many emotions over the past few weeks that I've found out that they're an item that I don't know *what* to think or feel anymore.

Unfortunately, enthusiasm, happiness, nor excitement are in the top ten.

"Yep." She quirks an eyebrow. "Me and Jason."

"Good. Great. He's a great guy." I don't know what to say next with her staring at me like this, so I go with what feels right given the situation. "You know, maybe this can be a fresh start. I think we should talk about what happened between us."

"No, you've got it wrong." Tiffany steps forward, waving her bottle at me. "You finally lost, and I finally won. This isn't a fresh start. It's payback."

I can't stop my jaw from dropping as she swerves around me and keeps walking, her hair shimmying over her back. Payback? That's what she wants to call it?

I don't care. Maybe it is. Fine, whatever.

Jason must've not told her about the conversation him and I had over the summer.

That thought alone is what keeps me from running after her and knocking her out. Instead, I slowly inhale and smile as I turn around to find Sterling.

Chapter 25

Jason

I drive us back to Clarity's house in silence, the shock and disappointment from our one-sided conversation with Ortiz hanging heavy between us.

It was bad enough walking away from hockey. At least that decision made sense. Did it suck? Sure it did. But it's not like I could argue. I knew I broke a rule or two, or five.

That's what makes this situation worse; we didn't do anything wrong. Ortiz simply decided that she couldn't foresee us progressing on her team and dropped us like we were nothing. She dropped *Clarity* like she's been nothing for the better part of a decade.

Thinking about that makes me angry all over again, and I choke the steering wheel to refrain from turning this car back around to go ram it through the side of Ortiz's SUV.

"Hey, Vick. Could you please call me back when you get a chance? I'm sorry to be bothering you, but something really big just happened and I think we should talk about it. It's not good news, so... Yeah. I don't know. Call me, please." Clarity ends her voicemail and sighs. "First Annabelle, now him. He usually picks up."

"Is he in class?" I glance over at her before turning into her neighborhood.

"No, he shouldn't be. His last one ends around four. He should be in his dorm."

"We could always drive over and tell him," I offer. That seems like the least we could do, given the situation.

"That's okay. Maybe he's busy. Besides, I'm starting to get a headache right here." She runs her fingertips over the top of her skull. "I should probably chill. Curl into a ball and disassociate. Pretend this day never happened."

"That's the spirit." I pull into their driveway, taking care to not park behind the car she shares with Cole. He's got to be leaving for practice any minute. I turn off the ignition and look at her. "Seriously though, when we get inside, you need to drink water and rest. Can you take ibuprofen yet?"

Clarity eyes me, her lips twisting into a smile. "Relax, doctor. My head isn't going to fall off my neck."

I tilt my head to the side and mirror her look of exasperation. "That's not what I asked."

My eyes trick me into thinking her gaze darts to my lips, just for a moment. Maybe I need to go get *my* head checked.

"Yes, I can take ibuprofen. The doctor told me to wait forty-eight hours, so I'm in the safe zone now."

"I'm sorry."

Clarity pauses as she reaches for the door handle and turns to face me. "Sorry?"

I unbuckle, taking a moment to gather my racing thoughts. "For everything. This. Your head hurting. I don't know."

"You have nothing to apologize for. None of this is your fault."

"It is," I reply. Now that I'm talking, I can't stop. "I am so sorry that I've never stepped up to help you in the past, especially when I started to notice something was wrong with your health. I'm sorry that I can't stop these terrible people out in the world from saying stupid shit. This is all new territory for me, and I've never known how to handle it."

"It's okay. Seriously. It's not your job to stand up for me, or protect me, or any of that."

"It is, though." I rest my hand on the center console, ducking my head to be at her eye-level. Those sweet brown eyes search mine. "I've known you and Cole longer than anyone on this earth, except for my dad. You're also my best friend, and my teammate. I want to look out for you, but I don't know how."

I run a hand through my hair, and she glances up to track the movement as I continue. "I don't want to stay on the outside this time, sitting here doing nothing like I've always done."

Clarity presses her tongue against her cheek. She's frozen, probably shocked by my outburst. Embarrassment causes me to wince.

"Sorry. I totally... shouldn't have said all of that. Let's see, what else am I sorry for?" I scratch my neck. "Well, I am still sorry for breaking Cole's foot in third grade."

That breaks the ice, making her laugh. "I don't think he's forgiven you for that."

I smile. "I don't blame him."

We both go silent for another heartbeat. A different version of me probably would've kept his mouth shut and held onto those thoughts, except I'm not the same person I was last year. I'm not even the same person I was last week. Given the look on Clarity's face, I think she's realizing that, too. She bites her lip.

"Should we go inside?" I offer quietly.

"Yeah, probably."

We get out at the same time, and I beat Clarity to grabbing her backpack, much to her dismay. I ignore her griping—it's all an act, anyway, because I don't miss the way she smiles—and walk behind her up the sidewalk. The snow we got over the weekend has turned into slick ice in some spots, so I watch every step she takes. I won't let her fall again, if I can help it.

Both of us make it to the door in one piece, and I exhale a sigh of relief for more than one reason. With the robin's egg blue door, the twinkling wind chimes that Aaron hasn't taken down yet, and the empty flower pots lining the porch that promise spring will return again, I can finally relax.

Clarity shoves her shoulder into the door, and it unsticks with a loud creak. The warmth of the house makes my cheeks tingle as they adjust from the cold. I shut the door behind us and slam my hip into it out of habit, pushing it back into place.

"That talk couldn't have gone well if you guys are back so soon," Lauren says from the dining room.

We kick off our shoes, and I hang Clarity's backpack on the coat rack before unzipping my jacket. She leads the way into the kitchen. Aaron has his back to us, chopping a head of lettuce on the counter. Lauren is bent over a laptop at the table, bills and papers strewn across the surface, and she looks up as Clarity wanders over.

"I say that it went so well, you came straight home to tell us the good news." Aaron spins around, wielding a massive knife.

"Mom hit the nail on the head with Option A." Clarity leans on the kitchen island and crosses her forearms before resting her head down on top, letting out a loud, guttural groan.

I go to the sink and pull down a glass from the cabinet, filling it with water.

"What? Seriously? Can she even follow through with this?" Lauren glances between all three of us, searching for an answer.

Aaron shrugs and waves his knife. "Alanna makes her own rules."

She watches the knifepoint nervously. "I can't focus when you're swinging that thing around."

I dig the ibuprofen bottle out of the medicine drawer as Cole walks into the kitchen and belts out, "That's what she said."

I can't stop the laugh that slips out.

"Cole Aaron Jansky, watch your mouth," Lauren scolds, then shakes her finger at me. "Don't egg him on."

Aaron is obviously trying to bite back his smile, so he quickly turns around and keeps chopping vegetables.

I put both hands in the air helplessly before grabbing the glass and returning to Clarity, setting everything down in front of her. She looks up from where she was buried in her arms, slowly tracing her eyes over my arms and face. Warmth fills her cheeks, and I turn away.

I can't function properly when she looks at me like that, full of gratitude and confusion, like she still can't understand why, after all these years, I'll go out of my way to help her.

"You said it, not me." Cole opens a cupboard and pulls out a bag of pretzels. He takes a handful and spins around to us. "So, you got the boot, huh?"

"Both boots, actually. Like a donkey kick to the face," I answer for the both of us as Clarity swallows the pills.

He whistles. "That's tough. What a week."

"Try month," Clarity retorts.

Try years. My life has been slowly falling apart since I started high school and realized I wanted Clarity in my life as more than a friend. That series of events was way worse than getting cut from the hockey team, but I can't exactly speak my mind on the matter.

Her phone starts to vibrate. She grabs it and gasps.

"It's Annabelle. I need to take this. Thank you for everything today," she says to me as she starts to step away.

Of course. I'd do anything for you. Say the word and I'll lay down my life if it meant saving yours.

I don't get the chance to say any of that—as if I would. She's already answering the phone and giggling at whatever Annabelle's saying on the other line. I watch her leave the room.

"I better get going myself. Almost time to shine." Cole pops the last pretzel in his mouth and walks over to me, knuckles raised. "Sorry to hear you're getting thrown in the can for the second time this year."

I bump my knuckles against his. "It was worth turning my limbs black and blue."

He scoffs, and I don't like that knowing twinkle in his eye. "Yeah, I'm sure it was, huh?"

I retort by punching him in the arm. He laughs and throws his knuckles at my head. I barely duck out of the way in time.

"Boys, please take it outside," Lauren says exasperatedly, like we're nine years old again.

"We're done." I grin even as Cole tries to take me out at the knees. I kick him away. "I should probably go home."

"Tell Jesse we said hello." Aaron glances at me.

Lauren looks up from her computer and waves. "Drive home safely, sweetheart. Don't be a stranger."

"No loving words of affection for your own flesh and blood? Your next of kin?" Cole frowns. "I see how it is."

"We see you every day." Aaron shrugs.

Lauren gasps. "Oh, don't start that. I love you, Cole. Please be safe at practice."

"Always am. Later." Cole salutes and walks out of the kitchen.

I say goodbye to his parents and follow him to the foyer, slipping my shoes back on. "Have you told them about Willie and his game of five-finger roulette with his hockey blades?"

"Shh, absolutely not." Cole puts on his sneakers. I zip up my coat as he grabs his gear bag, and I hold the door open to let him out first.

"Such a gentleman. I'll have to tell Clarity that she's not the only one getting princess treatment." He pretends to tuck a strand of hair behind his ear as I shut the door behind us.

I reach down to scoop a handful of snow off the stairs and shape it into a ball before throwing it at the back of his head. He yelps so loud that the sound echoes down the street.

"I'm sorry. What were you saying?" I grin as he bats the snow out of his hair, then spins around to give me a response that relies heavily on his middle finger.

"I hope you get a taste of your own medicine and end up in the ditch," Cole tries to say seriously. He ends up laughing as he throws his bag in the backseat of his car.

"Your mom already told me to drive safe, so those two requests are going to cancel each other out." I shrug and open my driver's side door.

"Then I hope you hit every red light on the way home."

"That's taking it too far." I hop in. "Later."

"*Ciao!*" We close our car doors at the same time. Cole backs out first, sending up a spray of muddy dirt as he hurries off to the rink. I take more care in leaving the driveway, sending one last longing look at the house. The last thing I want to do is leave, although there's no prolonging the inevitable.

The car rumbles as I pull into the driveway at home. Deja vu washes over me as I approach the garage and see that dad is already here. He hasn't beaten me home in a long time. I haven't even seen him since late last week since I spent the majority of my weekend at the Jansky's house.

I get out of the car and go inside, taking a moment to hang the car keys on the hook by the door and sliding off my shoes. I move them onto the shoe rack before creeping into the kitchen. It's empty.

The silence is almost mocking after the hustle and bustle of the Janskys', where the familiar sound of cooking, conversation, and laughter fills every room. Here it feels like a pin could drop and it would startle the birds out of the trees outside.

In the past I probably would've hightailed it up to my room, until I recently learned that it's better to take the bull by the horns. Even if me and this particular bull have been dancing around each other for a while.

My feet pad over the carpet as I walk through the sitting room and wrap around to my dad's office. I finally see the first sign of life. The lights are on, reflecting off his desk and the gleaming wooden shelves that line the room. The curtains are drawn over the massive windows on the back wall. He looks up from typing on his keyboard.

"You're home early."

"Yeah." I wander closer and inspect the files on the edge of his desk. How do I admit that after all the work I put into figure skating, it still went down the drain, anyway?

"How's Clarity doing? Is she still healing alright?"

"She's doing great, thankfully. I'm pretty sure she's going to start seeing a counselor later this week."

"Good. It's time she gets another person in her corner." He resumes typing.

The next words stick in my throat. "I wanted to let you know that wasn't the only thing that happened. Um." I scramble for the right words when he raises his eyebrow. He hates it when people don't get right to the point. "Ortiz—Coach Ortiz kicked us off the team today."

Now his eyebrows *really* go up. He turns to me. "Why? For losing?"

"No." My cheeks heat. "I'm sure that was part of it, but no. She thought Clarity's behavior was messing with her training environment, and I have a feeling that she didn't like the stuff coming out of my mouth. But she put it in more professional words."

"I see. That's too bad." His chair creaks as he leans back and crosses his arms. "But decent timing. I'm going with Paul to the boys' hockey practice on Friday to take those Hypershot prototypes for another test ride. Since you know how that equipment works, I'd appreciate it if you could help us out. We need the extra hand."

That's it? No fight? Nothing?

Every memory I've made with Clarity over the last two months fractures like glass, cracking under the heavy weight of reality. I knew that working with her was too good to be true, and I should've known that I would have to stop playing pretend at some point. It's time to wake up and smell the roses, as Dad would say. Nothing against Paul or the company.

I'm just not ready to be tied back to my job again. I'm not ready to give up my new dream, because that means giving up on her.

I have to breathe quickly and shallowly to keep my composure, like my last few gasps of oxygen before the water rises over my head.

"Sure." I cough and try again. "Okay. Fine."

"Great, I will let him know. This is a good thing, Jace. You gave it a good run, but it's time to get your head back in the game, yeah?" He grabs his phone and immediately starts texting, probably a message to Paul. "Everything happens for a reason."

"I guess so." I turn around and walk down the hall, dragging both hands through my hair to refrain from sending them through the drywall.

If only he would've been as encouraging for this venture from the start as he is for me getting out of it, maybe I wouldn't be in this position in the first place.

Chapter 26

Clarity

BREAKING: *The Ice Princess Melts! Jansky & Forbes OUT of Nationals*
Posted by: Skate Snaps Midwest
Published: November 19th — 2:02 PM CST

Some say she's a rising star who crumbled. Others say she was never the real deal to begin with. Either way, Clarity Jansky, Minnesota's Ice Princess, is officially out of Nationals contention, and so is her partner, ex-hockey golden boy Jason Forbes.

During Friday's high-stakes Invitational, the duo initiated a risky reverse rotational lift, only for it to end in catastrophe. Mid-air, Clarity reportedly lost consciousness, crashing headfirst onto the ice in front of a stunned crowd. Forbes attempted to catch her but was a beat too late.

They were disqualified on the spot for not completing their program. No final score = No Nationals.

The clip has since gone viral across skating forums and fan pages alike with new angles surfacing every day. Some blame Clarity's ongoing health struggles, which have long been speculated about but have never been confirmed. Others point to Jason's inexperience and the fact that he's still adjusting to figure skating after a decade on the ice as a hockey player. Whatever the reason, their Invitational campaign ended not with a flourish, but a stretcher.

In the days since, neither skater has spoken publicly. Forbes hasn't been spotted at the rink. Jansky's socials have gone silent. Rumor has it that Alanna Ortiz has had enough. As always, the fans are left filling in the blanks: was this a one-time medical emergency or the final unraveling of a team built on a shaky foundation?

The harsher critics say Clarity's always been more aesthetic than athletic. "Smoke and mirrors," one anonymous coach allegedly said. Another fan posted: "At some point, we have to stop pretending being fragile is the same thing as being good."

Meanwhile, Juliette McKenzie and Montgomery Baros skated clean. They closed out the event with a top five finish, earning their spot at Nationals this January. Neither athlete flinched as they skated over the same spot where Jansky bled only minutes prior.

Some might call it professionalism, we're calling it cold-blooded. No pun intended.

Either way, they're going to Nationals. But the Ice Princess? She'll be watching at home.

Want to see footage of the lift that ended it all? Click [here]. (Viewer discretion advised.) Was it a fluke, or was this fall bound to happen? Join the discussion in the comments.

- Skate Snaps Midwest

Rating: 2k comments | 10.1k likes | 6.7k shares

@skatesnapsmidwest
We understand this post stirred emotions. Our goal is always to spotlight the stories unfolding across the skating world. We care deeply about skater safety and performance. Stay tuned for Nationals coverage coming soon!
↳ **@annabellelloyd67**
You "care deeply"?? You ran an anonymous hit piece accusing her of starving herself the other week. Just say you wanted the attention because you couldn't get it without blasting her name.

↳ **@sk8fan456**
damn *@skatesnapsmidwest* y'all just got dragged
↳ **@skatesnapsmidwest**
We encourage respectful dialogue here. If you have concerns, feel
free to message us directly.

@amygazukskates
She couldn't even hold herself up in a basic lift. That's not pressure, it's incompetence. If I were Alanna, neither of them would've
been on the team in the first place
↳ **@kiki_lovexo**
Should've been Juliette from day ONE. At least she can stay on
her feet.
↳ **@vick_the_iceprince**
They had two months. TWO. MONTHS. Of choreography. The
fact that they even got that far is insane. Get off their backs.
↳ **@amygazukskates**
Victor sounds like he's still bitter she left him in the dust. Boo hoo.

@cherryslice67
I rewatched the footage. Guys... she buckles BEFORE Forbes
even lifts her. This isn't about nerves. This is someone who doesn't
belong in senior level competition!
↳ **@ilovemichigan444**
She's why ice dancing doesn't evolve. Same recycled moves, soft
arms, zero drive. She couldn't lift a paperclip let alone a Nation-
als-level routine HAHA
↳ **@brookyboo**
Nah let's talk about how dude had a whole ass future in hockey
and gave it up for this mess lol. She's dead weight and dragging him
down
↳ **@amygazukskates**

Not her thinking she was going to the Olympics when she can't even survive Invitationals... TBH she should be embarrassed. If I blacked out mid-lift, I'd change my name and flee the state. She's a liability

↳ **@icecole_bruh**
She's my sister, asshole.

↳ **@amygazukskates**
I heard USFSA pulled interest from *@offtheice* entirely. Word is Juliette's being watched now. Honestly thats deserved

↳ **@lottie.d.mac**
Jason can get it any day of the week, but the fact that he threw away hockey, his reputation, his GIRLFRIEND, all for Jansky is so embarrassing. He's the real clown

---

@twizzlequeen99
Clarity's blog hasn't updated in dayssss. Guess when the camera's not on she crumbles

↳ **@d.is.for.darika**
@twizzlequeen99 that's because she's been in the HOSPITAL, karen. maybe read something other than this comment section before spewing garbage?

↳ **@annabellelloyd67**
I'm so tired of this. That girl has been skating since she could walk. She has given her whole life to this sport, and you come in here with your anonymous usernames and zero medals to your name and talk shit? BYE.

↳ **@clarityj_luver**
If *@offtheice* doesn't go to Nationals, I'm done watching this sport. She was the only one with artistry

↳ **@ster_it_up**
Jason's probably relieved tbh. Now he can go back to tech bro land where he belongs lol

↳ **@icecole_bruh**

This thread is disgusting. She's RECOVERING. Anyone still typing hate here can come say it to my face.
　↳ **@skatesnapsmidwest**
@icecole_bruh Cole, would you like to give a statement on your sister's status post-competition? We've heard conflicting reports. DMs open.
　↳ **@icecole_bruh**
@skatesnapsmidwest Yeah here's your statement: LEAVE. HER. ALONE.

@_jasonforbes
Shut the hell up. Every last one of you keyboard warriors, shut up. You think you're tough piling on a girl who just got out of the hospital? You think you're clever picking apart a routine you couldn't survive five seconds of? You don't know a goddamn thing about Clarity or what she has sacrificed because she broke herself and still showed up with a smile for people like YOU.

You mock her blackout like it was intentional but she almost cracked her skull open trying to make something beautiful and you're out here whining about "aesthetic?" Are you kidding me?

If you want to talk about me, that's fine. Say I dropped her or fumbled or whatever. But don't act like you know the first thing about what it takes to skate at this level, refusing to quit even when you're assigned a partner that has to be taught EVERYTHING.

Clarity is the strongest person I've ever known. You don't get to speak her name. You don't get to look in her direction. So log off, sit the hell down, and think about something other than yourself for once.
　↳ **@icecole_bruh**
MIC DROP. You people pissed off the wrong Forbes #TeamJacity #ForbesFury
　↳ **@skatergirlzz**

It's the "you don't know a goddamn thing about her" for me!! He really came in swinging and didn't miss ONCE
  ↳ **@d.is.for.darika**
i'm literally printing this and hanging it in the locker room. also: everyone dragging Clarity can go do a triple axel face-first into traffic <3
  ↳ **@skatesnapsmidwest**
Due to recent violations of our community guidelines, comments on this post are now CLOSED. We do not tolerate bullying or targeted harassment. Further moderation actions may follow.

My friends came over on Sunday night to check in with me and help get my mind off the competition. Despite their best efforts, the topic came up while all of us were playing Catan, and Victor told me that if I truly cared for my sanity, I wouldn't go back and watch the recording of the performance.

The truth is the second everyone left, I ran upstairs to my room, hid under the covers, watched the video, and sobbed myself into exhaustion.

The announcers hyped up my name as we stepped onto the ice when they should've been highlighting Jason. He was the true star. Quite frankly, I'm shocked that Ortiz let me perform with him. From the moment my blades hit the ice until my skull followed a few minutes later, I looked like a zombie.

Jason was pulling words out of the announcers like, "*His strength and technicality is flawless,*" and "*Wow, look at him move!*" When they spoke about me, it was along the lines of, "*Jansky seems lost today. I've never seen her skate like this.*" No more than a minute later, they were all gasping in horror when I dropped, like I was an expensive China plate that slipped out of a child's hands.

It's been four days since I crashed on the ice, and twenty-four hours since Ortiz told us to leave her office for good. I've had to put my phone on Do Not Disturb at school, because if my injury and us falling short of Nationals wasn't enough, people have started to catch wind that we're off the team too.

I haven't gained online attention like this since I got the chance to interview Toni Denise at World Championships in freshman year when my parents surprised me with tickets. This situation is making that viral post look like a marketing students' class project.

I squint against the light of my phone that spills on my face and over my pillow as the taste of copper fills my mouth, and I run my tongue over the open wound I chewed inside my cheek. It's still not enough to make me flinch. Nothing compares to the pain deep inside of my chest as I scroll past the notifications from that godforsaken Skate Snaps post about me and Jason missing our shot at Nationals. I was tagged in the comments hundreds of times before they were turned off.

A message notification from the Overtime podcast makes me pause. What are the odds they're checking in with me to clear the air? To get information straight from the source before I go on their show next week? I tap it, and my gut plummets.

Hi Clarity! We hope you're recovering and taking time to rest. We wanted to reach out regarding your upcoming guest spot on our show. After careful internal discussion, we've decided to shift our coverage in a different direction this season...

I stop reading. Instead I roll over on my bed, throw my phone on the floor, stick my face in my pillow, and let out a guttural scream.

Is there anyone else who wants to take things a different direction this season? The only direction I want to go is down. Six feet into the dirt.

Everything is ruined, anyway. Shattered. Sitting in eleventh place on a sheet of paper.

My phone vibrates on the carpet. Not a social media notification buzz. Someone texted.

I groan in tandem with my empty stomach as I roll over again. Let's add that to my list of problems: I get to visit with my nutritional therapist for the first time on Friday. Just another person in my life to tell me what I'm doing wrong.

The mattress creaks as I slide halfway off, keeping my legs elevated and sliding my forearms across the carpet. I grab my phone and swipe over to my messages. I swear, if some hater found my number and is sending death threats again...

> **Hey C.J. Are you home? Can I come over?**

> **Please and thanks :)**

Jason.

My body falls to the ground. I inhale sharply and sit up, smoothing my hair back with one hand as I respond with the other.

> **Yeah I'm home. That's fine**

> **Cool. Then could you unlock your door?**

> **I'm outside**

"Outside?" I fling my head up, jump to my feet, and whip my bedroom door open. I go into Cole's room to look out his window. Sure enough, there's a sleek black car parked on the curb.

Cursing, I rush down the stairs and unlock the front door. I'm breathless as I throw it open.

Jason turns around from where he was inspecting our wind chimes, and he smiles sheepishly. His green eyes pop against his red cheeks, thanks to the brittle cold. His breath fogs the air. It's only been a few hours since I saw him, and I'm shocked at how much I missed his face.

"Hi."

"Oh, my god. Get in here." I grab his hand and pull him inside, slamming the door shut behind him. "Are you crazy? What if no one was home?"

"Then I would've left." He unzips his jacket. "I was only out there for a minute. Where is everyone?"

"Gone. My parents are at work, and Cole is at practice." I head into the living room as he takes off his shoes and follows me. "I'm surprised you didn't take the night to relax. You haven't had the chance to chill in months."

"Neither have you. That's actually what I wanted to talk about." Jason sits in an armchair and he watches as I pretend to fiddle with the thermostat. Anything so I don't have to sit across for him.

I don't trust myself to be alone with him anymore. There's no guessing what I'll say or do. Sometimes I want to kiss him until I'm breathless, solely relying on his breath for oxygen. Other times I want to fight him for being such a threat to my life, especially when I know he deserves so much better.

"Oh?" There's only so many times I can toggle the temperature between 70 and 71 degrees. I turn to face him, and he leans forward to rest his elbows on his knees, lacing his hands together.

"I talked to my dad last night, and I'm going to keep helping with some stuff at work over the next few weeks. But I'll still have plenty of time to skate. More than before."

"*Skate?*"

Jason straightens his spine and lets go of his hands. His eyebrows furrow. "Didn't the doctor say you can go back on the ice in a week?

Just because we aren't going to Nationals doesn't mean we can't start to prepare for next year. Would it be okay if we talked about next steps? We should make a game plan."

"Next steps." I laugh and nod, grabbing the ends of my hair to ball them at the base of my neck. I know he saw the comments online, because I saw him blow up on everyone. He should know that there are no next steps. The ten thousand people who liked that post made sure of it. "Yeah. Okay."

He blinks. I can tell he's trying to read me, see if I'm being sarcastic or not, so I turn away. He stands up. "Okay. Well, I was thinking..."

"Jason." I let go of my hair and turn back around. "There *are* no next steps. Don't get you get it? We're screwed!"

Actually, I think I *could* fight him right about now.

He flinches like I actually hit him. "No, we're not."

"What are you not understanding?" I raise my voice. "Nothing we did was enough. Now we're the joke of the skating world, my head hurts when I stand too fast, and you want to make a game plan? Are you kidding me?"

He stays quiet, pulling at his fingers.

"Skating was everything to me." My voice trembles as I step closer. "I gave my entire life to this sport, and it spit me out. No one cares that I haven't eaten a real meal in months, or that I'm always bruised, or scared, or exhausted. I worked my ass off to make this year *my* year, and now it's over."

I'm crying now. Hot, humiliated, messy tears race down my cheeks. "I have nothing left to give. No team to work for, no future to work toward. There's no point. No one is going to take me as I am anymore."

Jason's face shifts, like something inside of him is splitting. "Don't say that. You have—"

"Don't you *dare* say I have you." I slice my hand through the air. "That's not true."

"What are you talking about?"

I scoff and wipe my face. "I heard that Tiffany apologized. You always do this shit, splitting yourself in half for everyone around you. The second someone else needs you, you're laying at their feet. Maybe you should go back to her to fill your time, now that she's back on your radar."

I don't actually mean it, but it feels good to say. It's easier to argue and push him away rather than admit I'm still terrified to let him get too close.

My chest heaves as he strides forward, closing the space between us. The heat behind his eyes enraptures me, like a moth to a flame. I'm not scared because I can tell he's not angry. He's desperate.

"You think I don't see you? Do you seriously think I ever stopped?" His eyes search mine. "You were the first person who ever looked at me like I was worth something, you know. Not because of hockey. Not for my last name. Me. And I've spent every day since trying to be the same person that you see."

My breath catches. Jason keeps going.

"I still stand by what I said the first time we had this conversation: You are it, Clarity. Not Tiffany, or anyone else. You, because you make me feel like I can be more than my mistakes." He swallows. "If you're scared, fine. If you're exhausted or angry, fine. But don't you dare look me in the eyes and say there's nothing left. I'm still here, and I'm not going anywhere."

For a second, the silence is electric. Until I take a step back. "You should go."

Jason looks at me like he didn't hear me right. "What?"

"You're wrong. There's nothing left to save." Tears prick the back of my eye, threatening to spill more. I fold my arms across my chest in an attempt to keep from falling apart again. He's done more than enough for me, and he doesn't need to deal with another one of my breakdowns. He doesn't deserve to be associated with someone like me. "This is it. I've already brought you down with me. Leave before this gets worse and I ruin you."

"Absolutely not."

"Go home." I struggle to keep my voice flat. "Jesus, please, just go!" The tears start again. He doesn't move, and I'm terrified that I'll have to yell at him again, until he does the worst thing imaginable. He steps forward.

His arms wrap around me before I can stop him, nestling me in a tight hug. I hate him for holding together all the pieces I keep trying to shatter. I hate him for smelling like everything I love in life. It makes me want to hit something, so I do.

I slam my fist against his chest, once, hard. He doesn't even flinch.

"Go away." I choke on a sob.

Jason lets go. His eyes are red and glossy. "I don't want to."

"Please leave me alone," I say, even as my knees begin to give. "I want to be alone."

"You're sure?" His voice is barely audible. He takes a step away.

That's all it takes for the moment to cave in on itself, because I've heard him say that before. Different year, different wound. Same boy, and the same heartbreak that keeps rearing its ugly head.

I don't answer him. I can't anymore.

I'm actually *not* sure if I want him to go, but if he stays here, I'll make this worse. The tears are blinding me, and I blink rapidly as I turn away. There's a beat where I swear he might argue, except he knows better. He knows me too well. Right now, I despise that.

"You deserve to know that you didn't ruin me. You saved me."

He leaves me leaves his final words to hang in the air. His socked feet pad over the floor as he retreats to the foyer. My shoulders shake as I turn away, fighting the sobs that threaten to take me down.

When the door clicks shut, I crumble. I've burned through my anger and fear, and all that's left is a deep well of sadness. I cry as I collapse on the couch.

This is just like last time, and I'm the one who let him go. Again.

December 2015 - Age 16

Jason

I haven't really seen Clarity since that day in October when I showed up early to the rink and, like the coward I am, immediately left. I still haven't found the bravery to stop by their house, or smile at her in the hallway, or send her a text. It's nearly impossible with Tiffany constantly breathing down my neck, anyway. If anyone were to ask me, I don't even think she likes the fact that I still talk to Cole.

Tiffany can kiss my ass because I sit next to him on the bench behind the rink boards, skates in my hand. He smiles tightly and scoots over to make more room. It's a nice gesture, even though he's also been icy toward me lately. I'm starting to think that everyone hates me, including my girlfriend.

I bend down to pull on my hockey skates. "Ready for today?"

"As I'll ever be. Willie brought me a Redbull, so I'm hanging in there."

My chest tightens as I lace my skates. I'd have to be blind to not notice the way he, Willie, and Nick have become as close as brothers over the past few months Tiffany and I have started dating.

Almost as close as him and I are. Were. I don't even know anymore.

"Nice." There's nothing else for me to say. I pull on my other skate and glance up as movement on the other end of the rink catches my eye.

Speaking of Clarity...

She and Victor must have a different schedule this week because they're still skating, flying past the window. I watch, mesmerized, as Victor braces himself and swoops her into the air. She gotten impossibly smaller since being with Sterling. My heart skips a beat as I turn to Cole.

"Weird question, but how's Clarity been?"

Cole looks at me from under his eyelashes as he ties his skates. "What, *now* you're worried about her?"

"Clarity's fine." Annabelle jumps into our conversation as she comes over with her skates on, clipboard in hand. She scowls at me like I'm the problem. "Why do you ask? Who's talking?"

"Nobody is. She... I... Forget it." I push onto my feet, yanking my helmet off the bench with me. I don't miss the look that Annabelle and Cole share, and I get that same uncanny feeling that I am extremely out of the loop, as if it's my fault.

Everything's been going downhill since I started dating Tiffany.

Chapter 27
Jason

As I roll out two hard-shelled cases onto the ice of the West Rink with the boys' hockey team warming up around me, I glance up, catching Montgomery and Juliette on the other side of the glass. They're swept up in each other's arms as they float in a wide arc. My stomach aches with longing at the same time my heart twists in pain.

That should be me and Clarity. I don't care about what she said to me three nights ago. I don't believe her, anyway.

Did I ugly cry the whole way home and stay up all night trying to digest her words? Yes, I did. That scab from last year never healed over, and she ripped it right back off. At least she called me the next morning, apologizing profusely for speaking so irrationally.

I didn't tell her this, but I don't believe she's done skating. When she's done with something, she drops it and doesn't look back. She just needs some more time and space to think.

I hope.

"Careful with that. I'm sure that case right there could fund this entire building," Coach Lloyd jokes as he skates over.

"We're passing these sticks out to thirty high schoolers. I think it'll be fine." I push my blades to a stop. My ankles rub against the inside of these hockey skates, and I wince. Never thought I'd see the day where I'd miss the flexibility of leather figure skates, compared to the straight jackets my feet are currently stuffed in.

Paul carefully shuffles over the ice in his boots, the only part of his attire that's changed today. He didn't give up his khaki pants, and he's wearing a black jacket with the SporTech logo, the zipper drawn all the way up to his neck. Maybe if he put a hat over his bald head, he wouldn't be so cold. It's not like he has a head of hair to mess up.

"Retail cost is going to be over five hundred dollars per stick." Paul watches as I unlock the kickstand on both cases and set them up. "But these are just prototypes, so it's fine. We planned for an accident or two."

"We want to support our local high school teams where everything started." Dad follows Paul over, walking more confidently over the ice. "The U of M is still interested in testing these puppies, but we wanted to extend the offer to you guys, first. We're coming back tomorrow to work with Tracy and the ladies' team."

I bite my tongue to keep from showing my disdain as I unlatch the locks, keeping my back to all of them. Dad doesn't know it yet, but I'm going to be running a fever tomorrow morning, so it would probably be for the best if I stay home.

"We're very appreciative of everything that you guys do for us, so thank you." Lloyd approaches my shoulder to peer into the case. He lets out a low, appreciative whistle. "Now *that's* a stick."

"HyperShot Pro, SporTech's first artificially intelligent hockey training stick. Isn't she beautiful?" Dad gushes as he elbows me out of the way to be the first one to reach in, pulling out a sleek black stick, the blade reinforced with a rubber protector. "Made from carbon fiber composite, embedded with three different sensors, a Bluetooth transmitter, and wireless charging. My pride and joy. This technology is going to change the sport of hockey."

I awkwardly scratch behind my neck. Paul hands Lloyd one to look at himself, and I swear, I've never seen a handful of men look so deeply in love in my life. If this is the same way that I look at Clarity, then it's no wonder Cole has been warning me away the last few years.

Annabelle skates over to join us. I expect her to jump straight into a case herself, so I'm thrown off guard when she glides up on my other side. "Hey, Jason. Long time no see."

"What's up?" I side-eye her. She's bouncing on the balls of her heels, her blades clacking against the ground. Now I'm *really* thrown. I can't name one time where she's actually been excited to see me.

"Nothing. Do you have a minute to—"

I'm so distracted by this turn of events that I don't hear the hissing of blades approaching behind me, and I'm knocked off balance as someone slams into my back, wrapping their arms around my neck. It's been so long since I've been hit by a 180-pound boy that I nearly collapse face-first. Instinct kicks in and I plant my feet so I don't go down.

"Forbes! You hottie, you are a sight for sore eyes!" Willie crows and rubs his knuckles into my hair.

"Dude, what is your problem?" I jab my elbow into his ribs, connecting with the soft spot under his armpit where the chest protector doesn't reach. Annabelle backs off, chewing her lip.

He grunts and lets go with a loud laugh. I whip around as he exclaims, "It's been so long since you've been on this side of the ice. And in some Bauers!" He kicks my left foot. "That's my boy!"

"Reconnecting to your roots, huh?" Nick coasts over with Cole in tow.

"Let's call it that." I slap his shoulder before dapping up Cole. "You guys better be done horsing around, because if you break one of these, my dad will scalp you."

"And I'll hold you down." Coach Lloyd shakes his finger at the boys.

"Everyone can relax." Paul pulls out an armful of sticks. "These are just prototypes for field testing. We understand that accidents will happen. I'm not saying to go sword fight or beat each other with them, but they won't shatter if you look at them wrong. Here you go." He hands one to each of my friends, and they inspect them with varying degrees of awe. Dad watches with his hands on his hips, grinning like a new father in a hospital room.

I follow Paul's lead and start unloading more as the rest of the hockey team comes over, jostling and bumping each other out of the way to get their hands on one first.

Nick frowns as he moves off to the side, giving it a test swing. "I've been using the same brand of stick my entire career. This thing better not throw off my game."

"If you can't keep a puck out of the net because of this, I don't think it's the stick that's the problem," Cole retorts as he inspects the handle.

"It doesn't feel right."

"That's because you have the wrong one." I take Nick's stick and hand him one with a wider paddle meant for goalies. "Now you can quit whining."

He goes against Paul's words and smacks me on the hip. I use the stick he handed me to hit him in the knees while my dad's back is turned.

"You've been here for less than twenty minutes and you're already causing trouble?" Annabelle raises an eyebrow me. "The peewee boys' practice early on Saturday morning across town if you guys want to keep acting like children."

Willie holds out his hands for a high five. She gives him a cold stare, and he uses his other hand to give himself one. Cole laughs.

"Nice of you to come all the way out here to help when you're already so busy." Sterling glides around my friends, coming to a stop next to me. He holds out his hand. "I'll take one of those."

I consider shoving it down his throat, and from the look that flashes across Cole's eyes, I'm not the only one. I barely bless him with a passing glance as I hold one out, blade first. "Here you go."

"Thanks, Forbes." Sterling grins and yanks it away. "I'm glad to see that Clarity came to her senses. Do you feel like a hot potato yet?"

"Excuse me?" I tilt my head. *Her* senses? I'm about to come to mine and put a dent in his skull.

"Two hours, boys." Annabelle skates between us, lowering her voice to keep it from carrying as Paul and dad float amongst the team, droning on about the equipment. "That's it. Then you can go back to your spitting contest. Be civil, otherwise I'll put you on the bench for the rest of the night. You included." She points at me.

"I'm cool. Usually I'd say that we're back on the same level again, but that's not the case, is it? At least one of us is still on a team." Sterling smirks.

"At least when I call Clarity, it doesn't go straight to voicemail." I don't miss the way Sterling's nostrils flare, and that puts a smile on my face.

Cole raises his hand. "Don't you dare bring my sister into this."

"You're about eight months too late with that comment," Nick says. All three of us send him a withering glare as Lloyd blows into his whistle, the sharp note demanding everyone's attention.

As Paul and Dad thank everyone for their time today, Willie slowly approaches and cranes his neck to whisper, "I'm team Jason on this one."

"Tell Clarity that," I mutter. His lips twist upward. I don't know what's so funny. I don't get the chance to ask as Paul jumps into his next topic.

"What you're holding in your hands are smart hockey sticks designed to track real-time data on your performance. Think of them like fitness trackers built into your stick." He lifts the one he's holding in his hand and taps the shaft. "They have embedded sensors that measure swing speed, shot power, blade angle, even where the puck makes contact. We've also got accelerometers inside to track movement, and flex sensors to give us real-time feedback on how the stick responds to your shot."

Willie eyes his stick like a bomb that's about to detonate. Cole quietly quotes my dad from earlier, "Changing the game of hockey, all right."

"My net worth isn't nearly high enough to be handling this." Nick runs his hand over it.

"You're not even worth a McDonalds coupon," Willie says. Annabelle snaps her fingers at the boys when Nick goes to hit him this time.

"Now," Paul continues to speak, "like I said, these are still in the testing phase. That's why we're here. I want to see how they perform in real scenarios, and what adjustments we still need to make. We'll be tracking everything from the bench, so just play your game. I did ask Ralph to run you all through some specific drills. Breakaway shots, slap shots from the blue line, and passing accuracy. He will walk you through it, but if something feels off, just let us know." He glances at all the boys. "My goal is to make gear that works for you as the athlete. So give it your all, alright?"

He turns to Lloyd. "Coach, they're all yours."

"Thanks, Paul. Okay, boys! Get on the line. Jansky, pucks." Lloyd points at a bucket near the boards.

I nearly put a crick in my neck as I look over my shoulder to see what in the world Clarity is doing here, and my dreams are squashed when I realize Cole is skating away.

Wrong Jansky.

Willie bumps his shoulder into mine. "I saw that."

"Mind your own business." I turn away to retrieve the empty cases, my cheeks burning.

The ice sounds like it's coming to life as over thirty pairs of feet scratch against the surface, everyone going in separate directions. I ignore Sterling when he tries to make eye contact with me, tapping the top of his stick against his head in a silent recognition. I try not to think about the fact that he also saw me looking around like a broken bobblehead.

Paul gets off the ice first, making a beeline for the monitor that he brought to track the data. He takes a seat at the fold-up table that someone must've dragged out of the equipment room and immediately begins impersonating Tony Stark as he opens all the necessary databases. Dad follows him and stands behind his shoulder, crossing his arms as he watches Lloyd whip the boys into shape on the ice.

I do what I've been doing all week: sit and stay out of the way until someone needs me.

When practice ends, I do my due diligence and take the sticks from the players as they get off the ice, then stow them away safely in their cases. When everyone is off the ice, six slots are still empty. I mutter under my breath. Some players must've slipped past when I got caught up talking to my friends. Everyone is used to bringing their sticks home.

I go over to where Paul and Dad are leaning on the boards, talking to Coach Lloyd and Annabelle. They're caught up in their conversation. Might as well take matters into my own hands.

The hallway follows the curve of the building, and I push open the door to the boys' locker room. I'm immediately met with the stench of male body odor, topped off with loud chatter that accompanies inflated egos, and rap music that someone is playing at full volume.

A different boy that I recognize from Ortiz's team—Tyler, I think is his name—weaves his way past Cole and around the group, briefly dodging a loose puck that flies through the air before meeting my gaze as he approaches. He rolls his eyes, visibly annoyed, and mouths, *hockey players.*

I shrug as the teeth of guilt nip at me. During all my years of hockey practice, I can't ever recall acknowledging the figure skaters that came in and out. I'll give them credit. They're as silent as mice, except this is their locker room too. The hockey players act like they own it.

Unsettled, I continue to the benches and pick up an abandoned stick. One down, five to go.

"Here you go, man. I found these by the lockers." Willie approaches, holding two more sticks. His t-shirt is soaked with sweat, and he still has his hockey pants on.

"Thanks. You're a life saver." I take them from him at the same time Sterling's voice floats over the noise.

"...take it from me. It's a shame, huh? First it was the hockey semi-finals, and now Nationals. All that hard work, down the drain. I guess big competitions aren't for everyone." Sterling undoes the strap on his shoulder pad. "Maybe soon she'll find a man that can handle the pressure."

I catch the tail end of his conversation, and it's enough to douse my fire from earlier with more gasoline. Willie grunts as I shove the sticks in his arms.

Sterling turns around as I walk through the rows of benches toward him, and he laughs. "Perfect timing. Would you like to add to that?"

The corners of my vision turn red. His smile falters when I don't slow down, and he grunts when I put my hands on him, shoving him away. Hard.

"I'd love too," I say with a sneer, and push him again, making him stagger to catch his balance as he crashes into the lockers. Nick appears, his mouth moving soundlessly. I don't hear him. "She chose me. End of story."

Sterling's cheeks go red with anger and he steps into my face. "Actually, I'm pretty sure she chose *me* first. You were the charity case that she had to settle for."

A laugh of disbelief slips out of me. "The way I remember it, you chose to cheat on her. Who did she come running to when she needed help?"

He shakes his head dismissively. "Say what you want. That doesn't change the fact that you were the one who ruined her career. You're really good at dropping things: teams, partners, careers..." He shrugs.

I point at him, my hand shaking with rage. "Careful."

I'm never going to forget her tone when she told me she wanted me to leave the other night. She might've taken it back, but she still said it. My peace has been ruined since that goddamn competition because I've spent every waking hour trying to convince myself that there's no way I could've caught her, or changed the outcome.

"Or what?" Sterling cocks his head and smacks my hand away. "You'll knock me out the same way you knocked her out? Throw me onto my head? Let's be real, skating with you was the worst thing that ever happened to her."

His eyes flash with panic as I move forward. He stumbles over his feet to retreat, and his buddies jump out of the way.

I snarl, "One more word and you're eating through a straw until graduation."

Cole cuts between us, waving his arms like a referee.

"Time out! You guys need to stop using your asses as hats, right now." He presses his finger into my chest, and I back away. "You need to cool your jets."

Willie nods, and Nick presses his lips together. It's hard to tell whether they're enjoying the show with the rest of the locker room or on the verge of pulling us apart themselves.

Cole spins to Sterling. "And you need to stop. If I hear you talk about my sister one more time, you'll be picking your teeth off the ice."

"Your bark is bigger than your bite, Jansky." Sterling puffs up his chest again.

I push Cole out of the way, and something deep in my soul smiles as Sterling flinches away again. "Mine isn't. Get moving before you sit here wishing that I let Cole handle you."

"And you need to leave before I have to explain to Coach Lloyd why a brawl started in the locker room. I don't want his daughter to get involved." Nick grabs my elbow and drags me away.

Cole and I shudder at the thought of Annabelle getting into this argument, and Willie follows us, carrying all six sticks I was missing. If Sterling has anything else to say, I don't hear it as my friends all but kick me toward the door.

"You're the biggest idiot that I know." Cole starts to grab the door handle. "Seriously, you—"

The door flies open and cracks into the sticks that Willie is holding. He shrieks and jumps back to protect the thousands of dollars that he's holding onto, his face going pale with fear. Nick and I plaster ourselves to the wall as Montgomery nearly flies into us.

"Jason. God, you're still here." He's panting as he grabs the front of my shirt and drags me into the hallway.

I smack him away. "What's wrong?"

Cole, Nick, and Willie trickle out behind us. Montgomery lets go. "You're back in the game, dude. You and Clarity finished in tenth."

The floor spins under my feet. I reach out and grab the wall. "*What?*"

"Tenth?" Cole materializes alongside me. "How?"

Montgomery is practically vibrating. "Amy Gazuk couldn't keep her mouth shut." That name sounds familiar. She and her partner came in eighth place. "She was lighting you two up in the comments of that one post from Skate Snaps. Clarity's fangirls caught on and reported her for unsportsmanlike conduct, and the board dropped her."

"Holy shit," I breathe, and meet Cole's eyes. His excitement, his disbelief, matches my own. Goosebumps rake over my skin. I laugh. "Holy shit!"

"You're back in the game, baby!" Willie hoots and leaps forward, dumping the sticks on the floor to grab my shoulders and give them a hearty shake. I don't flinch, not even when Nick ruffles my hair.

"Clarity." I turn to Montgomery. "Does Clarity know? Did anyone tell her?"

"I don't know. Victor just texted me." Montgomery takes out his phone and holds it up for proof. "I'm assuming he's gotten ahold of her. This just happened, though."

"I have to tell her." I turn to my friends. "I should go."

"I'll be right behind you. Don't leave without me!" Cole runs back into the locker room, throwing off his shoulder pads as he goes.

"Willie and I will tell your dad and Lloyd that you left," Nick says as he picks the equipment off the floor. "Go get your woman, dude."

My cheeks flush. "We—She's not—"

"Oh, for the love of God." Willie shoves me. "Stop arguing and go!"

I can't help the laugh that slips out as I stumble away. "Thank you. Thank you, Montgomery."

He waves as I spin and run down the hallway. The sound of pounding footsteps approaching makes me jump out of the way, and Annabelle nearly sails right by.

"Jason, you guys are back on the roster!" She squeals and punches my arm as I screech to a stop. "You're going to Nationals!"

"How do you know?"

"I was trying to tell you earlier until Willie ruined the moment. I was going to tell you after practice, but your dad stopped me and you ran off." She grins. "Who's going to tell Clarity?"

"I'm going over to tell her now." I smack her shoulder appreciatively and take off again. "Meet you there!"

"You're the luckiest guy I know, Forbes!" Annabelle calls after me.

I know I am. Seriously, I feel like I just won the lottery.

My heart sings as I sail toward the lobby. If I weren't so giddy, I'd have half a mind to go down to Ortiz's rink and tell her the news. She can kick us while we're down all she wants, although she's never going to be able to stop us.

We're back on the road to Nationals.

Chapter 28

Clarity

I wish I could crawl into a cave and not come out until spring.

I've been exhausted all week. The shame of being stripped away from everything I've worked for and the regret of yelling at Jason weigh on my shoulders so heavily that it's a wonder I even drag myself out of bed every morning.

While Jason gracefully and selflessly accepted my apology, no one else seems to want to hear my side of the story leading up to the fall. Instead, the rumor mill continues to thrive.

I've known my new cognitive-behavioral therapist, Angela, for all of twenty minutes, however I don't hold back from telling her all of this. She reminds me of my grandma, who I lost a few years ago, and the words just fall out of me.

"Alright, then." Angela's armful of bangles jingle as she jots notes on her pad. "You've lived a lot of lives over the past few months."

"You can say that again." I run my fingertips over the fabric of the retro green couch I'm seated on. "Feels like I'm going on years, actually."

"I can imagine." She sets her pen down on her notepad and shuffles to the edge of her armchair to meet my eyes. "Before we go anywhere else, I want you to understand something. I'm not here to poke and prod and make you feel like a medical case. We're going to walk through this together, but you can set the pace, okay?"

"Sure." I've come to terms with this. It's not like I have much of a choice anymore.

Her face softens, and she leans back. "We're going to do a lot of uncomfortable work, but I won't let you give up on yourself. You're not alone here, not anymore."

"I don't want to stay on the outside this time, sitting here doing nothing like I've always done."

I recall the look in Jason's eyes when he said that to me. I wish I could tell Angela that I'm already not alone anymore. The lump in my throat keeps me from answering.

"I..." I swallow. "I don't even know where to start."

"How about the first moment you remember feeling like something shifted. What comes to the surface?" She clicks her pen.

I manage a shaky laugh despite myself. There's no telling when things changed from skipping a dessert here and there, to keeping a daily running list of how many calories I've consumed, and now taking drastic measures to manage the intake of those calories—or, well, the ejection.

"I don't know. My life has been fracturing since middle school. It's like a rock hit the windshield, and every day since then, the crack spreads wider. Now, everything feels..." I search for the right word. "Broken. My friendships, skating. Me."

Angela nods slowly, her gaze steady. Something about the way she's watching me makes me feel like she can read between the lines of my words. "Feeling broken isn't the same as *being* broken. People mistake the two all the time. You're sitting here, and that's proof you're stronger than you think."

My throat tightens again, much stronger this time. I don't know if she skipped over that part of Dr. Carlson's file, but I didn't exactly come here voluntarily.

"I don't feel very strong after everything that happened. Seriously, I cracked my head open on the ice." I point at the scar on my temple.

Angela lifts her hand, her bangles clinking again. "Hang on, I'm going to pause us there for a moment. Let's talk about the you that's in this room, not the version that fell quite yet." Her tone is so direct that it pulls me out of my spiraling thoughts.

I stare at her for a moment. "I can't just brush it off and forget everything that happened."

"I'm not asking you to," she says firmly. "We're going to reframe it and find a way to face what happened without letting it run the show."

"And how do we do that?" I ask with more attitude than I mean to, except my patience is thinning. I thought I was doing a damn good job living in the conditions that I made for myself until I found myself in the hospital.

"One step at a time. Today, we'll start small. Let's talk about your relationship with food." She notices the way I stiffen and waves her pen. "Unfortunately, we can't change what we don't understand. Tell me about a typical day. What does eating look like for you right now?"

Shame claws its way up my throat. There's a reason why I refuse to talk about this topic with anyone. This has always been my giant to face, alone.

Angela watches me, unflinching. I can't wiggle my way out of this, so I take a deep breath and prepare myself. "I'm generally not hungry in the morning. Or at least, I tell myself I'm not."

She nods and jots something down.

"At lunch, I eat something to stay strong enough for skating, but I try to keep my calorie intake as low as possible. I can't gain weight with what I do, so I try to pack lunches that are around one-thousand calories." The number sounds horrifying when I say it out loud. I fidget with the sleeve of my sweater, continuing despite the heavy weight of embarrassment sitting on my chest. "Dinner is harder to avoid, especially if my parents are home. I can't really get away with skipping it. Especially because I need to hit my daily threshold to stay healthy."

Thankfully Angela doesn't comment on the whole *staying healthy* bit, because we both know that if that were the case, I wouldn't be here right now. She glances up from writing. "So dinner feels required?"

I shrug and avoid her eyes. The couch fabric is much easier to look at. "Kind of. But I don't eat much. Just enough so no one will hound me about it."

She taps her pen thoughtfully. "What happens when you eat more than you planned?"

The question hits a nerve. I recall previous years where I'd skip multiple meals over multiple days to make up for high calorie counts until I became brave enough to start purging. My stomach tightens at the thought. "I feel out of control. Like I failed."

"Failed what?"

"Being better, I guess. I don't know." My voice wavers. "If I eat too much, it feels like proof that I'm weak and can't handle myself. And if I lose control there, then what's the point?"

"Clarity." She places her notebook on the side table before folding her hands in her lap and leaning forward. "Eating isn't a test you pass or fail. It's how your muscles repair, and how your heart beats. You don't earn it because your body needs it to stay alive."

I know this. I've been trying to tell myself that for years, and yet...

"It doesn't feel that simple."

"I know. But feelings aren't facts. We're going to work on separating the two," Angela says gently.

My vision blurs, and I blink back the tears. "It's just that skating is everything. It's all I've ever been good at. I can't keep losing control there, otherwise I might as well not even go back. If I can't compete, then what's the point?"

"The difference is that skating is something you do." She glances between my eyes. "It's not who you are. You're allowed to exist outside of it."

The room falls quiet, except for the soft ticking of the wall clock. Her words seep into the spaces I've left empty for almost ten years, touching something raw and fragile deep inside of me.

"What if I don't know who I am outside of skating?" I whisper as more tears spill over my cheeks. It hurts to admit, but it's the truth.

She picks up her notebook again, though not before sliding a tissue box toward me across the coffee table. "Then that's what we'll figure out together."

I've never been so happy to see my mom in my life. She's parked in the front row of the parking lot, and my love for her is solidified when I jump in and go to turn on the seat warmer. It's already on maximum heat.

"You're the best parent ever." I buckle my seatbelt. "Thank you for warming up my seat."

"Of course. It's colder than the dickens out there." Her eyes brighten with the compliment. She slides the gear shifter into reverse. "How was your first session?"

I readjust the air vents. Should I start by saying Angela made me, unintentionally, cry three different times? Or how angry she was when I mentioned my eating disorder started when I was nine years old because of an offhand comment from Ortiz? I'm sure Mom would love to hear that my breakup with Sterling motivated me to lose a few more pounds just to prove to myself that I was in control of my life, and so that I'd always be skinnier than the girl he cheated on me with.

Instead, I settle on saying, "It was interesting. My therapist is cool, but it's hard to strip down everything I've built my life around in an hour. She makes everything sound so simple when she explains it. My brain just can't comprehend that food is a tool, not a weapon."

"I bet it is hard." Her hands tighten around the wheel as we broach this subject. "You've spent nearly ten years convincing yourself that it *is* a weapon."

I nod in agreement and watch the snow-covered trees pass outside the window. I've done enough damage talking about and mulling over all of that today. Mom, always a saint, picks up on my mood change and turns the conversation around to rant about the way Maureen treated a young family at work today.

When she turns at the intersection to the house, my eyebrows raise when I see the driveway. It's no surprise that Cole is home—hockey practice ended a while ago.

What *is* a surprise is seeing Jason's car sitting on the curb, covered in salt from the roads. My heart leaps into my throat. He didn't tell me that he was coming over tonight. I thought he was doing side work for his dad. I don't have the chance to mentally prepare seeing him.

"Is there something about *that* situation that you're not telling me?" Mom motions at his car, trying and failing to hide her smirk. Her tone implies enough to make my face flush. "He's been a new man since breaking up with Tiffany."

"I would be too. That girl is a vampire, and we both know it."

"That's not what I meant." She pulls into the garage and turns the ignition off. I don't feed into her curiosity because, honestly, there's nothing to say. I hop out, and she's hot on my heels. "No comment from the crowd?"

"Nope. Nothing to say. Jason's just a friend, and you know it."

"Does Jason know that?" Mom asks, then laughs when I glare at her.

She beats me to the garage door and pushes it open with her shoulder. "Hi, we're home!"

Cole shuffles out of the kitchen. "You guys are home early." He's already changed out of his training clothes to don his finest attire: blue fuzzy pajama pants with reindeer on them and a baggy t-shirt he bought at our first freshman homecoming game.

"Nice pajamas. You must be feeling the holiday spirit." I quirk an eyebrow as I hang up my jacket. My attention snaps to movement behind Cole, and I immediately go still.

Jason steps around him, his physical presence like a magnet. I don't know what he's doing here, although it must not matter anymore to him because his shoulders drop and his eyes soften. He inhales slowly, chest expanding, like he finally has access to an oxygen mask. Heat fills my face, making my staples itch. Damn things.

"I am, actually," Cole responds with a huff and keeps walking to the living room. "The rest of my sweatpants are in the washer. If you'd prefer, I can take these off and walk around in my boxers."

"I'd like to see that," a fourth voice says and steps around Jason. I laugh and meet Victor halfway, wrapping him in a hug. Cole gags, and Annabelle prances down the stairs wearing one of my old sweatshirts.

"What in the world?" I pretend to not notice the irritation that flashes across Jason's face when I embrace Annabelle next. "What are you guys doing here? Where's your cars?"

"It's a long story. I'll tell you in a minute. At least take your shoes off first." Victor backs off and glances at Jason, his eyes brimming with unspoken words that I'm sure I'll hear in a minute. He splits off to the living room with Cole, and mom is grinning like a kid on Christmas as she slips into the kitchen.

"*Someone* took all the parking space." Annabelle shoots Jason a glare as she follows the boys. "I had to use the lot next door."

Jason rolls his eyes at her retreating back, then regards me. He smiles. "Hey, C.J."

"Hi, J.C." My heart performs beautiful twizzles as he approaches. He hesitates, his stride faltering as he comes to a stop right out of arm's reach. I want to hug him. I don't know if we're on good enough terms again *to* hug. I settle on scratching my neck. It's too late. I've already made this weird.

"Therapy. How was it?" Jason shakes his head, catching his mistake. His cheeks flush. "How was therapy?"

A smile tugs at my lips. "It was fine. Weird, and sad, and eye-opening, but fine."

"Clarity! Forbes!" Cole yells from across the house. "Get in here!"

"I'm glad. We can talk more about it later." Jason tips his head in the direction of the living room.

I follow, inhaling the scent of him, letting it wash over me. "Speaking of, what in the world are you doing here? Shouldn't you be with your dad?"

"That's another long story." At my pointed look, Jason scratches his jaw as he quietly admits, "Something came up."

"What? What happened?" I slow my pace to finish our conversation before we turn the corner.

He nudges me with his elbow. "You'll find out."

"Tell me."

"I can't."

"Yes, you can."

"No, I absolutely can't." He tilts his head. "Careful, your Italian is starting to show."

"What's that supposed to mean? Am I being stubborn?"

"You said it, not me."

I scoff and swat his arm, making him laugh. My heart grows two sizes.

Cole, Victor, and Annabelle look up as we walk in. I don't like the matching smirks on the boys' faces. Annabelle raises her eyebrows. I ignore all of them.

"So what's going on?" I weave around the sectional, taking the empty spot next to Victor.

Jason stands next to Cole on the other side of the room and crosses his arms. "Kerr, would you like to start?"

"How *did* you get here?" Annabelle turns to him.

It's not often that I see Victor blush, so my interest is piqued instantly. "Well, I got on Baros' good side, and he gave me a ride since my car is in the shop."

My jaw drops. "*Montgomery Baros?*"

"You're fraternizing with the enemy?" Annabelle shrieks and launches up from her armchair. She grabs a stuffed pillow and throws it at him. "You could've told us!"

"You guys are surprised?" Cole's comment gets lost in our shock. *My* shock.

"I *am* telling you guys! Let me explain." Victor holds up his hand.

"Oh, my God." The texts, and the comments, and the hovering. It all makes sense now, even if it was under my nose the entire time. I was too preoccupied with my life falling apart to notice.

"I'm sorry. Can you guys read my mind? No? Then let me talk." He dishes out a look that shuts everyone up. "We've been talking more ever since I've been on the sidelines. He's a really cool guy. Seriously, he's been opening up to me."

Cole quirks an eyebrow. "I'm sure he has."

I rub my eyes. "*Anyway.*"

"Anyway." Victor shoots Cole a dark look. "We talk a lot about skating and how it's affected our lives, especially since we've been athletes for so long. He told me that he's ready to break away from Juliette and that he wishes she never followed him over here because he wanted a fresh start. She's a control freak."

"I could've told you that, and I barely know her." Annabelle sits back down.

"No, it's bad." His eyes cut to mine. "He said that he hasn't known what to do or who to tell, so he's just been keeping to himself so he won't accidentally get himself in trouble. You don't have bad luck, Clarity. She's been ruining you."

I lay my hand flat on the couch cushion to keep from tipping over. "How?"

"What do you mean?" Jason asks, his tone suddenly sharp and dangerous.

Victor meets the eyes of everyone in the room. "She told Monty about sneaking upstairs to take those videos of you and Jason. When she sent them to Skate Snaps, she hoped someone from the USFSA would see them and pull you from the competition."

The videos.

This entire time, I thought Tiffany sicced one of her teammates on us. Juliette's been so kind, I never thought she would've had the balls to do something like that. Jason goes oddly still.

He's still not done talking. "Monty also said that she frayed your laces on your and Jason's first practice, and she was boasting about pulling the right threads on your dress to make sure the threads would eventually snap. I guess she was super pissed off when you managed to borrow Darika's."

I remember borrowing her my gloves the day before mine and Jason's first practice, and I told her to put them back when she was done. I can still picture her tight smile before we stepped onto the ice at the Invitational, her sharp voice. The way she seemed so remorseful, yet so mad.

"You're kidding me," Annabelle says curtly, her eyebrows bunched together. She's on the edge of her seat, hanging onto every word.

Victor looks at me and shrugs. "I guess Miss Juliette McKenzie wasn't leaving her competitive streak with you in the past, after all."

"She really hates you that much?" Cole asks me. "What did you do to her?"

"Nothing!" I sputter.

My mind races, flying through the possibilities. What have I ever done to Juliette that would make this treatment acceptable? What's so special about me, other than the fact that I'm one of the few girls in the state who can give her a run for her money on the ice?

Jason laughs bitterly. "Seriously? She caused all of this shit, and for what? To defend her title from when she was skating in novice competitions back in middle school? Give me a break."

"Don't say it like that." Annabelle crosses her arms. "People do crazy things for what they're passionate about. Wouldn't you have done anything to get back on the hockey team?"

"Maybe at one point." Jason puts his hands on his hips. "Not anymore. Sometimes a kick to the ego prepares you for something even better."

"I don't think you'd have that same opinion if Victor never got injured." Cole shrugs. Jason shoves him.

"So, what do we do now?" I talk over all of them to get us back on topic. "Just let her get away with ruining my life?" Quite literally. If it weren't for her, all of this drama on my blog would've never happened in the first place.

"Funny you mention that, because that's the real reason why we're all here." Annabelle pushes up the sleeves of her sweater, obviously battling a smile as she leans forward. "Hold on to your chair."

I groan. "Please don't tell me you killed her."

"Thinking about it," Jason mutters.

"When's the last time you checked your phone?" Victor starts to bounce his knee.

"It's been a few hours. I don't think I've taken it off Do Not Disturb in days." I pull it out of my pocket, and raise an eyebrow when all four of them lean closer. "Okay, actually though, what's going on?"

Victor looks at Annabelle, who looks at Cole, who looks at Jason. His eyes are shining as he speaks. "We're back on the roster. We're going to Nationals."

"What?" I jump to my feet and spin to face my best friend, and my brother. "What?"

I turn back around to look at Jason. He's glowing, and I swear, tonight I don't know whether I want to punch him for keeping this information from me or kiss him for being everything I could ever want in a boy. "*What?!*"

"You're going to Nationals!" Mom yells as she bounces into the living room, jumping up and down.

Suddenly everyone is on their feet, and I'm laughing from shock and adrenaline and pure elation. Our little group brings the same energy of the hockey team when they win state—laughing, crying, jumping in a circle.

I find Jason on instinct, and this time, I don't hesitate to wrap him in a hug. He squeezes his arms around me and picks me up off the floor to spin me around.

"Nationals!" I grab his shoulders when he sets me down and rattle him. "How did this happen?"

"Amy Gazuk couldn't keep her big mouth shut." Jason grins and grabs my face with both hands. My heart jumps into my throat. "She got herself and her partner disqualified. Unsportsmanlike conduct."

"What did she do?" I turn to look at everyone.

Cole flourishes his hand. "Check your phone. You're getting lit up for the billionth time this month."

I nearly drop my phone as I take it out of my pocket. Jason puts his hands on my shoulders as he stands behind me to read over my head. I turn off *DND*, and sure enough, my phone glitches as the notifications roll in like a tsunami wave.

Post by @skatesnapsmidwest:
THREAD: Jansky & Forbes: OUT to IN
You read that right: after last week's viral drama, the USFSA has removed Gazuk/Roland from the Nationals roster for unsports-manlike conduct. Guess who just snagged their spot? The come-back nobody saw coming... Not even us. Let's unpack.

Post by @icewireweekly:
The most chaotic Nationals roster change in YEARS.
• Gazuk/Roland: Disqualified for online trash talk.
• Jansky/Forbes: In by default.
• The fanbase: Losing their collective minds.
Click here for the full lowdown!

Post by @blades.edge.insider:
HEADLINE: Nationals shake-up after skatings "Mean Girls moment" goes nuclear. Jansky & Forbes just re-entered the chat.

@theofficialsilver:
JUSTICE. HAS. BEEN. SERVED.

@jtlaurie98:
If they couldn't qualify fair and square, they shouldn't be there at all. USFSA just wants drama for the ratings

@l.u.v.skating
Gazuk is about to post the longest Notes app apology of her career LOL

All I do is stare in disbelief. My world has completely flipped on its head in a matter of seconds, and my head is spinning with the aftermath. This isn't a joke.

"My god." I throw my phone onto the nearest couch, then gasp. My stomach drops as I turn to Victor. "But we don't have a coach. We can't just pull a routine out of our ass. No one is going to be able to take us on until the next season starts."

"You're in luck, because my calendar is open for the rest of the year."

"You?" I clarify. "*You* would coach us? Is that legal?"

"If that college kid from California can skate at a collegiate level with a student-led team, I think I can make sure Forbes never drops you again."

Jason sits on the couch next to me, his eyebrows drawing together. "It's never been on purpose."

"We'd have a problem if it was," Cole adds.

"You're serious?" I ask Victor again and search his eyes for an answer before I get my hopes up too much.

"Clarity." He pats my head. "I have recorded nearly every single one of your guys' practices. I skated with you for longer, and I've been on the ice since before we even met. I'm very serious. You need to finish healing, then we need to start practicing immediately."

I open my mouth. Annabelle cuts me off. "I already talked to my dad, and he's willing to let you guys borrow his sheet of ice in the morning. He's going to make sure the hockey boys don't take over."

"Once you're healed and ready next weekend, we can start." Victor waves his hands in the air. "I've already got some great ideas for choreography."

"Done. I'm ready. God, I'm so ready." I whirl around to face Jason and our chests nearly brush. I don't shy away. Right now, I'm tempted to smother him, but I settle for grabbing his hands. "Are you ready to lace back up? Give Juliette a run for her money?"

Jason squeezes my palms. If it weren't for the fact there are other people in the room, I think he'd be tempted to close the space between us and kiss me. I can't even think about it without getting light-headed.

"I've been waiting for you to say that."

March 2016 - Age 17

Jason

I overheard Clarity talking about wanting clip-on microphones to make more videos for her blog over the holidays, and I bought them for her that same week. The little box has been hidden under my bed for the past three months because I knew they'd make the perfect gift for her seventeenth birthday.

Cole and Clarity insisted that they didn't need a birthday party. Me and Annabelle refused to let them get away that easily. We—actually, Annabelle worked with Sterling on most of the planning. I just paid to cater the food. I refuse to be hands-on when he's around.

I wave at Tiffany as she drives away with her friend. I wasn't shocked when she told me she wanted to leave early, so thankfully she found someone to take her home. I was more surprised that she wanted to come at all when I pitched this idea to her.

I duck back into my car. Sliding my hand behind the drivers seat, I bump against the box. *Bingo*.

My heart gallops in my chest as I come up successful with the wrapped gift. Well, wrapped is a relative term. It looks like someone tied my dominant hand behind my back and forced me to wrap it with my left. And I'm starting to have second thoughts about my choice of the wrapping paper with the *Frozen* characters on it. I just thought it was funny considering that was Clarity's favorite movie when it came out a few years ago.

Tucking the box into my jacket pocket, I duck my head against the chilly wind and head back toward Sterling's house. Yeah. *Sterling's*.

My blood starts to boil even just picturing his face. It was bad enough earlier when Annabelle brought out the cake and started to sing happy birthday. When the song finished, Sterling swiped frosting on Clarity's mouth and kissed it off. I nearly leapt over the kitchen table and knocked him out until Tiffany distracted me with a question, except it was too late. That image is branded into my brain.

I close the door behind me as I enter the house and scan the living room. There was a ton of people here earlier—way more people than I recognized, considering I share the same friend group as the Jansky twins—but the crowd is starting to disperse. I still don't recognize anyone, and I scowl. Where did Cole and Clarity go? Our friends? They were in here when I walked Tiffany out.

As I weave toward the kitchen, the sound of feet pounding down the stairs makes me spin around.

"Hey, man. Where'd everyone go?" I ask Willie. I suddenly register the horror in his eyes, and my gut drops to the floor. I've never seen this kid so angry in my life. Scratch that—I've *never* seen him angry. My blood pressure skyrockets. "What happened?"

"Forbes. I need to talk to you." He grabs my arm and drags me toward the kitchen.

"Where's Cole and Clarity? Are they okay?" My fingertips start to tingle as my breath shallows.

Willie stays silent, which is also very uncharacteristic. I feel like I'm going to be sick by the time we enter the kitchen, which is empty.

He turns to me. "Let me preface this: don't yell at me."

"Oh, God. What did you do?"

"Listen to me." Willie grabs my hand. I try to pull it away. He keeps holding it and stares in my eyes. "I caught Sterling with Hattie. Like, *with* her."

I stare at him.

With...

No. Oh, no.

Raging heat burns through my body, turning my blood into flames. I rip my hand out of his grasp and whirl around. "Where is he? Willie, I swear to God, where the fuck is he?"

Who in their right mind would cheat on Clarity? Especially a Teletubby-lookalike son of a bitch like *Sterling*. He should consider himself lucky if he ever puts his hands on a donkey's ass, much less Clarity's, *much* less any other girl that's not her. He already won the jackpot with dating her, so the fact he threw her away is absolutely mind-boggling.

What's worse is that I saw this coming.

I called it. And I'm going to kill him.

"Jason. Bro, *stop*." Willie grabs my arm, and flinches when I turn on him.

"You listen to me." I don't hear myself speak because my blood is rushing so fast in my ears. "You're going to tell me where Sterling is, then you're going to tell me where Clarity went."

My voice cracks on Clarity's name. I must've been outside when this all happened. I should've been here to protect her.

Willie scratches his ear. "Nick and Cole have him cornered in the back yard. Just... don't go out there. They're handling him. Annabelle is upstairs with—wait—Jason!"

I'm already halfway to the stairs. I take them three at a time, rushing to find her.

As much as I'd love to go outside and tear Sterling's head off, my first priority is Clarity. It always has been, and always will be.

My eyes bounce from door to door as I go down the hall, making note of each dark room. I slow down as I approach what must be the bathroom. The door is shut, and light leaks out from underneath, along with ragged sobs.

I slam to a stop.

"Clarity, look at me. It's—"

"I don't understand!" Clarity's voice hits my heart and breaks it even further. "I don't understand. Is it because I wouldn't sleep with him? Am I not pretty enough? Not skinny enough? Not—"

Her words get cut off, muffled by the sound of shuffling feet and cloth. Annabelle must've cut her off with a tight hug.

Tears race down my cheeks as I pace outside the door. Do I knock? Do I leave them be? I don't know.

I do know that I want to tell Clarity she doesn't need to sleep with a single soul on this earth to gain their respect or validation. She is the most gorgeous girl that's ever graced this universe with their presence. Her beauty isn't based off her looks—it's because of her heart, and everything about her heart is enough.

Annabelle continues to hush her, mumbling words of affirmation, calming her down. Still, Clarity hiccups around her tears. I feel her heartbreak like it's my own.

I bite my hand to keep from making a noise as I gently, quietly, rest my forehead against the door. My body aches to hold her and comfort her, but I was too late.

Chapter 29

Jason

Last night felt like Christmas Eve, going to bed knowing that when I woke up this morning, I'd be skating with Clarity again.

We've been working with Victor every night for the past week, putting our heads together to come up with ideas for our programs, talking about what we did and didn't like about the way Ortiz coached. We watched replays of past practices until our eyes were dry and red-rimmed, breaking down every movement, every touch, each expression.

Between school and planning our comeback, I've barely had the chance to think about the snake in the grass: Juliette. She must know that we know because I haven't seen her once during school.

That's probably for the best because, if I had the chance, I wouldn't hesitate to tell her exactly what I think of her. I should've trusted my gut from the first time it rang the warning bell. Too late for that, I guess. All I can do now is make her wish she never even looked in Clarity's direction.

I brush my fingertips instinctively against her back as the thought crosses my mind, grounding myself with her presence. She's here, back on the ice, safe with me.

Clarity casts me a warm, playful side-eye. "Two weeks off the ice and you're already losing your balance?"

"Just trying to get you to loosen up." I purposely poke her harder in the side.

She lets out a loud giggle and smacks my hand away. "Quit that. You know my ribs are ticklish."

Everything in me wants to do it again so she'll keep laughing like that, but I'm not totally a monster. I hold up my hands in defeat and she reaches over, slapping her fist against my palm, making a hand puppet of a turkey. Her eyes shine when I'm the one who ends up laughing.

The door that leads onto the rink opens, the familiar creak instantly catching my attention. I haven't heard it since the springtime, although I've encountered it enough over the years to know that sound means Lloyd is coming out onto the ice, and Lloyd always means business. Clarity follows my gaze when I whip my head around, and she smiles as Victor steps out with his skates on.

"Well, well, well. There's a sight I never thought I'd see again." She splits away from me to meet him halfway. I'm right behind her.

Victor grins. "Just like riding a bike. As long as I don't trip and fall on my wrist again."

"You've got nothing to lose. I'm already here." I reach out to shake Clarity's shoulder. She purses her lips at me, though the look doesn't reach her eyes.

"I don't feel like paying that hospital bill a second time." He lifts up his phone as he changes the subject. "I got my Bluetooth hooked up to the speakers, so we should have music. I know we discussed something more modern, but I changed my mind. I want to throw it back."

Clarity sighs. "Is this choice up for discussion? Can we do a show of hands?"

"Please," I say with a groan. "No more of Ortiz's music."

"You've guys haven't even heard what I chose, so quit griping." He waves his hand dismissively. "I gave it more thought last night. Both of you guys are great skaters, that's obvious."

"I'm sorry. What was that?" Clarity digs in her ear. "Can you say that again? Slowly."

She's not even talking to me and my heart races at the connotation that her words could be taken at.

Victor doesn't even blink as he shoots her a look. "Ortiz kept you guys on a tight leash. Being able to stand on the sidelines and watch you these last few months made me realize that she likes to pair her skaters with the vision in her head, not the reality of the situation."

Clarity and I share a quizzical look.

He huffs. "What I'm saying is that she's not creative. Sure, she uses good choreography, but it never fits the picture. She came up with a program where all you guys did was skate together. Where's the passion? The spark?"

The passion has been simmering under my skin for so long that sometimes I'm surprised I haven't burst. If someone cut me and made me bleed, all I would bleed out is Clarity.

I don't dare look at her in case my face is giving away my thoughts.

"All we need to do is win," she says defensively, then catches herself and adds, "and have fun."

I almost start applauding for her sake.

"And you'll win to this song. It'll help you play to your strengths." Victor unlocks his phone and hits the play button.

All I need to hear is the first three guitar strums and I recognize the song. My stomach plummets. Not only does he want us to play to our strengths, he wants us to do it to one of the biggest love songs from the late '90s. I *really* don't dare look at Clarity as the breath freezes in my chest. I force myself to inhale, to not let the lyrics unravel me before we've taken a single step to this music.

"You want us to skate to the Goo Goo Dolls?" Clarity asks, exasperated.

"'*Iris*' is a classic! It's raw and emotional. Everything that I want you two to bring to the ice."

"As long as it's not another classical song, I don't care," I joke to break up the tension.

"Are we still sticking with the routine that we've been planning?"

Victor pauses the song. "Yes. For the most part."

I snort. "What's that supposed to mean?"

"I took some creative liberties. Instead of starting in a hand hold, I want you guys here." He pushes off and moves to the center of the rink, pointing down at the ice. We follow and stand in front of him.

"That's a start, but you two need to lie down."

I raise my eyebrows.

"Excuse me?" Clarity sputters. "It's cold!"

"Clarity, please." Victor rolls his head to the side and eyes her. "We've been skating for over ten years, and *now* you want to complain about it being cold?"

"What are you thinking?" I cut in to get us back on track.

"You'll lay on your back there" —Victor points— "and Clarity will do the same there. When the music starts, she'll roll over you, pause, then lay on your other side. You'll do the same, except when you go over her, you'll push up and grab her hand, pulling her up. Then you'll continue to do the routine like we've been planning."

"I'm sorry." Clarity shakes her head, her cheeks pink. "I think I'm missing something. What's the point of this?"

Victor gets this look on his face that I really don't appreciate. "We all know that passion starts on our backs."

I'm surprised that I am not melting the ice around my feet with the heat that's coming off my body.

"Oh, for the love of god." She groans. "Is this even competition legal?"

"It is, actually. I want a shocking intro. The judges need to feel what you're feeling." Victor shifts his weight onto his heels and slowly moves backward. "Let's at least try it. Introduction, lift, twirl. Get through those three elements, then we'll regroup."

"You're the boss," I respond despite my heart pounding in my ears.

"You got that right. Hop to it, we're wasting precious time." Victor claps his hands together before moving away, giving us plenty of room.

Clarity turns to me, her eyes wide and wild with intensity. "He's crazy."

"I think he's onto something." I give her a lop-sided smile and mentally prepare myself before sinking onto my knees, the cold biting into my bones. "No one else started their routine like this the other weekend."

"That's because everyone else still has their sanity intact." She follows suit and shivers. "Except for Juliette."

That reminder makes me grimace. "Don't remind me. I don't want to see her ever again." I shift onto the side of my hip and sharply inhale as I lie back, the warmth of my body heating the ice, soaking my back in cold water.

Clarity lies down beside me, our arms brushing. "Haven't you noticed she's been avoiding us since then? She probably knows that we know."

That passion Victor mentioned ripples through every nerve in my body. I curl my toes to keep it contained as she rolls her head over to look at me. I can see the thin ribbons of gold cutting across her brown eyes, the chapped skin of her lips, the flare of her nostrils. We've been working together for months, yet something about this moment feels so much more intimate than those other practices.

"C.J, let's not ruin this moment," I say lightly.

"You're right. Okay. Are you ready?"

I wiggle my fingers. I'm simultaneously sweltering hot and freezing cold. If I lie next to her for another moment longer, I fear I'll grab her by the waist and pull her over me for an entirely different reason.

I swallow. "Yes."

"I hope Victor is happy." She pushes off the ice, calibrating her movements to hover over me for a moment, pressing her palms into the ground. Her eyes find mine, and honest to God, she smiles at me deviously before rolling to my other side.

I don't know what comes over me, but I'm right behind her, a perfect mirror image as I launch off my elbow and lift my right foot, throwing it over her legs. I plant my blades on either side of her legs, brace my palms on the ice, and when I lean in, she inhales sharply. The look that flashes across her face almost sends me into a frenzy.

"I really want to kiss you," I admit so quietly that I almost believe that I kept that thought inside my head. She laughs, and her gaze flickers down to my lips.

She mocks Victor. "Passion starts on our backs."

I lift my hips, sliding my feet closer to Clarity's thighs. He didn't tell me to add this flair, but I can't stop myself from sliding my hands up her sides until I grab under her arms. I don't stop at just pulling her onto her feet—I sweep her into the air, twirling her around, making her giggle until I set her back down.

She regains her cool and mellows out. I don't miss the shimmer in her eye as I grab her hand and lead her into the next move. We are one body. Left leg, right, left, split. She stays in one place, flourishing her arms as I whirl around in a sharp circle, moving in a serpentine until I'm flying around her back. She holds out her right arm and I grab it, yanking her after me, forcing her to face me.

"Okay?" I ask for confirmation to make sure she's ready for the lift. We were joking earlier about taking time off, except it's not a joke anymore. I gauge her expression and I know the answer before she says a word.

"Perfect. Catch me." She grins and spins around, carrying herself backward into my arms. I grab her waist and pull her close, engaging in a small lift that sweeps her off her feet. I toss her up like a doll, spinning her in my hands so she can face me as I let her down. Our noses brush, and for a moment, we share the same breath.

Unfortunately, I have to let go of her, letting her have her moment before grabbing her outreached hand again and twirling her like a dancer. The moment dissolves around me when she lets go and back pedals away, another large grin splitting her face. I got so swept up in her that I forgot the whole point was to cut off right here.

I tune back in to reality, my hands shaking.

Victor looks way too smug as he sails over, clapping. "What did I say? I'm a goddamn genius. *That* is ice dancing. *That* is the Clarity and Jason that I know. Did you feel it?"

I glance at him and put my hands on my hips, unsure how to word that not only is he genuinely a genius, he's also my mortal enemy for putting me through this special type of hell. Or maybe it's heaven. I can't decide.

Clarity makes it more complicated by shrugging and meeting my gaze. "I'm definitely feeling something."

"Cold?" I offer.

She grins. "No. Passion." Her eyes flick to Victor for confirmation. "That's the word, right?"

He smirks. "Let's call it that. Sure." He waits until she turns her back to get my attention and mouths, *you're welcome.*

I roll my eyes. Passion, a job well done. It's all the same to me, and my soul clings to her partial acknowledgment. I hope that one day, she'll be able to call it what it actually is.

We continue to slowly break down the routine move by move. Victor follows in our shadows, calling out each upcoming maneuver. I have my hands on Clarity's waist when he asks for the curve lift, the first big lift of our routine. I feel the way her body locks up, as if his words have electrocuted her. I drag my heels into the ice, pulling us to a stop.

She spins around when I let go of her. "Why did you stop?"

"Why are you getting nervous?" I tilt my head.

Victor slows down to watch. I've never been so grateful to have a coach that actually lets us talk.

Her eyelashes flutter. I swear, if she brushes me off with another lie, I'm going to shake the truth out of her.

"I can't—" She cuts herself off with a shaky breath and presses her knuckles against her eyes for a moment. "I can't get out of my head. Every time you've gone to lift me for the last two months, I haven't remembered how to carry myself. All I think about is taking down Victor—or you—and now it's like I can feel myself falling again, hitting the ice. Maybe I am a liability." Her gaze flashes between us. "It was worth a shot."

"No. Shut up." Victor cuts between us before I can say anything. "First of all, you need to stop reading those stupid comments from those losers."

"They're not *wrong*—"

"Yes, they are."

Clarity glances at me for help as Victor continues to talk. I shrug. I couldn't say any of this better myself.

"The problem isn't just them. It's you."

"Okay." I start to move forward. "That's uncalled for."

Victor holds up his palm to me, and I stop. Clarity stares at him, stunned.

"I know that you care about me and Jason, but seriously, you need to get out of your head. What do you gain by trying to control the entire situation? Who are you helping by trying so hard to *not* fall? This dude used to run into and fight people for fun." Victor points at me. "He can handle your shit, Jansky. You know this."

Her eyes flicker to mine. I offer a soft smile. Victor gets between us again.

"We're not practicing tomorrow." He crosses his arms. "You guys need to do some team bonding, because I am not dragging you to Nationals by your bootstraps. *You* need to do the work, Clarity."

"I trust him." She lifts her chin defiantly.

"Great." Victor looks at me. "Let's do that lift again."

Clarity's expression falls, and I can't help my smirk when Victor gives her a knowing look. "That's what I thought. Figure out a way to get on the same page tomorrow, and let's start fresh on Monday."

"Come over to my house." I look at her. "The ice on the lake is deep enough to skate on. It can be like old times."

She grimaces. "Do you think skating is a good idea? That's my problem in the first place."

"I have a few ideas. It'll be fun." I grin when she frowns, unimpressed.

"I don't care what you guys do. Just get this" —Victor waves his hands— "figured out."

Oh, I'll make sure we get everything figured out, alright.

Chapter 30
Clarity

I haven't been to Jason's house in so long that I nearly drive past his driveway. My old car squeaks as I step on the brakes and put it in reverse to try again. I eye the gates as I pass by them, and I know the rust on the exterior of my car doors doesn't match the aesthetic of his dad's lake house. Well, lake mansion. I've never understood why two people live in such a big house when they're never home, anyway.

The car lets out a sigh of relief as I turn it off, get out, and gather my bag from the passenger seat. I follow the sidewalk to the front door. The stones are slick with the fog that drifted over the city last night and froze in place. Even the bare bushes and trees are glistening with icicles. Everything is hidden behind a water colored blur of grey.

I strategically place my feet on the porch stairs as I ascend, and glance up when movement catches my eye.

Jason opens the door and leans on the frame, a smile splitting his face. He's wearing black sweatpants and a red sweatshirt the shame shade that my cheeks just turned.

"Hey, stranger." His eyes drink me in.

"Hi, J.C." I grin when he chuckles. "Sorry I'm late. The roads were slippery, and it was hard to see."

"All I care about is that you got here safely." He steps back to let me in and takes my bag from me. I slip off my boots and glance around the foyer. It's been years since I've been here, yet nothing has changed. When Jesse hired an interior designer, he must've made *soulless* a requirement. Nothing about this place matches the Jason that I know.

"Is your dad home?" I whisper as I pick up my boots. I'm afraid to speak any louder.

"Yeah, he's in the kitchen. C'mon." He tips his head and leads the way into the living room. I unzip my jacket as I follow. We'll probably go back outside right away, however I'm already hot with all of my layers.

"Clarity's here," Jason announces as we round the corner.

Jesse gets up from where he's sitting at the island with his breakfast and stacks of papers, and he smiles. Nothing about this man has changed, either, except his hair is more silver than blond now. "I thought I recognized that voice. Hey, kid. It's been a while."

"No kidding." I laugh and meet him halfway, giving him a hug. No matter how many times I've wanted to throttle him over the last few months for the way he's treated Jason, he'll always be family to me. "How've you been?"

"Good, good." He taps the side of his head. "How's your noggin' holding up?"

Jason floats closer in my peripheral vision. I wave my hand dismissively. "Oh, I'm fine. It'll be a few more weeks before I'm back to one-hundred percent, but at least I can skate again. That's all that matters."

I expect some back-handed comment, so I'm surprised when Jesse agrees. "True. Nothing has ever been able to keep you kids off the ice for long. Not even when Cole broke his foot." He pauses and looks between us. "I'm really glad to hear you're doing well. I heard about the drama when it was going on the other week."

"I think everyone did." Jason crosses his arms.

I can feel his defensive energy growing, so I try to break it up by nudging him with my shoulder. "That's old news now."

"I was just impressed with the way you two handled it," Jesse says. "It took me a long time to learn when and how to get involved with situations like that, so I'm proud that you guys didn't add to the dumpster fire. Obviously it worked in your favor if you're back in the running."

He pauses, and I recognize the way he's scrambling for the right words. Jason's eyebrows furrow like that, too, when he's thinking.

"I know I wasn't the most supportive when you guys started out, but I'm hoping to change that." His eyes flash to Jason, just for a moment. "Let me know if you guys need anything while you're finishing out this season. Anything I can do to help out. Keep you guys safe. I'm in the business of improving conditions for athletes, so I don't want to see either of you get hurt again, okay?"

Jason stares at him. I answer for the both of us when I say, "Of course. Thank you, that means a lot."

"It's the least I could do. Be careful outside, it's brutal out there." Jesse returns to his chair.

"For sure." I grab Jason's arm and pull him toward the mud room at the back of the house. He stumbles after me.

"They need to do a scientific study on you," Jason says as he comes back to life.

"Me?" I let go and sit in a chair next to the back door to pull my boots back on.

"It's like you put a spell on everyone around you." He grabs his jacket. "I don't know what you did to my dad, but I don't know that man back there."

"Count your blessings. I think he's turning a corner." I tuck the loose ends of my scarf into my collar and pull gloves out of my bag, then my skates.

"About damn time," Jason mutters and puts on a hat before grabbing his skates out of the shoe closet. "Ready for this?"

"I think so." I mulled on Victor's words all night, and I've spent all morning wondering what Jason has up his sleeve. I'm still not sure how skating is going to fix me when that's my problem in the first place, but I'm about to find out.

We go outside and simultaneously curse the cold before starting the trek down to the lake. Jason must've woken up at dawn to come out here and shovel a path, and it's not until we reach the lake that I see he also shoveled off a large expanse of ice to skate on. It's about half the size of our normal rink.

"You must already be warmed up." I glance at the shovel and push broom that have been set off to the side. "Thank you for doing this."

"It was easy. The wind has been keeping the snow layer thin out here, so it wasn't a big deal." He shrugs off my compliment. I don't miss the smile on his face as he bends down to get his skates on.

I do the same and step onto the ice first. My blades roll over the subtle dips and curves from the water. It doesn't take much to get used to the texture.

"This brings back good memories," I say as Jason skates over to join me. The only difference is that when I look at him, I don't see my brother's best friend anymore. This particular Jason is all mine.

"I was just thinking the same thing. You used to skate over there while Cole and I played hockey." He points further down the shoreline, where the frozen fog is starting to lift. "It was so impressive to watch the way you twirled."

"That's cute." I bump into him, and he bumps me back. "You watched me skate?"

"I noticed everything that you did. Everything you do demands my attention."

I laugh as my pulse skitters. "Whatever. This scheme of yours has had me on the edge of my seat. What do you have in mind?"

Jason comes to a stop and shakes his finger. "Don't make this weird." He digs in his jacket pocket.

My blood pressure skyrockets. He better not be—

He pulls out a blindfold. I haven't seen that thing since his fifth grade birthday party when my mom brought a piñata.

I clear my throat to keep from laughing as one hundred different comments fly to the surface of my mind.

Jason's cheeks turn red. "I said don't make this weird."

"I didn't say anything!"

"It's written all over your face." He moves forward, his eyes shining. "Turn around. Please. If this is okay?"

Something about the way he says that makes it hard to breathe. We hold eye contact for a moment before I obey. My heart is about to pound out of my chest. "Whatever you say."

"Mhm." He hums in agreement, and that does nothing for the heat radiating off my body. His blades scratch over the ice as he approaches behind me, his body pressing against my back for a moment as he brings the blindfold over my eyes. I am so swept up in him that I didn't think about the fact I'd literally be *blinded*.

I flinch against the darkness as he ties a snug knot behind my head. I've never fallen over while standing on ice before, although there's a first time for everything. My knees immediately begin to tremble when I can't use my surroundings to balance myself.

"Jason. Jason, okay." My voice rises an octave as I fling out my hands. His hands grab my arm. "Breathe. I'm not going anywhere."

"Victor said to team bond, not traumatize each other." I laugh shakily. He tugs me forward, and I nearly collapse onto my knees. Instinct takes over, and I pick up my feet.

"I'm feeling very bonded, actually." Something about hearing his voice detached from his body makes my knees shake for a different reason. The moment is lost as my left blade snags against a bump in the ice, and I curse as I start to fall.

Jason pulls me back to my feet. "You need to skate, C.J."

I slowly run my hand up his arm, then swing with my other hand to punch him in the shoulder. He laughs so loud that it makes me laugh, too.

"This is ridiculous." I fumble for his hand again. He laces our fingers.

"You're doing great. Listen." He goes quiet, and I hear it. I must've tuned into him subconsciously because we sound like one body again, our blades striking down at the same time. I exhale slowly.

"There you go."

"I think I've had enough now."

"We haven't even gotten to the good part yet. I'm going to stop." He slows us down. "Okay, we're standing at the west side, closest to the house. I'm going to let go of you and stand a few feet away. On my word, you're going to skate backward and I'm going to catch you."

"No. No, no." I tighten my grip on his hand. "You're not leaving me."

"I've never left you once in my life, and I'm not starting today. You can let go." Jason loosens his grip.

I'm trembling. "That's not true. You dated Tiffany for an entire year." It's a lot easier to be brave when I can't see his expressions. He's silent for a second too long, and I immediately regret it. "I'm sorry. I shouldn't have said that." The adrenaline is making me crazy.

"You're right. I never should've gotten together with her."

My breath catches. "But you did."

"Because of you. Everything I've ever done is because of you. You know that." He squeezes my hand again.

"What? Come on." I slide my feet closer together. "I didn't tell you to date her. I would've told you the opposite, actually."

Jason inhales and exhales. My skin prickles. I know he's looking at me. "After everything that happened last summer, I wanted to make you so sick with jealousy that the only way you could remedy it would be by breaking up with Sterling and running back to me. Then I waited until it was too late and Tiffany was too involved, which made it harder to break up with her."

As the words fall out of his mouth, the memories come rushing back.

I don't know how to admit to him that I contemplated it. When I found out he and Tiffany were official, I locked myself in my room and cried. Partially because she never deserved a sweetheart like Jason. Mainly because I was so determined to pretend that I didn't care about him that it was the straw that broke the camels back.

I cared about him so deeply, except it was too late to do anything. He had her, and I had Sterling. I told myself that fate was keeping us apart, and I've continued to tell myself that every single day since.

Even now, I bite my tongue, because if I admit any of that, it'll mean that I'll have to face the truth. I'm not quite ready yet, and he doesn't deserve a half-assed version of me. I have my own shit to figure out, first, and it's not his responsibility to fix me. That's why I can't say a word.

"I didn't mean to put you through that." It's the truth, even if it's not what I actually want to say. It's not what he wants to hear, either, given the way he quietly sighs.

"You didn't make me do anything. But you deserve to know the truth." We hold hands for a moment longer. This time, I'm the first to let go.

"Okay. I'm ready."

"Alright." His touch lingers, then it's gone. The sound of his blades moves somewhere behind me. "Show me what you got."

I hold my tongue between my teeth as I push off, leaning into years of training to move backward. This whole mind-body disconnect thing is really messing with me. What if he's actually standing off to the side and—

I stumble, and my blades slip out from underneath me. A yelp escapes me. Pain doesn't follow. Jason swoops in, and I'm back on my feet before I take my next breath. My heart is galloping as I spin and wrap my arms around him.

"Thank you. Oh, my God." I press my forehead against his chest. He settles his arms around my shoulders.

"I've got you. It's okay. Let's do that again."

So we do. Again. And again, until it becomes a game of how fast I can skate backward.

He sets me up in my spot again, then grabs my waist and spins me around. "Let's try something else. You're facing forward now, okay? I want you to move forward as fast as you can, and when I say jump, you jump."

"This trust exercise is getting out of hand." I blindly move my hands in front of me, and feel my way up his chest until I have his face in my palms. I force him to bend down so he's on my eye level. "You're insane."

"And you are so talented, you're going to kill it." He's definitely smiling. His cheeks are rounded.

"I really don't like you right now." I drop my hands.

"I don't believe that for a second. Bye, C.J." He skates away. I give his retreating back the bird. The blood rushes in my ears when I don't hear him stop a few feet away. He must be going to the other side of our makeshift rink.

"I'm going to kill him," I mutter.

"Let's go!" he yells out. God, he's so far away.

"I hate this. I hate this." I shake out my arms and roll out my neck. "This sucks. Okay. Push through. Persevere. *Shit*."

Exhaling, I go against every instinct that's screaming at me to stop and race forward. The cold wind bites my face as I gain momentum. I have no idea where I am or what's going on. There's no room to confront the memory of taking down Victor. Besides, my trust in Jason outweighs the fear.

"Jump!"

I can't help but shriek as I push off my feet, launching into the air. This better not be how I die.

Jason doesn't miss a beat. His arms practically materialize under my knees and behind my back. He's giggling like a little kid, and his breath warms my face, sending a shock through my body. "Easy peasy."

"Says you." I reach behind my head as he sets me back on my feet and rip off this stupid blindfold. I blink against the bright light, and the thousand-watt smile on Jason's face. It takes a second for my eyes to adjust, and when they do, I gawk.

The fog is lifting around us. Sunlight is piercing through it, melting it away, making the crystallized trees on the shoreline and the snow on the lake shimmer like a trillion gems, and highlighting the deep lines we've engraved in the ice over the last fifteen minutes. Blue sky is starting to show through overhead.

I turn to face Jason, and he's easily the most beautiful part about the view. I never realized how much I loved to watch him while we skated, because I can't take my eyes off him as he approaches.

"How are you doing?" He reaches for the blindfold.

I grab his hand and pull him into a tight embrace. "Thank you. *Thank you.*"

It's like he doesn't know where to touch first. His hands graze my back, my waist, my hair. He settles for giving me a squeeze, momentarily pressing his cheek against my head.

I shut my eyes, unafraid of the darkness when I'm in his arms.

May 2016 - Age 17

Jason

Strobe lights spin across the dance floor, bouncing over the crowd of juniors and seniors who are enjoying this years' prom to the fullest. That much is obvious by the flash of prohibited flasks and hundreds of screaming voices as they jump up and down to the DJ's song.

Tiffany loops her hand through my elbow and tugs hard. "Come on, Jason. One song is all I'm asking for."

I plant my feet and shake my head. "I already told you, I don't dance."

"You don't dance. You don't drink the punch. You don't even talk to my friends." Her voice pitches higher, drawing a few curious glances as people swerve around us to slip out into the lobby of the venue. "Do you even want to be here?"

"I'm here, aren't I?"

"Barely." Her eyes narrow, lip gloss reflecting the flashing lights. "You've been wandering around like you're looking for an exit all night. Do you realize how this makes me look, having to keep babysitting you?"

I recoil, tugging my arm away from her. "This is about how you look? Not about the fact that I just... don't want to dance?"

"Then let's go do something else." Tiffany steps closer. The poison leaves her eyes, replaced with lust as she goes to slide her hands under my jacket.

My breath hitches as she leans in for a kiss. I turn my head away, pretending to cough for an excuse to step away. "I don't think that's a good idea."

"God!" She throws her hands up in the air. "I just can't win with you! Everyone else's boyfriend is with their girlfriends, actually trying. And you're" —she gestures at me with a sharp flick of her hand— "you're acting like you'd rather be anywhere else."

I clench my jaw. But she's not wrong, so I can't argue. Honestly, I don't know what to say, and I know I've been silent for too long.

Her eyes widen so far I can't even see her glittery red eyeshadow. Hurt flashes behind her anger. "Wow. Thanks. Good to know I dragged you into something you hate. You could've just said no, you know."

"I didn't want to fight." Plus I've gotten a kick out of watching Cole, Nick, and Willie tear up the dance floor.

And Clarity. My gaze flickers behind Tiffany's head, hoping for a glimpse of her shadow.

"Yeah, well, congratulations. You got one anyway." She glowers at me. "Brood in the damn corner all you want. I'm not letting you ruin my night."

Tiffany spins on her heel, her sequined dress catching the light before she disappears into the crowd, headed toward her teammates.

I stand for a second and give her words the chance to sink in. Unfortunately, they slide right off. Any normal boyfriend would run after their girlfriend to apologize, except I'm grateful for the excuse to leave. The music is too loud, and the air is too musty. I need some peace and quiet.

I follow a different couple out the door and into the lobby. Their hands are sliding all over each other, and the girl laughs as he whispers in her ear. I don't hide my grimace as I split off the other direction, toward the staircase.

The hallway is dim compared to the dance floor, and the thump of bass is still vibrating faintly through the walls. I can just sit on the stairs and count the tiles on the floor until I get my wits about me enough to find my buddies again.

I turn the corner, and notice that someone else had the same idea. It's her.

Clarity is sitting on the second-to-last stair, her strappy heels in a tangled mess on the floor. Her wine-colored satin dress pools around her legs like something out of a dream.

I genuinely stop in my tracks. She looks up, startled. I forget how to breathe as our eyes clash.

I haven't seen her up close like this in so long that she is a sight for my sore eyes. Since I haven't been at the rink over the last few months, my already-limited time of seeing her has been completely stripped. I've been so busy with my new internship that I haven't been over to the house with Cole in equally-as-many months. The only time I see her is when her posts pop up on my feed, which isn't nearly often enough.

Her sweet brown eyes soften. "Sorry, don't mind me. I might be able to skate on blades for hours, but these stupid heels are going to kill me."

A laugh—an actual laugh—slips out of me. My chest loosens as I walk over, leaning on the rail next to her. "I don't think they design those things for endurance. I'd say stick to sneakers, but something tells me they wouldn't go with that dress." I pause. "Actually, you'd make it look good. Because you can wear anything." My face flames. "Well—"

"Jason." She rubs her toes and glances up at me, fighting a smirk. "Just stop."

"Sorry." I blow out a breath and run my fingers through my hair.

Her gaze flickers from my hair to my... lips? No, that must've been a trick of the light. She quickly looks away, returning to massaging her bruised toes.

"Um," I break the awkward silence, "do you have any big plans for the summer?"

"I'll be busier than ever, actually. Ortiz wants Victor and me performing in the senior class starting this fall. No summer break for me."

I let out a low whistle. I don't know a lot about ice dancing, but I do know those senior classes are no joke. "Really? That's insane."

"Yeah." Clarity shrugs, and I catch a glimpse of pride in her eyes. She deserves it. God, she deserves everything.

She nods at me. "What about you?"

I bite my cheek. I don't have a good answer. Hockey's gone. My team's gone. The one thing that used to fill up every second of my life has been ripped away, and all that's left is an empty space I don't know how to fill.

"Working with my dad. I'll be focusing my internship."

"That's it?" A smile tugs at her lips like she's teasing me, though when she looks up to search my eyes, I'm taken aback at the pity on her face. I've always had a love-hate relationship with the way she's able to see right through me.

"Fortunately. Unfortunately. It's about time that I learn to take over for the future."

"You always talked about finishing college before doing that." She straightens, and a long strand of hair escapes her bun.

"I talked about a lot of things before I got kicked off the hockey team." I step around the railing. "Hold on. Your hair..."

I bend down before I even know what I'm doing.

Goosebumps rake over my skin as I lean toward her.

Clarity audibly inhales, her eyes sparking. She holds perfectly still as I grab the strand and bring it back up, gently running my fingertips near the crown of her head, feeling for a bobby pin. Her hair is so soft, and it still smells like roses. My hands tremble as I weave the strand through.

I don't want to move away. She doesn't move away, either.

The restroom door down the hall flies open, breaking the spell.

I jump backwards, nearly tumbling down the last stair. Clarity flies to her feet as Annabelle comes out, smoothing down her dress. Her unruly hair tumbles down her shoulders, matching the confused look in her eye as she stares at me.

"Hi, Jason," Annabelle says. It comes out like a question.

"Hi. I was just getting some air."

Her eyes bounce between me and Clarity, and I don't like the smirk on her face. "Uh-huh."

Clarity ties her heels back on and steps down, her smile softening for her friend. She adjusts her dress like nothing had happened. "We're going to keep dancing. Thanks for catching up, Forbes." She flits her fingers at me. "Good to see you."

"You too." My voice falls flat as I watch the girls twine their arms together. Annabelle practically skips away with Clarity in tow as they return to the dance.

I stay where I'm at, even as the door shuts behind them.

I don't know if I hate her for being able to walk away so easily, or if I hate myself more for still being in love.

Chapter 31
Clarity

The days turn into weeks, and those weeks steamroll through the remainder of the year. Jason sweet-talks his dad and family friend, Paul, into keeping an eye out for a figure skating jump harness so we could practice our difficult maneuvers confidently. One week later, he walks into the rink victoriously holding a box.

It's perfect timing because we spend every single day of our holiday break practicing in some capacity, whether in the gym, inside the yoga room, or on the ice. We utilize the new setup with the help of Annabelle on the other end of the pole harness until all three of us are dripping sweat and Victor is satisfied. I love that boy, I really do, but some days I wonder if he spent *too* much time with Ortiz because his critical eye for detail is almost as good as hers.

Christmas and the New Year pass by without a spoken word, and then suddenly it's January and we're twenty-four hours away from flying out to San Jose, California, for the USFSA National Championships.

Our deal with Annabelle's dad has worked swimmingly so far, and I relish the early morning silence as I finish changing out of my winter clothes in the locker room and grab my skates. I go to leave, and curse when the door hits something solid.

I start apologizing before I even know who it is. "Oh, my god. I'm so sorry." The words catch in my throat as Tiffany steps back, her red hair swept up in a ponytail. "I didn't see you coming."

"It's fine," she replies curtly and lets me through.

"Thanks." I get out of the way, my heart in my throat.

Since my accident in November, Tiffany and Juliette have kept their space. I'm occasionally on the receiving end of cold glares in the cafeteria, but I think all of us have learned our lesson, and we're tired of fighting. We all have better ways to spend our time and energy.

I stew on this as I begin to walk away. She doesn't move. We share so much history, and the part of me that will always care for her urges me to turn around.

"Hey, do you have a second?"

Tiffany glances over. "That depends."

"Okay, great. I want to say that I'm sorry."

She immediately masks her face, her eyebrows furrowing as she adjusts the bag strap on her shoulder.

I continue, undeterred. If I don't get this off my chest now, I don't think I'll ever be able to. "I am so sorry for everything that happened between us when we were kids. I regret not knowing how to handle the situation, and yes, we were just little girls that didn't know any better, but now I *do* know better. I know that I got you in trouble, and what happened at the pool changed everything at home for you. It's my fault that I turned your dad into a helicopter parent. I'm sorry it changed things, but I'm not sorry that I tried to keep us safe."

"It's not just that." Tiffany straightens.

"I understand that I also made Jason—"

"Don't start on him." She crosses her arms and leans against the door. I watch her hands to make sure she's not going to snap and hit me again. "You've always had everything. Don't you get it?"

I shake my head. "My life is nothing compared to yours."

"This is your problem, Clarity. You focus so much on what needs to be fixed that you miss what's right in front of you." Her voice shakes with sadness or anger. I can't tell anymore. "Your skating. Your family. Your friends and relationships. Nothing is quite good enough for you, and I hate you because of that. You have access to everything you could ever want in life, while I've always had to fight for it."

Her words make me blink. "I don't understand. You're an amazing athlete. Your family loves you."

"My parents don't see the point in me playing hockey in college if I can't go pro. They don't approve, so they won't help pay for college unless I do what they want. After we graduate, I'm done."

I snap my mouth shut. Thinking about her not playing hockey almost holds the same weight as when Jason couldn't anymore, either.

She must read my mind because she's not done. "The only reason why I pursued Jason and dated him for so long is because I wanted to see if there was one thing on this planet that would stop revolving around you. He had me convinced for a while that I had finally done it, but I should've seen that it was an act the entire time. That's my fault. I should have known that he was with me to get back at you. To make *you* jealous. If you had approached him and told him to stop seeing me, he would've dropped me right then and there."

That stings, especially knowing what I know now, getting as close to Jason as I have. He's become the most important person in my life again over the last few months, and he's told me many times that dating Tiffany was a mistake. She's so right that it hurts.

All I can say is, "I'm sorry. I didn't try."

"You don't have to. You do enough damage just by existing." Tiffany's eyes turn glassy. "I hope that you're happy. Are you happy?"

This seems like a trick question. I choose to answer honestly. "Yes. I am."

She nods slowly and looks me up and down. "Then please don't waste your breath on me to boost your ego. I don't want to make you feel any better. I'm over this, okay? You can keep doing you, but seriously, leave me out of it."

I bite my tongue again as I catch a tear slipping down her cheek before she turns away, her sneakers pounding over the floor. The door swings shut behind her, leaving me in the dust of her righteous anger. I don't know whether I should laugh or cry. That's not how I expected that conversation to go, but it's also not *not* what I was thinking.

Honestly, that sums up the rise and fall of my relationship with Tiffany. A few years ago—hell, even a few months ago—I would've been sick after that confrontation. I don't have those emotions or that time invested anymore. I'm supposed to be on the ice with her ex-boyfriend, my best friend, in a few minutes.

I start toward the rink, until movement catches my attention. Jason walks around the corner, looking guilty as sin wearing grey joggers and a black t-shirt.

My pulse skitters. "Did you hear any of that?"

"A little." He shrugs. "I'm sorry, I didn't mean to eavesdrop. I was just leaving the locker room. Are you okay?"

"Yeah, I'm fine. I just wanted to clear the air." I tuck a loose strand of hair behind my ear and continue toward the West Rink with him on my heels.

He scratches the side of his neck. "If I could go back in time, I would've never dated her. I'm sorry for making things more complicated between you guys."

"Thank you, but you don't need to apologize. Things were already complicated."

"And I made it worse."

I knock my shoulder into him. "And I'm not playing the blame game right now. We should be focusing on our last run through the routines. Head in the game."

He has that look on the face that means he's ready to keep arguing. There's no chance for that as we walk into the box and I glance up into the bleachers at movement that catches my eye. Willie is waving at us, Nick is trying to make him stop, and Cole has his hands on his hips.

Annabelle starts clapping. "There's our National winners!"

"We haven't won a single thing yet." I laugh as warmth spreads in my chest at the sight of our friends.

Jason shakes his head. "What are you all doing here? Shouldn't you be at home?"

"We're judging you." Willie gives us a double thumbs-up.

Nick scoffs. "Not *judging*. Watching. Willie and I can't exactly fly out to California with you guys, so we wanted to come support."

"I made Willie keep his sign in the car," Cole clarifies.

"But I'm definitely bringing it on the plane." Annabelle gives us a mischievous grin.

Jason quirks his eyebrow at me as Victor steps into the box behind us. "Can you all stop distracting my athletes? This is the most important practice they'll ever have and I could hear you jabbering all the way from the top of the stairs."

"Bro, this is all part of the practice. They need to get used to a loud crowd. I'm occasionally going to do this." Willie sticks his fingers in his mouth and makes an ear-splitting wolf whistle. Nick covers his ears.

Cole reaches around him to smack Willie on the back of the head. "You can go do that somewhere else, actually."

Victor appears tired as he turns to face us. "Get your skates on and let's get this over with."

I stifle my smile as Jason and I oblige. We're stepping onto the ice a few minutes later, and even though they're four of my closest companions, I feel like their stares are scrutinizing every move we make as we warm up.

Jason is as cool as a cucumber as he mirrors me around the rink. He knocks his arm into mine and gives me that signature grin of his that shows off his perfect teeth, and my stomach flips.

"You're nervous." He says it as a statement, not a question.

"I don't know why," I grumble. "It's not like I'm not used to crowds. And they're our friends."

"Some might argue that makes it worse. I felt more nervous having you and my dad at regular games than I did playing in brackets or at State."

"Oh, I'm sure you were." He gets nervous just when I look at him. I prove my point by flitting my eyes over his body, admiring the areas where the clothing clings to his muscles, and he blushes. He's saved from answering when Victor calls us over to run through the rest of our warm-up.

Either way, he's right. I've been skating with him for months, and yes, Annabelle has been helping us and Cole saw most of our performance during the Invitational until I fell. Otherwise, they have never actually seen us do this together. Something about having them watch feels overtly intimate.

Jason finds different ways to reassure me; fingers brushing my back here, squeezing my hand there. He meets my eyes whenever he can and gives me a small smile. I do my best to return the favor.

"Let's run through that reverse rotational lift before we start," Victor says as he skates around us, motioning at the ice with his hand. "That's your one sticking point. I want to make sure you're both confident going into the competition this weekend."

"I'm confident." Jason puts his hands on his hips. Both of them turn to me. I shrug.

"I am ninety-five percent there." Which is leaps and bounds better than I was two months ago. I would never admit this to their faces, but Victor and Jason made a good call with that team bonding day. My body feels tingly like it always does when I recall that memory.

"Then let's get you to one hundred. Come on." Jason holds out his hand. I take it.

"Relax, Jansky," Victor calls after us as Jason pulls me away. "You know what you're doing. Trust yourself."

"Trust me," Jason murmurs, now that we're alone. I don't let go of his hand.

I recall my latest conversation with Angela. All I can do is control myself right now. I breathe in slowly, letting my ribs expand, focusing on the cold oxygen seeping into my lungs.

We split as we reach the opposite end of the rink, taking this moment to go down the boards and gain momentum. Our paths meet again, going down the middle of the arena, and the ice flies by as Jason descends on me, scooping me over his shoulder like I weigh nothing. He was right, there's nothing except full confidence on his end.

Me? I catch Cole getting to his feet in the corner of my eye. I don't even know why I'm looking for him. Probably because the last time he saw us try this, blood was rushing out of my head. Thinking about that doesn't help, and I curse, bucking my legs to keep my balance.

Jason intercepts and tightens his grip on me before flipping me back around, as if that was his intention the entire time. He comes to a stop and turns me to face him before putting his hands on both sides of my face. My stomach tightens as he leans in, and I swear I can already feel his lips on mine.

Instead, he pauses a few inches from my face, his eyes heavy with concern. "Clarity Donna Jansky. Are you with me?"

My fingers tremble. I'm acutely aware of five different pairs of eyes staring at us.

"Yes," I lie.

"Don't lie to me."

"No."

"It's you and me. That's it. Always has been, always will be." He pauses, and for a moment, I question whether he's still talking about figure skating. "I need you here with me. Nobody else is going to help you, and unless you focus, they're going to have nothing to watch. Know what I mean?"

I nod, his hands still resting on my cheeks. "Yes. I'm sorry."

"I forgive you. Will you skate with me now?"

"After you." I flourish my hand.

"Atta girl." He pats my cheek with the palm of his hand, and I despise the way he grabs his bottom lip between his teeth as he turns away. Damn him.

We get back on the boards, gaining speed again. Sometimes I really hate how right he is. Also, I don't know if his intention was to frustrate me with that whole grabbing my face thing, but I'm suddenly acutely aware of him as we reenter the lift, his hands reaching for me again.

He's all I can think about as he throws me over his shoulder again, his hands pressing on my back. I put my whole heart and soul into trusting him as I split my legs in the air, choosing a spot on his legs to watch so I'll keep my balance. He stays steady as a rock even as the breeze from our momentum tugs at my limbs. I hold my core, smugly noticing that I'm finally strong enough to do so without my vision fading.

The seconds pass by way too quickly and we approach the new exit that Victor choreographed. I bring my legs around the backside of Jason's neck as his hands expertly guide me, curling me around his shoulders until I settle in a split in his arms. My left hand presses against his shoulder blade for balance as he grabs my thighs, spinning us in a fast series of rotations.

He keeps spinning as I slip expertly out of his arms, using the momentum to slip around his back again. I slide so softly onto the ice that I don't even notice my blades connecting with the surface until he's coming at me again, sweeping me off my feet.

This isn't part of our—*oh*.

Jason embraces me, squeezing me against his chest as he laughs. "There she is!"

"Thank you." I giggle breathlessly as I wrap my arms around his neck. Beyond the bubble of our moment, Willie is wolf whistling again. Our friends' applause echoes across the ice like a packed stadium.

I glance at Jason's mouth as he lets me go. If we were alone, I could kiss him for all the appreciation and gratitude spilling out of my heart. It takes a lot of strength to turn away and wave at the group. All of them are on their feet, and they're still clapping. I laugh when he takes a deep bow next to me.

My gaze flits to Victor, and he's joined them in applauding. He shakes his head when we make eye contact. His lips twist in a smile, and I know exactly what he's thinking. He and I are never going to compete together again. Not as long as I have Jason.

I catch my breath, the sweat cooling against the back of my neck, when I notice something out of the corner of my eye. There, a few yards down from the gate.

Sterling is leaning against the boards, slow clapping. His eyes spark when we make eye contact.

My stomach tightens, except it's not nerves. It's an angry heat. God, I am so sick of the space he's taking in my head, my ice, and now my morning.

Jason notices at the same time, and his jovial mood instantly switches, his smile collapsing. "I'll handle him."

"No." I push past. "I've got it."

I feel Jason's eyes on my back as I skate toward the boards. Sterling wanders over like he owns the place, his lips tugging up.

"What are you doing here?" I take a page out of Jason's book and put my hands on my hips.

"Same as always. I'm getting in my workout." He takes a beat, his eyes flashing over me, making me feel grimy. "You look good out there."

I bypass his compliment. "I don't believe for one second that you just happened to be walking by. The gym is that way." I nod my head toward the other side of the building.

"I was curious. It looks like I'm not the only one who wanted to see the big stars before they leave." His eyes flit to my friends who are all standing now, watching us talk. Cole and Annabelle look one second away from jumping over the railing to come down here. "Did they have to ask your permission to watch, too?"

"Here's the difference." I point back at them. "I want them here." I point at him. "Not you. You don't get my attention anymore. I'm sick of whatever game you're playing—"

"This isn't a game—"

"Ah." I cut him off this time and level a cold stare at him. I cherish the way irritation flashes across his face, his jaw tightening. "I'm talking right now. You've made it very clear what you think about me—about us—and I'm done giving you the benefit of the doubt. You don't get to hover and try to weasel into my head before the biggest competition of my life. You don't live there anymore. Rent's up."

"Clarity, I—"

I'm already turning away. "I need to practice. Bye, Sterling."

I should've known that Jason would follow. He's standing a few yards behind me, his arms crossed, eyebrows raised. He's smirking, and his eyes dance with pride as I approach.

"You..." He stops himself and laughs a little. "Never mind. Not saying it."

"You'd better not. C'mon." I grab his hand as I brush past, pulling him after me. He grins like a little boy, and I'm pretty sure he's flicking off Sterling as he turns around. I don't bother to look.

I've already gotten the last word, and man, does it feel good.

Chapter 32
Clarity

@ilov.eskating4evr
Four hours until MY girl Clarity takes the ice and proves she's the moment #TeamJacity
↳ **@chia4spill**
The "moment" better not be another face-plant. I hope Jason is ready to catch her this time lmao

@halfloophero
Plot twist they've been ghosting socials because the routine is THAT insane.
↳ **@coronamemecrazy**
Or because they're embarrassed

@maya_hen
McKenzie & Baros are in danger. I repeat McKenzie & Baros in DANGER

@cibemrem.56
I'm just here for the drama

When I pull my new performance dress out, I am more than happy to see it survived the trip this time. When I slip it on, my breath still stutters, just not in the same way it used to. The fabric lies snug across my hips and ribs, and the part of my brain that wants to panic wakes up like it always does in these moments.

I catch my breath to settle my heartbeat. As I recall my mantra about checking facts before feelings, I turn to the mirror and a smile pulls at my lips. I'm not a disaster, or a failure, or a girl who's letting herself go. I am an athlete who has worked hard to get here.

The devil on my shoulder prods my brain with a stick, trying to nit-pick the details and convince me that I should've eaten less at breakfast. I'm still learning when it deserves space in my head and when it doesn't. Right now, I'm merely pleased to finally wear a dress that I feel strong in.

Victor wanted us to keep our costumes simple, so I found a flowy pale lavender dress that's embedded with tiny sequins that don't glimmer unless they hit the light just right. It was stunning on the rack, however it's more breathtaking on my body.

Now that I'm dressed, I leave the stall for someone else. I pull a partially-consumed protein shake out of my bag as I find an open section of countertop to finish preparing. My gut retaliates as I polish it off, but it goes down.

I can hear Angela in the back of my head as I throw the empty bottle into the trashcan next to the counter: drink one before every practice or competition. Old habits make my fingers twitch to pull the bottle back out to make note of the calorie count. I don't give in. Besides, Cole and Jason have made it their personal mission to scribble out every single nutrition label on everything in the house with a Sharpie.

I finish styling my hair into a half up do, and dig the eyeliner pencil out of my makeup bag. Maybe focusing on not poking my eye out will help me forget about eating.

The pencil bumps against the zipper as I take it out, and slips out of my fingers. I mutter under my breath when it hits the floor and rolls away. Bending down, I flinch as I nearly grab someone's hand, instead.

"Thanks. Slippery little— Oh. Hi." I straighten my spine to look Juliette in the eye.

Her eyes go wide as she quickly passes over my eyeliner, blonde wispy baby hairs escaping her tight braid. "I'm sorry, I didn't realize this was yours." She hesitates. "Not a good way to start your day. Dropping something."

I think she means to be funny, except it's not.

"It's okay." I set it down in my makeup bag. I've stayed up more nights than I could count on both hands thinking about what I would say if I got the chance to confront Juliette, but the words have now escaped me.

She's still rooted in place, looking just as much in shock as I feel. I'm tempted to go back to pretending she doesn't exist. That didn't get me very far with Tiffany, so instead I blurt out, "I've got to ask. Why did you do all of that to me? The video, the dress, everything. I've been trying to figure out what I ever did to you."

Her face stiffens. A group of girls run past, laughing and shouting. Someone turns on a hair dryer further down the wall.

"It's what you didn't do." She runs her hands over the front of her dress. Hand-stitched, by the looks of it.

"What?" Confusion bubbles inside me.

"You never failed. You never stumbled, or had to look up at me from further down on the podium." Juliette finds my eyes as her voice wavers. "Even everything you post is flawless. Everyone loved you, because you were untouchable. When I moved to Minneapolis with Monty, when we joined Ortiz's team, I thought this would be our chance to finally stand out. If she trained you to be the best, I thought she could train us to be better. I wanted to shake things up, you know?"

I watch embarrassment flicker over her face, and irritation pulls her brows together. "But the more I got to know you, the more I realized you're not that person." She hesitates and clarifies, "Not the villain I made you out to be."

"Oh." I don't know what else to say. First Tiffany, now her. I had no idea that they had such strong opinions about me. I am the most imperfect, flawed person that I know. "I never meant to be the enemy."

"It was easier to tear you down than admit I was wrong." She inhales shakily. "I wanted to talk to you after the Invitational, but the universe chewed you up and spit you out. I didn't want to add to your problems."

I can't help the bitter laugh that escapes me. "That's a small mercy."

Juliette allows a small, strained smile. "I'm sorry. I know I should go online and fess up, but..." She fades off. I don't care how badly anyone messes up. I wouldn't wish the wrath of strangers online on my worst enemy.

"It's okay. I'm over it. I forgive you." God, Angela would be so proud of me.

Juliette nearly snaps her neck looking up at me, shock rimming her eyes.

I hold out my hand. "I hope you skate clean today. Give it your best effort, okay? I'd hate for this to be an easy win."

She makes a sound that's a mixture between a scoff and a laugh, and I finally recognize the girl behind her eyes as she shakes my hand. "You too. It's not the same without some real competition."

"Be careful what you wish for." I smile as she steps away. "See you on the podium."

"Tell Jason and Victor I say hello." She flits her fingers as she walks away, relief visible on her face with that conversation behind her.

My smile falls. Yeah, right. If I told Jason I talked to her, he would blow a gasket. I'll save that tidbit for a different day.

Regardless, I feel like a weight has been lifted off my shoulders as I quickly finish touching up my makeup. I didn't realize how badly I wanted to say something to her. I glance at the clock on the wall. Five minutes to spare. Unfortunately, I'll have to finish stewing on that conversation a different day.

I use the five minutes to throw my belongings in the locker set aside for me, grab my skates, and run out of the locker room. As I jog down the hallway to the warmup rink, the speakers crackle overhead.

"Good morning, contestants! Welcome to day two of the U.S. Figure Skating National Championships. Our rink crew is leaving the ice now, and senior ice dancing will be kicking off shortly. Mr. John Herber and Miss Sabine Yang, please be ready. May the following pairs be warmed up and ready to perform. Montgomery Baros and Juliette McKenzie, Evan Smith and..."

I turn the corner, panting as I jog up to Victor, who's pacing near the entry to the warm-up rink. He turns and sees me, his shoulders dropping. "There you are! Are you trying to kill me?"

"I'm sorry, I needed touch-ups. Is my costume okay?" I do a full spin. I'll tell him about Juliette another day, too.

"Hang on." He steps behind me, straightening a piece of fabric near my lower back. He pulls on a strand of hair and comes around my side with a smile. "There. You look great. Why have you never cleaned up like this for me?"

"I have. You've always been too focused on yourself to notice. Where's Jason?"

He shrugs and doesn't argue. Instead, he points. "Over there."

I follow his finger and find Jason standing off to the side of the rink, flourishing his hands as he speaks to his audience standing on the other side of the barrier.

He always looks amazing, but today, he's stunning.

Everything about him is polished and handsome: his black satin shirt with the collar unbuttoned just one button too low. Black slacks that fit snugly over the perfect lines of his legs. Black figure skates polished to a shine. At our last competition, he styled his hair. It was cute, but man, do I prefer the natural look he's got going on. My heart lets all the butterflies out of their cage, the gust of their wings making it impossible to catch my breath.

I finally notice who he's talking to. Darika managed to find him. Her class isn't until tomorrow, so she's wearing simple clothes, standing next to my parents, Cole, Annabelle, and a random blonde man. No, not any man. For the love of God, that's Jesse Forbes.

"His dad is here?" I blurt.

"I guess so. We were all surprised when he walked over."

"I can't believe it. California must be the twilight zone. What time is it?"

Victor looks at his phone and scowls. "Time to get you two on the ice. Everyone can catch up later. Forbes, let's go!"

I look toward the group again and catch Jesse's attention, giving him a wave. I grin when he returns the favor.

My attention is immediately swooped up by his son as he walks over, a gauzy grin on his face as he looks—no, not looks. This boy straight up checks me out. If I keep blushing like this, the makeup is going to melt off my face.

I put my hands on my hips as Jason approaches. "What in the world is daddy dearest doing here? I didn't know he was coming."

"Me either. Making up for lost time, if I had to guess." Jason pauses in front of me, waving one hand. "Wow, Clarity. You are... Wow. Gorgeous."

"Thank you." I take the compliment and immediately deflect away from the topic before I can accidentally tell him that he can wear satin any time he wants. "I can't believe he came all the way out here. That seems like an olive branch, if I've ever seen one."

"Actually, he flew in early this morning. Just got here. He claims he had to come out this direction for a work trip, but I don't know if I believe that," Jason says. With the smile he's got on his face, I know he's just happy to have him here.

Victor claps his hands, nearly spooking the two of us out of our socks. "Okay, team! Get your skates on and take a few laps to get limber. Don't try to compete out in the warm-up rink; save your energy for the judges."

We oblige. Jason waits for me as I finish tying my skates and takes my hand as we step onto the ice. We push off on the same leg, slipping into the current of the crowd that's moving counterclockwise around the boards. Heads immediately turn our direction.

"Are you ready for this?" I squeeze his hand.

He returns the gesture. "Very ready. Actually, you know what, I was born ready."

I breathe this moment in—the feeling of his hand in mine, the ice chipping away under our blades, the universal passion and talent and skill that's whizzing by all around us. I have never overlooked the fact that I'm one of the lucky ones to turn my childhood dream into reality. Despite everything that was stacked against me, I got to the other side. Yet...

I suddenly speak, turning my thoughts into words. "Without you, I wouldn't be here, Jason."

He jolts at my sudden outburst, looking at me again. I keep going before I lose my nerve, not giving him the chance to speak. "You need to know how much it means to me that you're here. No, I take that back. You've *always* been there. But when Victor got hurt, you came. When we asked you to skate, I was terrified you were going to say no. Despite everything else that was going on, you stepped up so well and so completely that I don't think I'll ever be able to repay you. Without you, I'd be done."

Jason slows down to a stop, turning to face me, his green eyes drinking me in.

"You were there as I battled my anorexia," I choke out, the words sticking to my throat. "You didn't shame me or force me through it. I never felt less than, or incapable."

"That's because you never were."

"That's my point." A lifetime of gratitude and love causes the breath to hitch in my chest. My hand clasps around his, trembling. I meant to shut up about eight sentences ago, however, he deserves to hear this.

I've always been afraid of my feelings for him, especially over the last few months. I needed to take the time to heal and start to figure out my own issues, separate facts from fiction, and I did. The fact is, I won't be able to live with myself if I don't finally tell him the truth now.

"Jason, I... see Ortiz."

His head tilts, eyebrows furrowing as our moment is stolen. He blinks at me before looking over his shoulder, directly at the woman who told us we weren't good enough to be here.

She's looking at us. Actually, not just looking. She's watching us. I don't know what she sees, but she looks mad. Dare I say, a little disappointed.

Jason nods his head up in a subtle greeting. She turns away.

"Real mature," he grumbles and glances at me. "What were you saying?"

"Alright, you two, let's go!" Victor's voice cuts through the noise. "Just a few more pairs, then you're up."

"Later." I hustle toward the exit, dragging him with me. He mutters under his breath.

Victor found water bottles, and he passes them over as we step off the ice. I don't argue, and neither does Jason as we take this final moment to get a drink and prepare ourselves. We walk down the mats in his wake as he leads. My heart begins to pound.

"Trust yourselves and each other out there." Victor looks over his shoulder at us. "Neither of you are here by happenstance. You're here for a reason, and that reason is because you're damn great skaters that deserve to be on the ice. Don't worry about doing anything extra. Just get on the ice. Have fun. Enjoy it."

"Thank you," Jason says as we stop behind the boards. The pair in front of us steps onto the ice, their introduction blasted over the speakers as the announcers begin to talk.

I swallow as I look past Victor's shoulder, glancing at the white ice and the packed bleachers. There are cameras to record every angle of our routine, and a panel of judges to scrutinize every second.

"What score did Montgomery and Juliette get?" I ask.

"Nothing that you two can't beat." Victor steps forward to take our bottles. "This isn't about them. This is about you and him." He points at Jason, who smiles sheepishly, which makes me laugh as I turn to Victor.

"Thank you. For everything. You're the best coach I've ever had."

"Considering you've only had one other coach, this isn't a hard race to win," he says gruffly, although I don't miss the twinkle in his eye.

"You know what I mean." I step forward and pull him into a hug. "It's been weird being out there without you, but this is the next best thing. I really appreciate it."

Victor isn't a hugger, so he surprises me by giving me a quick squeeze. "Trust me, Jansky. You never needed me. But I'm glad to be here. You're going to knock their socks off." He lets go, his eyes glassy. Mine are, too, until he eyes Jason and adds, "For the love of God, point your goddamn toes out there. Don't lose just because your Achilles heel is tight."

"I appreciate the vote of confidence, Vick. Great speech." Jason rolls his eyes but doesn't stop smiling as they bump fists. We wait a few more minutes until the music fades over the speakers. Despite all my years of experience, my heart starts jackrabbiting faster.

"Alright. This is it. Go get 'em!" Victor slaps our shoulders as we pass.

The gate attendant opens it, letting the other couple off. We step onto the ice next. Jason grabs my hand, squeezing my palm as we step into the spotlight and skate off. He lets go to split in the opposite direction, yet that moment, that memory of his hand in mine, grounds me.

I glance beyond the Plexiglass as the announcers rattle off the previous couple's score, searching for my parents, using them as an excuse to not listen to the previous couples score and get in my head.

I find them right behind the glass, grinning and waving like fools. Annabelle and Darika are jumping up and down, holding a sign that says *NATIONALS? FORBES & JANSKY CALL IT TUESDAY*. Cole seems embarrassed to stand next to them, but grins and gives two thumbs up when we make eye contact. And Jesse actually seems happy to be here, nostalgia written all over his face as he watches his son. I keep smiling as I turn away.

"Now on the ice, Clarity Jansky and Jason Forbes!" The announcer says, and the crowd cheers their approval. "Jansky suffered a hard fall a few months ago..."

I tune out again and look over at Jason as we turn the corner, mirroring each other, stopping in the middle of the arena. He's smiling like a groom at the end of the aisle as I approach. The lights dim for our routine, backlighting his body, painting him as my only focus.

We move in tandem, sinking down to the ice. The bitter cold is a welcome shock, clearing my head as I lie on my side, facing away from Jason. I can hear him breathing as silence falls for one perfect moment. *Inhale. Exhale.*

The music starts. It's second nature to count the beats, and I roll over, hoisting myself perfectly over him. My hands rest on the ice beside his ears, my skates balanced next to his.

Jason's eyes are the perfect shade of green, never leaving mine. His mouth tilts in a teasing smile as he chases my body when I roll onto his other side, my spine pressing into the ice.

He swings his leg over mine and hovers right above my body. The breath hitches in my lungs.

Damn it, Victor was right. Passion does start on our backs.

"I really want to kiss you," Jason had whispered so quietly, I thought it was my intrusive thoughts speaking. I laughed it off when all I wanted to do was grab his face and kiss him until there was no breath left in my lungs.

That conversation plays in his eyes as he moves his skates in line with my ribcage, pressing them in a wide V-stance and scooping his hands under my armpits, lifting me with vigor. I love how he always picks me up and handles me like a rag doll, and places me down like a vase.

The music is a distant hum, and the spotlight cuts across my eyes as Jason grabs my hand to lead the way into the next move. His palm is warm in contrast to my skin, cool from the ice. I let him be the guide, our bodies synchronizing. I let go of him to come to a stop as he keeps moving past me, cutting back around.

I flourish my arms to the music, and I know I'm supposed to hold a certain facial expression for this part, so I fight down a smile as I watch Jason approach. It's hard to believe this is the same boy that could barely do a simple spin a few months ago. The knowledge that he worked so hard—for me, out of all people—is humbling.

His eyes find mine. My heart swells as he flashes me a hidden grin, and I can't hold down my smile anymore. I look the other way as I hold out my arm and he grabs it, pulling me behind him. Something about the force he uses makes my heart beat a little faster, paired with the heat behind his gaze.

Jason grabs my waist for the first lift, lifting me effortlessly, the air crisp and cool against my skin. I extend my arms, feeling like I could touch the rafters. The moment feels timeless. He lowers me back down and the audience cheers, nearly spooking me. I'm so lost in this moment with him that I completely forgot we were competing.

The music swells. We pick up speed, our movements more daring as we continue through the routine.

When Jason grips my hand for the reverse rotational lift, he gives it a reassuring squeeze. Victor talked about trust, and I trust him implicitly as I'm launched into the air and flipped over his shoulder. I focus on holding my position until its time to curl around his shoulders. He catches me, spinning us out of the lift. It feels less like landing and more like coming home.

The crowd erupts with applause. My adrenaline surges, and yet all I hear is my breath mingling with his as the next move causes us to brush noses. He changes the movement of his hands, tracing them down my face to tuck a piece of hair behind my ear that was stuck across my face. This isn't the time to verbally thank him. I know he can see it on my face because of the way he catches my eye and winks. My face flushes as we continue seamlessly through sequence.

By the time the final notes of the music play, we find ourselves back where we began—lying on the ice, side by side, our chests heaving, faces flushed. I reach for Jason's hand, and he squeezes mine. I laugh breathlessly as he gets up, pulling me up with him.

The stadium is roaring, the noise echoing over the ice. Jason takes my other hand, his fingers trembling with adrenaline and a job well done. He's grinning like a mad man, eyes sparkling, mouth moving soundlessly. I can't hear over the sound of the crowd.

I glide closer, tilting my ear toward him as I yell, "What?"

"It's later!" Jason replies. "What was your point earlier?"

I laugh. It's time to let the past be the past and look at the future, untouched, like a fresh layer of ice.

There was a time where I didn't believe in soul mates. It felt silly, because out of all the people on the planet, how could one person be made for me? I don't know if him becoming my partner was divine intervention. And him asking this question right now isn't just chance. No, I knit the threads of fate myself until they spelled his name.

"I love you," I shout over the clamor. "That's my point, Jason."

For a moment, he looks utterly stunned, his breath catching as the words sink in.

Then, with a joyous laugh, he pulls me into his arms. His hands cradle my face, and mine rest on his neck. Before I can say another word, his lips are on mine, soft and warm, and everything I've been dreaming of.

I let this kiss speak for every shared dream, every unspoken word, and every moment we've fought for. I made myself think that my dream was skating, but he's always been my dream, and choosing him is the best decision I've ever made.

The crowd's roar fades into the background, replaced by the pounding of my heart and the sheer euphoria of this moment.

We pull apart, breathless and giddy. Jason's smile is the brightest thing in the world. His eyes, gleaming with love and relief, search mine as if committing this moment to memory.

"I love you, too," he whispers, his voice thick with emotion. "God, I've been waiting so long to say that."

I laugh again, feeling the weight of the world lift from my shoulders as I trace my fingers in a circle behind his neck. "Was it worth the wait?" I tilt my head mischievously.

"More than you can imagine." He presses his forehead to mine. "I love you, Clarity. Always have, always will."

The audience's cheers surge back into focus, the sound of clapping and whistles filling the arena as I grab the back of his head and pull him down to kiss him again.

My boy.

Epilogue

Clarity - One Year Later

UPDATE: WE'RE ALMOST TO THE OLYMPICS!
Posted by: *Off the Ice*
Published: January 10th — 10:05 AM CST

From the first time I stepped onto the ice at a local state competition, to now, a few weeks out from standing under the five most iconic rings in the world in PyeongChang, nearly ten years have passed.

It's been more than a decade since I started skating, and the ice has given me so much joy and sadness. I've always dreamed of stepping onto Olympic ice, and I didn't want to stop trying, even knowing it might never happen. Hell, it almost didn't happen! Failure is part of the journey and the learning process. Without it, it's impossible for success to come — true, genuine, gratifying success.

The last year has been a storm, and I owe so much to Victor Kerr and Anya Kovalenko. They never focused on the end result of being here but rather the desire and passion that Jason and I put into everything. These two saw us at our worst, never stopped believing, and have held our hands through every step of this journey over the last few months. Without them and their faith, we wouldn't be here.

I never meant to become a skating icon. I started this page in hopes that I would make a few friends along the way. All I wanted to do was share the joy of skating with someone, and the fact that so many of you have been here since the very beginning is amazing. This upcoming performance is for you. Thank you. You kept me going when I wanted to give up. You believed in me when I didn't even believe in myself. This dream, this moment, is ours. I hope I can do you justice.

People always ask me where I get my work ethic from, and my answer is the same every time: my family.

I was motivated to work hard watching my parents constantly confront and conquer life's challenges. Watching them get up early, work long hours, come home, and run me and Cole around all in the name of chasing our dreams... never with a complaint, mind you, is the reason why I am the way I am. I'm brave enough to show up, to fight, and believe because of them.

Although, my brother is the real force of nature who makes me feel like I need to work twice as hard to keep up. He never missed a beat on or off the ice growing up, and he continues to bust his ass every day for his college hockey team. I am so proud of him, and I'd like to think he's proud of me, too. Though honestly, he's probably most excited to be coming with to the Olympics because of the amazing kimchi.

My family's laughter, strength, and endless support is my foundation. I'm nothing without them.

To my dear friends—Annabelle, Willie, Nick, Darika, and everyone else who's been by my side—you guys have always been my biggest supporters, but you've filled the cracks of my life more over the past twelve months than ever before. You've been there whenever we needed you, and pushed us when everyone else was afraid to. Part of our success is due to your commitment and love.

Jason... Where do I even begin? I know you told me to not write anything to you, but let me have my moment. I know you'll forgive me ;)

For so long, I thought this dream was just about the Olympics. I've come to realize over the last few years that I have dual dreams. One is to be the best skater that I can be. The other is learning to be there for you the way you have ALWAYS been there for me.

You were the missing piece of every routine, and every moment on the ice. You saw the parts of me no one else did—the cracks, the scars, the wild, broken hope—and you stayed. It's because of you that I'm not afraid anymore. Because of you, I'm stronger than I ever dreamed I could be. It's because of you that we're here today.

YOU are the heart and soul of everything that we do out there. I am so lucky that I get to do my favorite sport with my favorite person. *Ti amo*. You are the other half of me. You've seen me at my worst and at my best, and soon, we get to lace up our skates on the biggest stage in the world. Not because we're perfect, but because we fought through the broken parts to get here, together. As fun as the Olympics will be, I am more excited to tie my skates alongside you for the rest of my life.

Everything about these upcoming performances is proof that even when the world tries to break you, even when you fall so hard you think you'll never rise again... you can. You *will* rise. You will find love, strength, and light in the most unexpected places. You will be more than your mistakes. You will be more than the noise.

This isn't just my story anymore. It's yours too. Thank you for being part of it. Thank you for believing when I couldn't. Thank you for helping me find my way back to myself. All of you.

Let's go and show them what it means to never give up.

See you there.

— Clarity Jansky

Rating: 167k likes | 57.2k shares
Comments disabled.

"Three, two, one!"

The backlights flash, and my eyes burn as I resist the urge to blink. Jason's hand instinctually tightens around my waist.

"Okay, let's see how that turned out." The photographer clicks buttons on her camera, humming to herself for a moment. Then, she gasps. "Perfect. You guys are just perfect."

"I could've told you that without looking." Jason grins and brings his hand to the other side of my head, running his hand over my hair while simultaneously kissing the top of my head.

We started to officially date after cleaning house at Nationals. It's been one year since then, yet my body still releases hundreds of butterflies with every kiss. They always feel like the first. I smile up at him, and the unbridled love on his face mirrors my own.

"Stop that." I playfully swat him away. He swings right back at me, which makes me laugh as the hairstylist approaches for the millionth time today.

"Jason," Victor says from where he's sitting in his director chair behind the camera, "keep your hands to yourself, would you? These poor cosmetic artists are going to go through all of their supplies if you keep ruining her hair and makeup."

"We don't mind." The hairstylist catches my eye and winks as she spritz's my hair with more hairspray, touching up the spot that he flattened. "I'd much rather do what I'm paid to do for a happy couple than stand in the corner and watch them argue."

"I second that." The photographer tucks a piece of her blonde hair behind her ear. "You guys are making this easy."

"As long as the photos look good for the cover of the magazine. I mean, come on. The Olympics!" Anya raises her hands triumphantly as she walks around the corner, balancing bottles in her hands. "These photos will be plastered everywhere, on every single ad we can get our hands on."

"Can I get a copy of every single one?" Jason asks.

I stuff down my smile so he doesn't get the satisfaction of making me laugh. The hairstylist and I make eye contact as she backs away, and she laughs for me.

"I've already got you CC'ed in the email. Here. Drink, stay hydrated. God, these lights are hot." Anya grimaces as she steps on the platform with us. She gives a bottle to Jason, and I take the Vitamin Water. Flipping it over, I read the label.

"Zero sugar lemonade." I spin it out of habit, but the nutrition label is already scribbled out with Sharpie. "This is my favorite. Where did it come from?"

"I have a few little birdies on my shoulders." Anya puts her hands on her hips.

I turn to look at Jason. He's already chugging his drink. We make eye contact, and he shrugs. Water dribbles out of the corner of his mouth as he smiles, and I laugh. "You do too much. Thank you."

He lowers his bottle and swallows, dabbing his mouth before stepping forward and giving me a kiss. "Anything for you."

"Love you." I crack open my bottle and let my eyes drift over his outfit, admiring every sharp line and clean angle.

The costume designer made every single one of my dreams come true with the maroon shirt he has on, tucked into his black pants. And something about those shiny black skates do it for me every time.

"*Ti amo di più.*" He passes his bottle over to Anya, and I do the same when I'm finished. My ears tingle pleasantly with his Italian words.

"How many more poses do we need?" Anya glances at her watch as she returns to her chair next to Victor, handing him a water bottle, too. "We have to go for our interviews with ESPN in an hour."

When she came to us last spring asking to be our coach, the biggest change was the fact that she actually took care of us. I thought it was to get on our good sides at first, but she never fails to Mother Hen us—all of us. Including Victor, who refused to be demoted from his original role. It turns out they make a pretty good team.

The photographer glances at her clipboard. "At least two, but they won't take long. We already got a lift, so let's do a dip."

"Don't mess up." Victor points his bottle at Jason. "They can only photoshop so much. It's bad enough that they're going to have to totally rework your face."

"You should come closer and say that again. Then we'll see whose face needs to be reworked." Jason gives him a cool glare as he steps up behind me, but his tone lacks venom.

"His face is perfect," I say to Victor.

"Listen to my girlfriend. She's never wrong."

"Okay." The photographer steps out from behind the camera, obviously having heard enough. "Let's get in position. I don't want a classic dip, I want to spice it up a little."

Jason looks at me and wiggles his eyebrows.

I mouth, *focus*. But I can't hide my smile this time. I love how much he's eating this up.

"Jason, act like you're on the ice. Place your feet here." The photographer points at the floor, making him stand in a wide stance on the edge of his blades. "You're going to place your left arm around Clarity's back. Clarity, just lean back like you would during a performance, okay?"

"Sure." I move closer to him as she goes back to her camera. He slides his hand over my back, making sure to linger his fingertips on my bare skin. All of my senses fire up, especially when he smiles at me like that, all devilish and coy.

I step out with my left foot, balancing precariously on the edge of my blade as I push it into the mat on the floor. Lifting my right foot, I dig the toe pick into the ground and balance the majority of my weight on Jason's arm as I lean back. I stretch my left arm toward the ground, and my right arm toward the ceiling.

Finally, I make eye contact with Jason. He's still watching me like I'm the only person in the world, his eyes shimmering.

"Great! Jason, drop your left shoulder a little... perfect. Bend your left knee, just like that. Okay, I hate to say this, but don't smile guys. I want straight faces." The photographer fiddles with something on the top of her camera. "Hold that pose."

Him and I inhale slowly, simultaneously, like we're one body. I watch the way his smile melts away, replaced with an expert expression of confidence and adoration.

I tilt my chin back to meet his gaze with the same passion, going as far as quirking an eyebrow. His eyes instantly heat. God, I used to mistake that expression as being annoyed with me. I quickly learned that it's because he was a few moments away from devouring me. If his tongue could never speak again, his eyes would do all of the talking.

"That's wonderful. Perfect." The photographer pauses, probably checking the images. "Let's move forward with the last pose."

Jason gently puts me back on my feet as she keeps explaining.

"I want Jason to stand normally. Clarity, stand in front of him, and back up close enough so you can rest the back of your head against his left shoulder. Yes, like that. Put your left hand down, and reach up with your right to put it on his neck. Jason, put your hands wherever it feels natural."

He immediately rests his right hand on my waist, then slides his left hand over mine, lacing my fingers. My heart starts to pound.

Victor whistles. We ignore him.

"Yes, oh my god, okay. Hold those expressions." The photographer rushes off to her camera, and I stare off to the side of the photo studio as the shutter clicks rapidly. I can feel the weight of Jason's eyes as he looks down at me. I start sweating, and not because I'm nervous.

"Let's get one of you guys smiling at each other. Jason, maybe say something to make her laugh. Do you have any jokes?"

"He's absolutely full of them," Victor deadpans.

Jason hums thoughtfully. Goosebumps crawl over my skin as he leans down to my ear. I *really* start sweating when he says, "*Non veto l'ora di toglierti questo vestito stasera.*"

I know no one in this room besides me knows what he's saying, yet I still gasp. "Jason, oh my *god*."

The intention of his words makes me laugh in shock, and he grins, way too proud with himself. The camera shutter clicks rapidly.

"She said make her laugh, not melt her makeup off," the makeup artist says from the corner with a laugh.

"Nope, that was awesome. I think we're all done, thank you. You guys are great." The photographer steps up to Anya and Victor to shake their hands.

I turn to face Jason and hold up my hand. "We made it!"

He gives me a high five, then takes my hand before I can put it down, pulling me close for a kiss. He proceeds by peppering kisses over my nose, then all over my cheeks and up my hairline.

I start to giggle. My heart swells as I run my hands down his arms. "You're going to ruin my makeup."

"We're done here, C.J. I've been waiting all morning for this." Jason finally steps away, but not without lifting my hand that he's holding and kissing my knuckles. He holds my gaze while doing it, and my stomach somersaults.

"Great job. I'm proud of you for making it through." I pull him into a side hug as we head over to the chairs at the side of the backdrop, where our normal shoes are waiting for us.

"Thanks, you too. You're going to steal the show, I already know it." He rubs my shoulder before letting go. I smile at him, although his face is already ducked down as he sits to untie his laces.

He can say that all he wants but no matter the outcome of this journey, as long as I have him, I've already won.

Acknowledgements

Who knew that writing this would be the hardest part of the book? Laugh all you want, but I'm dead serious. I have no idea where to start, so I guess I'll go back to the beginning.

Jason and Clarity were once nothing more than characters born from childish imagination. I never thought I'd expand on that idea as an adult, but I'm so glad I did. There isn't any other story I'd want to share as my debut except for theirs.

They were begging to be put out into the world, and my biggest hope—*my* dream—is that they would find readers that resonate with them. It took a lot of literal blood, sweat, and tears to get to this point, but we're on the other side. Finally!

To my readers: thank you. There's over 100,000 words in this story, but I can't write another word to appropriately express my gratitude for you. It's one thing to keep an idea tucked away in the back of my head, and another to share that idea with the world. Without your support as a reader, I'd be left to fangirl over this story alone! Thank you for giving it a chance.

Mom, Dad, I'll take a line from Clarity's epilogue and express that without you guys modeling such amazing strength and perseverance with everything you do in life, I'd be nothing. Thank you for being the perfect role models for Aaron and Lauren in this story. Especially to Mom: you've cheered me on every step of the way, and you've been willing to read every terrible draft, and that love and care doesn't go unnoticed.

Speaking of terrible drafts... my beta readers. Do they give out Olympic medals for putting up with the worst plot lines in the written language? Joking. Kind of. Tessy, Bree, Kate, and Charline, this story wouldn't be half of what it is without your feedback and support. Thank you from the bottom of my heart.

Jami, I owe you a piece of my soul. Thank you for wadding through the sloppy mess of my drafts alongside me and for pointing out the nuggets of gold. Without your expertise and encouragement, I probably would've left this book inside of a Word Doc and never touched it again. You are a gem!

Emily, I am forever grateful for your exacting eye and your ability to straighten out my sentences. The way you were able to wave your magic wand on this story makes me forever grateful for your talents. Without you, the words "Mom" and "Dad" would've stayed lowercase forever. I should've paid more attention in English class...

To my friends: Leah, Carrie, Malana, Maria, Anna (both Anna's!), Alice, and the countless others who have been there for me in different ways throughout this journey, I'd be nothing without your support. You all kept me motivated, and the way you all live your lives inspires me every day. Thank you, thank you, thank you.

I can't close out without shedding light on the rest of my family: my siblings, grandparents, aunts, uncles, cousins, and everyone else who has made an impact on me.

The only reason why I am able to write such a compelling family dynamic is because of the stage you guys have set throughout my life. Family is everything to me, blood and built, and I'm so honored to be able to bring it to life in this art form. Thank you for always supporting me in everything I do. Even if that means risking our family name by publishing stories for the world to consume. Lol.

Lastly, I'd like to thank the only one who made this entire thing possible: my Lord and Savior. Sharing stories has been a lifelong dream of mine, and to be able to have the time, skills, and ability to do so is absolutely incredible. It's a privilege I don't take for granted.

This is just the beginning, and I can't wait to see what's next!

Isabelle Martens is a Minnesota-based author who finds her inspiration in the simple joys of life—family, friends, and time spent outdoors in every season. Writing has been her passion since childhood, and she strives to craft stories that move readers to feel more, think deeper, and dream a little bigger.

Skating the Line is her debut novel.

Connect Online:
isabellemartensauthor.com
Instagram: @isabellemauthor